William Harrison Ainsworth

Rockwood

A romance

William Harrison Ainsworth

Rockwood
A romance

ISBN/EAN: 9783337019662

Printed in Europe, USA, Canada, Australia, Japan

Cover: Foto ©Andreas Hilbeck / pixelio.de

More available books at **www.hansebooks.com**

RESCUE OF LADY ROOKWOOD.

ROOKWOOD

A ROMANCE

BY

WILLIAM HARRISON AINSWORTH

I see how Ruin, with a palsied hand,
Begins to shake our ancient house to dust.
YORKSHIRE TRAGEDY

AUTHOR'S COPYRIGHT EDITION

LONDON
GEORGE ROUTLEDGE AND SONS, Limited
BROADWAY, LUDGATE HILL
GLASGOW, MANCHESTER, AND NEW YORK

CONTENTS.

———

                                                              PAGE

MEMOIR OF WILLIAM HARRISON AINSWORTH. BY LAMAN
    BLANCHARD vii

BIOGRAPHICAL SKETCH BY JAMES CROSSLEY, ESQ., F.S.A. . . xx

———

ROOKWOOD.

DEDICATION xxv

PREFACE xxvii

BOOK I. THE WEDDING RING 1

  „ II. THE SEXTON 99

  „ III. THE GIPSY 143

  „ IV. THE RIDE TO YORK 274

  „ V. THE OATH 336

MEMOIR

OF

WILLIAM HARRISON AINSWORTH.

BY LAMAN BLANCHARD.

A RECENT review in a leading journal of France bears
testimony to the great popularity which has been obtained in
that romance-reading nation by the writer of whom we are
now to offer some account. The estimation in which he is
held by his own countrymen is evinced by the large sale
which each new production of his pen successively commands.
In America his writings have been extensively read. They have
all been translated into German, and some of them into Dutch
and Spanish. Dramas have been founded upon them; their
more striking passages have become as familiar as household
words; and their subjects, in some important instances at least,
are associated with the most memorable features of English
history. The biography of a writer who has secured so prominent a position may be supposed calculated to awaken a
more than ordinary curiosity; not merely with respect to
those early dawnings of intellect, and those traits of personal
character, to which a deep interest always attaches, but in
relation to the family from which he has sprung. Happily,
in the present instance, we are able to gratify the reader's
curiosity.

WILLIAM HARRISON AINSWORTH unites in his own name
the names of two families which in the eminent success of
various members of them, had obtained celebrity long prior
to the present generation. Amongst his paternal ancestors

are Robert Ainsworth, the well-known scholar and author of
the Latin Dictionary, and Henry Ainsworth, the Brownist,
who flourished at the commencement of the seventeenth
century.   The latter was one of the most profound Hebrew
scholars of his time, and author of " Annotations upon the
Old Testament," and of a translation of the Pentateuch.
From these we come to the father of the living descendant
from the learned stock, Thomas Ainsworth, of Manchester, a
solicitor in very extensive practice.

This gentleman, though descended from a family residing at Plessington, in Lancashire, was born at Rosthorne,
in Cheshire, a village which he always remembered with
affection, and where, dying in June, 1824, he was interred.
Manchester, however, the stage on which his active life was
passed, benefited most largely by the ardour and zeal with
which he devoted himself to the promotion of public improvements.   He was one of the main instruments in causing the
rebuilding and widening of one of the principal thoroughfares
—Market-street ; and though he did not live to see the work
accomplished, his name must always be honourably connected
with it.   Of rather an irritable temperament, perhaps he was
known extensively for a singular liberality of character and
generosity of disposition.   He was a man of taste and virtu ;
uniting, with a fair degree of classical scholarship, considerable proficiency in botany, and a general fondness for scientific
pursuits ; and thus the excellent library he possessed was
throughout life a source of pleasure and recreation that
lightened the graver duties he so faithfully discharged.

Thomas Ainsworth married, in 1802, Ann, daughter of the
Rev. Ralph Harrison, a Presbyterian divine, and Ann Touchet.
This divine, himself the son of a minister, and great-grandson
to the Rev. Cuthbert Harrison, who, as a famous Nonconformist
teacher, is noticed in Dr. Calamy's account of ejected ministers, attained a high reputation in Manchester as a preacher,
an author, and a scholar.   In the Academy there, he was
appointed professor of the Greek and Latin languages, and of
polite literature.   He produced many able works of an educa-
tional character ; and left behind him a volume of discourses
that fully bear out his claim to the affectionate regard in
which his character and ministrations were held.   Of these
sermons, which, with a biographical memoir, were first printed
in 1813, a new edition appeared in 1827.   It may here be
mentioned, as a somewhat rare occurrence in the life of a

Presbyterian minister, that this reverend person, the grand-father of the subject of this sketch, realised, by fortunate speculations in land and building, a large fortune, leaving behind him upwards of 60,000*l*. Of this union, two sons were born ; the elder named William Harrison, the younger Thomas Gilbert, who distinguished himself at Cambridge, and taking a scholarship there, unfortunately fell into ill-health from over-study, which so affected his nervous system that he never took his degree, and his intention of going into the Church was therefore abandoned.*

William Harrison Ainsworth was born on the 4th of February, 1805, at the house of his father, in King-street, Manchester; but not long after, the family removed to a very commodious and pleasantly-situated country-house, called Beech-hill, about two miles from the town, on the Chetham side. Here was a very extensive garden; and here all the time that could be spared by its possessor from pro-fessional pursuits was devoted to the studies and recreations of which he was so passionately fond. The grounds were laid out under his own eye, and several of the trees were planted by the young brothers.

To the education of the elder of these it is now necessary to refer. The early part of it was undertaken by his uncle, the Rev. William Harrison; and then, while still very young, he was placed at the free grammar-school in Manchester, in one of the classes of the Rev. Robinson Elsdale.

In this school, which was founded early in the six-teenth century, many persons eminent for science and learn-ing have been educated. The list extends as far back as the reign of Mary, opening with the well-known name of John Bradford, who suffered martyrdom in 1555. Reginald Heber (the father of the bishop) was here, Cyril Jackson, and his brother the Bishop of Oxford, the first Lord Alvanley, Mr. Morritt of Rokeby, David Latouche, the celebrated banker, Mr. Justice Williams, and many others. Here our youthful student so far distinguished himself as to have received very flattering testimonials from Dr. Smith (the then head-master of the school), and his colleague, Dr. Elsdale. He wrote several translations from the Latin and Greek poets, which obtained their approbation. In this school he remained, gathering honour and advantage, until he reached

* Thomas Gilbert Ainsworth died on the 9th of April, 1876, at Hill View Lodge, Reigate, and was interred in the Kensal Green Cemetery.

the first form, when his father, who designed his son to be his successor, placed him as a clerk with an eminent solicitor in the town.

It had been his father's wish, when the period of the youth's law-studies commenced, that he should devote himself chiefly to that branch of the profession which it was intended he should practise—conveyancing; but no great progress was made in this study. Byron, Scott, and Shelley had charms that title-deeds could never boast; writing verses was far more attractive than making abstracts, and drawing drafts bore no comparison to sketching for magazines. It was the old story—he was literally

> A youth foredoom'd his father's hopes to cross,
> Who penn'd a stanza when he should engross.

The nameless editor of a magazine was, in his enchanted view, greater by far than the greatest of the whole tribe of lawyers; and the occupation of the editorial chair appeared in his fanciful dream an object worthier of a loftier ambition than a seat on the woolsack.

On his father's death, which occurred, as we have said, in 1824, he awakened to a sense of the expediency of completing his term as a conveyancer, and qualifying himself for assuming the professional responsibility which this bereavement devolved upon him. With this view he repaired to London, to finish his term with Mr. Jacob Phillips, of the Inner Temple. Yet it does not appear that he devoted himself with the adequate diligence and zeal to professional study. The literary enthusiasm was still the stronger feeling, though less productive in its immediate results than before; for the metropolis was a novel scene, and some time was spent in acquainting himself with its amusements.

Not long before the completion of his appointed stay in town, he commenced an acquaintance with Mr. Ebers, at that time the manager of the Opera House, and a constant attendance there was, of course, included among the young law-student's London pleasures.

We now have to record an important event in life—the marriage of Mr. Ainsworth to Fanny, the youngest daughter of Mr. Ebers. This event occurred in the autumn of 1826. Three daughters, still living, were the offspring of this union. They lost their mother in the spring of 1838.

The connexion thus formed with Mr. Ebers had a material influence in deciding the young man as to the course he should pursue. His repugnance to "conveyancing" being insuperable, and his tastes and inclinations being decidedly literary, he readily listened to the suggestions of Mr. Ebers, to make an experiment as a publisher. The sacrifice, to be sure, was considerable. It involved the relinquishment of his share in his father's lucrative business, which had been carried on, meanwhile, by two partners, at the head of whom he would necessarily be placed; it was the exchanging a certainty for a chance. Yet, on the other hand, he was to secure the advantage of Mr. Ebers's extensive connexion, and of his practical knowledge of business, which as yet was a "book sealed" to him. There were other temptations, not unworthy of a high literary ambition, and a generous zeal for the interests of authors. The period, that of 1828-9, was the season of the (exclusively) "fashionable novels," when what was most ephemeral was most triumphant, and when works of a more enduring though less winning character had fewer charms than usual in a publisher's eye. Let us here pause for a moment to consider what his aims were, and, at the same time, what were his qualifications for giving effect to them.

Mr. Ainsworth entered upon his speculation doubtless with literary feelings not very dissimilar to those with which he may be supposed to have recently originated his Magazine. His was not the speculation of an ordinary publisher: his aim was to promote the interests of literature, to advance his own reputation as a writer, and to surround himself with such authors as it was alike honourable to serve and to be associated with; he thought that he might bring forward sterling works, rejected, perhaps, as not "fashionable," and assist writers of a better class than those who aspired to a merely fleeting popularity; in any case, he should succeed in showing that such an enterprise might be conducted on liberal and gentlemanlike principles. These, as we believe, were his objects; but he mistook the practicability of the scheme, and misconceived his own qualifications for conducting it. He had great liberality, a highly cultivated literary taste, ripe scholarship, and popular manners; he was borne up by the spirit of youth, and the love of books for their own sake, to make an experiment, and his entering upon it was the best proof of the sacrifices he could cheerfully incur, and that he thought of no selfish or mercenary bargain. But with these fine qualities he wanted some that are not always found in their company and in that of youth—forethought, deliberation, patience under disappointment, submission to repugnant tasks, and indifference to the trifling circumstance of being always unthanked and generally misapprehended. What young man of one-and-twenty understands his own character sufficiently to justify such an attempt? His principles were but partially recognised by the writers with whom he was brought into connexion, and he was of too impatient a temperament to afford them time to understand him. His pride speedily revolted from the position he had voluntarily chosen, and at the expiration of about a year and a half he abandoned the experiment; the result was—neither good nor harm, beyond loss of time. During this period, and up to the year 1830, a few trifles had been written; a tragedy on the subject of Philip van Artevelde was planned, and two acts composed; a melodrame or two, never acted, swelled the stock; but nothing was published. A change of scene was now resolved upon: in the summer of that year Mr. Ainsworth started on a tour in Switzerland and Italy.

It was in the following year, during a visit to Chesterfield, that he first thought of writing a three-volumed tale, and the idea of "Rookwood" arose. He has told us his object. "Wishing," he says, "to describe somewhat minutely the trim gardens, the picturesque domains, the rook-haunted groves, the gloomy chambers, and gloomier galleries of an ancient hall with which I was acquainted, I resolved to attempt a story in the bygone style of Mrs. Radcliffe; substituting an old English squire, an old manorial residence and an old English highwayman, for the Italian marchese, the castle, and the brigand of that great mistress of romance."

"Rookwood" was commenced, but many and serious pauses occurred in the completion of the story; nor was it until May, 1834, that it was published; but the power with which the design was worked out, the success with which it was accomplished, was instantaneously recognised. The "Edinburgh Review" described the novel achievement—"What Mr. Ainsworth has ventured to do, and successfully, was to revive the almost exploded interest afforded by the supernatural; and to preserve this, too, not in connexion with days long gone by, but side by side with the sober realities of 1737, with the convivialities of Yorkshire squires and country attorneys, with the humours of justices of the peace and the feats of Dick Turpin the highwayman." The same writer describes, also, the influences of all this upon the reader. "Strange as it may seem, the author has contrived to present the terrors of burial vaults and the blood-stained mysteries of family crime side by side with the most familiar scenes of the every-day life of the eighteenth century, without exciting the slightest feeling of the ludicrous—nay, more, with a character of earnestness and solemnity with which, *à priori*, we should have hardly thought such subjects could have been invested."

But the truth is, as the critic seems to have felt, that the reader is never allowed to pause for an instant to think at all. The famous picture of the ride to York, now as well known as the name of Turpin himself, is but an image of the reader's course as he leaps the abrupt gaps and turns the picturesque corners of this singular tale. He goes through it hurried, yet noting everything, and with breathless interest; and it is not until after a pause at the close that he bethinks him of the songs and ballads whose lively or solemn chimes struck his ear as he passed rapidly; when he is sure to turn back to read them leisurely over one by one, enjoying the true spirit of the old minstrelsy with which they are embued, and wishing for a whole volume of such tuneful rarities. The effect of this publication was to place Mr. Ainsworth in the first rank of writers of romantic fiction. The first edition was speedily sold off; a second followed. In 1836 Mr. Macrone issued a beautiful volume with designs by Cruikshank.

"Crichton" was the next work meditated; and as soon as projected Mr. Macrone offered 350*l.* for the manuscript. It appeared in the spring of 1837, and a rapid sale betokened the now established reputation of the writer. This historical romance afforded, in some respects, indications of a higher aim and more elaborate finish than the happiest pictures of the preceding work. Extensive and curious reading—a minute acquaintance with the modes, usages, intrigue, and philosophy of the time—a capacity at once to analyse and combine—an eye for grand effects as well as the smallest details—were everywhere recognised. Many rare qualities united in the composition of this work. Its pictures of the times and persons it treats of are " finished sketches," the effect of which, by a truly artist-like skill, is heightened instead of diminished by the small fine touches that denote a thorough familiarity with every incidental particular of the subject. Thus, not only are the king's jester and the king's cook as vividly set

before us as Henri himself; but Henri's lineaments are not
more accurately painted than is the quaint figure of a piece
of embroidery, the fashion of a jewel, or the cut of a garment.
In spite of a most hurried and effect-marring termination, this
romance has in it the seeds of life, and contains some of its
author's soundest and most brilliant writing.   Here, again,
we see a lyrical genius in full flow; some of the songs are of
a most dainty fashion, and charm equally by their structure
and their fancy.

The "Admirable Crichton" was yet winning admiration
when his untired historian commenced another romance,
which he originally intended to call "Thames Darrell," and
under that name it was announced by its publisher.   After
considerable delays, the opening chapters of the work made
their appearance in "Bentley's Miscellany," under the title
of "Jack Sheppard."   This was in January, 1839.   Two
months afterwards, on the retirement of Mr. Dickens, the
author of the new romance was installed as editor of the
"Miscellany"—the terms agreed upon being 51l. per month.

As the story month by month developed itself, the circle
of its success widened; not an audible objection to its hero
or to its author—to his plot, scenery, or persons—their life,
character, or behaviour—was raised, as far as we are aware,
in the most fastidious coterie; but, on the contrary, many
established critics of high character, fully cognisant of the
significant fact that the hero of the tale was the veritable
housebreaker, welcomed him with winged pens as he broke
limb by limb out of the Magazine, and shook him heartily by
the hand as a legitimate historical acquaintance.   When he
stood before them, whole, in the autumn of the same year,
he met with astonishing success, and became the "rage" for
months.   The three volumes were produced in a dramatic
form simultaneously at eight different theatres; and George
Cruikshank's inimitable designs became set scenes east and
west.   At last, however, the prison-breaker's popularity
became all at once an offence in people's eyes greater than
any of which he was ever convicted.   He was denounced as
something worse than the monster in "Frankenstein."
Critics, who had always a passion for heroes in fetters before,
now found out that housebreakers are disreputable characters.
They were in raptures with the old-established brigand still,
and the freebooter of foreign extraction; they could hug
Robin Hood as fondly as ever, and dwell with unhurt morals
on the little peccadilloes of *Rob Roy;* nay, they had no

objection to ride behind *Turpin* to York any day, and would never feel ashamed of their company; but they shook their heads at *Sheppard*, because low people began to run after him at the theatres; he was a housebreaker!

We are here recording facts, and have small space for opinions. It may be observed, however, that the outcry, to have served any moral end, should have been raised much sooner. Why did it not break out when the housebreaker first broke out in January amidst public plaudits? Why was it silent for a whole twelvemonth? But this is not the only question. Why was not that moral outcry raised long before this culprit ever made a literary appearance at all? He had some remarkably suspicious precursors—heroes selected only for their ruffianism; yet the storm falls on this offender, probably because he comes late in the field. In answer to the charge of choosing a Newgate hero, the romancer is surely entitled to say, "I did not select him because he was a housebreaker, but because he was a *prison-breaker*." And if mischief arise from the delineation of the characters of such criminals—which is a separate question, and would lead us as far afield as the "Robbers" of Schiller led the young reprobate nobles who turned thieves in imitation, and might suggest a committee of inquiry concerning *Bardolph* and Company, amongst a crowd of others; but if mischief arise, which course has the directest tendency to produce it—that which introduces the criminal into the story to play off his brutalities unrestricted, and, as it were, under cover of false dates and places—or that which avows the heroship on the title-page, and warns off those of timid tastes and trembling morals? People seem to object to no atrocity, no vulgarity, so that it be unexpected, and not concentrated in the hero. We take up the most innocent-looking Arcadian sort of books, and find ourselves in the heart of Newgate. Of this we may have some cause to complain; but we cannot complain of going to Tyburn, when the hero's very name tells us we shall be taken there in the end, wheresoever the story may previously wind.

Gay has been libelled for his "Beggar's Opera," and Fielding has been abused for his "Jonathan Wild the Great" (excellent company wherein to sin or to suffer martyrdom!); but those exquisite satires, if liable to be misunderstood by the dull, are as innocent of evil as they are brave in purpose and profound in wit. They are what they profess to be, and do not cheat the reader with a promise of some-

thing different. It is so, in its degree, with the romance to
which we have referred. It can have injured or imposed
upon no family on earth, except the Fudge Family.

We now approach the consideration of works on which
their author has unquestionably employed his best powers,
and in which at least he has not sinned in point of subject.
With the new year he commenced two new romances. "Guy
Fawkes" appeared in the "Miscellany," and was completed
in eighteen monthly numbers, when it was reprinted in three
volumes. The sum received during this period from the
publisher exceeded 1500*l.* Of the several romances that
have been founded partly or entirely upon the same subject,
it is by far the most striking. The bold and simple painting of character, the felicitous description, the hair-breadth
'scapes which the reader follows with an interest tremblingly
alive, the constant fertility of invention, while the stream of
historical truth flows on in the midst of all, denote the
abundance of the resources which this writer always brings
to his task. The time and subject seem new in his hands,
because his manner and his materials (save the simple truth
upon and around which he works them) are entirely his own.

The "Tower of London"—the twin-born romance, running
chapter by chapter with the foregoing—is a work of yet more
remarkable power, because it is more fully and consistently
sustained to the close. It had been the author's wish—if we
are not misinformed—from the hour when he first saw the
old fortress, to write a romance on one of the thousand almost
incredible truths with which the memory that sanctifies it is
peopled. The companion-thought to this was the hope to
connect another historical legend with the Castle of Windsor
—both so picturesque in themselves, and both so surpas-
singly rich in historical recollections. The one object is
accomplished, the other is on the eve of commencement.

The project of the "Tower" brought together author and
artist—Ainsworth and Cruikshank—in partnership, on equal
terms, and on their own responsibility. Considerations, however, connected with publication, led to an arrangement with
Mr. Bentley, who was appointed to publish the work in
monthly parts. It is still as popular as ever, as it must long
remain. "Desirous," says Mr. Ainsworth, "of exhibiting
the Tower in its triple light of a palace, a prison, and a
fortress, the author has shaped his story with reference to
that end ; and he has also contrived such a series of incidents
as should naturally introduce every relic of the old pile—its

towers, chapels, halls, chambers, gateways, arches, and draw-bridges, so that no part of it should remain unillustrated."
It is curious to observe how this purpose is worked out in entire consistency with an unbroken and uninterrupted narra-tive. With every necessity imposed upon the historian for going out of his way in order to realise previously resolved upon effects, there is no appearance of his ever doing so, and, indeed, the scene being circumscribed and the locality fixed, there is in this work fewer abrupt turns and changes than in the majority of its predecessors. The historical events chosen for illustration are happily suited for the design : they admit of every variety of agency, and embrace an enormous field in a small space ; they involve the throne and the block, the siege and the stake, the secret plot and the fiery storm of revolt ;—" the mad battle and the ghastly grave." They comprise the cold, insidious foreign bigot, wily as a serpent, and the hot-gospeller, frantic in his fanaticism ; the haughty, daring noble and the brutal gaoler ; the courtly knight and the headsman—a goodly company, with an infinite train of " dwarf and giant auxiliaries." The characters are extremely numerous ; but they are not more skilfully grouped than they are artfully discriminated. Two of them seem to us of first-rate rank in that grand human gallery to which this author has now contributed several noble portraitures ; these are, Mary the queen, and the subtle Spaniard, Simon Renard. But the whole space allotted to this Memoir would not be too wide a limit for a comprehensive review of the characteristics of this admirable romance.

One remark may be allowed. Mr. Ainsworth, in his intro-ductory observations, says—" Opposite the matchless White Tower—William of Orange by the side of William the Con-queror—is that frightful architectural abomination, the Grand Store-House. It may not be impossible to remove this ugly and incongruous structure." Not long after this was written the abused building was burnt down. Should not cant or prejudice, when it traces robberies to novels, have traced the conflagration to this romance ?

In the first week of 1841, " Old Saint Paul's" was com-menced. The proprietors of the *Sunday Times* newspaper had proposed to Mr. Ainsworth to write a romance to be pub-lished in their journal weekly throughout the year, for which they very liberally offered 1000*l*. This was a new feature in newspaper management and romance-writing. The offer was accepted : the Tale appeared in successive numbers, and at the close of the year (the copyright reverting to Mr. Ainsworth) it was re-issued in three handsome volumes, lavishly illustrated by Franklin. A large edition was disposed of. This work, "a tale of the Plague and the Fire," abounds, as this explanation denotes, in the terrible and the sublime. The time extends from April, 1665, to September in the following year, embracing the two most fearful and fatal calamities that ever London was visited with. With what grasping power Mr. Ainsworth has seized upon the prominent points arising out of these scenes of devastation and dismay, those best may judge who can most vividly recall past examples of his art in stirring men's blood and lifting the imagination to a point of horror; but they may not so readily surmise with what a gentle and reconciling humanity he has detained us amidst what was loathsome, to exhibit to us, as it were, the lily in the charnel-house; and carried us through the pestilence and the flame, to vindicate the severity of human trials, to inculcate salutary lessons of exertion and endurance, and track the course of faith, and courage, and happiness, through all. From the insupportable and unredeemed ghastliness of Defoe's astonishing narrative, we turn to this *peopled* story, and discover a vitality amidst the shadows of death, and hope stealing silently on through the desolation and the ruin.

Mr. Ainsworth's engagement as editor of "Bentley's Miscellany" terminated with the year 1841, and in February, 1842, appeared the first number of "Ainsworth's Magazine," a Journal of Romance, Literature, and Art. Its success, measured by the sale of the first volume, now completed, surpasses, it is said, by many degrees, that of any similar periodical that ever made its appearance. Its editor had surrounded himself by many able writers, but his reliance, perhaps, was upon a new tale from his own pen, "The Miser's Daughter." Public opinion seems to have set its seal upon this fine-toned and charmingly-coloured story, as "the favourite and the flower;" but Mr. Ainsworth, it seems, purposes to keep the imagination of a second artist employed, for in July he opens, in his Magazine, a new tale, entitled "Windsor Castle," for which the celebrated Tony Johannot is to furnish steel engravings, and Alfred Delamotte woodcuts.

Here we draw to a close, with the observation, that, should these new romances, now in a state of progress, share the good fortune of their predecessors, they will not only be extensively read, but dramas will be founded upon them in this country; the Paris press will give them a new shape; America will spread them over her surface; the German translator will insure them a wide circulation in that land of the mysteries; and even the Dutch, as in the case of "Rookwood" and "Crichton," will mark them for their own.

There is one event of a domestic nature that should be mentioned in a more saddened tone at the close. On the 15th of March, 1842, it was Mr. Ainsworth's affliction to lose his surviving parent—the revered mother who had taken pride in his rising fame, and had found joy in his constant affection. A beautiful monumental tribute to both parents has just been erected in the cemetery at Kensal Green.

What have we to add to what we have here ventured to record, which the engraving that accompanies this Memoir will not more happily embody? Should that fail to do justice to our author's face—to its regularity and delicacy of feature, its manly glow of health, and the cordial nature which lightens it up, we must refer the dissatisfied beholder to Mr. Pickersgill's masterly full-length portrait, exhibited last year; in which the author of "The Miser's Daughter" may be seen, not as some pale, worn, pining scholar—some fagging, half-exhausted, periodical romancer—but, as an English gentleman, of goodly stature and well-set limb, with a fine head on his shoulders, and a heart to match.*

If to this we add a word, it must be to observe, that, though the temper of our popular author may be marked by impatience on some occasions, it has never been upon any occasion marked by a want of generosity, whether in conferring benefits or atoning for errors. His friends regard him as a man with as few failings, blended with fine qualities, as most people; and his enemies know nothing at all about him. He is liberal towards his contemporaries, and quick to feel a kindness rendered to himself. He writes rapidly, and finds leisure, we are told, for a full portion of social enjoyment and relaxation; so that, at Kensal Manor-House, hospitality is a virtue that is always at home.

---

* Pickersgill's portrait has recently been presented by Mr. Ainsworth to the Chetham Hospital, Manchester, and is placed in the library. 1878.

WILLIAM HARRISON AINSWORTH.

BY JAMES CROSSLEY, ESQ., F.S.A.,

PRESIDENT OF THE CHETHAM SOCIETY.

WILLIAM HARRISON AINSWORTH was born in King-street, Manchester, at the house of his father, who was a solicitor of high standing and extensive practice, on the 4th February, 1805. His paternal grandfather was Jeremiah Ainsworth, one of the founders of the Lancashire School of Geometry. By the side of his mother, Ann, the daughter of the Rev. Ralph Harrison, he was descended from a line of Nonconformists, some of whom Calamy has embalmed in his pages.

William Harrison, who was gifted by nature with a fine constitution, high spirits, and a most joyous temperament, after receiving elementary tuition from his uncle, the Rev. William Harrison, who held a highly respectable rank as a teacher, became on the 20th March, 1817, a scholar of the Manchester Free Grammar School, where he remained for some years. A vivid sketch, in which he has brought the school and its masters with such life and spirit before us, appears in *Mervyn Clitheroe*. At the annual recitations he appeared to great advantage, and his remarkably handsome face, excellent delivery, and perfect self-possession are still recollected by the surviving attenders of those interesting occasions, and never failed to bring down plaudits from the audience. Of Dr. Smith he was always a great favourite, and that sagacious master well understood that he was no common boy. While at school and afterwards he went through a large amount of miscellaneous reading, in which, beside recourse to his father's collection, which was a good one, he had the advantage, a benefit which Thomas de Quincey had availed himself of before him, of the old Exchange Circulating Library, now broken up and dispersed, in which there was an ample if not select table provided with dishes of all sorts, from *Amadis of Gaul* and *Palmerin of England* to Bryant's *Mythology*, and Cudworth's *Intellectual System*. On leaving the Free Grammar School he was placed by his father with Mr. Alexander Kay, an able and experienced solicitor, afterwards Mayor of Manchester, with a view to his succeeding to the well-established business which his father carried on in partnership with his son's early and intimate friend, the present President of the Chetham Society.

Mr. Thomas Ainsworth, the father, to whose energy and public spirit the improvements in Manchester were materially indebted, died at a comparatively speaking early age, in 1824. His son, William Harrison, went through the regular legal curriculum, and from Mr. Kay's office in Manchester proceeded to Mr. Jacob Phillips's chambers in King's Bench Walk, to be perfected in the higher mysteries of conveyancing. Here he copied precedents, and we have a folio volume in which his labours are embodied, but the rule in Shelley's case and Fearne's contingent remainders had no charms for him. His aspirations were of another kind—to give new associations to the name of Ainsworth unconnected with Law, Mathematics, or Lexicography—in short, to enter upon a literary career; and to know and be known by the leading authors of the day, exchanging Manchester with all its prospects for the great metropolis. In this resolve he was confirmed by marrying (October, 1826) Ann Frances, the beautiful daughter of Mr. John Ebers, of Old Bond-street, then lessee of the Opera House, whose London connexions were large and extensive; and the young man accordingly became settled in the midst of the world of letters and fashion. For some time he carried on the business of a publisher, and several works of interest and value may be found with his name attached; but this, after giving it a full and fair trial, he thought fit for wise reasons to discontinue; having, however, acquired an experience from his publishing operations which was afterwards undoubtedly beneficial to him. During all this period—at school, while going through his professional education in Manchester and London, and the years which immediately followed—he devoted the greater part of his leisure to contributing, sometimes solely, sometimes with a friendly collaborateur, to various periodicals; commencing with Arliss's little but elegantly illustrated magazine, and proceeding onward to those of larger size and greater pretensions. But, leaving these prolusions, as well as the separate works in poetry and prose, of what we may style the præ-Rookwoodian Era, to be indicated and enumerated by his future biographer—and biography has nothing more interesting than the examination of the early works of successful writers—we must come to the production which first gave Mr. Ainsworth a solid footing as an author. This was the striking story of *Rookwood*, which contained what was at once acknowledged to be a masterpiece of descriptive power; we need not add that we refer to Turpin's celebrated Ride to York, which at once, delighting the young and the old, established the writer as a favourite of the reading public.

Rookwood was followed by *Crichton*, which sustained, if it did not increase, the reputation Mr. Ainsworth had acquired. Most of the works which succeeded appeared originally in a serial form either in *Bentley's Miscellany*, *Ainsworth's Magazine*, the *Sunday Times*, or in monthly numbers, and were afterwards collected into volumes. The first of these was the wonderfully popular and much calumniated *Jack Sheppard*, which, admirably illustrated by George Cruikshank, was universally read; and, by its extraordinary success, called forth attacks on all sides, and a spirit which, to lovers of fair play, looked very much like persecution. On this subject, we cannot do better than refer to Laman Blanchard's very sensible remarks in his *Memoir*.

The storm which *Jack Sheppard* had evoked was in a great measure appeased by the *Tower of London*, which deals with a higher class of criminals, and must always be placed amongst the best, if it be not indeed *the* best of the author's historical novels. During nearly forty years it has certainly lost none of its original popularity. Its great success gave occasion to a large dinner, which we well remember, in which were present, by Mr. Ainsworth's invitation, the leading authors, critics, artists, and publishers of London, at which Serjeant Talfourd presided. We doubt much whether, amongst the many similar celebrations which have since occurred in London, there has been any which went off more brilliantly, or with which the author, in compliment of whom the gathering took place, had better reason to be satisfied.

The narrow limits of this sketch necessarily prevent more than a simple enumeration of the titles of the novels which Mr. Ainsworth's creative power and extraordinary fertility have produced, from the date of *Rookwood* (1834) to the present time. One of them we must not, however, omit to single out from the rest—*Mervyn Clitheroe*—as it gives many graphic sketches of the friends and scenes with which he was familiar in boyhood. Another, *The Lancashire Witches*, dedicated to his old friend, the President of the Chetham Society, in which, with great artistic skill, he has worked up the materials contained in two works in the Chetham series of very different character—Potts's *Discovery* and

Nicolas Assheton's Journal—will always have a peculiar interest
as a powerful and striking delineation of the grand superstition
of his native county. Nor should it be omitted that to
the very pleasing story, the *Flitch of Bacon*, we owe, under the
auspices of Mr. Ainsworth, the temporary revival of one of
the most curious and interesting of the old customs of England,
the giving of the Flitch at Great Dunmow. We proceed
to the list:

Rookwood, 1834.
Crichton, 1837.
Jack Sheppard, 1839.
Tower of London, 1840.
Guy Fawkes, 1841.
*Old St. Paul's, a Tale of the
  Plague and the Fire of
  London*, 1841.
The Miser's Daughter, 1842.
Windsor Castle, 1843.
*St. James's, or the Court of
  Queen Anne*, 1844.
Lancashire Witches, 1848.
Star-Chamber, 1854.
*The Flitch of Bacon, or the
  Custom of Dunmow*, 1854.
Spendthrift, 1856.
Mervyn Clitheroe, 1857.
*Ovingdean Grange, a Tale of
  the South Downs*, 1860.
Constable of the Tower, 1861.
The Lord Mayor of London,
  1862.
Cardinal Pole, 1863.

John Law the Projector, 1864.
*The Spanish Match, or Charles
  Stuart in Madrid*, 1865.
Myddleton Pomfret, 1865.
The Constable de Bourbon,
  1866.
Old Court, 1867.
The South Sea Bubble, 1868.
Hilary St. Ives, 1869.
Talbot Harland, 1870.
Tower Hill, 1871.
Boscobel, 1872.
*The Manchester Rebels of the
  Fatal '45*, 1873
Merry England, 1874.
The Goldsmith's Wife, 1874.
*Preston Fight, or the Insur-
  rection of 1715*, 1875.
Chetwynd Calverley, 1876.
*The Leaguer of Lathom, a
  Tale of the Civil War in
  Lancashire*, 1876.
The Fall of Somerset, 1877.
Beatrice Tyldesley, 1878.

That in so long a series, and dealing with scenes and
periods and subjects so diversified, Mr. Ainsworth should
still have retained his hold upon public favour, as is sufficiently evidenced by the continually repeated impressions of
his works both here, on the Continent, in America, and our
colonial dependencies, and the translations of them into most
of the languages of Europe, is an ample proof that he pos-
sesses those sterling qualities, as a writer of fiction, which
will ensure permanence to his name as an author. To continue to please the public by successive productions during

a period of more than forty years is a distinction accorded to few.

We must not forget to notice the collection of Mr. Ainsworth's ballads, published in 1855, which makes us regret that he has not continued to cultivate a species of composition for which he seems to have a peculiar talent. Nor can we pass by *The Combat of the Thirty, from an old Breton Lay of the 14th Century*, 1859, 8vo, a most spirited and excellent version which we should be glad to see in an illustrated form, which is all that is needed to give it an extensive popularity.

Mr. Forster, in his *Life of Charles Dickens*, has referred with evident pleasure to the kindly intercourse which existed between the far-famed Boz, himself, and Mr. Ainsworth, in the days gone by. We believe there is no one connected with literature, who has been brought within the range of the genial sympathy, the considerate feeling, and hearty and liberal hospitality of the subject of this sketch, who will not have equal pleasure in looking back to the occasions when they met. We are sure there are no reminiscences that dwell more agreeably on our minds than of the days when Kensal Manor House, on the Harrow Road, where Mr. Ainsworth resided for many years, was a central point for literary men; and when, after sitting under an admirable host and enjoying the conversation of men whom it was always a delight to meet, the guests were serenaded on those fine summer evenings as they went homewards by the nightingales which had not then deserted that part of the suburbs of London.

One of the advantages of the eminent authors of the present day is the admirable manner in which, as a rule, they have been represented pictorially. The portraits by Pickersgill and Maclise will always give, as far as painting can, to those unacquainted with the original, a perfect idea of the author of *Rookwood* when in the full bloom of age and authorship.

Mr. Ainsworth was present at the grand banquet in October, 1871, commemorating the new erections of the Manchester Free Grammar School, the Earl of Derby presiding; and, in an interesting and very appropriate speech, from which, if our space had allowed, we should have given some extracts, took a review of the alumni, who in former days had done honour to the School.

DEDICATION.

TO MY MOTHER.

WHEN I inscribed this Romance to you, my dear Mother, on its first appearance, I was satisfied that, whatever reception it might meet with elsewhere, at your hands it would be sure of indulgence.

Since then, the approbation your partiality would scarcely have withheld, has been liberally accorded by the public; and I have the satisfaction of reflecting, that in following the dictates of affection, which prompted me to select the dearest friend I had in the world as the subject of a Dedication, I have not overstepped the limits of prudence; nor, in connecting your honoured name with this trifling production, involved you in a failure which, had it occurred, would have given you infinitely more concern than myself.

After a lapse of three years, during which my little bark, fanned by pleasant and prosperous breezes, has sailed, more than once, securely into port, I again commit it to the waters, with more confidence than heretofore, and with a firmer reliance that, if it should be found "after many days," it may prove a slight memorial of the warmest filial regard.

Exposed to trials of no ordinary difficulty, and visited by domestic affliction of no common severity, you, my dear Mother, have borne up against the ills of life with a fortitude and resignation which those who knew you best can best appreciate, but which none can so well understand, or so thoroughly appreciate, as myself. Suffering is the lot of all. Submission under the dispensation is permitted to few. And it is my fervent hope that my own children may emulate your virtues, if they are happily spared your sorrows.

Hereafter, if I should realise a design, which I have always entertained, of illustrating the early manners and customs, as well as the local peculiarities, of the great commercial town to which I owe my birth, I would inscribe that book to my Father —"*une pauvre feuille de papier, tout ce que j'ai, en regrettant de n'avoir pas de granit ;"*—as a fit tribute to the memory of one whose energies were so unremittingly and so successfully directed towards the promotion of the public improvements in Manchester, that his name may, with propriety, be associated with its annals. Would that he had lived to see the good work he so well began entirely accomplished!

But the present Dedication, and that which I meditate, are inseparably connected together in my mind by the same ties of reverence and love. I would offer one to both, and both to one.

The tenderness lavished on my childhood, the guidance bestowed upon my youth, and the counsel afforded me in maturer years,

> All these, still legible in memory's page,
> And still to be so to my latest age,
> Add joy to duty, make me glad to pay
> Such honours to thee as my numbers may :
> Perhaps a frail memorial, but sincere,
> Not scorned in heaven, though little noticed here!

That you may be long spared to him* is the earnest wish of

Your very affectionate son,

WILLIAM HARRISON AINSWORTH.

October 18, 1837.

---

* The prayer was not granted. My venerated Mother was lost to me in little more than four years from the date of this dedication. She died 15th March, 1842.

PREFACE.

During a visit to Chesterfield, in the autumn of the year 1831, I first conceived the notion of writing this story. Wishing to describe, somewhat minutely, the trim gardens, the picturesque domains, the rook-haunted groves, the gloomy chambers, and gloomier galleries, of an ancient hall with which I was acquainted, I resolved to attempt a story in the bygone style of Mrs. Radcliffe (which had always inexpressible charms for me), substituting an old English squire, an old English manorial residence, and an old English highwayman, for the Italian marchese, the castle, and the brigand of the great mistress of Romance.

While revolving this subject, I happened, one evening, to enter the spacious cemetery attached to the church with the queer, twisted steeple, which, like the uplifted tail of the renowned Dragon of Wantley, to whom " houses and churches were as capons and turkeys," seems to menace the good town of Chesterfield with destruction. Here an incident occurred, on the opening of a vault, which it is needless to relate, but which supplied me with a hint for the commencement of my romance, as well as for the ballad entitled " The Coffin." Upon this hint I immediately acted ; and the earlier chapters of the book, together with the description of the ancestral mansion of the Rookwoods, were completed before I quitted Chesterfield.

Another and much larger portion of the work was written during a residence at Rottingdean, in Sussex, in the latter part of 1833, and owes its inspiration to many delightful walks over the Downs adjoining the sea-coast. Romance-writing was pleasant occupation then.

The Ride to York was completed in one day and one night. This feat—for a feat it was, being the composition of a hun-

dred ordinary novel pages in less than twenty-four hours—
was achieved at "The Elms"—a house I then occupied at
Kilburn. Well do I remember the fever into which I was
thrown during the time of composition. My pen literally
scoured over the pages. So thoroughly did I identify myself
with the flying highwayman, that, once started, I found it
impossible to halt. Animated by kindred enthusiasm, I
cleared every obstacle in my path with as much facility as
Turpin disposed of the impediments that beset his flight. In
his company, I mounted the hill-side, dashed through the
bustling village, swept over the desolate heath, threaded the
silent street, plunged into the eddying stream, and kept an
onward course, without pause, without hindrance, without
fatigue. With him I shouted, sang, laughed, exulted, wept.
Nor did I retire to rest till, in imagination, I heard the bell
of York Minster toll forth the knell of poor Black Bess.

The supernatural occurrence, forming the groundwork of
one of the ballads which I have made the harbinger of doom
to the house of Rookwood, is ascribed, by popular superstition,
to a family resident in Sussex; upon whose estate the
fatal tree (a gigantic lime, with mighty arms and huge girth
of trunk, as described in the song) is still carefully preserved.
Cuckfield Place, to which this singular piece of timber is
attached, is, I may state, for the benefit of the curious, the
real Rookwood Hall; for I have not drawn upon imagination,
but upon memory, in describing the seat and domains of that
fated family. The general features of the venerable structure,
several of its chambers, the old garden, and, in particular,
the noble park, with its spreading prospects, its
picturesque views of the hall, "like bits of Mrs. Radcliffe"
(as the poet Shelley once observed of the same scene), its
deep glades, through which the deer come lightly tripping
down, its uplands, slopes, brooks, brakes, coverts, and groves,
are carefully delineated.

The superstition of a fallen branch affording a presage of
approaching death is not peculiar to the family I have mentioned.
Many other old houses have been equally favoured
in fact, there is scarcely an ancient family in the kingdom
without a boding sign. For instance, the Breretons of Brereton,
in Cheshire, were warned by the appearance of stocks
of trees floating, like the swollen bodies of long-drowned
men, upon the surface of a sombre lake (called Blackmere,
from the inky colour of its waters) adjoining their residence;
and numerous other examples might be given. The death-

presage of the Breretons is alluded to by Drayton in the "*Polyolbion*."

It has been well observed by Barry Cornwall, "that the songs that occur in dramas are more natural than those which proceed from the author in person." With equal force does the reasoning apply to the romance, which may be termed the drama of the closet. It would seem strange, on a first view, that an author should be more at home in an assumed character than his own. But experience shows the position to be correct. Conscious he is no longer individually associated with his work, the writer proceeds with all the freedom of irresponsibility. His idiosyncrasy is merged in that of the personages he represents. He thinks with their thoughts; sees with their eyes; speaks with their tongues. His strains are such as he himself (*per se*) would not—perhaps could not—have originated. In this light he may be said to bring to his subject not one mind, but several; he becomes not one poet, but many; for each actor in his drama has a share, and an important share, in the lyrical *estro* to which he gives birth. This it is which has imparted any verve, variety, or dramatic character they possess, to the ballads contained in this production. Turpin I look upon as the real songster of " Black Bess;" to Jerry Juniper I am unquestionably indebted for a flash melody which, without his hint, would never have been written; while to the Sexton I owe the solitary gleam of light I have been enabled to throw upon the horrors and mystery of the churchyard.

As I have casually alluded to the flash song of Jerry Juniper, I may, perhaps, be allowed to make a few observations upon this branch of versification. It is somewhat curious, with a dialect so racy, idiomatic, and plastic as our own cant, that its metrical capabilities should have been so little essayed. The French have numerous *chansons d'argot*, ranging from the time of Charles Bourdigné and Villon down to that of Vidocq and Victor Hugo, the last of whom has enlivened the horrors of his " *Dernier Jour d'un Condamné*" by a festive song of this class. The Spaniards possess a large collection of *Romances de Germania*, by various authors, amongst whom Quevedo holds a distinguished place. We, on the contrary, have scarcely any slang songs of merit. With a race of depredators so melodious and convivial as our highwaymen, this is the more to be admired. Had they no bards amongst their bands? Was there no minstrel at hand to record their exploits? I can only call to mind one robber

who was a poet—Delany, and *he* was an Irishman. This
barrenness, I have shown, is not attributable to the poverty
of the soil, but to the want of due cultivation. Materials are
at hand in abundance, but there have been few operators.
Dekker, Beaumont and Fletcher, and Ben Jonson, have all
dealt largely in this jargon, but not lyrically; and one of
the earliest and best specimens of a canting-song occurs in
Brome's "*Jovial Crew;*" and in the "*Adventures of Bam-
fylde Moore Carew*" there is a solitary ode, addressed by the
mendicant fraternity to their newly-elected monarch; but it
has little humour, and can scarcely be called a genuine canting-song. This ode brings us down to our own time; to the
effusions of the illustrious Pierce Egan: to Tom Moore's
Flights of "*Fancy;*" to John Jackson's famous chant, "*On
the High Toby Spice flash the Muzzle,*" cited by Lord Byron
in a note to "*Don Juan;*" and to the glorious Irish ballad,
worth them all put together, entitled "*The Night before
Larry was stretched.*" This facetious performance is attributed to the late Dean Burrowes, of Cork. It is worthy of note,
that almost all modern aspirants to the graces of the *Musa
Pedestris* are Irishmen. Of all rhymesters of the "*Road,*"
however, Dean Burrowes is, as yet, most fully entitled to the
laurel. Larry is quite "the potato!"

And here, as the candidates are so few, and their pretensions so humble,

I can't help putting in my claim for praise.

I venture to affirm that I have done something more than
has been accomplished by my predecessors, or contemporaries, with the significant language under consideration.   I
have written a purely flash song; of which the great and
peculiar merit consists in its being utterly incomprehensible
to the uninformed understanding, while its meaning must be
perfectly clear and perspicuous to the practised *patterer* of
Romany, or *Pedlar's French.* I have, moreover, been the
first to introduce and naturalise amongst us a measure which,
though common enough in the Argotic minstrelsy of France,
has been hitherto utterly unknown to our *pedestrian* poetry.
Some years afterwards the song alluded to, better known
under the title of "*Nix my dolly, pals,—fake away!*" sprang
into extraordinary popularity, being set to music by Rodwell,
and chanted by glorious Paul Bedford and clever little Mrs.
Keeley.

Turpin was the hero of my boyhood. I had always a

strange passion for highwaymen, and have listened by the
hour to their exploits, as narrated by my father, and especially to those of "Dauntless Dick," that "chief minion of
the moon." One of Turpin's adventures in particular, the
ride to Hough Green, which took deep hold of my fancy, I
have recorded in song. When a boy, I have often lingered
by the side of the deep old road where this robbery was committed, to cast wistful glances into its mysterious windings;
and when night deepened the shadows of the trees, have
urged my horse on his journey, from a vague apprehension of
a visit from the ghostly highwayman. And then there was
the Bollin, with its shelving banks, that Turpin cleared at a
bound; the broad meadows over which he winged his flight;
the pleasant bowling-green of the pleasant old inn at Hough,
where he produced his watch to the Cheshire squires, with
whom he was upon terms of intimacy; all brought something
of the gallant robber to mind. No wonder, in after-years, in
selecting a highwayman for a character in a tale, I should
choose my old favourite, Dick Turpin.

In reference to two of the characters here introduced, and
drawn from personages living at the time the tale was written,
it may be mentioned that poor Jerry Juniper met his death
from an accident at Chichester, while he was proceeding to
Goodwood races; and that the knight of Malta (Mr. Tom, a
brewer of Truro, the self-styled Sir William Courtenay, who
played the strange tricks at Canterbury chronicled in a song
given in these pages), after his release from Barming Heath
Asylum, was shot through the head while leading on a mob
of riotous Kentish yeomen, whom he had persuaded that he
was the Messiah!

If the design of Romance be, what it has been held, the
exposition of an useful truth by means of an interesting
story, I fear I have but imperfectly fulfilled the office imposed
upon me; having, as I will freely confess, had, throughout,
an eye rather to the reader's amusement than his edification.
One wholesome moral, however, may, I trust, be gathered
from a perusal of this Tale; namely, that, without due
governance of the passions, high aspirations and generous
emotions will little avail their possessor. The impersonations
of the Tempter, the Tempted, and the Better Influence, may
be respectively discovered, by those who care to cull the
honey from the flower, in the Sexton, in Luke, and in Sybil.

But the chief object I had in view in making the present

essay, was to see how far the infusion of a warmer and more genial current into the veins of old Romance would succeed in reviving her fluttering and feeble pulses. The attempt has succeeded beyond my most sanguine expectation. Romance, if I am not mistaken, is destined shortly to undergo an important change. Modified by the German and French writers—by Hoffman, Tieck, Victor Hugo, Alexandre Dumas, Balzac, and Paul Lacroix—the structure commenced in our own land by Horace Walpole, Monk Lewis, Mrs. Radcliffe, and Maturin, but left imperfect and inharmonious, requires, now that the rubbish which choked up its approach is removed, only the hand of the skilful architect to its entire renovation and perfection.

And now, having said my say, I must bid you, worthy reader, farewell, beseeching you, in the words of old Rabelais, "to interpret all my sayings and doings in the perfectest sense. Reverence the cheese-like brain that feeds you with all these jolly maggots; and do what lies in you to keep me always merry. Be frolic now, my lads! Cheer up your hearts, and joyfully read the rest, with all ease of your body, and comfort of your reins."

KENSAL MANOR HOUSE,
    December 15, 1849.

ROOKWOOD.

Book the First.

THE WEDDING RING.

It has been observed, and I am apt to believe it is an observation which will generally be found true, that before a terrible truth comes to light, there are certain murmuring whispers fly before it, and prepare the minds of men for the reception of the truth itself.—*Gallick Reports.* *Case of the Count Saint Geran.*

I.

THE VAULT.

Let me know, therefore, fully the intent
Of this thy dismal preparation—
This talk fit for a charnel.   WEBSTER.

WITHIN a sepulchral vault, and at midnight, two persons were seated. The chamber was of singular construction and considerable extent. The roof was of solid stone masonry, and rose in a wide semicircular arch to the height of about seventeen feet, measured from the centre of the ceiling to the ground floor, while the sides were divided by slight partition-walls into ranges of low narrow catacombs. The entrance to each cavity was surmounted by an obtusely-pointed arch, resting upon slender granite pillars; and the intervening space was filled up with a variety of tablets, escutcheons, shields, and inscriptions, recording the titles and heraldic honours of the departed. There were no doors to the niches; and within might be seen piles of coffins, packed one upon another, till the floor groaned with the weight of lead. Against one of the pillars, upon a hook, hung a rack of tattered, time-out-of-mind hatchments; and in the centre of the tomb might be seen the effigies of Sir Ranulph de Roke-wode, the builder of the mausoleum, and the founder of the race who slept within its walls. This statue, wrought in black marble, differed from most monumental carved-work, in that its posture was erect and life-like. Sir Ranulph was represented as sheathed in a complete suit of mail, decorated

B

with his emblazoned and gilded surcoat, his arm leaning upon
the pommel of a weighty curtal-axe. The attitude was that
of stern repose. A conically-formed helmet rested upon the
brow ; the beaver was raised, and revealed harsh, but commanding features. The golden spur of knighthood was fixed
upon the heel ; and, at the feet, enshrined in a costly sarcophagus of marble, dug from the same quarry as the statue,
rested the mortal remains of one of " the sternest knights to
his mortal foe that ever put speare in the rest."

Streaming in a wavering line upon the roof, the sickly
flame of the candle partially fell upon the human figures
before alluded to, throwing them into darkest relief, and casting their opaque and fantastical shadows along the ground.
An old coffin upon a bier, we have said, served the mysterious
twain for a seat. Between them stood a bottle and a glass ;
evidences that, whatever might be the ulterior object of their
stealthy communion, the immediate comfort of the creature
had not been altogether overlooked. At the feet of one of
the personages were laid a mattock, a horn lantern (from
which the candle had been removed), a crowbar, and a bunch
of keys. Near to these implements of a vocation which the
reader will readily surmise, rested a strange superannuated
terrier, with a wiry back and frosted muzzle, a head minus
an ear, and a leg wanting a paw. His master, for such we
shall suppose him, was an old man, with a lofty forehead,
covered with a singularly-shaped nightcap, and clothed, as
to his lower limbs, with tight, ribbed, grey worsted hose,
ascending externally, after a bygone fashion, considerably
above the knee. The old man's elbow rested upon the handle
of his spade, his wrist supported his chin, and his grey,
glassy eyes, glimmering like marsh-meteors in the candle-
light, were fixed upon his companion with a glance of searching scrutiny.

The object of his investigation, a much more youthful and
interesting person, seemed lost in reverie, and alike insensible to time, place, and the object of the meeting. With
both hands grasped round the barrel of a fowling-piece, and
his face leaning upon the same support, the features were
entirely concealed from view ; the light, too, being to the
back, and shedding its rays over, rather than upon his person,
aided his disguise. Yet, even thus imperfectly defined, the
outline of the head and the proportions of the figure were
eminently striking and symmetrical. Attired in a rough
forester's costume, of the mode of 1737, and of the roughest

texture and rudest make, his wild garb would have determined his rank as sufficiently humble in the scale of society, had not a certain loftiness of manner, and bold, though reckless deportment, argued pretensions on the part of the wearer to a more elevated station in life, and contradicted, in a great measure, the impression produced by the homely appearance of his habiliments. A cap of shaggy, brown fur, fancifully, but not ungracefully fashioned, covered his head, from beneath which, dropping, in natural clusters, over his neck and shoulders, a cloud of raven hair escaped. Subsequently, when his face was more fully revealed, it proved to be that of a young man, of dark aspect, and grave, melancholy expression of countenance, approaching even to the stern, when at rest; though sufficiently animated and earnest when engaged in conversation, or otherwise excited. His features were regular, delicately formed, and might be characterised as singularly handsome, were it not for a want of roundness in the contour of the face, which gave the lineaments a thin, worn look, totally distinct, however, from haggardness or emaciation. The nose was delicate and fine, the nostril especially so; the upper lip was short, curling, graceful, and haughtily expressive. As to complexion, his skin had a truly Spanish warmth and intensity of colouring. His figure, when raised, was tall and masculine, and though slight, exhibited great personal vigour.

We will now turn to his companion, the old man with the great grey glittering eyes. Peter Bradley, of Rookwood (comitatû Ebor), where he had exercised the vocation of sexton for the best part of a life already drawn out to the full span ordinarily allotted to mortality, was an odd caricature of humanity. His figure was lean, and almost as lank as a skeleton. His bald head reminded one of a bleached skull, allowing for the overhanging and hoary brows. Deepseated, and sunken within their sockets, his grey orbs gleamed with intolerable lustre. Few could endure his gaze; and, aware of his power, Peter seldom failed to exercise it. He had likewise another habit, which, as it savoured of insanity, made him an object of commiseration with some, while it rendered him yet more obnoxious to others. The habit we allude to was the indulgence of wild screaming laughter at times when all merriment should be checked, and when the exhibition of levity must proceed from utter disregard of human grief and suffering, or from mental alienation.

Wearied with the prolonged silence, Peter at length condescended to speak. His voice was harsh and grating as a rusty hinge.

"Another glass?" said he, pouring out a modicum of the pale fluid.

His companion shook his head.

"It will keep out the cold," continued the sexton, pressing the liquid upon him; "and you, who are not so much accustomed as I am to the damps of a vault, may suffer from them. Besides," added he, sneeringly, "it will give you courage."

His companion answered not. But the flash of his eye resented the implied reproach.

"Nay, never stare at me so hard, Luke," continued the sexton; "I doubt neither your courage nor your firmness. But if you won't drink, I will. Here's to the rest eternal of Sir Piers Rookwood! You'll say amen to that pledge, or you are neither grandson of mine, nor offspring of his loins."

"Why should I reverence his memory," answered Luke, bitterly, refusing the proffered potion, "who showed no fatherly love for me? He disowned *me* in life; in death I disown *him*. Sir Piers Rookwood was no father of mine."

"He was as certainly your father, as Susan Bradley, your mother, was my daughter," rejoined the sexton.

"And, surely," cried Luke, impetuously, "*you* need not boast of the connection! 'Tis not for you, old man, to couple their names together—to exult in your daughter's disgrace and your own dishonour. Shame! shame! Speak not of them in the same breath, if you would not have me invoke curses on the dead! *I* have no reverence (whatever *you* may have) for the seducer—for the murderer of my mother."

"You have choice store of epithets, in sooth, good grandson," rejoined Peter, with a chuckling laugh. "Sir Piers a murderer!"

"Tush!" exclaimed Luke, indignantly, "affect not ignorance. You have better knowledge than I have of the truth or falsehood of the dark tale that has gone abroad respecting my mother's fate; and unless report has belied you foully, had substantial reasons for keeping sealed lips on the occasion. But to change this painful subject," added he, with a sudden alteration of manner, "at what hour did Sir Piers Rookwood die?"

"On Thursday last in the night-time. The exact hour I know not," replied the sexton.

"Of what ailment?"

"Neither do I know that. His end was sudden, yet not without a warning sign."

"What warning?" inquired Luke.

"Neither more nor less than the death omen of the house. You look astonished. Is it possible you have never heard of the ominous Lime-Tree and the Fatal Bough? Why, 'tis a common tale hereabouts, and has been for centuries. Any old crone would tell it you. Peradventure, you *have* seen the old avenue of lime-trees leading to the hall, nearly a quarter of a mile in length, and as noble a row of timber as any in the West Riding of Yorkshire. Well, there is one tree—the last on the left hand before you come to the clock-house—larger than all the rest—a huge piece of timber, with broad spreading branches, and of I know not what girth in the trunk. The tree is, in some mysterious manner, connected with the family of Rookwood, and immediately previous to the death of one of that line, a branch is sure to be shed from the parent stem, prognosticating his doom. But you shall hear the legend. And in a strange sepulchral tone, not inappropriate, however, to his subject, Peter chanted the following ballad:

THE LEGEND OF THE LIME-TREE.

Amid the grove o'er-arched above with lime-trees old and tall
(The avenue that leads unto the Rookwood's ancient hall),
High o'er the rest its towering crest one tree rears to the sky,
And wide out-flings, like mighty wings, its arms umbrageously.

Seven yards its base would scarce embrace—a goodly tree I ween,
With silver bark, and foliage dark of melancholy green;
And mid its boughs two ravens house, and build from year to year,
Their black brood hatch—their black brood watch—then screaming disappear.

In that old tree when playfully the summer breezes sigh,
Its leaves are stirred, and there is heard a low and plaintive cry;
And when in shrieks the storm blast speaks its reverend boughs among,
Sad wailing moans, like human groans, the concert harsh prolong.

But whether gale or calm prevail, or threatening cloud hath fled,
By hand of Fate, predestinate, a limb that tree will shed:
A verdant bough—untouched, I trow, by axe or tempest's breath—
To Rookwood's head an omen dread of fast-approaching death.

Some think that tree instinct must be with preternatural power,
Like 'larum bell Death's note to knell at Fate's appointed hour;
While some avow that on its bough are fearful traces seen,
Red as the stains from human veins commingling with the green.

Others, again, there are maintain that on the shattered bark,
A print is made, where fiends have laid their scathing talons dark ;
That, ere it falls, the raven calls thrice from that wizard bough ;
And that each cry doth signify what space the Fates allow.

In olden days, the legend says, as grim Sir Ranulph view'd
A wretched hag her footsteps drag beneath his lordly wood,
His blood-hounds twain he called amain, and straightway gave her chase ;
Was never seen in forest green, so fierce, so fleet a race !

With eyes of flame to Ranulph came each red and ruthless hound,
While mangled, torn—a sight forlorn !—the hag lay on the ground ;
E'en where she lay was turned the clay, and limb and reeking bone
Within the earth, with ribald mirth, by Ranulph grim were thrown.

And while as yet the soil was wet with that poor witch's gore,
A lime-tree stake did Ranulph take, and pierced her bosom's core ;
And, strange to tell, what next befel !—that branch at once took root,
And richly fed, within its bed, strong suckers forth did shoot.

From year to year fresh boughs appear—it waxes huge in size ;
And, with wild glee, this prodigy Sir Ranulph grim espies.
One day, when he, beneath that tree, reclined in joy and pride,
A branch was found upon the ground—the next, Sir Ranulph died !

And from that hour a fatal power has ruled that Wizard Tree,
To Ranulph's line a warning sign of doom and destiny ;
For when a bough is found, I trow, beneath its shade to lie,
Ere suns shall rise thrice in the skies a Rookwood sure shall die !

"And such an omen preceded Sir Piers's demise ?" said
Luke, who had listened with some attention to his grandsire's song.

"Unquestionably," replied the sexton. "Not longer ago
than Tuesday morning, I happened to be sauntering down
the avenue I have just described. I know not what took me
thither at that early hour, but I wandered leisurely on till I
came nigh the Wizard Lime-Tree. Great Heaven! what a
surprise awaited me ! a huge branch lay right across the path.
It had evidently just fallen ; for the leaves were green and
unwithered ; the sap still oozed from the splintered wood ;
and there was neither trace of knife nor hatchet on the bark.
I looked up among the boughs to mark the spot from whence
it had been torn by the hand of Fate—for no human hand
had done it—and saw the pair of ancestral ravens perched
amid the foliage, and croaking as those carrion fowl are wont
to do when they scent a carcase afar off. Just then a livelier
sound saluted my ears. The cheering cry of a pack of
hounds resounded from the courts, and the great gates being
thrown open, out issued Sir Piers, attended by a troop of his
roystering companions, all on horseback, and all making the
welkin ring with their vociferations. Sir Piers laughed as
loudly as the rest, but his mirth was speedily checked. No
sooner had his horse (old Rook, his favourite steed, who never

swerved at stake or pale before) set eyes upon this accursed branch, than he started as if the fiend stood before him, and, rearing backwards, flung his rider from his saddle. At this moment, with loud screams, the wizard ravens took flight. Sir Piers was somewhat hurt by the fall, but he was more frightened than hurt; and though he tried to put a bold face on the matter, it was plain that his efforts to recover himself were fruitless. Doctor Titus Tyrconnel and that wild fellow Jack Palmer (who has lately come to the hall, and of whom you know something) tried to rally him. But it would not do. He broke up the day's sport, and returned dejectedly to the hall. Before departing, however, he addressed a word to me, in private, respecting you; and pointed, with a melancholy shake of the head, to the fatal branch. ' *It is my death-warrant*,' said he, gloomily. And so it proved; two days afterwards his doom was accomplished."

"And do you place faith in this idle legend?" asked Luke, with affected indifference, although it was evident, from his manner, that he himself was not so entirely free from a superstitious feeling of credulity as he would have it appear.

"Certes," replied the sexton. "I were more difficult to be convinced than the unbelieving disciple else. Thrice hath it occurred to my own knowledge, and ever with the same result; firstly, with Sir Reginald; secondly, with thy own mother; and lastly, as I have just told thee, with Sir Piers."

"I thought you said, even now, that this death-omen, if such it be, was always confined to the immediate family of Rookwood, and not to mere inmates of the mansion."

"To the heads only of that house, be they male or female."

"Then how could it apply to my mother? Was *she* of that house? Was *she* a wife?"

"Who shall say she was *not?*" rejoined the sexton.

"Who shall say she *was* so?" cried Luke, repeating the words with indignant emphasis—"who will avouch *that?*"

A smile, cold as wintry sunbeam, played upon the sexton's rigid lips.

"I will bear this no longer," cried Luke; "anger me not, or look to yourself. In a word, have you anything to tell me respecting her? if not, let me begone."

"I have. But I will not be hurried by a boy like you," replied Peter, doggedly. "Go, if you will, and take the consequences. My lips are sealed for ever, and I have much to say—much that it behoves you to know."

"Be brief, then. When you sought me out this morning, in my retreat with the gipsy gang at Davenham Wood, you bade me meet you in the porch of Rookwood Church at midnight. I was true to my appointment."

"And I will keep my promise," replied the sexton. "Draw closer, that I may whisper in thine ear. Of every Rookwood who lies around us— and all that ever bore the name, except Sir Piers himself (who lies in state at the hall), are here—not one—mark what I say—not one male branch of the house but has been suspected——"

"Of what?"

"Of murder!" returned the sexton, in a hissing whisper.

"Murder!" echoed Luke, recoiling.

"There is one dark stain—one foul blot on all. Blood—blood hath been spilt."

"By all?"

"Ay, and *such* blood! theirs was no common crime. Even murder hath its degrees. Theirs was of the first class."

"Their wives! you cannot mean that?"

"Ay, their wives!—I do. You have heard it, then. Ha! ha! 'tis a trick they had. Did you ever hear the old saying?

> No mate ever brook would
> A Rook of the Rookwood!

A merry saying it is, and true. No woman ever stood in a Rookwood's way but she was speedily removed—that's certain. They had all, save poor Sir Piers, the knack of stopping a troublesome woman's tongue, and practised it to perfection. A rare art, eh?"

"What have the misdeeds of his ancestry to do with Sir Piers," muttered Luke, "much less with my mother?"

"Everything. If he could not rid himself of his wife (and she is a match for the devil himself), the *mistress* might be more readily set aside."

"Have you absolute knowledge of aught?" asked Luke, his voice tremulous with emotion.

"Nay, I but hinted."

"Such hints are worse than open speech. Let me know the worst. Did he kill her?" And Luke glared at the sexton as if he would have penetrated his secret soul.

But Peter was not easily fathomed. His cold, bright eye returned Luke's gaze steadfastly, as he answered composedly:

"I have said all I know."

"But not all you *think*."

"Thoughts should not always find utterance, else we might often endanger our own safety, and that of others."

"An idle subterfuge—and, from you, worse than idle. I will have an answer, yea or nay. Was it poison—was it steel?"

"Enough—she died."

"No, it is not enough. When? where?"

"In her sleep—in her bed."

"Why, that was natural."

A wrinkling smile crossed the sexton's brow.

"What means that horrible gleam of laughter?" exclaimed Luke, grasping the shoulder of the man of graves with such force as nearly to annihilate him. "Speak, or I will strangle you. She died, you say, in her sleep?"

"She did so," replied the sexton, shaking off Luke's hold.

"And was it to tell me that I had a mother's murder to avenge, that you brought me to the tomb of her destroyer—when he is beyond the reach of my vengeance?"

Luke exhibited so much frantic violence of manner and gesture, that the sexton entertained some little apprehension that his intellects were unsettled by the shock of the intelligence. It was, therefore, in what he intended for a soothing tone that he attempted to solicit his grandson's attention.

"I will hear nothing more," interrupted Luke, and the vaulted chamber rang with his passionate lamentations. "Am I the sport of this mocking fiend?" cried he, "to whom my agony is derision—my despair a source of enjoyment—beneath whose withering glance my spirit shrinks—who, with half-expressed insinuations, tortures my soul, awakening fancies that goad me on to dark and desperate deeds? Dead mother! upon thee I call. If in thy grave thou canst hear the cry of thy most wretched son, yearning to avenge thee—answer me, if thou hast the power. Let me have some token of the truth or falsity of these wild suppositions, that I may wrestle against this demon. But no," added he, in accents of despair, "no ear listens to me, save his to whom my wretchedness is food for mockery."

"Could the dead hear thee, thy mother might do so," returned the sexton. "She lies within this space."

Luke staggered back, as if struck by a sudden shot. He spoke not, but fell with a violent shock against a pile of coffins, at which he caught for support.

" What have I done !" he exclaimed, recoiling.

A thundering crash resounded through the vault. One of the coffins, dislodged from its position by his fall, tumbled to the ground, and. alighting upon its side, split asunder.

"Great Heavens! what is this?" cried Luke, as a dead body, clothed in all the hideous apparel of the tomb, rolled forth to his feet.

"It is your mother's corpse," answered the sexton, coldly ; "I brought you hither to behold it. But you have anticipated my intentions."

" *This* my mother?" shrieked Luke, dropping upon his knees by the body, and seizing one of its chilly hands, as it lay upon the floor, with the face upwards.

The sexton took the candle from the sconce.

" Can this be death?" shouted Luke. " Impossible! Oh, God! she stirs—she moves. The light!—quick. I see her stir! This is dreadful!"

" Do not deceive yourself," said the sexton, in a tone which betrayed more emotion than was his wont. " 'Tis the bewilderment of fancy. She will never stir again."

And he shaded the candle with his hand, so as to throw the light full upon the face of the corpse. It was motionless as that of an image carved in stone. No trace of corruption was visible upon the rigid, yet exquisite tracery of its features. A profuse cloud of raven hair, escaped from its swathements in the fall, hung like a dark veil over the bosom and person of the dead, and presented a startling contrast to the waxlike hue of the skin and the pallid cereclothes. Flesh still adhered to the hand, though it mouldered into dust within the gripe of Luke, as he pressed the fingers to his lips. The shroud was disposed like night-gear about her person, and from without its folds a few withered flowers had fallen. A strong aromatic odour, of a pungent nature, was diffused around; giving evidence that the art by which the ancient Egyptians endeavoured to rescue their kindred from decomposition had been resorted to, to preserve the fleeting charms of the unfortunate Susan Bradley.

A pause of awful silence succeeded, broken only by the convulsive respiration of Luke. The sexton stood by, apparently an indifferent spectator of the scene of horror. His eye wandered from the dead to the living, and gleamed with a peculiar and indefinable expression, half apathy, half abstraction. For one single instant, as he scrutinised the features of his daughter, his brow, contracted by anger, immediately afterwards was elevated in scorn. But otherwise you would have sought in vain to read the purport of that cold, insensible glance, which dwelt for a brief space on the face of the mother, and settled eventually upon her son. At length the withered flowers attracted his attention. He stooped to pick up one of them.

"Faded as the hand that gathered ye—as the bosom on which ye were strewn!" he murmured. "No sweet smell left—but—faugh!" Holding the dry leaves to the flame of the candle, they were instantly ignited, and the momentary brilliance played like a smile upon the features of the dead. Peter observed the effect. "Such was thy life," he exclaimed; "a brief, bright sparkle, followed by dark, utter extinction!"

Saying which, he flung the expiring ashes of the floweret from his hand.

II.

THE SKELETON HAND.

> *Duch.* You are very cold.
> I fear you are not well after your travel.
> Ha! lights.—Oh horrible!
> *Fer.* Let her have lights enough.
> *Duch.* What witchcraft doth he practise, that he hath left
> A dead hand here?   *Duchess of Malfy.*

THE sexton's waning candle now warned him of the progress of time, and having completed his arrangements, he addressed himself to Luke, intimating his intention of departing. But receiving no answer, and remarking no signs of life about his grandson, he began to be apprehensive that he had fallen into a swoon. Drawing near to Luke, he took him gently by the arm. Thus disturbed, Luke groaned aloud.

"I am glad to find you can breathe, if it be only after that melancholy fashion," said the sexton; "but come, I have wasted time enough already. You must indulge your grief elsewhere."

"Leave me," sighed Luke.

"What, here? It were as much as my office is worth. You can return some other night. But go you must, now— at least, if you take on thus. I never calculated upon a scene like this, or it had been long ere I brought you hither.

So come away; yet, stay; but first lend me a hand to replace the body in the coffin."

"Touch it not," exclaimed Luke; "she shall not rest another hour within these accursed walls. I will bear her hence myself." And, sobbing hysterically, he relapsed into his former insensibility.

"Poh! this is worse than midsummer madness," said Peter; "the lad is crazy with grief, and all about a mother who has been four-and-twenty years in her grave. I will e'en put her out of the way myself."

Saying which, he proceeded, as noiselessly as possible, to raise the corpse in his arms, and deposited it softly within its former tenement. Carefully as he executed his task, he could not accomplish it without occasioning a slight accident to the fragile frame. Insensible as he was, Luke had not relinquished the hold he maintained of his mother's hand. And when Peter lifted the body, the ligaments connecting the hand with the arm were suddenly snapped asunder. It would appear afterwards, that this joint had been tampered with, and partially dislocated. Without, however, entering into further particulars in this place, it may be sufficient to observe that the hand, detached from the socket at the wrist, remained within the gripe of Luke; while, ignorant of the mischief he had occasioned, the sexton continued his labours unconsciously, until the noise, which he of necessity made in stamping with his heel upon the plank, recalled his grandson to sensibility. The first thing that the latter perceived, upon collecting his faculties, were the skeleton fingers twined within his own.

"What have you done with the body? Why have you left this with me?" demanded he.

"It was not my intention to have done so," answered the sexton, suspending his occupation. "I have just made fast the lid, but it is easily undone. You had better restore it."

"Never," returned Luke, staring at the bony fragment.

"Pshaw! of what advantage is a dead hand? 'Tis an unlucky keepsake, and will lead to mischief. The only use I ever heard of such a thing being turned to, was in the case of Bowlegged Ben, who was hanged in irons for murder, on Hardchase Heath, on the York Road, and whose hand was cut off at the wrist the first night to make a Hand of Glory, or Dead Man's Candle. Hast never heard what the old song says?" And without awaiting his grandson's response, Peter broke into the following wild strain:

THE HAND OF GLORY.*

From the corse that hangs on the roadside tree
(A murderer's corse it needs must be),
Sever the right hand carefully :—
Sever the hand that the deed hath done,
Ere the flesh that clings to the bones be gone,
In its dry veins must blood be none.
Those ghastly fingers white and cold,
Within a winding-sheet enfold ;
Count the mystic count of seven ;
Name the Governors of heaven †
Then in earthen vessel place them,
And with dragon-wort encase them,
Bleach them in the noonday sun,
Till the marrow melt and run,
Till the flesh is pale and wan,
As a moon-ensilvered cloud,
As an unpolluted shroud.
Next within their chill embrace
The dead man's Awful Candle place :
Of murderer's fat must that candle be
(You may scoop it beneath the roadside tree),
Of wax, and of Lapland sisame.
Its wick must be twisted of hair of the dead,
By the crow and her brood on the wild waste shed.
Wherever that terrible light shall burn
Vainly the sleeper may toss and turn ;
His leaden lids shall he ne'er unclose
So long as that magical taper glows.
Life and treasure shall he command
Who knoweth the charm of the Glorious Hand !
But of black cat's gall let him aye have care,
And of screech-owl's venomous blood beware !

"Peace!" thundered Luke, extending his mother's hand towards the sexton. "What seest thou?"

"I see something shine. Hold it nigher the light. Ha! that is strange, truly. How came that ring there?"

"Ask of Sir Piers! ask of her *husband*!" shouted Luke, with a wild burst of exulting laughter. "Ha! ha! ha! 'tis a wedding-ring! And look! the finger is bent. It must have been placed upon it in her lifetime. There is no deception in this—no trickery—ha!"

"It would seem not ; the sinew must have been contracted in life. The tendons are pulled down so tightly, that the ring could not be withdrawn without breaking the finger."

"You are sure that coffin contains her body?"

"As sure as I am that this carcase is my own."

"The hand—'tis hers. Can any doubt exist?"

* See the celebrated recipe for the Hand of Glory in "Les Secrets du Petit Albert."
† The seven planets, so called by Mercurius Trismegistus.

"Wherefore should it? It was broken from the arm by accident within this moment. I noticed not the occurrence, but it must have been so."

"Then it follows that she was wedded, and I am not——"

"Illegitimate. For your own sake I am glad of it."

"My heart will burst. Oh! could I but establish the fact of this marriage, her wrongs would be indeed avenged."

"Listen to me, Luke," said the sexton, solemnly. "I told you, when I appointed this midnight interview, I had a secret to communicate. That secret is now revealed—that secret was your mother's marriage."

"And was it known to you during her lifetime?"

"It was. But I was sworn to secrecy."

"You have proofs then?"

"I have nothing beyond Sir Piers's word—and he is silent now."

"By whom was the ceremony performed?"

"By a Romish priest—a Jesuit—one Father Checkley, at that time an inmate of the hall; for Sir Piers, though he afterwards abjured it, at that time professed the Catholic faith; and this Checkley officiated as his confessor and counsellor; as the partner of his pleasures, and the prompter of his iniquities. He was your father's evil genius."

"Is he still alive?"

"I know not. After your mother's death he left the hall. I have said he was a Jesuit, and I may add, that he was mixed up in dark political intrigues, in which your father was too feeble a character to take much share. But though too weak to guide, he was a pliant instrument, and this Checkley knew. He moulded him according to his wishes. I cannot tell you what was the nature of their plots. Suffice it, they were such as, if discovered, would have involved your father in ruin. He was saved, however, by his wife."

"And her reward——" groaned Luke.

"Was death," replied Peter, coldly. "What Jesuit ever forgave a wrong—real or imaginary? Your mother, I ought to have said, was a Protestant. Hence, there was a difference of religious opinion (the worst of differences that can exist between husband and wife.) Checkley vowed her destruction, and he kept his vow. He was enamoured of her beauty. But while he burnt with adulterous desire, he was consumed by fiercest hate—contending, and yet strangely-reconcileable passions—as you may have reason, hereafter, to discover."

"Go on," said Luke, grinding his teeth.

"I have done," returned Peter. "From that hour your father's love for his supposed mistress, and unacknowledged wife, declined; and with his waning love declined her health. I will not waste words in describing the catastrophe that awaited her union. It will be enough to say, she was found one morning a corpse within her bed. Whatever suspicions were attached to Sir Piers were quieted by Checkley, who distributed gold, largely and discreetly. The body was embalmed by Barbara Lovel, the Gipsy Queen."

"My foster-mother!" exclaimed Luke, in a tone of extreme astonishment.

"Ay," replied Peter, "from her you may learn all particulars. You have now seen what remains of your mother. You are in possession of the secret of your birth. The path is before you, and if you would arrive at honour you must pursue it steadily, turning neither to the right nor to the left. Opposition you will meet at each step. But fresh lights may be thrown upon this difficult case. It is in vain to hope for Checkley's evidence, even should the caitiff priest be living. He is himself too deeply implicated—ha!"

Peter stopped, for at this moment the flame of the candle suddenly expired, and the speakers were left in total darkness. Something like a groan followed the conclusion of the sexton's discourse. It was evident that it proceeded not from his grandson, as an exclamation burst from him at the same instant. Luke stretched out his arm. A cold hand seemed to press against his own, communicating a chill like death to his frame.

"Who is between us?" he ejaculated.

"The devil!" cried the sexton, leaping from the coffin-lid with an agility that did him honour. "Is aught between us?"

"I will discharge my gun. Its flash will light us."

"Do so," hastily rejoined Peter. "But not in this direction."

"Get behind me," cried Luke. And he pulled the trigger.

A blaze of vivid light illumined the darkness. Still nothing was visible, save the warrior figure, which was seen for a moment, and then vanished like a ghost. The buck-shot rattled against the further end of the vault.

"Let us go hence," ejaculated the sexton, who had rushed to the door and thrown it wide open. "Mole! Mole!" cried he, and the dog sprang after him.

"I could have sworn I felt something," said Luke; "whence issued that groan?"

"Ask not whence," replied Peter. "Reach me my mattock and spade, and the lantern; they are behind you. And stay, it were better to bring away the bottle."

"Take them, and leave me here."

"Alone in the vault—no, no, Luke, I have not told you half I know concerning that mystic statue. It is said to move—to walk—to raise its axe—be warned, I pray."

"Leave me, or abide, if you will, my coming in the church. If there is aught that may be revealed to my ear alone, I will not shrink from it, though the dead themselves should arise to proclaim the mystery. It may be—but—go—there are your tools." And he shut the door with a jar that shook the sexton's frame.

Peter, after some muttered murmurings at the hardihood and madness, as he termed it, of his grandson, disposed his lanky limbs to repose upon a cushioned bench without the communion railing. As the pale moonlight fell upon his gaunt and cadaverous visage, he looked like some unholy thing suddenly annihilated by the presiding influence of that sacred spot. Mole crouched himself in a ring at his master's feet. Peter had not dozed many minutes when he was aroused by Luke's return. The latter was very pale, and the damp stood in big drops upon his brow.

"Have you made fast the door?" inquired the sexton.

"Here is the key."

"What have you seen?" he next demanded.

Luke made no answer. At that moment the church clock struck two, breaking the stillness with an iron clang. Luke raised his eyes. A ray of moonlight, streaming obliquely through the painted window, fell upon the gilt lettering of a black mural entablature. The lower part of the inscription was in the shade, but the emblazonment and the words—

Orate pro anima Reginaldi Rookwood equitis aurati,

were clear and distinct. Luke trembled, he knew not why, as the sexton pointed to it.

"You have heard of the handwriting upon the wall," said Peter. "Look there!—'His kingdom hath been taken from him.' Ha, ha! Listen to me. Of all thy monster race—of all the race of Rookwood I should say—no demon ever stalked the earth more terrible than him whose tablet you now behold. By him a brother was betrayed; by him a brother's wife was dishonoured. Love, honour, friendship, were with him as words. He regarded no ties; he defied and set at naught all human laws and obligations—and yet he was religious, or esteemed so—received the *viaticum*, and died full of years and honours, hugging salvation to his sinful heart. And after death he has yon lying epitaph to record his virtues. *His* virtues! ha! ha! Ask him who preaches to the kneeling throng gathering within this holy place, what shall be the murderer's portion—and he will answer—*Death!* And yet Sir Reginald was long-lived. The awful question, 'Cain, where is thy brother?' broke not his tranquil slumbers. Luke, I have told you much—but not all. You know not, as yet—nor shall you know your destiny; but you shall be the avenger of infamy and blood. I have a sacred charge committed to my keeping, which, hereafter, I may delegate to you. You *shall* be Sir Luke Rookwood, but the conditions it must be mine to propose."

"No more," said Luke; "my brain reels. I am faint. Let us quit this place, and get into the fresh air." And striding past his grandsire, he traversed the aisles with hasty steps. Peter was not slow to follow. The key was applied, and they emerged into the churchyard. The grassy mounds were bathed in the moonbeams, and the two yew-trees, throwing their black, jagged shadows over the grave-hills, looked like evil spirits brooding over the repose of the righteous.

The sexton noticed the deathly paleness of Luke's countenance, but he fancied it might proceed from the tinge of the sallow moonlight.

"I will be with you at your cottage, ere daybreak," said Luke. And turning an angle of the church, he disappeared from view.

"So," exclaimed Peter, gazing after him, "the train is laid; the spark has been applied; the explosion will soon follow. The hour is fast approaching when I shall behold this accursed house shaken to dust, and when my long-delayed vengeance will be gratified. In that hope I am content to drag on the brief remnant of my days. Meanwhile, I must not omit the stimulant. In a short time I may not require it." Draining the bottle to the last drop, he flung it from him, and commenced chanting, in a high key and cracked voice, a wild ditty, the words of which ran as follow:

c

THE CARRION CROW.*

The Carrion Crow is a sexton bold,
He raketh the dead from out of the mould;
He delveth the ground like a miser old,
Stealthily hiding his store of gold.   *Caw! Caw!*

The Carrion Crow hath a coat of black,
Silky and sleek like a priest's to his back;
Like a lawyer he grabbeth—no matter what way—
The fouler the offal, the richer his prey.
                    Caw! Caw! the Carrion Crow!
                    Dig! Dig! in the ground below!

The Carrion Crow hath a dainty maw,
With savory pickings he crams his craw;
Kept meat from the shambles to please well his whim,
It never can hang too long for him!   *Caw! Caw!*

The Carrion Crow sees with powder, 'tis said,
Like a soldier each with the taste of cold lead;
No jester, or no one again servy service of;
For, wherever he fights ah, he caws with him!
                    Caw! Caw! the Carrion Crow!
                    Dig! Dig! in the ground below!

Shouldering his spade, and whistling to his dog, the sexton
quitted the churchyard.

Peter had not been gone many a little, when a dark figure,
muffled in a wide flowing mantle, emerged from among the
tombs surrounding the church; gazed after him for a few
seconds, and then, with a menacing gesture, retreated behind
the ivied buttresses of the grey old pile.

III.

THE PARK.

Brian. Ralph! hearest thou any stirring?
Ralph. I heard one speak here hard by in the hollow. Peace! master,
speak low. Nouns! if I do not hear a bow go off, and the buck bray, I never
heard deer in my life.
Bri. Stand, or I'll shoot.
Sir Arthur. Who's there?
Bri. I am the keeper, and do charge you stand.
        You have stolen my deer.   *Merry Devil of Edmonton.*

LUKE's first impulse had been to free himself from the
restraint imposed by his grandsire's society. He longed to
commune with himself. Leaping the small boundary-wall,
which defended the churchyard from a deep green lane, he
hurried along in a direction contrary to that taken by the

* Set to music by Mr. F. Romer.

sexton, making the best of his way until he arrived at a gap in the high-banked hazel hedge, which overhung the road. Heedless of the impediments thrown in his way by the undergrowth of a rough ring-fence, he struck through the opening that presented itself, and, climbing over the moss-grown paling, trod presently upon the elastic sward of Rookwood Park.

A few minutes' rapid walking brought him to the summit of a rising ground crowned with aged oaks, and, as he passed beneath their broad shadows, his troubled spirit, soothed by the quietude of the scene, in part resumed its serenity.

Luke yielded to the gentle influence of the time and hour. The stillness of the spot allayed the irritation of his frame, and the dewy chilliness cooled the fever of his brow. Leaning for support against the gnarled trunk of one of the trees, he gave himself up to contemplation. The events of the last hour—of his whole existence—passed in rapid review before him. The thought of the wayward, vagabond life he had led; of the wild adventures of his youth; of all he had been; of all he had *done*; of all he had endured—crowded his mind; and then, like the passing of a cloud flitting across the autumnal moon, and occasionally obscuring the smiling landscape before him, his soul was shadowed by the remembrance of the awful revelations of the last hour, and the fearful knowledge he had acquired of his mother's fate — of his father's guilt.

The eminence on which he stood was one of the highest points of the park, and commanded a view of the hall, which might be a quarter of a mile distant, discernible through a broken vista of trees, its whitened walls glimmering in the moonlight; and its tall chimney spiring far from out the round masses of wood in which it lay embosomed. The ground gradually sloped in that direction, occasionally rising into swells, studded with magnificent timber—dipping into smooth dells, or stretching out into level glades, until it suddenly sank into a deep declivity, that formed an effectual division, without the intervention of a haw-haw, or other barrier, between the chase and the home-park. A slender stream strayed through this ravine, having found its way thither from a small reservoir, hidden in the higher plantations to the left; and further on, in the open ground, and in a line with the hall, though, of course, much below the level of the building, assisted by many local springs, and restrained by a variety of natural and artificial embankments, this

brook spread out into an expansive sheet of water. Crossed
by a rustic bridge, the only communication between the
parks, the pool found its outlet into the meads below; and
even at that distance, and in that still hour, you might almost
catch the sound of the brawling waters, as they dashed down
the weir in a foaming cascade; while, far away, in the spreading valley, the serpentine meanderings of the slender current
might be traced, glittering like silvery threads in the moonshine. The mild beams of the queen of night, then in her
meridian, trembled upon the topmost branches of the tall
timber, quivering like diamond spray upon the outer foliage;
and, penetrating through the interstices of the trees, fell
upon the light wreaths of vapour, then beginning to arise
from the surface of the pool, steeping them in misty splendour, and lending to this part of the picture a character of
dreamy and unearthly beauty.

All else was in unison. No sound interrupted the silence
of Luke's solitude, except the hooting of a large grey owl,
that, scared at his approach, or in search of prey, winged its
spectral flight in continuous and mazy circles round his
head, uttering at each wheel its startling whoop; or a deep
distant bay, that ever and anon boomed upon the ear, proceeding from a pack of hounds kennelled in a shed adjoining
the pool before mentioned, but which was shrouded from
view by the rising mist. No living objects presented themselves, save a herd of deer, crouched in a covert of brown
fern beneath the shadow of a few stunted trees, immediately
below the point of land on which Luke stood; and although
their branching antlers could scarcely be detected from the
ramifications of the wood itself, they escaped not his practised ken.

"How often," murmured Luke, "in years gone by, have I
traversed these moonlit glades, and wandered amidst these
woodlands, on nights heavenly as this—ay, and to some purpose, as you thinned herd might testify! Every dingle,
every dell, every rising brow, every bosky vale and shelving
covert, have been as familiar to my track as to that of the
fleetest and freest of their number: scarce a tree amidst the
thickest of yon outstretching forest with which I cannot
claim acquaintance; 'tis long since I have seen them. By
heavens! 'tis beautiful! and it is all my own! Can I forget
that it was here I first emancipated myself from thraldom?
Can I forget the boundless feeling of delight that danced
within my veins when I first threw off the yoke of servitude,

and roved unshackled, unrestrained, amidst these woods?
The wild intoxicating bliss still tingles to my heart. And
they are all my own — my own! Softly, what have we
there!"

Luke's attention was arrested by an object which could not
fail to interest him, sportsman as he was. A snorting bray
was heard, and a lordly stag stalked slowly and majestically
from out the copse. Luke watched the actions of the noble
animal with great interest, drawing back into the shade. A
hundred yards, or thereabouts, might be between him and
the buck. It was within range of ball. Luke mechanically
grasped his gun; yet his hand had scarcely raised the piece
half way to his shoulder, when he dropped it again to its
rest.

"What am I about to do?" he mentally ejaculated.
"Why, for mere pastime, should I take away yon noble
creature's life, when his carcase would be utterly useless to
me? Yet such is the force of habit, that I can scarce resist
the impulse that tempted me to fire; and I have known the
time, and that not long since, when I should have shown no
such self-control."

Unconscious of the danger it had escaped, the animal
moved forward with the same stately step. Suddenly it
stopped with ears pricked, as if some sound had smote them.
At that instant the click of a gun-lock was heard, at a little
distance to the right. The piece had missed fire. An instantaneous report from another gun succeeded; and, with a
bound high in air, the buck fell upon his back, struggling in
the agonies of death. Luke had at once divined the cause;
he was aware that poachers were at hand. He fancied that
he knew the parties; nor was he deceived in his conjecture.
Two figures issued instantly from a covert on the right, and
making to the spot, the first who reached it put an end to
the animal's struggles by plunging a knife into its throat.
The affrighted herd took to their heels, and were seen darting
swiftly down the chase.

One of the twain, meantime, was occupied in feeling for the
deer's fat, when he was approached by the other, who pointed
in the direction of the house. The former raised himself
from his kneeling posture, and both appeared to listen atten-
tively. Luke fancied he heard a slight sound in the distance;
whatever the noise proceeded from, it was evident the deer-
stealers were alarmed. They laid hold of the buck, and,
dragging it along, concealed the carcase among the tall fern;

they then retreated, halting for an instant to deliberate, within a few yards of Luke, who was concealed from their view by the trunk of the tree, behind which he had ensconced his person. They were so near, that he lost not a word of their muttered conference.

"The game's spoiled this time, Rob Rust, anyhow," growled one, in an angry tone; "the hawks are upon us, and we must leave this brave buck to take care of himself. Curse him!—who'd a' thought of Hugh Badger's quitting his bed to-night? Respect for his late master might have kept him quiet the night before the funeral. But look out, lad. Dost see 'em?"

"Ay, thanks to old Oliver—yonder they are," returned the other. "One—two—three—and a muzzled bouser to boot. There's Hugh at the head on 'em. Shall we stand and show fight. I have half a mind for it."

"No, no," replied the first speaker; "that will never do, Rob—no fighting. Why run the risk of being grabb'd for a haunch of venison? Had Luke Bradley or Jack Palmer been with us, it might have been another affair. As it is, it won't pay. Besides, we've that to do at the hall to-morrow night that may make men of us for the rest of our nat'ral lives. We've pledged ourselves to Jack Palmer, and we can't be off in honour. It won't do to be snabbled in the nick of it. So let's make for the prad in the lane. Keep in the shade as much as you can. Come along, my hearty." And away the two worthies scampered down the hill-side.

"Shall I follow," thought Luke. "and run the risk of falling into the keeper's hand, just at this crisis, too? No, but if I am found here, I shall be taken for one of the gang. Something must be done—ha!—devil take them, here they are already."

Further time was not allowed him for reflection. A hoarse baying was heard, followed by a loud cry from the keepers. The dog had scented out the game; and, as secrecy was no longer necessary, his muzzle had been removed. To rush forth now were certain betrayal; to remain, was almost equally assured detection; and, doubting whether he should obtain credence if he delivered himself over in that garb and armed, Luke at once rejected the idea. Just then it flashed across his recollection that his gun had remained unloaded, and he applied himself eagerly to repair this negligence, when he heard the dog in full cry, making swiftly in his direction. He threw himself upon the ground, where the fern was thickest; but this seemed insufficient to baffle the sagacity of the hound—the animal had got his scent, and was baying close at hand. The keepers were drawing nigh. Luke gave himself up for lost. The dog, however, stopped where the two poachers had halted, and was there completely at fault: snuffing the ground, he bayed, wheeled round, and then set off with renewed barking upon their track. Hugh Badger and his comrades loitered an instant at the same place, looked warily round, and then, as Luke conjectured, followed the course taken by the hound.

Swift as thought, Luke arose, and keeping as much as possible under cover of the trees, started in a cross line for the lane. Rapid as was his flight, it was not without a witness; one of the keepers assistants, who had lagged behind, gave the view-halloo in a loud voice. Luke pressed forward with redoubled energy, and aiming to gain the shelter of the plantation, and this he could readily have accomplished had no impediment been in his way. But his rage and vexation were boundless, when he heard the keeper's cry echoed by shouts immediately below him, and the tongue of the hound resounding in the hollow. He turned sharply round, steering a middle course, and still aiming at the fence. It was evident from the cheers of his pursuers, that he was in full view, and he heard them encouraging and directing the dog.

Luke had gained the park palings, along which he rushed, in the vain quest of some practicable point of egress, for the fence was higher in this part of the park than elsewhere, owing to the inequality of the ground. He had cast away his gun as useless. But even without that incumbrance he dared not hazard the delay of climbing the palings. At this juncture a deep breathing was heard close behind him. He threw a glance over his shoulder. Within a few yards was a ferocious bloodhound, with whose savage nature Luke was well acquainted; the breed, some of which he had already seen, having been retained at the Hall ever since the days of grim old Sir Ranulph. The eyes of the hound were glaring, blood-red; his tongue was hanging out, and a row of keen white fangs were displayed, like the teeth of a shark. There was a growl—a leap—and the dog was close upon him.

Luke's courage was undoubted. But his heart failed him as he heard the roar of the remorseless brute, and felt that he could not avoid an encounter with the animal. His reso-

lution was instantly taken; he stopped short with such suddenness, that the dog, when in the act of springing, flew past
him with great violence, and the time, momentary as it was,
occupied by the animal in recovering himself, enabled Luke
to drop on his knee, and to place one arm, like a buckler,
before his face, while he held the other in readiness to grapple
his adversary. Uttering a fierce yell, the hound returned to
the charge, darting at Luke, who received the assault without
flinching; and in spite of a severe laceration of the arm, he
seized his foe by the throat, and hurling him upon the
ground, jumped with all his force upon his belly. There was
a yell of agony—the contest was ended, and Luke was at
liberty to pursue his flight unmolested.

Brief as had been the interval required for this combat, it
had been sufficient to bring the pursuers within sight of the
fugitive. Hugh Badger, who from the acclivity had witnessed
the fate of his favourite, with a loud oath discharged the
contents of his gun at the head of its destroyer. It was
fortunate for Luke, that at this instant he stumbled over the
root of a tree—the shot rattled in the leaves as he fell, and
the keeper, concluding that he had at least winged his bird,
descended more leisurely towards him. As he lay upon the
ground, Luke felt that he was wounded; whether by the teeth
of the dog, from a stray shot, or from bruises inflicted by the
fall, he could not determine. But, smarting with pain, he
resolved to wreak his vengeance upon the first person who
approached him. He vowed not to be taken with life—to
strangle any one who should lay hands upon him. At that
moment he felt a pressure at his breast. It was the dead
hand of his mother!

Luke shuddered. The fire of revenge quenched. He
mentally cancelled his rash oath; yet he could not bring
himself to surrender at discretion, and without further effort.
The keeper and his assistants were approaching the spot
where he lay, and searching for his body. Hugh Badger was
foremost, and within a yard of him.

"Confound the rascal," cried Hugh, "he's not half killed;
he seems to breathe."

The words were scarcely out of his mouth ere the speaker
was dashed backwards, and lay sprawling upon the sod.
Suddenly and unexpectedly, as an Indian chief might rush
upon his foes, Luke arose, dashing himself with great violence
against Hugh, who happened to stand in his way, and before
the startled assistants, who were either too much taken by

surprise, or unwilling to draw a trigger, could in any way lay hands upon him, exerting all the remarkable activity which he possessed, he caught hold of a projecting branch of a tree, and swung himself, at a single bound, fairly over the paling.

Hugh Badger was shortly on his legs, swearing lustily at his defeat. Directing his men to skirt alongside the fence, and make for a particular part of the plantation, which he named, and snatching a loaded fowling-piece from one of them, he clambered over the pales, and guided by the crashing branches, and other sounds conveyed to his quick ear, he was speedily upon Luke's track.

The plantation through which the chase now took place was not, as might be supposed, a continuation of the ring-fence which Luke had originally crossed, on his entrance into the park, though girded by the same line of paling, but, in reality, a close pheasant preserve, occupying the banks of a ravine, which, after a deep and tortuous course, terminated in the declivity heretofore described as forming the park boundary. Luke plunged into the heart of this defile, fighting his way downwards, in the direction of the brook. His progress was impeded by a thick undergrowth of brier, and other matted vegetation, as well as by the entanglements thrown in his way by the taller bushes of thorn and hazel, the entwined and elastic branches of which, in their recoil, galled and fretted him, by inflicting smart blows on his face and hands. This was a hardship he usually little regarded. But, upon the present occasion, it had the effect, by irritating his temper, of increasing the thirst of vengeance raging in his bosom.

Through the depths of the ravine welled the shallow stream before alluded to, and Hugh Badger had no sooner reached its sedgy margin than he lost all trace of the fugitive. He looked cautiously round, listened intently, and inclined his ear to catch the faintest echo. All was still: not a branch shook, nor a leaf rustled. Hugh looked aghast. He had made sure of getting a glimpse, and, perhaps, a stray shot at the " poaching rascal," as he termed him, " in the open space, which he was sure the fellow was aiming to reach ; and now, all at once, he had disappeared, like a will-o'-the-wisp, or a boggart of the clough." However, he could not be far off, and Hugh endeavoured to obtain some clue to guide him in his quest. He was not long in detecting recent marks deeply indented in the mud on the opposite bank.

Hugh leaped thither at once. Further on, some rushes were trodden down, and there were other indications of the course the fugitive had taken.

"Hark forward!" shouted Hugh, in the joy of his heart at this discovery; and, like a well-trained dog, he followed up, with alacrity, the scent he had opened. The brook presented still fewer impediments to expedition than the thick copse, and the keeper pursued the wanderings of the petty current, occasionally splashing into the stream. Here and there, the print of a foot on the sod satisfied him he was in the right path. At length he became aware, from the crumbling soil, that the object of his pursuit had scaled the bank, and he forthwith moderated his pace. Halting, he perceived what he took to be a face peeping at him from behind a knot of alders that overhung the steep and shelving bank immediately above him. His gun was instantly at his shoulder.

"Come down, you infernal deer-stealing scoundrel," cried Hugh, "or I'll blow you to shivers."

No answer was returned: expostulation was vain; and, fearful of placing himself at a disadvantage if he attempted to scale the bank, Hugh fired without further parley. The sharp discharge rolled in echoes down the ravine; and a pheasant, scared at the sound, answered the challenge from a neighbouring tree. Hugh was an unerring marksman, and on this occasion his aim had been steadily taken. The result was not precisely such as he had anticipated. A fur cap, shaken by the shot from the bough on which it hung, came rolling down the bank, proclaiming the trick that had been practised upon the keeper. Leech time was allowed him for reflection. Scarce had he stooped to pick it up, he felt himself collared by his incensed opponent.

Hugh Badger was a man of great personal strength—

shins, and struggling v h... ntly, Hugh succeeded in extri-
cating himself from his throttling grasp: he then closed with
his foe, and they were locked together like a couple of bears
at play. Straining, tugging, and practising every sleight and
stratagem coming within the scope of feet, knees, and thighs
—now tripping, now j rking, now advancing, now retreating,
they continued the strife, but all with doubtful result.
Victory, at length, seemed to declare itself in favour of the
sturdy keeper. Aware of his opponent's strength, it was
Luke's chief endeavour to keep his lower limbs disengaged,
and to trust more to skill than force for ultimate success.
To prevent this was Hugh's grand object. Guarding himself
against every feint, he ultimately succeeded in firmly grap-
pling his agile assailant. Luke's spine was almost broken by
the shock, when he suddenly gave way; and, without losing
his balance, drew his adversary forward, kicking his right
leg from under him. With a crash like that of an uprooted
oak, Hugh fell, with his foe upon him, into the bed of the
rivulet.

Not a word had been spoken during the conflict. A convulsive groan burst from Hugh's hardy breast. His hand
sought his girdle, but in vain; his knife was gone. Gazing
upwards, his glaring vision encountered the glimmer of the
blade. The weapon had dropped from its case in the fall.
Luke brandished it before his eyes.

"Villain!" gasped Hugh, ineffectually struggling to free
himself, "you will not murder me?" And his efforts to
release himself became desperate.

"No," answered Luke, flinging the uplifted knife into the
brook. "I will not do *that*, though thou hast twice aimed at
my life to-night. But I will silence thee, at all events."
Saying which, he dealt the keeper a blow on the head that
terminated all further resistance on his part.

Leaving the inert mass to choke up the current, with whose
waters the blood, oozing from the wound, began to commingle,
Luke prepared to depart. His perils were not yet past.
Guided by the firing, the report of which alarmed them, the
keeper's assistants hastened in the direction of the sound,
presenting themselves directly in the path Luke was about to
take. He had either to retrace his steps, or face a double
enemy. His election was made at once—he turned and fled.

For an instant the men tarried with their bleeding companion; they then dragged him from the brook, and with
loud oaths followed in pursuit.

Threading, for a second time, the bosky labyrinth, Luke sought the source of the stream. This was precisely the course his enemies would have desired him to pursue; and when they beheld him take it, they felt confident of his capture.

The sides of the hollow became more and more abrupt as they advanced, though they were less covered with brushwood. The fugitive made no attempt to climb the bank, but still pressed forward. The road was tortuous, and wound round a jutting point of rock. Now he was a fair mark—no, he had swept swiftly by, and was out of sight before a gun could be raised. They reached the same point. He was still before them, but his race was nearly run. Steep, slippery rocks, shelving down to the edges of a small, deep pool of water, the source of the stream formed an apparently insurmountable barrier in that direction. Rooted (Heaven knows how!) in some reft or fissure of the rock, grew a wild ash, throwing out a few boughs over the solitary pool; this was all the support Luke could hope for, should he attempt to scale the rock. The rock was sheer—the pool deep—yet still he hurried on. He reached the muddy embankment, mounted its sides, and seemed to hesitate. The keepers were now within a hundred yards of him. Both guns were discharged; and, sudden as the reports, with a dead splashless plunge, like a diving otter, the fugitive dropped into the water.

The pursuers were at the brink. They gazed at the pool. A few bubbles floated upon its surface, and burst. The water was slightly discoloured with sand. No ruddier stain crimsoned the tide; no figure rested on the naked rock; no hand clung to the motionless tree.

"Devil take the rascal," growled one; "I hope he har'n't escaped us, arter all."

"Noa, noa, he be fast enough, never fear," rejoined the other, "sticking like a snig at the bottom o' the pond; and dang him he deserves it, for he's slipp'd out of our fingers like a snig often enough to-night. But come, let's be stumping, and give poor Hugh Badger a helping hand."

Whereupon, they returned to the assistance of the wounded and discomfited keeper.

IV.

THE HALL.

1 am right against my house—seat of my ancestors.—Yorkshire Tragedy.

ROOKWOOD PLACE was a fine, old, irregular pile, of considerable size, presenting a rich, picturesque outline, with its innumerable gable ends, its fantastical coigns, and tall crest of twisted chimneys. There was no uniformity of style about the building, yet the general effect was pleasing and beautiful. Its very irregularity constituted a charm. Nothing except convenience had been consulted in its construction: additions had from time to time been made to it, but everything dropped into its proper place, and, without apparent effort or design, grew into an ornament, and heightened the beauty of the whole. It was, in short, one of those glorious manorial houses that sometimes unexpectedly greet us in our wanderings, and gladden us like the discovery of a hidden treasure. Some such ancestral hall we have occasionally encountered, in unlooked-for quarters, in our native county of Lancaster, or in its smiling sister shire; and never without feelings of intense delight, rejoicing to behold the freshness of its antiquity, and the greenness of its old age. For, be it observed in passing, a Cheshire or Lancashire hall, time-honoured though it be, with its often-renovated black and white squares, fancifully filled up with trefoils and quatrefoils, rosettes, and other figures, seems to bear its years so lightly, that its age, so far from detracting from its beauty, only lends it a grace; and the same mansion, to all outward appearance, fresh and perfect as it existed in the days of good Queen Bess, may be seen in admirable preservation in the days of the youthful Victoria. Such is Bramall—such Moreton, and many another we might instance; the former of these houses may, perhaps, be instanced as the best specimen of its class (and its class, in our opinion, *is* the best) to be met with in Cheshire, considered with reference either to the finished decoration of its exterior, rich in the chequered colouring we have alluded to, preserved with a care and neatness almost Dutch, or to the consistent taste exhibited by its possessor in the restoration and maintenance of all its original and truly national beauty within doors. As an illustration of old English hospitality (that real, hearty hospitality for which the squirearchy of this country was once so famous—ah! why have they bartered it for other ust ms. less s stentialr (lodal?). It m y be mention d, that a road c l ted th pa ger irectly through the great hall of l h e, lt erti ment," where, if he listed, trong ale and ther r fr shm nts awaited his acceptan ; an courted his stay. W ll m ht old King, the Chishire historian, in the pride of his honest heart, exclaim, "*I know these men. who are but farmers, that in their housekeeping may compare with a lord or lord in some countries beyond the sea;—* ,t , I act ed a higher degree. I are able j st , . have no such "golden farmers" in these last days.

The mansion was o lly l lt y ir Ranulph de Rook-wood (or, h s the r b r, Rookwode the first of t name, a stout Y o , who h n t e re n of Edward the Fourth, and r d th f t om e and br d l d pon which th e l th ws r ed fr m his e t l, in r ward for good serv e; r ing tl r in th e l t of l the close of the wars of the R ses to seq t te h f rom scenes of str fe, and to c uslt h s e at l d t the erection an l nds m nt of th n i h ring hurch It was of mixed ch t re, and comb d the p l res of each success ve era. Retaining some of the t rted forms of earlier days, the period ere yet the mb ttl d manor-house peculiar to the reigns of the later Henrys had be n merged in the graceful and peaceable hall, the pride of the Rook-woods had early anticipated th gentler characteristics of a later day, though it could boast little of that exuberance of external ornament, luxuriance of design, and prodigality of beauty, which, under the sway of the virgin queen, dis-tinguished the residence of the w lth r E l h l downer, and rendered the hall of Elizabeth, pr p r so called, the pride and boast of our dom sti arch t t re.

The site selected by Sir Ranulph r his habitation had been already occupied by a vast fabric of oak, which be in part removed, though some vestiges might still be traced of that ancient pile. A massive e lifice suc ceeded with gate and tower, court and moat complete, substantial enough, one would have thought, to have endured for centuries. But even this ponderous structure grew into disuse, and Sir Ranulph's successors, remodelling, repairing, al ost r b lding th r mansion, in the end so m tamorphosed its aspect, that at last little of its original and distinctive character remained. Still, as we said before, it was a fine old house; though some changes had taken place for the worse, which could not be

readily pardoned by the eye of taste; as, for instance, the
deep embayed windows had dwindled into modernised case-
ments, of lighter construction; the wide porch, with its flight
of steps leading to the great hall of entrance, had yielded to
a narrow door; and the broad, quadrangular court was succeeded by a gravel drive. Yet, despite of all these changes,
the house of the Rookwoods, for an old house (and, after all,
what is like an old house?), was no undesirable, or uncon-
genial abode for any worshipful country gentleman, " who
had a great estate."

The hall was situated near the base of a gently declining
hill, terminating a noble avenue of limes, and partially
embosomed in an immemorial wood of the same timber, which
had given its name to the family that dwelt amongst its
rook-haunted shades. Descending the avenue, at the point
of access afforded by a road that wound down the hill-side,
towards a village distant about half a mile, as you advanced,
the eye was first arrested by a singular external turret of
brick, of more recent construction than the house; and in all
probability occupying the place where the battlemed gateway
stood of yore. This tower rose to a height corresponding
with the roof of the mansion; and was established on the
side of the house with a flauntingly solid air, peering, like
an impudent observer, at all that passed within doors. Two
apartments, which it contained, were appropriated to the
house-porter. Despoiled of its martial honours, the gateway
still displayed the achievements of the family—the rook and
the fatal branch—carved in granite, which had resisted the
storms of two centuries, though stained green with moss, and
mapped over with lichens. To the left, overgrown with ivy,
and peeping from out a tuft of trees, appeared the hoary
summit of a dovecot, indicating the neighbourhood of an
ancient barn, contemporary with the earliest dwelling-house;
and of a little world of offices and out-buildings buried in the
thickness of the foliage. To the right was the garden—
the pleasaunce of the place—formal, precise, old fashioned,
artificial, yet exquisite—(for commend us to the bygone,
beautiful English garden—really a garden—not that mixture
of park, meadow, and wilderness,* brought up to one's very

* Payne Knight, the scourge of Repton and his school, speaking of the
licence indulged in by the modern landscape gardeners, thus vents his indignation:

But here, once more, ye rural muses weep
The ivy'd balustrade, and terrace steep;
Walls, mellowed into harmony by time,
On which fantastic creepers used to climb;

windows—which, since the days of the innovators, Kent, and
his "bold associates," Capability Brown and Co., has obtained
so largely)—this *was* a garden! There might be seen the
stately terraces, such as Watteau, and our own Wilson, in
his earlier works, painted—the trim alleys exhibiting all the
triumphs of Topiarian art—

> The sidelong walls
> Of shaven yew ; the holly's prickly arms,
> Trimm'd into high arcades ; the tonsile box
> Wove in mosaic mode of many a curl,
> Around the figured carpet of the lawn.*

the gayest of parterres and greenest of lawns, with its ad-
monitory sun-dial, its marble basin in the centre, its fountain,
and conched water-god, the quaint summer-house, surmounted
with its gilt vane, the statue, glimmering from out its covert
of leaves, the cool cascade, the urns, the bowers, and a
hundred luxuries beside, suggested and contrived by Art to
render Nature most enjoyable, and to enhance the recreative
delights of home-out-of-doors (for such a garden should be),
with least sacrifice of in-door comfort and convenience.

> When Epicurus to the world had taught,
> That pleasure was the chiefest good
> (And was perhaps i' th' right, if rightly under.tood),
> His life he to his doctrine brought—
> And in his garden's shade that sovereign pleasure soug't.†

All these delights might once have been enjoyed. But at
the time of which we write, this fair garden was for the most
part a waste. Ill kept, and unregarded, the gay parterres
were disfigured with weeds ; grass grew on the gravel walk ;
several of the urns were overthrown ; the hour upon the dial
was untold ; the fountain was choked up, and the smooth-
shaven lawn only rescued, it would seem, from the general
fate, that it might answer the purpose of a bowling-green,
as the implements of that game, scattered about, plainly
testified.

Diverging from the garden to the house, we have before
remarked that the more ancient and characteristic features of
the place had been, for the most part, destroyed ; less by the

> While statues, labyrinths, and alleys pent
> Within their bounds, at least were innocent ! —
> Our modern taste (alas !) no limit knows :
> O'er hill, o'er dale, through wood and field it fows :
> Spreading o'er all its unprolific spawn,
> In never-ending sheets of vapid lawn. —
>   *The Landscape, a didactic Poem,*
>   *addressed to Uvedale Price, Esq.*

* Mason's English Garden.   † Cowley.

hand of time than to suit the tastes of different proprietors. This, however, was not so observable in the eastern wing, which overlooked the garden. Here might be discerned many indications of its antiquity. The strength and solidity of the walls, which had not been, as elsewhere, masked with brickwork; the low, Tudor arches; the mullioned bars of the windows—all attested its age. This wing was occupied by an upper and lower gallery, communicating with suites of chambers, for the most part deserted, excepting one or two, which were used as dormitories; and another little room on the ground-floor, with an oriel window opening upon the lawn, and commanding the prospect beyond—a favourite resort of the late Sir Piers. The interior was curious for its honeycomb ceiling, deeply moulded in plaster, with the arms and alliances of the Rookwoods. In the centre was the royal blazon of Elizabeth, who had once honoured the hall with a visit during a progress, and whose cipher Œ. R. was also displayed upon the immense plate of iron which formed the fire-grate.

To return, for a moment, to the garden, which we linger about as a bee around a flower. Below the lawn there was another terrace, edged by a low balustrade of stone, commanding a lovely view of park, water, and woodland. High-hanging woods waved in the foreground, and an extensive sweep of flat, champaign country, stretched out to meet a line of blue, hazy hills bounding the distant horizon.

CHAPTER V.

SIR REGINALD ROOKWOOD.

Un homme qui changeait de femmes, comme une femme de robes. Il répudia la première, il fit couper la tête à la seconde, il fit ouvrir le ventre à la troisième : quant à la quatrième, il lui fit grâce, il la chassa ; mais en revanche il fit couper la tête à la cinquième. Ce n'est pas le conte de Barbe-Bleue que je vous fais là, c'est l'histoire.—VICTOR HUGO.—*Marie Tudor.*

FROM the house to its inhabitants, the transition is natural. Besides the connection between them, there were many points of resemblance; many family features in common; there was the same melancholy grandeur, the same character of romance, the same fantastical display. Nor were the secret passages, peculiar to the one, wanting to the history of the other. Both had their mysteries. One blot there was in the otherwise proud escutcheon of the Rookwoods, that dimmed its splendour, and made pale its pretensions: their sun was eclipsed in blood from its rising to its meridian; and so it seemed would be its setting. This foul reproach attached to all the race; none escaped it. Traditional rumours were handed down from father to son, throughout the county, and, like all other rumours, had taken to themselves wings, and flown abroad: their crimes became a byword. How was it they escaped punishment? How came they to evade the hand of justice? Proof was ever wanting; justice was ever baffled. They were a stern and stiff-necked people of indomitable pride and resolution, with, for the most part, force of character sufficient to enable them to breast difficulties and dangers that would have overwhelmed ordinary individuals. No quality is so advantageous to its possessor as firmness; and the determined energy of the Rookwoods bore them harmless through a sea of troubles. Besides, they were wealthy; lavish even to profusion; and gold will do much, if skilfully administered. Yet, despite all this, a dark ominous cloud settled over their house, and men wondered when the vengeance of Heaven, so long delayed, would fall, and consume it.

Possessed of considerable landed property, once extending over nearly half the West Riding of Yorkshire, the family increased in power and importance for an uninterrupted series of years, until the outbreak of that intestine discord which ended in the civil wars, when the espousal of the royalist party, with sword and substance, by Sir Ralph Rookwood, the then lord of the mansion (a dissolute, depraved personage, who, however, had been made a Knight of the Bath at the coronation of Charles the First), ended in his own destruction at Naseby, and the wreck of much of his property; a loss which the gratitude of Charles the Second on his restoration did not fail to make good to Sir Ralph's youthful heir, Reginald.

Sir Ranulph Rookwood left two sons, Reginald and Alan. The fate of the latter was buried in obscurity. It was even a mystery to his family. He was, it was said, a youth of much promise, and of gentle manners; who, having made an imprudent match, from jealousy, or some other motive, deserted his wife, and fled his country. Various reasons were assigned for his conduct. Amongst others, it was stated that the object of Alan's jealous suspicions was his elder brother, Reginald; and that it was the discovery of his wife's infidelity in this quarter, which occasioned his sudden disappearance with his infant daughter. Some said he died abroad. Others, that he had appeared again for a brief space at the hall. But all now concurred in a belief of his decease. Of his child nothing was known. His inconstant wife, after enduring for some years the agonies of remorse, abandoned by Sir Reginald, and neglected by her own relatives, put an end to her existence by poison. This is all that could be gathered of the story, or the misfortunes of Alan Rookwood.

The young Sir Reginald had attended Charles, in the character of page, during his exile; and if he could not requite the devotion of the son, by absolutely reinstating the fallen fortunes of the father, the monarch could at least accord him the fostering influence of his favour and countenance; and bestow upon him certain lucrative situations in his household, as an earnest of his good-will. And thus much he did. Remarkable for his personal attractions in youth, it is not to be wondered at, that we should find the name of Reginald Rookwood recorded in the scandalous chronicles of the day, as belonging to a cavalier of infinite address and discretion, matchless wit, and marvellous pleasantry; and eminent beyond his peers for his successes with some of the most distinguished beauties who ornamented that brilliant and voluptuous court.

A career of elegant dissipation ended in matrimony. His first match was unpropitious. Foiled in his attempts upon the chastity of a lady of great beauty and high honour, he was rash enough to marry her; rash, we say, for from that fatal hour all became as darkness; the curtain fell upon the comedy of his life, to rise to tragic horrors. When passion subsided, repentance awoke, and he became anxious for deliverance from the fetters he had so heedlessly imposed on himself, and on his unfortunate dame.

The hapless lady of Sir Reginald was a fair and fragile creature, floating in the eddying current of existence, and hurried to destruction as the summer gossamer is swept away by the rude breeze, and lost for ever. So beautiful, so gentle was she, that if

> Sorrow had not made
> Sorrow more beautiful than Beauty's self,

it would have been difficult to say whether the charm of softness and sweetness was more to be admired than her faultless personal attractions. But when a tinge of melancholy came saddening and shading the once smooth and smiling brow; when tears dimmed the blue beauty of those deep and tender eyes; when hot, hectic flushes supplied the place of healthful bloom, and despair took possession of her heart, then was it seen *what* was the charm of Lady Rookwood, if charm that could be called, which was a saddening sight to see, and melted the beholder's soul within him. All acknowledged, that exquisite as she had been before, the sad, sweet lady was now more exquisite still.

Seven moons had waned and flown—seven bitter, tearful moons—and each day Lady Rookwood's situation claimed more soothing attention at the hand of her lord. About this time his wife's brother, whom he hated, returned from the Dutch wars. Struck with his sister's altered appearance, he readily divined the cause; indeed, all tongues were eager to proclaim it to him. Passionately attached to her, Lionel Vavasour implored an explanation of the cause of his sister's griefs. The bewildered lady answered evasively, attributing her wobegone looks to any other cause than her husband's cruelty; and pressing her brother, as he valued her peace, her affection, never to allude to the subject again. The fiery youth departed. He next sought out his brother-in-law, and taxed him sharply with his inhumanity, adding threats to his upbraidings. Sir Reginald listened silently and calmly. When the other had finished, with a sarcastic obeisance, he replied, " Sir, I am much beholden for the trouble you have taken in your sister's behalf. But when she intrusted herself to my keeping, she relinquished, I conceive, all claim on *your* guardianship: however, I thank you for the trouble you have taken; but, for your own sake, I would venture to caution you against a repetition of interference like the present."

" And I, sir, caution *you*. See that you give heed to my words, or, by the Heaven above us, I will enforce attention to them."

" You will find me, sir, as prompt at all times to defend my conduct, as I am unalterable in my purposes. Your sister is my wife. What more would you have? Were she a harlot, you should have her back and welcome. The fool is virtuous. Devise some scheme, and take her with you hence—so you rid *me* of her I am content."

" Rookwood, you are a villain." And Vavasour spat upon his brother's cheek.

Sir Reginald's eyes blazed. His sword started from its

scabbard. "Defend yourself," he exclaimed furiously attacking Vavasour. Pass after pass was exchanged. Fierce thrusts were made and parried. Feint and appeal, the most desperate and dexterous, were resorted to. Their swords glanced like lightning flashes. In the struggle the blades became entangled. There was a moment's cessation. Each glanced at the other with deadly, inextinguishable hate. Both were admirable masters of the art of defence. Both were so brimful of wrath as to be regardless of consequences. They tore back their weapons. Vavasour's blade shivered. He was at the mercy of his adversary—an adversary who knew no mercy. Sir Reginald passed his rapier through his brother's body. The hilt struck against his ribs.

Sir Reginald's ire was kindled, not extinguished, by the deed he had done. Like the tiger, he had tasted blood—like the tiger he thirsted for more. He sought his home. He was greeted by his wife. Terrified by his looks, she yet summoned courage sufficient to approach him. She embraced his arm—she clasped his hand. Sir Reginald smiled. His smile was cutting as his dagger's edge.

"What ails you, sweetheart?" said he.

"I know not; your smile frightens me."

"My smile frightens you—fool! be thankful that I frown not."

"Oh! do not frown. Be gentle, my Reginald, as you were when I first knew you. Smile not so coldly, but as you did then, that I may, for one instant, dream you love me."

"Silly wench! There—I do smile."

"That smile chills me—freezes me. Oh, Reginald! could you but know what I have endured this morning, on your account. My brother Lionel has been here."

"Indeed!"

"Nay, look not so. He insisted on knowing the reason of my altered appearance."

"And no doubt you made him acquainted with the cause. You told him your version of the story."

"Not a word, as I hope to live."

"A lie!"

"By my truth, no."

"A lie, I say. He avouched it to me himself."

"Impossible! He could not—would not disobey me."

Sir Reginald laughed bitterly.

"He would not, I am sure, give utterance to any scandal," continued Lady Rookwood. "You say this but to try me, do you not?—ha! what is this? Your hand is bloody. You have not harmed him? He is safe? Whose blood is this?"

"Your brother spat upon my cheek. I have washed out the stain," replied Sir Reginald, coldly.

"Then it *is* his," shrieked Lady Rookwood, pressing her hands shudderingly before her eyes. "Is he dead—dead?"

Sir Reginald turned away.

"Stay," she cried, exerting her feeble strength to retain him, and becoming white as ashes, "abide and hear me. You have killed me, I feel, by your unkindness. I have striven against it, but it would not avail. I am sinking fast—dying. I, who loved you, only you; yea, one beside—my brother, and you have slain *him*. Your hands are dripping in his blood, and I have kissed them—have clasped them. And now," continued she, with an energy that shook Sir Reginald, "I hate you—I abhor you—I renounce you—for ever! May my dying words ring in your ears on your deathbed, for that hour *will* come. You cannot shun *that*. Then, think of *him!* think of *me!*"

"Away!" interrupted Sir Reginald, endeavouring to shake her off.

"I will *not* away! I will cling to you—will curse you. My unborn child shall live to curse you—to requite you—to visit my wrongs on you and yours. Weak as I am, you shall not cast me off. You shall learn to fear even *me*."

"I fear nothing living, much less a frantic woman."

"Fear the *dead*, then."

"Hence! or by the God above us——"

"Never!"

There was a struggle—a blow—and the wretched lady sank, shrieking, upon the floor. Convulsions seized her. A mother's pains succeeded fierce and fast. She spoke no more, but died within the hour, giving birth to a female child.

Eleanor Rookwood became her father's idol—her father's bane. All the love he had to bestow was centred in her. She returned it not. She fled from his caresses. With all her mother's beauty, she had all her father's pride. Sir Reginald's every thought was for his daughter—for her aggrandisement. In vain. She seemed only to endure him, and while his affection waxed stronger, and entwined itself round her alone, she withered beneath his embraces as the shrub withers in the clasping folds of the parasite plant. She grew towards womanhood. Suitors thronged around her—gentle and noble ones. Sir Reginald watched them with a jealous eye. He was wealthy, powerful, high in royal favour,—and could make his own election. He did so. For the first time, Eleanor promised obedience to his wishes. They accorded with her own humour. The day was appointed. It came. But with it came not the bride. She had fled, with the humblest and the meanest of the pretenders to her hand— with one upon whom Sir Reginald supposed she had not deigned to cast her eyes. He endeavoured to forget her, and, to all outward seeming, was successful in the effort. But he felt that the curse was upon him, the undying flame scorched his heart. Once and once only they met again, in France, whither she had wandered. It was a dread encounter terrible to both; but most so to Sir Reginald. He spoke not of her afterwards.

Shortly after the death of his first wife, Sir Reginald had made proposals to a dowager of distinction, with a handsome jointure, one of his early attachments, and was, without scruple, accepted. The power of the family might then be said to be at its zenith; and but for certain untoward circumstances, and the growing influence of his enemies, Sir Reginald would have been elevated to the peerage. Like most reformed spendthrifts, he had become proportionately avaricious, and his mind seemed engrossed in accumulating wealth. In the mean time, his second wife followed her predecessor; dying, it was said, of vexation and disappointment.

The propensity to matrimony, always a distinguishing characteristic of the Rookwoods, largely displayed itself in Sir Reginald. Another dame followed—equally rich, younger, and far more beautiful than her immediate predecessor. She was a prodigious flirt, and soon set her husband at defiance. Sir Reginald did not condescend to expostulate. It was not his way. He effectually prevented any recurrence of her indiscretions. She was removed, and with her expired Sir Reginald's waning popularity. So strong was the expression of odium against him, that he thought it prudent to retire to his mansion in the country, and there altogether seclude himself. One anomaly in Sir Reginald's otherwise utterly selfish character was uncompromising devotion to the house of Stuart; and shortly after the abdication of James the Second, he followed that monarch to St. Germains, having previously mixed largely in secret political intrigues; and only returned from the French court to lay his bones with those of his ancestry, in the family vault at Rookwood.

VI.

SIR PIERS ROOKWOOD.

My old master kept a good house, and twenty
Or thirty tall sword and buckler men about
Him: and in faith his son differs not much;
He will have metal too; though he has no
Store of cutlers' blades, he will have plenty
Of vintners' pots. His father kept a good
House for honest men, his tenants that brought
Him in part; and his son keeps a bad house
With knaves that help to consume all: 'tis but
The change of time: why should any man repine
At it? Crickets, good loving and lucky worms,
Were wont to feed, sing, and rejoice in the
Father's chimney; and now carrion crows build
In the son's kitchen.
                    WILKINS.—*Miseries of Enforced Marriage.*

SIR REGINALD died, leaving issue three children, a daughter,
the before-mentioned Eleanor (who, entirely discountenanced
by the family, had been seemingly forgotten by all but her
father), and two sons by his third wife. Reginald, the eldest,
whose military taste had early procured him the command of
a company of horse, and whose politics did not coalesce with
those of his sire, fell, during his father's lifetime, at Killie-
crankie, under the banners of William. Piers, therefore, the
second son, succeeded to the title.

A very different character, in many respects, from his
father and brother, holding in supreme dislike courts and
courtiers, party warfare, political intrigue, and all the subtle-
ties of Jesuitical diplomacy; neither having any inordinate
relish for camps or campaigns; Sir Piers Rookwood yet displayed in early life one family propensity, viz., unremitting
devotion to the sex. Among his other mistresses was the
unfortunate Susan Bradley, to whom by some he was supposed to have been clandestinely united. In early youth, as
has been stated, Sir Piers professed the faith of Rome, but
shortly after the death of his beautiful mistress (or wife, as it
might be), having quarrelled with his father's confessor,
Checkley, he publicly abjured his heresies. Sir Piers subsequently allied himself to Maud, only daughter of Sir Thomas
D'Aubeny, the last of a line as proud and intolerant as his
own. The tables were then turned. Lady Rookwood usurped
sovereign sway over her lord, and Sir Piers, a cipher in his
own house, scarce master of himself, much less of his dame,
endured an existence so miserable, that he was often heard to

regret, in his cups, that he had not inherited, with the estate of his forefathers, the family secret of shaking off the matrimonial yoke, when found to press too hardly.

At the onset, Sir Piers struggled hard to burst his bondage. But in vain—he was fast fettered; and only bruised himself, liked the caged lark, against the bars of his prison house. Abandoning all further effort at emancipation, he gave himself up to the usual resource of a weak mind, debauchery; and drank so deeply to drown his cares, that, in the end, his hale constitution yielded to his excesses. It was even said, that remorse at his abandonment of the faith of his fathers had some share in his misery; and that his old spiritual, and if report spoke truly, sinful adviser, Father Checkley, had visited him secretly at the hall. Sir Piers was observed to shudder, whenever the priest's name was mentioned.

Sir Piers Rookwood was a good-humoured man in the main, had little of the old family leaven about him, and was esteemed by his associates. Of late, however, his temper became soured, and his friends deserted him; for, between his domestic annoyances, remorseful feelings, and the inroads already made upon his constitution by constant inebriety, he grew so desperate and insane in his revels, and committed such fearful extravagances, that even his boon companions shrank from his orgies. Fearful were the scenes between him and Lady Rookwood upon these occasions—appalling to the witnesses, dreadful to themselves. And it was, perhaps, their frequent recurrence, that, more than anything else, banished all decent society from the hall.

At the time of Sir Piers's decease, which brings us down to the date of our story, his son and successor, Ranulph, was absent on his travels. Shortly after the completion of his academical education, he had departed to make the tour of the Continent, and had been absent rather better than a year. He had quitted his father in displeasure, and was destined never again to see his face while living. The last intelligence received of young Rookwood was from Bordeaux, whence it was thought he had departed for the Pyrenees. A special messenger had been despatched in search of him, with tidings of the melancholy event. But, as it was deemed improbable by Lady Rookwood that her son could return within any reasonable space, she gave directions for the accomplishment of the funeral rites of her husband on the sixth night after his decease (it being the custom of the Rookwoods ever to inter their dead at midnight), intrusting their solemnization entirely to the care of one of Sir Piers's hangers-on (Doctor Titus Tyrconnel), for which she was greatly scandalized in the neighbourhood.

Ranulph Rookwood was a youth of goodly promise. The stock from which he sprang would on neither side warrant such conclusion. But it sometimes happens, that from the darkest elements are compounded the brightest and subtlest substances; and so it occurred in this instance. Fair, frank, and free—generous, open, unsuspicious—he seemed the very opposite of all his race—their antagonizing principle. Capriciously indulgent, his father had allowed him ample means, neither curbing nor restraining his expenditure; acceding at one moment to every inclination; and the next irresolutely opposing it. It was impossible, therefore, for him, in such a state of things, to act decidedly, without incurring his father's displeasure; and the only measure he resolved upon, which was to absent himself for a time, was conjectured to have brought about the result he had endeavoured to avoid. Other reasons, however, there were, which secretly influenced him, which it will be our business in due time to detail.

VII.

THE RETURN.

> *Flam.* How croaks the raven?
> Is our good Duchess dead?
> *Lod.* Dead.   WEBSTER.

THE time of the sad ceremonial drew nigh. The hurrying of the domestics to and fro; the multifarious arrangements for the night; the distribution of the melancholy trappings, and the discussion of the "funeral baked meats" furnished abundant occupation within doors. Without, there was a constant stream of the tenantry, thronging down the avenue, mixed with an occasional horseman, once or twice intercepted by a large lumbering carriage, bringing friends of the deceased, some really anxious to pay the last tribute of regard, but the majority attracted by the anticipated spectacle of a funeral by torchlight. There were others, indeed, to whom it was not matter of choice; who were compelled, by a vassal tenure of their lands, held of the house of Rookwood, to lend a shoulder to the coffin, and a hand to the torch, on the burial of its lord. Of these there was a plentiful muster collected in the hall; they were to be marshalled by Peter Bradley, who was deemed to be well skilled in the proceedings, having been present at two solemnities of the kind. That mysterious personage, however, had not made his appearance—to the great dismay of the assemblage. Scouts were sent in search of him, but they returned with the intelligence that the door of his habitation was fastened, and its inmate apparently absent. No other tidings of the truant sexton could be obtained.

It was a sultry August evening. No breeze was stirring in the garden; no cool dews refreshed the parched and heated earth; yet from the languishing flowers rich sweets exhaled. The plash of a fountain fell pleasantly upon the ear, conveying in its sound a sense of freshness to the fervid air; while deep and drowsy murmurs hummed heavily beneath the trees, making the twilight slumbrously musical. The westering sun, which had filled the atmosphere with flame throughout the day, was now wildly setting; and, as he sank behind the hall, its varied and picturesque tracery became each instant more darkly and distinctly defined against the crimson sky.

At this juncture a little gate, communicating with the chase, was thrown open, and a young man entered the garden, passing through the shrubbery, and hurrying rapidly forward till he arrived at a vista opening upon the house. The spot at which the stranger halted was marked by a little basin, scantily supplied with water, streaming from a lion's kingly jaws. His dress was travel-soiled and dusty; and his whole appearance betokened great exhaustion, from heat and fatigue. Seating himself upon an adjoining bench, he threw off his riding cap, and unclasped his collar, displaying a finely-turned head and neck; and a countenance which, besides its beauty, had that rare nobility of feature which seldom falls to the lot of the aristocrat, but is never seen in one of an inferior order. A restless disquietude of manner showed that he was suffering from over-excitement of mind, as well as from bodily exertion. His look was wild and hurried; his black ringlets were dashed heedlessly over a pallid, lofty brow, upon which care was prematurely written, while his large melancholy eyes were bent, with a look almost of agony, upon the house before him.

After a short pause, and as if struggling against violent emotions, and some overwhelming remembrance, the youth arose, and plunged his hand into the basin, applying the moist element to his burning brow. Apparently becoming more calm, he bent his steps towards the hall, when two figures suddenly issuing from an adjoining copse, arrested his progress; neither saw him. Muttering a hurried farewell, one of the figures disappeared within the shrubbery, and the other, confronting the stranger, displayed the harsh features and gaunt form of Peter Bradley. Had Peter encountered the dead Sir Piers in corporeal form, he could not have manifested more surprise than he exhibited, for an instant or two, as he shrunk back from the stranger's path.

VIII.

AN IRISH ADVENTURER.

Scapin. A most outrageous, roaring fellow, with a swelled red face inflamed with brandy.—*Cheats of Scapin.*

An hour or two prior to the incident just narrated, in a small cosy apartment of the hall, nominally devoted to justiciary business by its late owner, but, in reality, used as a sanctum, snuggery, or smoking-room, a singular trio were assembled, fraught with the ulterior purpose of attending the obsequies of their deceased patron and friend, though immediately occupied in the discussion of a magnum of excellent claret, the bouquet of which perfumed the air, like the fragrance of a bed of violets.

This little room had been poor Sir Piers's favourite retreat. It was, in fact, the only room in the house that he could call his own; and thither would he often, with pipe and punch, beguile the flagging hours, secure from interruption. A snug, old-fashioned apartment it was; wainscoted with rich black oak; with a fine old cabinet of the same material, and a line or two of crazy, worm-eaten book-shelves, laden with sundry dusty, unconsulted law tomes, and a slight sprinkling of the elder divines, equally neglected. The only book, indeed, Sir Piers ever read was the "Anatomie of Melancholy," and he merely studied Burton because the quaint, racy style of the learned old hypochondriac suited his humour at seasons, and gave a zest to his sorrows, such as the olives lent to his wine.

Four portraits adorned the walls; those of Sir Reginald Rookwood and his wives. The ladies were attired in the flowing drapery of Charles the Second's day, the snow of their radiant bosoms being somewhat sullied by over-exposure, and the vermeil tinting of their cheeks darkened by the fumes of tobacco. There was a shepherdess, with her taper crook, whose large, languishing eyes, ripe, pouting lips, ready to melt into kisses, and air of voluptuous abandonment, scarcely suited the innocent simplicity of her costume. She was portrayed tending a flock of downy sheep, with azure ribands rounds their necks, accompanied by one of those invaluable little dogs, whose length of ear, and silkiness of skin, evinced him perfect in his breeding; but whose large-eyed indifference to his charge proved him to be as much out of character with his situation as the refined and luxuriant charms of his mistress were out of keeping with her artless attire. This was Sir Piers's mother, the third wife, a beautiful woman, answering to the notion of one who had been somewhat of a flirt in her day. Next to her was a magnificent dame, with the throat and arm of a Juno, and a superb bust (the bust was then what the bustle is now — a paramount attraction — whether the modification be an improvement, we leave to the consideration of the lovers of the beautiful)—this was the dowager. Lastly, there was the lovely and ill-fated Eleanor. Every gentle grace belonging to this unfortunate lady had been stamped in undying beauty on the canvas by the hand of Lely, breathing a spell on the picture, almost as powerful as that which had dwelt around the exquisite original. Over the high carved mantelpiece was suspended the portrait of Sir Reginald. It had been painted in early youth; the features were beautiful, disdainful—with a fierceness breaking through the courtly air. The eyes were very fine, black as midnight, and piercing as those of Cæsar Borgia, in Raphael's wonderful picture of the fratricide duke, in the Borghese Palace at Rome. They seemed to fascinate the gazer—to rivet his glances—to follow him whithersoever he went—and to search into his soul, as did the dark orbs of Sir Reginald in his lifetime. It was the work likewise of Lely, and had all the fidelity and graceful refinement of that great master; nor was the haughty countenance of Sir Reginald unworthy the patrician painter.

No portrait of Sir Piers was to be met with. But, in lieu thereof, depending from a pair of buck's horns, hung the worthy knight's stained scarlet coat (the same in which he had ridden forth, with the intent to hunt, on the eventful occasion detailed by Peter Bradley), his velvet cap, his buck-handled whip, and the residue of his equipment for the chase.

This attire was reviewed with melancholy interest and unaffected emotion by the company, as reminding them forcibly of the departed, of which it seemed a portion.

The party consisted of the vicar of Rookwood, Doctor Polyphemus Polycarp Small, Doctor Titus Tyrconnel, an emigrant, and empirical professor of medicine, from the sister isle, whose convivial habits had first introduced him to the hall, and afterwards retained him there, and Mr. Codicil Coates, clerk of the peace, attorney-at-law, bailiff, and receiver. We were wrong in saying that Tyrconnel was *retained*. He was an impudent, intrusive fellow, whom, having once gained a footing in the house, it was impossible to dislodge. He cared for no insult; perceived no slight, and professed, in her presence, the profoundest respect for Lady Rookwood: in short, he was ever ready to do anything but depart.

Sir Piers was one of those people who cannot dine alone. He disliked a solitary repast almost as much as a *tête-à-tête* with his lady. He would have been recognised at once as the true Amphitryon, had any one been hardy enough to play the part of Jupiter. Ever ready to give a dinner, he found a difficulty arise, not usually experienced on such occasions— there was no one upon whom to bestow it. He had the best of wine; kept an excellent table; was himself no niggard host; but his own merits, and those of his *cuisine*, were forgotten in the invariable *pendant* to the feast; and the best of wine lost its flavour when the last bottle found its way to the guest's head. Dine alone Sir Piers would not. And as his old friends forsook him, he plunged lower in his search of society; collecting within his house a class of persons whom no one would have expected to meet at the hall, nor even its owner have chosen for his companions, had any choice remained to him. He did not endure this state of things without much outward show of discontent. " Anything for a quiet life," was his constant saying; and, like the generality of people with whom those words form a favourite maxim, he led the most uneasy life imaginable. Endurance, to excite commiseration, must be uncomplaining—an axiom the aggrieved of the gentle sex should remember. Sir Piers endured, but he grumbled lustily, and was on all hands voted a bore; domestic grievances, especially if the husband be the plaintiff, being the most intolerable of all mentionable miseries. No wonder that his friends deserted him; still there was Titus Tyrconnel; his ears and lips were ever open to pathos and to punch; so Titus kept his station. Immediately after

her husband's demise, it had been Lady Rookwood's intention
to clear the house of all the "vermin," so she expressed herself, that had so long infested it; and forcibly to eject Titus,
and one or two other intruders of the same class. But, in
consequence of certain hints received from Mr. Coates, who
represented the absolute necessity of complying with Sir
Piers's testamentary instructions, which were particular in
that respect, she thought proper to defer her intentions until
after the ceremonial of interment should be completed, and,
in the mean time, strange to say, committed its arrangement to Titus Tyrconnel; who, ever ready to accommodate,
accepted, nothing loth, the charge, and quitted himself
admirably well in his undertaking: especially, as he said, "in
the *aiting* and drinking department—the most essential part
of it all." He kept open house—open dining-room—open
cellar; resolved that his patron's funeral should emulate as
much as possible an Irish burial on a grand scale, "the finest
sight," in his opinion, "in the whole world."

Inflated with the importance of his office, inflamed with
heat, sat Titus, like a "robustious perriwig-pated" alderman
after a civic feast. The natural rubicundity of his countenance was darkened to a deep purple tint, like that of a
full-blown peony, while his ludicrous dignity was augmented
by a shining suit of sables, in which his portly person was
invested.

The first magnum had been discussed in solemn silence;
the cloud, however, which hung over the conclave, disappeared under the genial influence of "another and a better"
bottle, and gave place to a denser vapour, occasioned by the
introduction of the pipe and its accompaniments.

Ensconced in a comfortable old chair (it is not every old
chair that *is* comfortable), with pipe in mouth, and in full
unbuttoned ease, his bushy cauliflower wig laid aside, by
reason of the heat, reposed Doctor Small. Small, indeed, was
somewhat of a misnomer, as applied to the worthy doctor,
who, besides being no diminutive specimen of his kind, entertained no insignificant opinion of himself. His height
was cetainly not remarkable; but his width of shoulder—his
sesquipedality of stomach—and obesity of calf—these were
unique! Of his origin we know nothing; but presume he
must in some way or other have been connected with the
numerous family of "the Smalls," who, according to Christopher North, form the predominant portion of mankind. In
appearance, the doctor was short-necked and puffy, with a

sodden, pasty face, wherein were set eyes, whose obliquity of
vision was, in some measure, redeemed by their expression
of humour. He was accounted a man of parts and erudition,
and had obtained high honours at his university. Rigidly
orthodox, he abominated the very names of Papists and
Jacobite; amongst which heretical herd he classed his
companion, Mr. Titus Tyrconnel—Ireland being with him
synonymous with superstition and Catholicism—and every
Irishman rebellious and schismatical. On this head he was
inclined to be disputatious. His prejudices did not prevent
him from passing the claret, nor from laughing as heartily as
a plethoric asthma and sense of the decorum due to the occasion would permit, at the quips and quirks of the Irishman,
who, he admitted, notwithstanding his heresies, was a pleasant
fellow in the main. And when, in addition to the flattery, a
pipe had been insinuated by the officious Titus, at the precise
moment that Small yearned for his afternoon's solace, yet
scrupled to ask for it; when the door had been made fast,
and the first whiff exhaled, all his misgivings vanished, and
he surrendered himself to the soft seduction. In this elysian
state we find him.

"Ah! you may say that, Doctor Small," said Titus, in
answer to some observation of the vicar, "that's a most
original apophthegm. We all of us hould our lives by a thrid.
Och! many's the sudden finale I have seen. Many's the fine
fellow's heels tripped up unawares, when least expected.
Death hangs over our heads by a single hair, as your
reverence says, precisely like the sword of Dan Maclise,* the
flatterer of Dinnish what-do-you-call-him, ready to fall at a
moment's notice, or no notice at all—eh?—Mr. Coates. And
that brings me back again to Sir Piers—poor gentleman—
ah! we shan't soon see the like of him again!"

"Poor Sir Piers!" said Mr. Coates, a small man, in a
scratch wig, with a face red and round as an apple, and
almost as diminutive. "It is to be regretted that his over
conviviality should so much have hastened his lamented
demise."

"Conviviality!" replied Titus; "no such thing—it was
apoplexy—extravasation of *sarum*."

"Extra vase-ation of rum-and-water, you mean," replied
Coates, who, like all his **tribe**, rejoiced in a quibble.

"The squire's ailment," continued Titus, "was a sangui-
neous effusion, as we call it—positive determination of blood

* Query, Damocles?—*Printer's Devil.*

to the head, occasioned by a low way he got into, just before his attack—a confirmed case of hypochondriasis, as that *ould* book Sir Piers was so fond of terms the blue devils. He neglected the bottle, which, in a man who has been a hard drinker all his life, is a bad sign. The lowering system never answers—never. Doctor, I'll just trouble you"—for Small, in a fit of absence, had omitted to pass the bottle, though not to help himself. "Had he stuck to *this*"—holding up a glass ruby bright—"the elixir vitæ—the grand panacea—he might have been hale and hearty at this present moment, and as well as any of us. But he wouldn't be advised. To my thinking, as that was the case, he'd have been all the better for a little of your reverence's *sperretual* advice; and his conscience having been relieved, by confession and absolution, he might have opened a fresh account with an aisy heart and clane breast."

"I trust, sir," said Small, gravely withdrawing his pipe from his lips, "that Sir Piers Rookwood addressed himself to a higher source than a sinning creature of clay like himself for remission of his sins; but, if there was any load of secret guilt that might have weighed heavy upon his conscience, it is to be regretted that he refused the last offices of the church, and died incommunicate. I was denied all admittance to his chamber."

"Exactly my case," said Mr. Coates, pettishly. "I was refused entrance, though my business was of the utmost importance—certain dispositions—special bequests—matter connected with his sister—for though the estate is entailed, yet still there are charges—you understand me—very strange to refuse to see *me*. Some people may regret it—may live to regret it, I say—that's all. I've just sent up a package to Lady Rookwood, which was not to be delivered till after Sir Piers's death. Odd circumstance that—been in my custody a long while—some reason to think Sir Piers meant to alter his will—ought to have seen *me*—sad neglect!"

"More's the pity. But it was none of poor Sir Piers's doing!" replied Titus; "he had no will of his own, poor fellow, during his life, and the devil a will was he likely to have after his death. It was all Lady Rookwood's doing," added he, in a whisper. "I, his medical adviser and confidential friend, was ordered out of the room; and, although I knew it was as much as his life was worth to leave him for a moment in that state, I was forced to comply; and, would you believe it, as I left the room, I heard high words. Yes,

E

doctor, as I hope to be saved, words of anger from her at that awful juncture."

The latter part of this speech was uttered in a low tone, and very mysterious manner. The speakers drew so closely together that the bowls of their pipes formed a common centre, whence the stems radiated. A momentary silence ensued, during which each man puffed for very life. Small next knocked the ashes from his tube, and began to replenish it, coughing significantly. Mr. Coates expelled a thin, curling stream of vapour from a minute orifice in the corner of his almost invisible mouth, and arched his eyebrows, in a singular manner, as if he dared not trust the expression of his thoughts to any other feature. Titus shook his huge head, and, upon the strength of a bumper which he swallowed, mustered resolution enough to unburden his bosom.

"By my *sowl*," said he, mysteriously, "I've seen enough lately to frighten any quiet gentleman out of his senses. I'll not get a wink of sleep, I fear, for a week to come. There must have been something dreadful upon Sir Piers's mind; sure—nay, there's no use in mincing the matter with *you*— in a word, then, some crime too deep to be divulged."

"Crime!" echoed Coates and Small, in a breath.

"Ay, crime!" repeated Titus. "Whist! not so loud, lest any one should overhear us. Poor Sir Piers, he's dead now. I'm sure you both loved him as I did; and pity and pardon him if he was guilty; for certain am I that no soul ever took its flight more heavily laden than did that of our poor friend. Och! it was a terrible ending. But you shall hear *how* he died, and judge for yourselves. When I returned to his room, after Lady Rookwood's departure, I found him quite delirious. I knew death was not far off then. One minute he was in the chase, cheering on the hounds. 'Halloo! tallyho!' cried he; 'who clears that fence!—who swims that stream?' The next, he was drinking, carousing, and hurraing, at the head of his table, 'Hip! hip! hip!'—as mad, and wild, and frantic as ever he used to be when wine had got the better of him; and then all of a sudden, in the midst of his shouting, he stopped, exclaiming, 'What! here again?—who let her in?—the door is fast—I locked it myself. Devil! why did you open it!—you have betrayed me—she will poison me—and I cannot resist. Ha! another! Who—who is that?—her face is white—her hair hangs about her shoulders. Is she alive again? Susan! Susan! why that look? You loved me well—too well. *You* will not drag me to perdition! *You* will not appear against me! No, no, no—it is not in your nature—you whom I doated on, whom I loved—whom I—but I repented—I sorrowed—I prayed—*prayed!* Oh! oh! no prayers would avail. Pray for me, Susan—for ever! *Your* intercession may avail. It is not too late. I will do justice to all. Bring me pen and ink—paper—I will confess—*he* shall have all. Where is my sister? I would speak with her—would tell her—tell her. Call Alan Rookwood—I shall die before I can tell it. Come hither,' said he to me. 'There is a dark, dreadful secret on my mind—it must forth. Tell my sister—no, my senses swim—Susan is near me—fury is in her eyes—avenging fury—keep her off. What is this white mass in my arms? what do I hold? is it the corpse by my side, as it lay that long, long night? It is—it is. Cold, stiff, stirless as then. White—horribly white—as when the moon, that would not set, showed all its ghastliness. Ah! it moves, embraces me, stifles, suffocates me. Help! remove the pillow. I cannot breathe—I choke—oh!' And now I am coming to the strangest part of my story—and, strange as it may sound, every word is as true as the Holy Gospel."

"Ahem!" coughed Small.

" Well, at this moment—this terrible moment—what should I hear but a tap against the wainscot. Holy Virgin! how it startled me. My heart leapt to my mouth in an instant, and then went thump, thump, against my ribs. But I said nothing, though you may be sure I kept my ears wide open—and then presently I heard the tap repeated somewhat louder, and shortly afterwards a third—I should still have said nothing, but Sir Piers heard the knock, and raised himself at the summons, as if it had been the last trumpet. 'Come in,' cried he, in a dying voice, and Heaven forgive me if I confess that I expected a certain person, whose company one would rather dispense with upon such as occasion, to step in However, though it wasn't the *ould* gentleman, it was somebody near akin to him; for a door I had never seen, and never even dreamed of, opened in the wall, and in stepped Peter Bradley—aye, you may well stare, gentlemen; but it was Peter, looking as stiff as a crowbar, and as blue as a mattock. Well, he walked straight up to the bed of the dying man, and bent his great diabolical grey eyes upon him—laughing all the while—yes, laughing—you know the cursed grin he has. To proceed. 'You have called me,' said he to Sir Piers; 'I am here. What would you with me?'—'We are not alone,' groaned the dying man. 'Leave us, Mr. Tyrconnel—leave me for five minutes—only five, mark me.'—'I'll go,' thinks I, 'but I shall never see you again alive.' And true enough it was—I never did see him again with breath in his body. Without more ado, I left him, and I had scarcely reached the corridor when I heard the door bolted behind me. I then stopped to listen; and I am sure you'll not blame me when I say I clapped my eye to the keyhole; for I suspected something wrong. But, Heaven save us! that crafty gravedigger had taken his precautions too well. I could neither see nor hear anything, except, after a few minutes, a wild unearthly screech. And then the door was thrown open, and I, not expecting it, was precipitated head foremost into the room, to the great damage of my nose. When I got up, Peter had vanished, I suppose, as he came; and there was poor Sir Piers leaning back upon the pillow, with his hands stretched out as if in supplication; his eyes unclosed and staring; and his limbs stark and stiff!"

A profound silence succeeded Tyrconnel's narrative. Mr. Coates would not venture upon a remark. Doctor Small seemed, for some minutes, lost in painful reflection; at length he spoke. "You have described a shocking scene, Mr. Tyrconnel, and in a manner that convinces me of its fidelity. But I trust you will excuse me, as a friend of the late Sir Piers, in requesting you to maintain silence in future on the subject. Its repetition can be productive of no good, and may do infinite harm, by giving currency to unpleasant reports, and harrowing the feelings of the survivors. Every one acquainted with Sir Piers's history must be aware, as I dare say you are already, of an occurrence which cast a shade over his early life, blighted his character, and endangered his personal safety. It was a dreadful accusation. But I believe, nay, I am sure, it was unfounded. Dark suspicions attach to a Romish priest of the name of Checkley. He, I believe, is also beyond the reach of human justice. Erring, Sir Piers was undoubtedly. But I trust he was more weak than sinful. I have reason to think he was the tool of others, especially of the wretch I have named. And it is easy to perceive how that incomprehensible lunatic, Peter Bradley, has obtained an ascendancy over him. His daughter, you are aware, was Sir Piers's mistress. Our friend is now gone, and with him let us bury his offences, and the remembrance of them. That his soul was heavily laden, would appear from your account of his last moments; yet I fervently trust, that his repentance was sincere, in which case there is hope of forgiveness for him. 'At what time soever a sinner shall repent him of his sins, from the bottom of his heart, I will blot out all his wickedness out of my remembrance, said the Lord.' God's mercy is greater than man's sins. And there is hope of salvation even for Sir Piers."

"I trust so, indeed," said Titus, with emotion; "and as to repeating a syllable of what I have just said, devil a word more will I utter on the subject. My lips shall be shut and sealed, as close as one of Mr. Coates's bonds, for ever and a day: but I thought it just right to make you acquainted with the circumstances. And now, having dismissed the bad for ever, I am ready to speak of Sir Piers's good qualities, and not few they were. What was there becoming a gentleman that he couldn't do, I'd like to know? Couldn't he hunt as well as ever a one in the county? and hadn't he as good a pack of hounds? Couldn't he shoot as well, and fish as well, and drink as well, or better—only he couldn't carry his wine, which was his misfortune, not his fault. And wasn't he always ready to ask a friend to dinner with him, and didn't he give him a good dinner when he came, barring the cross-cups afterwards? And hadn't he everything agreeable about him, except his wife, which was a great drawback? And with all his peculiarities and humours, wasn't he as kind-hearted a man as needs be? and an Irishman at the core? And so, if he wern't dead, I'd say long life to him. But as he is, here's peace to his memory!"

At this juncture, a knocking was heard at the door, which some one without had vainly tried to open. Titus rose to unclose it, ushering in an individual known at the hall as Jack Palmer.

IX.

AN ENGLISH ADVENTURER.

Mrs. Peachum. Sure the captain's the finest gentleman on the road.
Beggar's Opera.

JACK PALMER was a good-humoured, good-looking man, with immense bushy, red whiskers, a freckled, florid complexion, and sandy hair, rather inclined to scantiness towards the scalp of the head, which garnished the nape of his neck with a ruff of crisp little curls, like the ring on a monk's shaven crown. Notwithstanding this tendency to baldness, Jack could not be more than thirty, though his looks were some five years in advance. His face was one of those inexplicable countenances, which appear to be proper to a peculiar class of men—a regular Newmarket physiognomy—compounded chiefly of cunning and assurance; not low cunning, nor vulgar assurance, but crafty sporting subtlety, careless as to results, indifferent to obstacles, ever on the alert for the main chance, game and turf all over, eager, yet easy, keen, yet quiet. He was somewhat showily dressed, in such wise that he looked half like a fine gentleman of that day, half like a jockey of our own. His nether man appeared in well-fitting, well-worn buckskins, and boots with tops, not unconscious of the saddle; while the airy extravagance of his broad-skirted, sky-blue riding coat, the richness of his vest (the pockets of which were beautifully exuberant, according to the mode of 1737), the smart luxuriance of his shirt-frill, and a certain curious taste in the size and style of his buttons, proclaimed that, in his own esteem at least, his person did not appear altogether unworthy of decoration; nor, in justice to Jack, can we allow that he was in error. He was a model of a man for five feet ten: square, compact, capitally built in every particular, excepting that his legs *were slightly* imbowed, which defect probably arose from his being almost constantly on horseback; a sort of exercise in which Jack greatly delighted, and was accounted a superb rider. It was, indeed, his daring horsemanship, upon one particular occasion, when he had outstripped a whole field, that had procured him the honour of an invitation to Rookwood. Who he was, or whence he came, was a question not easily answered—Jack, himself, evading all solution to the inquiry. Sir Piers never troubled his head about the matter: he was a " d——d good fellow—rode devilish well, and stood on no sort of ceremony;" that was enough for him. Nobody else knew anything about him, save that he was a capital judge of horseflesh, kept a famous black mare, and attended every hunt in the West Riding—that he could sing a good song, was a choice companion, and could drink three bottles without feeling the worse for them.

Sensible of the indecorum that might attach to his appearance, Doctor Small had hastily laid down his pipe, and arranged his wig. But when he saw who was the intruder, with a grunt of defiance, he resumed his occupation, without returning the bow of the latter, or bestowing further notice upon him. Nothing discomposed at the churchman's displeasure, Jack greeted Titus cordially, and carelessly saluting Mr. Coates, threw himself into a chair. He next filled a tumbler of claret, and drained it at a draught.

"Have you ridden far, Jack?" asked Titus, noticing the dusty state of Palmer's azure attire.

"Some dozen miles," replied Palmer; "and that, on such a sultry afternoon as the present, makes one feel thirstyish. I'm as dry as a sandbed. Famous wine this—beautiful tipple—better than all your red fustian. Ah, how poor Sir Piers used to like it! Well, that's all over—a glass like this might do him good in his present quarters! I'm afraid I'm intruding. But the fact is, I wanted a little information about the order of the procession, and missing you below, came hither in search of you. You're to be chief mourner, I suppose, Titus—*rehearsing* your part, eh?"

"Come, come, Jack, no joking," replied Titus; "the subject's too serious. I am to be chief mourner—and I expect you to be a mourner—and everybody else to be mourners. We must all mourn at the proper time. There'll be a power of people at the church."

"There *are* a power of people here already," returned Jack, "if they all attend."

"And they all *will* attend, or what is the eating and drinking to go for? I sha'n't leave a soul in the house."

"Excepting one," said Jack, slyly. "*She* won't attend, I think."

"Ay, excepting one—Lady Rookwood and her abigail. All the rest go with me, and form part of the procession. You go too."

"Of course. What time do you start?"

"Twelve precisely. As the clock strikes, we set out—all in a line, and a long line we'll make. I'm waiting for that *ould* coffin-faced rascal, Peter Bradley, to arrange the order."

"How long will it occupy, think you," asked Jack, carelessly.

"That I can't say," returned Titus; "possibly an hour, more or less. But we shall start to the minute—that is, if we can get all together, so don't be out of the way. And hark ye, Jack, you must contrive to change your toggery. That sky-blue coat won't do. It's not the thing at all, at all."

"Never fear that," replied Palmer. "But who were those in the carriages?"

"Is it the last carriage you mean? Squire Forester and his sons. They're dining with the other gentlefolk, in the great room up-stairs, to be out of the way. Oh, we'll have a grand *berrin'*. And by Saint Patrick! I must be looking after it."

"Stay a minute," said Jack; "let's have a cool bottle first. They are all taking care of themselves below, and Peter Bradley has not made his appearance, so you need be in no hurry. I'll go with you presently. Shall I ring for the claret?"

"By all means," replied Titus.

Jack accordingly arose; and a butler answering the summons, a long-necked bottle was soon placed before them.

"You heard of the affray last night, I presume," said Jack, renewing the conversation.

"With the poachers? To be sure I did. Wasn't I called in to examine Hugh Badger's wounds the first thing this morning; and a deep cut there was, just over the eye, besides other bruises."

"Is the wound dangerous?" inquired Palmer.

"Not exactly mortal, if you mean that," replied the Irishman; "dangerous, certainly."

"Humph!" exclaimed Jack; "they'd a pretty hardish bout of it, I understand. Anything been heard of the body?"

"What body?" inquired Small, who was half-dozing.

"The body of the drowned poacher," replied Jack; "they were off to search for it this morning."

"Found it—not they!" exclaimed Titus. "Ha, ha!—I can't help laughing, for the life and *sowl* of me; a capital trick he played 'em,—capital—ha, ha! What do you think the fellow did? Ha, ha!—after leading 'em the devil's dance, all round the park, killing a hound as savage as a wolf, and breaking Hugh Badger's head, which is as hard and thick as a butcher's block, what does the fellow do but dive into a pool, with a great rock hanging over it, and make his way to the other side, through a subterranean cavern, which nobody knew anything about, till they came to drag it, thinking him snugly drowned all the while—ha, ha!"

"Ha, ha, ha!" chorused Jack; "bravo! he's a lad of the right sort—ha, ha!"

"He! who?" inquired the attorney.

"Why, the poacher, to be sure," replied Jack; "who else were we talking about?"

"Beg pardon," returned Coates; "I thought you might

have heard some intelligence. We've got an eye upon him. We know who it was."

"Indeed!" exclaimed Jack; "and who was it?"

"A fellow known by the name of Luke Bradley."

"Zounds!" cried Titus; "you don't say it was he? Murder in Irish! that *bates* everything; why he was Sir Piers's——"

"Natural son," replied the attorney; "he has not been heard of for some time—shockingly incorrigible rascal—impossible to do anything with him."

"You don't say so," observed Jack. "I've heard Sir Piers speak of the lad; and, by his account, he's as fine a fellow as ever crossed tit's back; only a little wildish and unreasonable, as the best of us may be; wants breaking, that's all. Your skittish colt makes the best horse, and so would he. To speak the truth, I'm glad he escaped."

"So am I," rejoined Titus; "for, in the first place, I've a foolish partiality for poachers, and am sorry when any of 'em come to hurt; and, in the second, I'd be mightily displeased if any ill had happened to one of Sir Piers's flesh and blood, as this young chap appears to be."

"Appears to be!" repeated Palmer; "there's no *appearing* in the case, I take it. This Bradley's an undoubted offshoot of the old squire. His mother was a servant-maid at the hall, I rather think. You, sir," continued he, addressing Coates, "perhaps can inform us of the real facts of the case."

"She was something better than a servant," replied the attorney, with a slight cough and a knowing wink. "I remember her quite well, though I was but a boy then; a lovely creature, and so taking, I don't wonder that Sir Piers was smitten with her. He was mad after the women in those days, and pretty Sue Bradley above all others. She lived with him quite like his lady."

"So I've heard," returned Jack; "and she remained with him till her death. Let me see, wasn't there something rather odd in the way in which she died, rather suddenish and unexpected—a noise made about it at the time, eh?"

"Not that I ever heard," replied Coates, shaking his head, and appearing to be afflicted with an instantaneous ignorance; while Titus affected not to hear the remark, but occupied himself with his wine-glass. Small snored audibly. "I was too young, then, to pay any attention to idle rumours," continued Coates. "It's a long time ago. May I ask the reason of your inquiry?"

"Nothing further than simple curiosity," replied Jack, enjoying the consternation of his companions. "It is, as you say, a long while since. But it's singular how those sort of things are remembered. One would think people had something else to do than talk of one's private affairs for ever. For my part, I despise such tattle. But there *are* persons in the neighbourhood who still say it was an awkward business. Amongst others, I've heard that this very Luke Bradley talks in pretty plain terms about it."

"Does he, indeed?" said Coates. "So much the worse for him. Let me once lay hands upon him, and I'll put a gag in his mouth that shall spoil his talking in future."

"That's precisely the point I desire to arrive at," replied Jack; "and I advise you by all means to accomplish that, for the sake of the family. Nobody likes his friends to be talked about. So I'd settle the matter amicably, were I you. Just let the fellow go his way, he won't return here again in a hurry, I'll be bound. As to clapping him in quod, he might prattle—turn stag."

"Turn stag!" replied Coates, "what the deuce is that? In my opinion he has 'turned stag' already. At all events, he'll pay *deer* for his night's sport, you may depend upon it. What signifies it what *he* says? Let me lay hands upon him, that's all."

"Well, well," said Jack, "no offence. I only meant to offer a suggestion. I thought the family, young Sir Ranulph, I mean, mightn't like the story to be revived. As to Lady Rookwood, she don't, I suppose, care much about idle reports. Indeed, if I've been rightly informed, she bears this youngster no particular goodwill to begin with, and has tried hard to get him out of the country. But, as you say, what *does* it signify what he says, he can *only* talk. Sir Piers is dead and gone."

"Humph!" muttered Coates, peevishly.

"But it does seem a little hard that a lad should swing for killing a bit of venison in his own father's park."

"Which he'd a *nat'ral* right to do," cried Titus.

"He had no natural right to bruise, violently assault, and endanger the life of his father's, or anybody else's, gamekeeper," retorted Coates. "I tell you, sir, he's committed a capital offence, and if he's taken——"

"No chance of that, I hope," interrupted Jack.

"That's a wish I can't help wishing myself," said Titus; "on my conscience these poachers are fine boys, when all's said and done."

"The finest of all boys," exclaimed Jack, with a kindred enthusiasm, "are those birds of the night, and minions of the moon, whom we call, most unjustly, poachers. They are, after all, only *professional sportsmen*, making a business of what we make a pleasure; a nightly pursuit of what is to us a daily relaxation; there's the main distinction. As to the rest, it's all in idea; they merely thin an overstocked park, as *you* would reduce a plethoric patient, doctor; or as *you* would work a moneyed client, if you got him into Chancery, Mister Attorney. And then how much more scientifically and systematically they set to work than we amateurs do; how noiselessly they bag a hare, smoke a pheasant, or knock a buck down with an air-gun; how independent are they of any license, except that of a good eye, and a swift pair of legs; how unnecessary is it for them to ask permission to shoot over Mr. So-and-So's grounds, or my Lord That's preserves; they are free of every cover, and indifferent to any alteration in the game laws. I've some thoughts, when everything else fails, of taking to poaching myself. In my opinion, a poacher's a highly respectable character. What say you, Mr. Coates?" turning very gravely to that gentleman.

"Such a question, sir," replied Coates, bridling up, "scarcely deserves a serious answer. I make no doubt you will next maintain that a highwayman is a gentleman."

"Most undoubtedly," replied Palmer, in the same grave tone, which might have passed for banter, had Jack ever bantered. "I'll maintain and prove it. I don't see how he can be otherwise. It is as necessary for a man to be a gentleman before he can turn highwayman, as it is for a doctor to have his diploma, or an attorney his certificate. Some of the finest gentlemen of their day, as Captains Lovelace, Hind, Hannum, and Dudley, were eminent on the road, and they set the fashion. Ever since their day a real highwayman would consider himself disgraced, if he did not conduct himself in every way like a gentleman. Of course, there are pretenders, in this line, as in everything else. But these are only exceptions, and prove the rule. What are the distinguishing characteristics of a fine gentleman?—perfect knowledge of the world—perfect independence of character—notoriety—command of cash—and inordinate success with the women. You grant all these premises. First, then, it is part of a highwayman's business to be thoroughly acquainted with the world. He is the easiest and pleasantest fellow going. There is Tom King, for example; he is the handsomest man about town, and the best-bred fellow on the road. Then whose inclinations are so uncontrolled as the highwayman's, so long as the mopuses last? Who produces so great an effect by so few words?—' *Stand and deliver*,' is sure to arrest attention. Every one is captivated by an address so *taking*. As to money, he wins a purse of a hundred guineas as easily as you would the same sum from the faro table. And wherein lies the difference? Only in the name of the game. Who so little need of a banker as he? all he has to apprehend is a check—all he has to draw is a trigger. As to the women, they dote upon him: not even your red-coat is so successful. Look at a highwayman mounted on his flying steed, with his pistols in his holsters, and his mask upon his face. What can be a more gallant sight? The clatter of his horse's heels is like music to his ear—he is in full quest—he shouts to the fugitive horseman to stay—the other flies all the faster— what chase can be half so exciting as that? Suppose he overtakes his prey, which ten to one he will, how readily his summons to deliver is obeyed; how satisfactory is the appro- priation of a lusty purse or corpulent pocket-book—getting the brush is nothing to it. How tranquilly he departs, takes off his hat to his accommodating acquaintance, wishes him a pleasant journey, and disappears across the heath. England, sir, has reason to be proud of her highwaymen! They are peculiar to her clime, and are as much before the brigand of Italy, the contrabandist of Spain, or the cut-purse of France— as her sailors are before all the rest of the world. The day will never come, I hope, when we shall degenerate into the footpad, and lose our *night errantry*. Even the French borrow from us—they have only one highwayman of eminence, and he learnt and practised his art in England."

"And who was he, may I ask?" said Coates.

"Claude Du-Val," replied Jack; "and though a French- man, he was a deuced fine fellow in his day—quite a tip-top macaroni—he could skip and twirl like a figurant, warble like an opera singer, and play the flageolet better than any man of his day—he always carried a lute in his pocket, along with his snappers. And then his dress—it was quite beau- tiful to see how smartly he was rigg'd out, all velvet and lace; and even with his vizard on his face, the ladies used to cry out to see him. Then he took a purse with the air and grace of a receiver-general. All the women adored him—and that, bless their pretty faces, was the best proof of his gentility. I wish he'd not been a Mounseer. The women never mistake. *They* can always discover the true gentleman, and they were all, of every degree, from the countess to the kitchen-maid, over head and ears in love with him."

" But he was taken, I suppose?" asked Coates.

" Ay," responded Jack, " the women were his undoing as they've been many a brave fellow's before, and will be again." Touched by which reflection, Jack became for once in his life sentimental, and sighed. " Poor Duval! he was seized at the Hole-in-the-Wall in Chandos-street by the bailiff of Westminster when dead drunk, his liquor having been drugged by his dells—and was shortly afterwards hanged at Tyburn."

" It was a thousand pities," said Mr. Coates, with a sneer, " that so fine a gentleman should come to so ignominious an end."

" Quite the contrary," returned Jack. " As his biographer, Doctor Pope, properly remarks, ' Who is there worthy of the name of man, that would not prefer such a death before a mean, solitary, inglorious life?' By the bye, Titus, as we're upon the subject, if you like, I'll sing you a song about highwaymen!"

" I should like it of all things," replied Titus, who entertained a favourable opinion of Jack's vocal powers, and was by no means an indifferent performer; " only let it be in a minor key."

Jack required no further encouragement, but, disregarding the hints and looks of Coates, sang with much unction the following ballad to a good old tune, then very popular—the merit of which " nobody can deny."

A CHAPTER OF HIGHWAYMEN.

Of every rascal of every kind,
The most notorious to my mind,
Was the Cavalier Captain, gay JEMMY HIND!*
Which nobody can deny.

But the pleasantest coxcomb among them all
For lute, coranto, and madrigal,
Was the galliard Frenchman, CLAUDE DU-VAL!†
Which nobody can deny.

And Tobygloak never a coach could rob,
Could lighten a pocket or empty a fob,
With a neater hand than OLD MOB, OLD MOB!‡
Which nobody can deny.

---

* James Hind (the " Prince of Prigs"), a royalist captain of some distinction, was hanged, drawn, and quartered, in 1652. Some good stories are told of him. He had the credit of robbing Cromwell, Bradshaw, and Peters. His discourse to Peters is particularly edifying.

† See Du-Val's life by Doctor Pope, or Leigh Hunt's brilliant sketch of him in *The Indicator.*

‡ We cannot say much in favour of this worthy, whose name was Thomas

Nor did housebreaker ever deal harder knocks
On the stubborn lid of a good strong box,
Than that prince of good fellows, TOM COX, TOM COX!*
       Which nobody can deny.

A blither fellow on broad highway,
Did never with oath bid traveller stay,
Than devil-may-care WILL HOLLOWAY!†
       Which nobody can deny.

And in roguery nought could exceed the tricks
Of GETTINGS and GREY, and the five or six,
Who trod in the steps of bold NEDDY WICKS!‡
       Which nobody can deny.

Nor could any so handily break a lock
As SHEPPARD, who stood on the Newgate dock,
And nicknamed the gaolers around him "*his flock!*"§
       Which nobody can deny.

Nor did highwayman ever before possess,
For ease, for security, danger, distress,
Such a mare as DICK TURPIN's Black Bess! Black Bess!
       Which nobody can deny.

"A capital song, by the powers!" cried Titus, as Jack's ditty came to a close. "But your English robbers are nothing at all, compared with our Tories|| and Rapparees—

Simpson. The reason of his *sobriquet* does not appear. He was not particularly scrupulous as to his mode of appropriation. One of his sayings is, however, on record. He told a widow whom he robbed, "that the end of a woman's husband begins in tears, but the end of her tears is another husband." "Upon which," says his chronicler, "the gentlewoman gave him about fifty guineas."

* Tom was a sprightly fellow, and carried his sprightliness to the gallows; for just before he was turned off he kicked Mr. Smith, the ordinary, and the hangman, out of the cart—a piece of pleasantry which created, as may be supposed, no small sensation.

† Many agreeable stories are related of Holloway. His career, however, closed with a murder. He contrived to break out of Newgate, but returned to witness the trial of one of his associates; when, upon the attempt of a turnkey, one Richard Spurling, to seize him, Will knocked him on the head in the presence of the whole court. For this offence he suffered the extreme penalty of the law in 1712.

‡ Wicks's adventures with Madame Toly are highly diverting. It was this hero, not Turpin, as has been erroneously stated, who stopped the celebrated Lord Mohun. Of Gettings and Grey, and "the five or six," the less said the better.

§ One of Sheppard's recorded *mots*. When a Bible was pressed upon his acceptance by Mr. Wagstaff, the chaplain, Jack refused it, saying, "that in his situation one file would be worth all the Bibles in the world." A gentleman who visited Newgate asked him to dinner; Sheppard replied, "that he would take an early opportunity of waiting upon him." And we believe he kept his word.

|| The word Tory, as here applied, must not be confounded with the term of party distinction now in general use in the political world. It simply means a thief on a grand scale, something more than "a snapper up of unconsidered trifles," or petty larceny rascal. We have classical authority for this:— TORY—"an advocate for absolute monarchy, *also an Irish vagabond, robber, or rapparee.*"—GROSE's *Dictionary.*

nothing at all. They were the *raal* gentlemen—they were the boys to cut a throat *asily*."

"Pshaw!" exclaimed Jack in disgust, "the gentlemen I speak of never maltreated any one, except in self-defence."

"Maybe not," replied Titus, "I'll not dispute the point—but these Rapparees were true brothers of the blade, and gentlemen every inch. I'll just sing you a song I made about them myself. But meanwhile don't let's forget the bottle—talking's dry work—my service to you, doctor!" added he, winking at the somnolent Small. And, tossing off his glass, Titus delivered himself with much joviality of the following ballad; the words of which he adapted to the tune of the *Groves of the Pool*:—

THE RAPPAREES.

Let the Englishman boast of his Turpins and Sheppards, as cocks of the walk,
His Mulsacks, and Cheneys, and Swiftnecks *—it's all botheration and talk ;
Compared with the robbers of Ireland, they don't come within half a mile,
There never were yet any rascals like those of my own native isle !

First and foremost comes REDMOND O'HANLON, allowed the first thief of
the world,†
That O'er the broad province of Ulster the Rapparee banner unfurled ;
Och ! he was an elegant fellow, as ever you saw in your life,
At fingering the blunderbuss trigger, or handling the throat-cutting knife.

---

* A trio of famous High-Tobygloaks. Swiftneck was a captain of *Irish* dragoons, by the bye.

† REDMOND O'HANLON was the Rob Roy of Ireland, and his adventures, many of which are exceedingly curious, would furnish as rich *materials* for the novelist, as they have already done for the ballad-mongers : some of them are, however, sufficiently well narrated in a pleasant little tome, published at Belfast, entitled *The History of the Rapparees*. We are also in possession of a funeral discourse preached at the obsequies of the " noble and renowned" Henry St. John, Esq., who was unfortunately killed by the *Tories* (the *Destructives* of those days), in the induction to which we find some allusion to Redmond. After describing the thriving condition of the north of Ireland, about 1680, the Rev. Lawrence Power, the author of the sermon, says, " One mischief there was, which indeed in a great measure destroyed all, and that was, a pack of insolent bloody outlaws, whom they here call *Tories*. These had so rivetted themselves in these parts, that by the interest they had among the natives, and some English, too, *to their shame be it spoken*, they exercise a kind of separate sovereignty in three or four counties in the north of Ireland. REDMOND O'HANLON is their chief, and has been these many years ; a cunning, dangerous fellow, who, though proclaimed an outlaw with the rest of his crew, and sums of money set upon their heads, yet he reigns still, and keeps all in subjection, so far that 'tis credibly reported *he raises more in a year by contribution à-la-mode de France than the king's land taxes and chimney-money come to, and thereby is enabled to bribe clerks and officers,* IF NOT THEIR MASTERS, (!) *and makes all too much truckle to him.*" Agitation, it seems, was not confined to our own days—but the " finest country in the world" has been, and ever will be the same. The old game is played under a new colour—the only difference being, that had Redmond lived in our

And then such a dare-devil squadron as that which composed REDMOND's
 tail!
Meel, Mactigh, Jack Reilly, Shan Bernagh, Phil Galloge, and Arthur O'Neal;
Shure never were any boys like 'em, for rows, *agitation*, and sprees:
Not a *rap* did they leave in the country, and hence they were called *Rap-
 parees.**

Next comes POWER, the great TORY† of Munster, a gentleman born every
 inch,
And strong JACK MACPHERSON, of Leinster, a horse-shoe who broke at a
 pinch;
The last was a fellow so *lively*, not death e'en his courage could damp,
For as he was led to the gallows, he played his own "march to the camp."‡

PADDY FLEMMING, DICK BALF, and MULHONI, I think are the next on my
 list,
All adepts in the beautiful science of giving a pocket a twist;
JEMMY CARRICK must follow his leaders, ould PURNEY who put in a huff,
By dancing a hornpipe at Tyburn, and bothering the hangman for snuff.

There's PAUL LIDDY, the curly-pate Tory, whose noddle was stuck on a
 spike,
And BILLY DELANY, the "*Songster*,"§ we never shall meet with his like;
For his neck by a witch was anointed, and warranted safe by her charm,
No hemp that was ever yet twisted his wonderful throttle could harm.

---

time, he would, in all probability, not only have pillaged a county, but *represented* it in parliament. The spirit of the Rapparee is still abroad—though
we fear there is little of the *Tory* left about it. We recommend this note to
the serious consideration of the declaimers against the sufferings of the "six
millions."

 * Here Titus was slightly in error. He mistook the cause for the effect.
"They were called Rapparees," Mr. Malone says, "from being armed with
a half-pike, called by the Irish a *rapparee*."—TODD'S JOHNSON.

 † *Tory*, so called from the Irish word *Toree*, give me your money.—TODD'S
JOHNSON.

 ‡ As he was carried to the gallows, Jack played a fine tune of his own
composing on the bagpipe, which retains the name of Macpherson's tune to
this day.—*History of the Rapparees.*

 § "Notwithstanding he was so great a rogue, Delany was a handsome
portly man, extremely diverting in company, and could behave himself before
gentlemen very agreeably. *He had a political genius* (not altogether surprising in so eminent a *Tory*), and would have made a great proficiency in
learning if he had rightly applied his time. He composed several songs, and
put tunes to them; and by his skill in music gained the favour of some of the
leading musicians in the country, who endeavoured to get him reprieved."—
History of the Rapparees. The particulars of the *Songster's* execution are
singular:—" When he was brought into court to receive sentence of death,
the judge told him that he was informed he should say 'that there was not
a rope in Ireland sufficient to hang him. But,' says he, 'I'll try if Kilkenny
can't afford one strong enough to do your business; and if that will not do,
you shall have another and another. Then he ordered the sheriff to choose
a rope, and Delany was ordered for execution the next day. The sheriff
having notice of his mother's boasting that no rope could hang her son (and
pursuant to the judge's desire), provided two ropes, but Delany broke them
one after another! The sheriff was then in a rage, and went for three bed
cords, which he plaited three-fold together, *and they did his business!* Yet
the sheriff was afraid he was not dead; and in a passion, to make trial,
stabbed him with his sword in the soles of his feet, and at last cut the rope.
After he was cut down, his body was carried into the court-house, where it

And lastly, there's CAHIR NA CAPPUL, the handiest rogue of them all,
Who only need whisper a word, and your horse will trot out of his stall;
Your tit is not safe in your stable, though you or your groom should be near,
And devil a bit in the paddock, if CAHIR gets *hould* of his ear.

Then success to the Tories of Ireland, the generous, the gallant, the gay!
With them the best *Rumpads** of England are not to be named the
    same day!
And were further proof wanting to show what precedence we take with
    our *prigs*,
Recollect that our robbers are TORIES, while those of your country are
    WHIGS!

"Bravissimo!" cried Jack, drumming upon the table.

"Well," said Coates, "we've had enough about the Irish
highwaymen, in all conscience. But there's a rascal on our
side of the Channel, whom you have only incidentally
mentioned, and who makes more noise than them all put
together."

"Who's that?" asked Jack, with some curiosity.

"Dick Turpin," replied the attorney: "he seems to me
quite as worthy of mention as any of the Hinds, the Du-Vals,
or the O'Hanlons, you have either of you enumerated."

"I did not think of him," replied Palmer, smiling;
"though if I had, he scarcely deserves to be ranked with
those illustrious heroes."

"Gads bobs!" cried Titus; "they tell me Turpin keeps
the best nag in the United Kingdom, and can ride faster and
further in a day than any other man in a week."

"So I've heard," said Palmer, with a glance of satisfaction. "I should like to try a run with him. I warrant me,
I'd not be far behind."

"I should like to get a peep at him," quoth Titus.

"So should I," added Coates. "*Vastly!*"

"You may both of you be gratified, gentlemen," said
Palmer. "Talking of Dick Turpin, they say, is like speaking of the devil, he's at your elbow ere the word's well out
of your mouth. He may be within hearing at this moment,
for anything we know to the contrary."

"Body o' me!" ejaculated Coates, "you don't say so.
Turpin in Yorkshire! I thought he confined his exploits
to the neighbourhood of the metropolis, and made Epping
Forest his head-quarters."

remained in the coffin for two days, standing up, till the judge and all the
spectators were fully satisfied that he was stiff and dead, and then permission
was given to his friends to remove the corpse and bury it."—*History of the
Rapparees.*

  * Highwaymen, as contradistinguished from footpads.

F

"So he did," replied Jack, "but the cave is all up now. The whole of the great North Road, from Tottenham Cross to York gates, comes within Dick's present range; and Saint Nicholas only knows in which part of it he is most likely to be found. He shifts his quarters as often and as readily as a Tartar; and he who looks for him may chance to *catch a Tartar*—ha! ha!"

"It's a disgrace to the country that such a rascal should remain unhanged," returned Coates, peevishly. "Government ought to look to it. Is the whole kingdom to be kept in a state of agitation by a single highwayman?—Sir Robert Walpole should take the affair into his own hands."

"Fudge!" exclaimed Jack, emptying his glass.

"I have already addressed a letter to the editor of the *Common Sense* on the subject," said Coates, "in which I have spoken my mind pretty plainly: and I repeat, it is perfectly disgraceful that such a rascal should be suffered to remain at large."

"You don't happen to have that letter by you, I suppose," said Jack, "or I should beg the favour to hear it?—I am not acquainted with the newspaper to which you allude;—I read *Fog's Journal*."

"So I thought," replied Coates, with a sneer; "that's the reason you are so easily mystified. But luckily I *have* the paper in my pocket; and you are quite welcome to my opinions. Here it is," added he, drawing forth a newspaper. "I shall waive my preliminary remarks, and come to the point at once."

"By all means," said Jack.

"'I thank God,'" began Coates, in an authoritative tone, "'that I was born in a country that hath formerly emulated the Romans in their public spirit; as is evident from their conquests abroad, and their struggles for liberty at home.'"

"What has all this got to do with Turpin?" interposed Jack.

"You will hear," replied the attorney—"no interruptions, if you please. 'But this noble principle,'" continued he, with great emphasis, "'though not utterly lost, I cannot think at present so active as it ought to be in a nation so jealous of her liberty.'"

"Good!" exclaimed Jack. "There is more than '*common sense*' in that observation, Mr. Coates."

"'My suspicion,'" proceeded Coates, "'is founded on a late instance. I mean the flagrant, undisturbed success of the notorious TURPIN, who hath robb'd in a manner scarce ever known before for several years, and is grown so insolent and impudent as to threaten particular persons, and become openly dangerous to the lives as well as fortunes of the people of England.'"

"Better and better," shouted Jack, laughing immoderately. "Pray go on sir."

"'That a fellow,'" continued Coates, "'who is known to be a thief by the whole kingdom, shall for so long a time continue to rob us, and not only rob us, but make a jest of us.'"

"Ha—ha—ha—capital! Excuse me, sir," roared Jack, laughing till the tears ran down his cheeks—"pray, pray, go on."

"I see nothing to laugh at," replied Coates, somewhat offended; "however, I will conclude my letter, since I have begun it—' not only rob us, but make a jest of us, shall defy the laws, and laugh at justice, argues a want of public spirit, which should make every particular member of the community sensible of the public calamity, and ambitious of the honour of extirpating such a notorious highwayman from society, since he owes his long success to no other cause than his immoderate impudence, and the sloth and pusillanimity of those who ought to bring him to justice.' I will not deny," continued Coates, "that, professing myself, as I do, to be a stanch new Whig, I had not some covert political object in penning this epistle.* Nevertheless, setting aside my principles——"

"Right," observed Jack; "you Whigs, new or old, always set aside your principles."

"Setting aside any political feeling I may entertain," continued Coates, disregarding the interruption, "I repeat, I am ambitious of extirpating this modern Cacus—this Autolycus of the eighteenth century."

"And what course do you mean to pursue?" asked Jack, "for I suppose you do not expect to catch this ' *ought-to-lick-us*,' as you call him, by a line in the newspapers."

"I am in the habit of keeping my own counsel, sir," replied

* Since Mr. Coates here avows himself the writer of this diatribe against Sir Robert Walpole, attacked under the guise of *Turpin* in the *Common Sense* of July 30th, 1737, it is useless to inquire further into its authorship. And it remains only to refer the reader to the *Gents. Mag.*, vol. vii., p. 138, for the article above quoted; and for a reply to it in the *Daily Gazetteer*, contained in p. 499 of the same volume.

Coates, pettishly; "and to be plain with you I hope to finger all the reward myself."

"Oons, is there a reward offered for Turpin's apprehension?" asked Titus.

"No less than two hundred pounds," answered Coates, "and that's no trifle, as you will both admit. Have you not seen the king's proclamation, Mr. Palmer?"

"Not I," replied Jack, with affected indifference.

"Nor I," added Titus, with some appearance of curiosity; "do you happen to have *that* by you too?"

"I always carry it about with me," replied Coates, "that I may refer to it in case of emergency. My father, Christopher, or Kit Coates, as he was familiarly called, was a celebrated thief-taker. He apprehended Spicket and Child, and half a dozen others, and always kept their descriptions in his pocket. I endeavour to tread in my worthy father's footsteps. I hope to signalise myself by capturing a highwayman. By the bye," added he, surveying Jack more narrowly, "it occurs to me that Turpin must be rather like you, Mr. Palmer?"

"Like me," said Jack, regarding Coates askance; "like me—how am I to understand you, sir, eh?"

"No offence; none whatever, sir. Ah! stay, you won't object to my comparing the description. That *can* do no harm. Nobody would take you for a highwayman—nobody whatever—ha! ha! Singular resemblance—he—he! These things *do* happen sometimes: not very often, though. But here is Turpin's description in the *Gazette, June 28th,* A.D. 1737:—'*It having been represented to the King that Richard Turpin did, on Wednesday, the 4th of May last, rob on his Majesty's highway Vavasour Mowbray, Esq., Major of the 2nd troop of Horse Grenadiers*' (that Major Mowbray, by the bye, is a nephew of the late Sir Piers, and cousin of the present baronet), '*and commit other notorious felonies and robberies near London, his Majesty is pleased to promise his most gracious pardon to any of his accomplices, and a reward of two hundred pounds to any person or persons who shall discover him, so as he may be apprehended and convicted.*'"

"Odsbodikins!" exclaimed Titus, "a noble reward! I should like to lay hands upon Turpin," added he, slapping Palmer's shoulder: "I wish he were in your place at this moment, Jack."

"Thank you!" replied Palmer, shifting his chair.

"'*Turpin,*'" continued Coates, "'*was born at Thacksted,*

in Essex; is about thirty'—you, sir, I believe, are about thirty?" added he, addressing Palmer.

"Thereabouts," said Jack, bluffly. "But what has my age to do with that of Turpin?"

"Nothing—nothing at all," answered Coates—"suffer me, however, to proceed?—*'Is by trade a butcher,'*—you, sir, I believe, never had any dealings in that line?"

"I have some notion how to dispose of a troublesome calf," returned Jack. "But Turpin, though described as a butcher, is, I understand, a lineal descendant of a great French archbishop of the same name."

"Who wrote the chronicles of that royal robber Charlemagne; I know him," replied Coates—"a terrible liar!—The modern Turpin *'is about five feet nine inches high'*—exactly your height, sir—exactly!"

"I am five feet ten," answered Jack, standing bolt upright.

"You have an inch, then, in your favour," returned the unperturbed attorney, deliberately proceeding with his examination—"'*he has a brown complexion, marked with the small-pox.'*"

"My complexion is florid—my face without a seam," quoth Jack.

"Those whiskers would conceal anything," replied Coates, with a grin. "Nobody wears whiskers now-a-days, except a highwayman."

"Sir!" said Jack, sternly. "You are personal."

"I don't mean to be so," replied Coates; "but you must allow the description tallies with your own in a remarkable manner. Hear me out, however—'*his cheek-bones are broad—his face is thinner towards the bottom—his visage short—pretty upright—and broad about the shoulders.'* Now I appeal to Mr. Tyrconnel if all this does not sound like a portrait of yourself?"

"Don't appeal to me," said Titus, hastily, "upon such a delicate point. I can't say that I approve of a gentleman being likened to a highwayman. But if ever there was a highwayman I'd wish to resemble, it's either Redmond O'Hanlon or Richard Turpin; and may the devil burn me if I know which of the two is the greater rascal!"

"Well, Mr. Palmer," said Coates, "I repeat, I mean no offence. Likenesses are unaccountable. I am said to be like my Lord North, whether I am or not, the Lord knows. But if ever I meet with Turpin I shall bear you in mind—he

—he! Ah! if ever I *should* have the good luck to stumble
upon him, I've a plan for his capture which couldn't fail. Only
let me get a glimpse of him, that's all. You shall see how
I'll dispose of him."

"Well, sir, we *shall* see," observed Palmer. "And for
your own sake, I wish you may never be nearer to him than
you are at this moment. With his friends, they say Dick
Turpin can be as gentle as a lamb; with his foes, especially
with a limb of the law like yourself, he's been found but an
ugly customer. I once saw him, as I told you, at Newmarket,
where he was collared by two constable culls, one on each
side. Shaking off one, and dealing the other a blow in the
face with his heavy-handled whip, he stuck spurs into his
mare, and though the whole field gave chase, he distanced
them all easily."

"And how came you not to try your pace with him, if
you were there, as you boasted a short time ago?" asked
Coates.

"So I did, and stuck closer to him than any one else. We
were neck and neck. I was the only person who could have
delivered him into the hands of justice, if I'd felt inclined."

"Zounds!" cried Coates; "if I had a similar opportunity
it should be neck or nothing. Either he or I should reach
the scragging-post first. I'd take him, dead or alive."

"*You* take Turpin!" cried Jack, with a sneer.

"I'd engage to do it," replied Coates. "I'll bet you a
hundred guineas I take him, if I ever have the same chance."

"Done!" exclaimed Jack, rapping the table at the same
time, so that the glasses danced upon it.

"That's right," cried Titus. "I'll go your halves."

"What's the matter—what's the matter?" exclaimed
Small, awakening from his doze.

"Only a trifling bet about a highwayman," replied Titus.

"A highwayman!" echoed Small. "Eh! what? there
are none in the house, I hope."

"I hope not," answered Coates. "But this gentleman has
taken up the defence of the notorious Dick Turpin in so singular a manner, that——"

"*Quod factu fœdum est, idem est et Dictu Turpe,*" returned
Small. "The less said about that rascal the better."

"So I think," replied Jack. "The fact is as you say, sir
—were Dick here, he would, I am sure, take the *freedom to
hide 'em.*"

Further discourse was cut short by the sudden opening of
the door, followed by the abrupt entrance of a tall, slender

young man, who hastily advanced towards the table, around which the company were seated. His appearance excited the utmost astonishment in the whole group : curiosity was exhibited in every countenance—the magnum remained poised midway in the hand of Palmer—Doctor Small scorched his thumb in the bowl of his pipe ; and Mr. Coates was almost choked, by swallowing an inordinate whiff of vapour.

" Young Sir Ranulph !" ejaculated he, so soon as the syncope would permit him.

" Sir Ranulph here ?" echoed Palmer, rising.

" Angels and ministers !" exclaimed Small.

" Odsbodikins !" cried Titus, with a theatrical start ; " this is more than I expected."

" Gentlemen," said Ranulph, " do not let my unexpected arrival here discompose you. Doctor Small, you will excuse the manner of my greeting ; and you, Mr. Coates. One of the present party, I believe, was my father's medical attendant, Doctor Tyrconnel."

" I had that honour," replied the Irishman, bowing profoundly—" I am Doctor Tyrconnel, Sir Ranulph, at your service."

" When, and at what hour, did my father breathe his last, sir ?" inquired Ranulph.

" Poor Sir Piers," answered Titus, again bowing, " departed this life on Thursday last."

" The hour—the precise minute ?" asked Ranulph, eagerly.

" Troth, Sir Ranulph, as nearly as I can recollect, it might be a few minutes before midnight."

" The very hour !" exclaimed Ranulph, striding towards the window. His steps were arrested as his eye fell upon the attire of his father, which, as we have before noticed, hung at that end of the room. A slight shudder passed over his frame. There was a momentary pause, during which Ranulph continued gazing intently at the apparel. " The very dress, too !" muttered he ; then turning to the assembly, who were watching his movements with surprise, " Doctor," said he, addressing Small, " I have something for your private ear. Gentlemen, will you spare us the room for a few minutes ?"

" On my conscience," said Tyrconnel to Jack Palmer, as they quitted the sanctum, " a mighty fine boy is this young Sir Ranulph !—and a chip of the *ould* block !—he'll be as good a fellow as his father."

" No doubt," replied Palmer, shutting the door. " But what the devil brought him back, just in the nick of it ?"

X.

RANULPH ROOKWOOD.

Fer. Yes, Francisco,
    He hath left his curse upon me.
Fran. How?
Fer. His curse! do-t comprehend what that word carries,
    Shot from a father's angry breath?   Unless
    I tear poor Felisarda from my heart,
    He hath pronounced me heir to all his curses.
            SHIRLEY.—*The Brothers.*

"THERE is nothing, I trust, my dear young friend, and quondam pupil," said Doctor Small, as the door was closed, " that weighs upon your mind, beyond the sorrow naturally incident to an affliction, severe as the present. Forgive my apprehensions if I am wrong. You know the affectionate interest I have ever felt for you—an interest which, I assure you, is nowise diminished, and which will excuse my urging you to unburden your mind to me; assuring yourself, that whatever may be your disclosure, you will have my sincere sympathy and commiseration. I may be better able to advise with you, should counsel be necessary, than others, from my knowledge of your character and temperament. I would not anticipate evil, and am, perhaps, unnecessarily apprehensive. But I own, I am startled at the incoherence of your expressions, coupled with your sudden and almost mysterious appearance at this distressing conjuncture. Answer me: has your return been the result of mere accident? is it to be considered one of those singular circumstances which almost look like fate, and baffle our comprehension? or were you nearer home than we expected, and received the news of your father's demise through some channel unknown to us? Satisfy my curiosity, I beg of you, upon this point."

"Your curiosity, my dear sir," replied Ranulph, gravely and sadly, "will not be decreased, when I tell you, that my return has neither been the work of chance (for I came fully anticipating the dread event, which I find realised), nor has it been occasioned by any intelligence derived from yourself, or others. It was only, indeed, upon my arrival here that I received full confirmation of my apprehensions. I had another, a more terrible summons to return."

"What summons? you perplex me!" exclaimed Small,

gazing with some misgiving into the face of his young friend.

"I am myself perplexed—sorely perplexed," returned Ranulph. "I have much to relate; but I pray you bear with me to the end. I have that on my mind which, like guilt, must be revealed."

"Speak, then, fearlessly to me," said Small, affectionately pressing Ranulph's hand; "and assure yourself, beforehand, of my sympathy."

"It will be necessary," said Ranulph, "to preface my narrative by some slight allusion to certain painful events (and yet I know not why I should call them painful, excepting in their consequences) which influenced my conduct in my final interview between my father and myself—an interview which occasioned my departure for the Continent—and which was of a character so dreadful, that I would not even revert to it, were it not a necessary preliminary to the circumstance I am about to detail

"When I left Oxford, I passed a few weeks alone, in London. A college friend, whom I accidentally met, introduced me, during a promenade in St. James's Park, to some acquaintances of his own, who were taking an airing in the Mall at the same time—a family whose name was Mowbray, consisting of a widow lady, her son, and daughter. This introduction was made in compliance with my own request. I had been struck by the singular beauty of the younger lady, whose countenance had a peculiar and inexpressible charm to me, from its marked resemblace to the portrait of the Lady Eleanor Rookwood, whose charms, and unhappy fate, I have so often dwelt upon and deplored. The picture is there," continued Ranulph, pointing to it: "look at it, and you have the fair creature I speak of before you; the colour of the hair—the tenderness of the eyes. No—the expression is not so sad, except when—but no matter! I recognised her features at once.

"It struck me, that upon the mention of my name, the party betrayed some surprise, especially the elder lady. For my own part, I was so attracted by the beauty of the daughter, the effect of which upon me seemed rather the fulfilment of a predestined event, originating in the strange fascination which the family portrait had wrought in my heart, than the operation of what is called 'love at first sight,' that I was insensible to the agitation of the mother. In vain I endeavoured to rally myself; my efforts at conversation

were fruitless; I could not talk—all I could do was silently
to yield to the soft witchery of those tender eyes: my admiration increasing each instant that I gazed upon them.

"I accompanied them home. Attracted as by some irresistible spell, I could not tear myself away; so that, although
I fancied I could perceive symptoms of displeasure in the
looks of both the mother and the son, yet, regardless of consequences, I ventured, uninvited, to enter the house. In
order to shake off the restraint which I felt my society imposed, I found it absolutely necessary to divest myself of
bashfulness, and to exert such conversational powers as I
possessed. I succeeded so well that the discourse soon
became lively and animated; and what chiefly delighted me
was, that *she*, for whose sake I had committed my present
rudeness, became radiant with smiles. I had been all eagerness to seek for some explanation of the resemblance to which
I have just alluded, and the fitting moment had, I conceived,
arrived. I called attention to a peculiar expression in the
features of Miss Mowbray, and then instanced the likeness
that subsisted between her and my ancestress. 'It is the
more singular,' I said, turning to her mother, 'because there
could have been no affinity, that I am aware of, between
them, and yet the likeness is really surprising.'—'It is not so
singular as you imagine,' answered Mrs. Mowbray; 'there *is*
a close affinity. That Lady Rookwood was my mother.
Eleanor Mowbray *does* resemble her ill-fated ancestress.'

"Words cannot paint my astonishment. I gazed at Mrs.
Mowbray, considering whether I had not misconstrued her
speech—whether I had not so shaped the sounds, as to suit
my own quick and passionate conceptions. But no! I read
in her calm, collected countenance—in the downcast glance
and sudden sadness of Eleanor, as well as in the changed
and haughty demeanour of the brother, that I had heard her
rightly. Eleanor Mowbray was my cousin—the descendant
of that hapless creature whose image I had almost wor-
shipped.

"Recovering from my surprise, I addressed Mrs. Mowbray,
endeavouring to excuse my ignorance of our relationship, on
the plea that I had not been given to understand that such
had been the name of the gentleman she had espoused. 'Nor
was it,' answered she, 'the name he bore at Rookwood; circumstances forbad it then. From the hour I quitted that
house until this moment, excepting one interview with my—
with Sir Reginald Rookwood—I have seen none of my family

—have held no communication with them. My brothers have been strangers to me; the very name of Rookwood has been unheard, unknown; nor would you have been admitted here, had not accident occasioned it.' I ventured now to interrupt her, and to express a hope that she would suffer an acquaintance to be kept up, which had so fortunately commenced, and which might most probably bring about an entire reconciliation between the families. I was so earnest in my expostulations, my whole soul being in them, that she inclined a more friendly ear to me. Eleanor, too, smiled encouragement. Love lent me eloquence; and, at length, as a token of my success and her own relenting, Mrs. Mowbray held forth her hand: I clasped it eagerly. It was the happiest moment of my life.

"I will not trouble you with any lengthened description of Eleanor Mowbray. I hope, at some period or other, you may still be enabled to see her, and judge for yourself; for though adverse circumstances have hitherto conspired to separate us, the time for a renewal of our acquaintance is approaching, I trust, for I am not yet altogether without hope. But thus much I may be allowed to say, that her rare endowments of person were only equalled by the graces of her mind.

"Educated abroad, she had all the vivacity of our livelier neighbours, combined with every solid qualification which we claim as more essentially our own. Her light and frolic manner was French, certainly; but her gentle, sincere heart was as surely English. The foreign accent that dwelt upon her tongue communicated an inexpressible charm, even to the language which she spoke.

"I will not dwell too long upon this theme. I feel ashamed of my own prolixity. And yet I am sure you will pardon it. Ah, those bright, brief days! too quickly were they fled! I could expatiate upon each minute—recal each word—revive each look. It may not be. I must hasten on. Darker themes await me.

"My love made rapid progress—I became each hour more enamoured of my new-found cousin. My whole time was passed near her; indeed, I could scarcely exist in absence from her side. Short, however, was destined to be my indulgence in this blissful state. One happy week was its extent. I received a peremptory summons from my father to return home

"Immediately upon commencing this acquaintance, I had written to my father, explaining every particular attending

it. This I should have done of my own free will; but I was
urged to it by Mrs. Mowbray. Unaccustomed to disguise, I
had expatiated upon the beauty of Eleanor, and in such
terms, I fear, that I excited some uneasiness in his breast.
His letter was laconic. He made no allusion to the subject
upon which I had expatiated when writing to him. He commanded me to return.

"The bitter hour was at hand. I could not hesitate to
comply. Without my father's sanction, I was assured Mrs.
Mowbray would not permit any continuance of my acquaintance. Of Eleanor's inclinations I fancied I had some
assurance; but without her mother's consent, to whose will
she was devoted, I felt, had I even been inclined to urge it,
that my suit was hopeless. The letter which I had received
from my father made me more than doubt whether I should
not find him utterly adverse to my wishes. Agonized, therefore, with a thousand apprehensions, I presented myself on
the morning of my departure. It was then I made the
declaration of my passion to Eleanor; it was then that every
hope was confirmed, every apprehension realized. I received
from her lips a confirmation of my fondest wishes; yet were
those hopes blighted in the bud, when I heard, at the same
time, that their consummation was dependent on the will of
two others, whose assenting voices, she feared, could never be
obtained. From Mrs. Mowbray I received a more decided
reply. All her haughtiness was aroused. Her farewell words
assured me that it was indifferent to her whether we met
again as relatives or as strangers. Then was it that the
native tenderness of Eleanor displayed itself, in an outbreak
of feeling peculiar to a heart keenly sympathetic as hers.
She saw my suffering—the reserve natural to her sex
gave way—she flung herself into my arms—and so we
parted.

" With a heavy foreboding, I returned to Rookwood; and,
oppressed with the gloomiest anticipations, endeavoured to
prepare myself for the worst. I arrived. My reception was
such as I had calculated upon; and, to increase my distress,
my parents had been at variance. I will not pain you and
myself with any recital of their disagreement. My mother
had espoused my cause, chiefly, I fear, with the view of
thwarting my poor father's inclinations. He was in a terrible
mood, exasperated by the fiery stimulants he had swallowed,
which had not, indeed, drowned his reason, but roused and
inflamed every dormant emotion to violence. He was as one
insane. It was evening when I arrived. I would willingly

have postponed the interview till the morrow. It could not
be. He insisted upon seeing me.

"My mother was present. You know the restraint she
usually had over my father, and how she maintained it. On
this occasion she had none. He questioned me as to every
particular; probed my secret soul; dragged forth every
latent feeling, and then thundered out his own determination that Eleanor never should be bride of mine; nor would
he receive under his roof her mother, the discountenanced
daughter of his father. I endeavoured to remonstrate with
him. He was deaf to my entreaties. My mother added
sharp and stinging words to my expostulations. 'I had her
consent,' she said; 'what more was needed? The lands
were entailed. I should at no distant period be their master,
and might then please myself.' This I mention, in order to
give you my father's strange answer.

"'Have a care, madam,' replied he, 'and bridle your
tongue; they *are* entailed, 'tis true, but I need not ask *his*
consent to cut off that entail. Let him dare to disobey me
in this particular, and I will so divert the channel of my
wealth, that no drop shall reach him. I will—but why
threaten?—let him do it, and approve the consequences.'

"On the morrow I renewed my importunities with no
better success. We were alone.

"'Ranulph,' said he, 'you waste time in seeking to change
my resolution. It is unalterable. I have many motives
which influence me; they are inexplicable, but imperative.
Eleanor Mowbray never can be yours. Forget her as speedily
as may be, and I pledge myself, upon whomsoever else your
choice may fix, I will offer no obstacle.'

"'But why,' exclaimed I, with vehemence, 'do you object
to one whom you have never beheld? At least, consent to
see her.'

"'Never!' he replied. 'The tie is sundered, and cannot
be reunited; my father bound me by an oath never to meet
in friendship with my sister; I will not break my vow. I
will not violate its conditions, even in the second degree. We
never can meet again. An idle prophecy which I have heard
has said, "*that when a Rookwood shall marry a Rookwood
the end of the house draweth nigh.*" That I regard not. It
may have no meaning, or it may have much. To me it
imports nothing further, than that if you wed Eleanor, every
acre I possess shall depart from you. And assure yourself
this is no idle threat. I can, and will do it. My curse shall
be your sole inheritance.'

"I could not avoid making some reply, representing to him how unjustifiable such a procedure was to me, in a case where the happiness of my life was at stake, and how inconsistent it was with the charitable precepts of our faith, to allow feelings of resentment to influence his conduct. My remonstrances, as in the preceding meeting, were ineffectual. The more I spoke, the more intemperate he grew. I therefore desisted. But not before he had ordered me to quit the house. I did not leave the neighbourhood, but saw him again on the same evening,

"Our last interview took place in the garden. I then told him that I had determined to go abroad for two years, at the expiration of which period I proposed returning to England; trusting that his resolution might then be changed, and that he would listen to my request, for the fulfilment of which I could never cease to hope. Time, I hoped, might befriend me. He approved of my plan of travelling, requesting me not to see Eleanor before I set out; adding, in a melancholy tone—'We may never meet again, Ranulph, in this life; in that case, farewell for ever. Indulge no vain hopes. Eleanor never can be yours, but upon one condition, and to that you would never consent!'—'Propose it!' I cried; 'there is no condition I could not accede to.'—'Rash boy!' he replied; 'you know not what you say; that pledge you would never fulfil, were I to propose it to you; but no— should I survive till you return, you shall learn it then—and now, farewell.'—'Speak now, I beseech you!' I exclaimed; 'anything, everything—what you will!'—'Say no more,' replied he, walking towards the house; 'when you return we will renew this subject; farewell—perhaps for ever.' His words were prophetic—that parting *was* for ever.' I remained in the garden till nightfall. I saw my mother, but *he* came not again. I quitted England without beholding Eleanor."

"Did you not acquaint her by letter with what had occurred, and your consequent intentions?" asked Small.

"I did," replied Ranulph; "but I received no reply. My earliest inquiries will be directed to ascertain whether the family are still in London. It will be a question for our consideration, whether I am not justified in departing from my father's express wishes, or whether I should violate his commands in so doing."

"We will discuss that point hereafter," replied Small, adding as he noticed the growing paleness of his companion, "you are too much exhausted to proceed—you had better defer the remainder of your story to a future period."

"No," replied Ranulph, swallowing a glass of water; "I am exhausted, yet I cannot rest—my blood is in a fever, which nothing will allay. I shall feel more easy when I have made the present communication. I am approaching the sequel of my narrative. You are now in possession of the story of my love—of the motive of my departure. You shall learn what was the occasion of my return.

"I had wandered from city to city during my term of exile—consumed by hopeless passion—with little that could amuse me, though surrounded by a thousand objects of interest to others, and only rendering life endurable by severest study, or most active exertion. My steps conducted me to Bordeaux; there I made a long halt, enchanted by the beauty of the neighbouring scenery. My fancy was smitten by the situation of a villa on the banks of the Garonne, within a few leagues of the city. It was an old château, with fine gardens bordering the blue waters of the river, and commanding a multitude of enchanting prospects. The house, which had in part gone to decay, was inhabited by an aged couple, who had formerly been servants to an English family, the members of which had thus provided for them on their return to their own country. I inquired the name. Conceive my astonishment to find that this château had been the residence of the Mowbrays. This intelligence decided me at once—I took up my abode in the house; and a new and unexpected source of solace and delight was opened to me. I traced the paths *she* had traced; occupied the room *she* had occupied; tended the flowers *she* had tended; and, on the golden summer evenings, would watch the rapid waters, tinged with all the glorious hues of sunset, sweeping past my feet, and think how *she* had watched them. Her presence seemed to pervade the place. I was now comparatively happy, and, anxious to remain unmolested, wrote home that I was leaving Bordeaux for the Pyrenees, on my way to Spain.

"That account arrived," observed Small.

"One night," continued Ranulph—"'tis now the sixth since the occurrence I am about to relate—I was seated in a bower that overlooked the river. It had been a lovely evening—so lovely, that I lingered there, wrapped in the heavenly contemplation of its beauties. I watched each rosy tint reflected upon the surface of the rapid stream—now fading into yellow—now shining silvery white. I noted the mystic mingling of twilight with darkness—of night with day, till the bright current on a sudden became a black mass of waters. I could scarcely discern a leaf—all was darkness—when, lo! another change! The moon was up—a flood of light deluged all around—the stream was dancing again in reflected radiance, and I still lingering at its brink.

"I had been musing for some moments, with my head resting upon my hand, when, happening to raise my eyes, I beheld a figure immediately before me. I was astonished at the sight, for I had perceived no one approach—had heard no footstep advance towards me, and was satisfied that no one besides myself could be in the garden. The presence of the figure inspired me with an undefinable awe! and, I can scarce tell why, but a thrilling presentiment convinced me that it was a supernatural visitant. Without motion—without life—without substance, it seemed; yet still the outward character of life was there. I started to my feet. God! what did I behold? The face was turned to me—*my father's face.* And what an aspect—what a look! Time can never efface that terrible expression; it is graven upon my memory—I cannot describe it. It was not anger—it was not pain; it was as if an eternity of woe were stamped upon its features. It was too dreadful to behold. I would fain have averted my gaze—my eyes were fascinated—fixed—I could not withdraw them from the ghastly countenance. I shrank from it, yet stirred not—I could not move a limb. Noiselessly gliding towards me, the apparition approached. I could not retreat. It stood obstinately beside me. I became as one half dead. The phantom shook its head with the deepest despair; and as the word 'Return!' sounded hollowly in my ears, it gradually melted from my view. I cannot tell how I recovered from the swoon into which I fell, but daybreak saw me on my way to England. I am here. On that night—at that same hour my father died."

"It was, after all, then, a supernatural summons that you received?" said Small.

"Undoubtedly," replied Ranulph.

"Humph!—the coincidence, I own, is sufficiently curious," returned Small, musingly; "but it would not be difficult, I think, to discover a satisfactory explanation of the delusion."

"There was no delusion," replied Ranulph, coldly; "the figure was as palpable as your own. Can I doubt, when I behold this result? Could any deceit have been practised

upon me at that distance?—the precise time, moreover,
agreeing. Did not the phantom bid me return?—I *have* returned—he is dead. I have gazed upon a being of another
world. To doubt were impious, after that look."

" Whatever my opinions may be, my dear young friend,"
returned Small, gravely, "I will suspend them for the present. You are still greatly excited. Let me advise you to
seek some repose."

"I am easier," replied Ranulph; "but you are right, I
will endeavour to snatch a little rest. Something within tells
me all is not yet accomplished. What remains? I shudder
to think of it. I will rejoin you at midnight. I shall myself
attend the solemnity. Adieu!"

Ranulph quitted the room. Small sighingly shook his
head, and having lighted his pipe, was presently buried in a
profundity of smoke and metaphysical speculation.

XI.

LADY ROOKWOOD.

Fran. de Med.	Your unhappy husband
	Is dead.
Vit. Cor.	Oh, he's a happy husband!
	Now he owes nature nothing.
Mon.	And look upon this creature as his wife.
	She comes not like a widow—she comes armed
	With scorn and impudence. Is this a mourning habit?

The White Devil.

THE progress of our narrative demands our presence in
another apartment of the hall—a large, lonesome chamber,
situate in the eastern wing of the house, already described as
the most ancient part of the building—the sombre appearance of which was greatly increased by the dingy discoloured
tapestry that clothed its walls; the record of the patience
and industry of a certain Dame Dorothy Rookwood, who
flourished some centuries ago, and whose skilful needle had
illustrated the slaughter of the Innocents, with a severity of
gusto, and sanguinary minuteness of detail, truly surprising
in a lady so amiable as she was represented to have been.
Grim-visaged Herod glared from the ghostly woof, with his
shadowy legions, executing their murderous purposes, grouped
like a troop of Sabbath-dancing witches around him. Mysterious twilight, admitted through the deep, dark, mullioned

G

windows, revealed the antique furniture of the room, which still boasted a sort of mildewed splendour, more imposing, perhaps, than its original gaudy magnificence; and showed the lofty hangings, and tall, hearse-like canopy of a bedstead, once a couch of state, but now destined for the repose of Lady Rookwood. The stiff crimson hangings were embroidered in gold, with the arms and cipher of Elizabeth, from whom the apartment, having once been occupied by that sovereign, obtained the name of the "Queen's Room."

The sole tenant of this chamber was a female, in whose countenance, if time and strong emotion had written strange defeatures, they had not obliterated its striking beauty and classical grandeur of expression. It was a face majestical and severe. Pride was stamped in all its lines; and though each passion was, by turns, developed, it was evident that all were subordinate to the sin by which the angels fell. The contour of her face was formed in the purest Grecian mould, and might have been a model for Medea; so well did the gloomy grandeur of the brow, the severe chiselling of the lip, the rounded beauty of the throat, and the faultless symmetry of her full form, accord with the beau ideal of antique perfection. Shaded by smooth folds of raven hair, which still maintained its jetty dye, her lofty forehead would have been displayed to the greatest advantage, had it not been at this moment knit and deformed, by excess of passion, if that passion can be said to deform which only calls forth strong and vehement expression. Her figure, which wanted only height to give it dignity, was arrayed in the garb of widowhood; and if she exhibited none of the desolation of heart, which such a bereavement might have been expected to awaken, she was evidently a prey to feelings scarcely less harrowing. At the particular time of which we speak, Lady Rookwood, for she it was, was occupied in the investigation of the contents of an escritoir. Examining the papers which it contained with great deliberation, she threw each aside, as soon as she had satisfied herself of its purport, until she arrived at a little package, carefully tied up with black riband, and sealed. This, Lady Rookwood hastily broke open, and drew forth a small miniature. It was that of a female, young and beautiful, rudely, yet faithfully executed—faithfully, we say, for there was an air of sweetness and simplicity—and, in short, a look of *reality* and nature about the picture (it is seldom, indeed, that we mistake a *likeness*, even if we are unacquainted with the original), that attested the artist's fidelity. The face was as radiant with smiles as a bright day with sunbeams. The portrait was set in gold, and behind it was looped a lock of the darkest and finest hair. Underneath the miniature were written, in Sir Piers's hand, the words "*Lady Rookwood.*" A slip of folded paper was also attached to it.

Lady Rookwood scornfully scrutinized the features for a few moments, and then unfolded the paper, at the sight of which she started, and turned pale. "Thank God!" she cried, "this is in my possession—while I hold this, we are safe. Were it not better to destroy this evidence at once? No, no, not *now*—it shall not part from me. I will abide Ranulph's return. This document will give me a power over him such as I could never otherwise obtain." Placing the marriage certificate, for such it was, within her breast. and laying the miniature upon the table, she next proceeded, deliberately, to arrange the disordered contents of the box.

All outward traces of emotion had, ere this, become so subdued in Lady Rookwood, that although she had, only a few moments previously, exhibited the extremity of passionate indignation, she now, apparently without effort, resumed entire composure, and might have been supposed to be engaged in a matter of little interest to herself. It was a dread calm, which they who knew her would have trembled to behold. "From these letters I gather," exclaimed she, "that their wretched offspring knows not of his fortune. So far well. There is no channel whence he can derive information, and my first care shall be to prevent his obtaining any clue to the secret of his birth. I am directed to provide for him—ha! ha! I will provide—a grave! There will I bury him and his secret. My son's security and my own wrong demand it. I must choose surer hands—the work must not be half done, as heretofore. And now I bethink me, he is in the neighbourhood, connected with a gang of poachers—'tis as I could wish it."

At this moment a knock at the chamber door broke upon her meditations. "Agnes, is it you?" demanded Lady Rookwood.

Thus summoned, the old attendant entered the room.

"Why are my orders disobeyed?" asked the lady, in a severe tone of voice. "Did I not say, when you delivered me this package from Mr. Coates, which he himself wished to present, that I would not be disturbed?"

"You did my lady, but——"

"Speak out," said Lady Rookwood, somewhat more mildly, perceiving from Agnes's manner, that she had something of importance to communicate. "What is it brings you hither?"

"I am sorry," returned Agnes, "to disturb your ladyship, but—but——"

"But what?" interrupted Lady Rookwood, impatiently.

"I could not help it, my lady—he would have me come; he said he was resolved to see your ladyship, whether you would or not."

"*Would* see me, ha! is it so? I guess his errand, and its object—he has some suspicion. No, that cannot be; he would not dare to tamper with these seals. Agnes, I will *not* see him."

"But he swears, my lady, that he will not leave the house without seeing you—he would have forced his way into your presence, if I had not consented to announce him."

"Insolent!" exclaimed Lady Rookwood, with a glance of indignation; "*force* his way! I promise you he shall not display an equal anxiety to repeat the visit. Tell Mr. Coates I *will* see him."

"Mr. Coates! Mercy on us, my lady, it's not he. He'd never have intruded upon you unasked. No such thing. He knows his place too well. No, no; it's not Mr. Coates——"

"If not he—who is it?"

"Luke Bradley; your ladyship knows whom I mean."

"He here—now?——"

"Yes, my lady; and looking so fierce and strange, I was quite frightened to see him. He looked so like his—his——"

"His father, you would say. Speak out."

"No, my lady, his grandfather—old Sir Reginald. He's the very image of him. But had not your ladyship better ring the alarm bell? and when he comes in, I'll run and fetch the servants—he's dangerous, I'm sure."

"I have no fears of him. He will see me, you say——"

"Ay, *will*," exclaimed Luke, as he threw open the door, and shut it forcibly after him, striding towards Lady Rookwood, "nor abide longer delay."

It was an instant or two ere Lady Rookwood, thus taken by surprise, could command speech. She fixed her eyes, with a look of keen and angry inquiry, upon the bold intruder, who, nothing daunted, confronted her glances with a gaze as stern and steadfast as her own.

"Who are you, and what seek you?" exclaimed Lady

Rookwood, after a brief pause, and, in spite of herself, her voice sounded tremulously. "What would you have, that you venture to appear before me at this season, and in this fashion?"

"I might have chosen a fitter opportunity," returned Luke, "were it needed. My business will not brook delay—you must be pleased to overlook this intrusion on your privacy at a *season of sorrow* like the present. As to the fashion of my visit, you must be content to excuse *that*. I cannot help myself. I may amend hereafter. *Who* I am, you are able, I doubt not, to divine. *What* I seek, you shall hear, when this old woman has left the room, unless you would have a witness to a declaration that concerns you as nearly as myself."

An indefinite feeling of apprehension had, from the first instant of Luke's entrance, crossed Lady Rookwood's mind. She, however, answered with some calmness—

"What you can have to say is of small moment to me—nor does it signify who may hear it. It shall not, however, be said that Lady Rookwood feared to be alone, even though she endangered her life."

"I am no assassin," replied Luke, "nor have sought the destruction of my deadliest foe—though 'twere but retributive justice to have done so."

Lady Rookwood started.

"Nay, you need not fear me," replied Luke; "my revenge will be otherwise accomplished."

"Go," said Lady Rookwood to Agnes—"yet—stay without, in the antechamber."

"My lady," said Agnes, scarcely able to articulate, "shall I——"

"Hear me, Lady Rookwood," interrupted Luke. "I repeat, I intend you no injury. My object here is solely to obtain a private conference. You can have no reason for denying me this request. I will not abuse your patience. Mine is no idle mission. Say you refuse me, and I will at once depart. I will find other means of communicating with you—less direct, and therefore less desirable. Make your election. But we *must* be alone—undisturbed. Summon your household—let them lay hands upon me, and I will proclaim aloud what you would gladly hide, even from yourself."

"Leave us, Agnes," said Lady Rookwood. "I have no fear of this man. I can deal with him myself, should I see occasion."

"Agnes," said Luke, in a stern, deep whisper, arresting the ancient handmaiden as she passed him, "stir not from the door till I come forth. Have you forgotten your former mistress!—my mother? Have you forgotten Barbara Lovel, and *that night?*"

"In Heaven's name, hush!" replied Agnes, with a shudder.

"Let that be fresh in your memory. Move not a footstep, whatever you may hear," added he, in the same tone as before.

"I will not—I will not." And Agnes departed.

Luke felt some wavering in his resolution when he found himself alone with the lady, whose calm, collected, yet haughty demeanour, as she resumed her seat, prepared for his communication, could not fail to inspire him with a certain degree of awe. Not unconscious of her advantage, nor slow to profit by it, Lady Rookwood remained perfectly silent, with her eyes steadily fixed upon his face, while his embarrassment momentarily increased. Summoning, at length, courage sufficient to address her, and ashamed of his want of nerve, he thus broke forth—

"When I entered this room, you asked my name and object. As to the first I answer to the same designation as your ladyship. I have long borne my mother's name. I now claim my father's. My object is the restitution of my rights."

"Soh!—it is as I suspected," thought Lady Rookwood, involuntarily casting her large eyes down. "Do I hear you rightly?" exclaimed she, aloud; "your name is——"

"Sir Luke Rookwood. As my father's elder born; by right of *his* right to that title."

If a glance could have slain him, Luke had fallen lifeless at the lady's feet. With a smile of ineffable disdain, she replied, "I know not why I hesitate to resent this indignity, even for an instant. But I would see how far your audacity will carry you. The name you bear is Bradley?"

"In ignorance I have done so," replied Luke. "I am the son of her whose maiden name was Bradley. She was——"

"'Tis false—I will not hear it—she was *not*," cried Lady Rookwood; her vehemence getting the master of her prudence.

"Your ladyship anticipates my meaning," returned Luke. "Susan Bradley was the first wife of Sir Piers Rookwood."

"His minion—his mistress, if you will; nought else. Is it new to you, that a village wench, who lends herself to

shame, should be beguiled by such shallow pretences? That
she was so duped I doubt not. But it is too late now to
complain, and I would counsel you not to repeat your idle
boast. It will serve no other purpose, trust me, than to
blazon forth your own, your mother's dishonour."

"Lady Rookwood," sternly answered Luke, "my mother's
fame is as free from dishonour as your own. I repeat, she
was the first wife of Sir Piers; and that I, her child, am first
in the inheritance; nay, sole heir to the estates and title of
Rookwood, to the exclusion of your son. Ponder upon that
intelligence. Men say they fear you, as a thing of ill. *I*
fear you not. There *have* been days when the Rookwoods
held their dames in subjection. Discern you nought of that
in me?"

Once or twice during this speech Lady Rookwood's glances
had wandered towards the bell-cord, as if about to summon
aid; but the intention was abandoned almost as soon as
formed, probably from apprehension of the consequences of
any such attempt. She was not without alarm as to the
result of the interview, and was considering how she could
bring it to a termination without endangering herself, and, if
possible, secure the person of Luke, when the latter, turning
sharply round upon her, and drawing a pistol, exclaimed—

"Follow me!"

"Whither?" asked she, in alarm.

"To the chamber of death!"

"Why there? what would you do? Villain! I will not
trust my life with you. I will *not* follow you."

"Hesitate not, as you value your life. Do aught to alarm
the house, and I fire. Your safety depends upon yourself.
I would see my father's body, ere it be laid in the grave. I
will not leave you here."

"Go," said Lady Rookwood; "if that be all, I pledge
myself you shall not be interrupted."

"I will not take your pledge; your presence shall be my
surety. By my mother's unavenged memory, if you play me
false, though all your satellites stand around you, you die
upon the spot! Obey me, and you are safe. Our way leads
to the room by the private staircase—we shall pass unobserved—you see I know the road. The room, by your own
command, is vacant—save of the dead. We shall, therefore,
be alone. This done, I depart. You will then be free to
act. Disobey me, and your blood be upon your own
head."

"Lead on," said Lady Rookwood, pressing towards the antechamber.

"The door I mean is there," pointing to another part of the room—"that panel——"

"Ha! how know you that?"

"No matter; follow."

Luke touched a spring, and the panel, flying open, disclosed a dim recess, into which he entered; and, seizing Lady Rookwood's hand, dragged her after him.

XII.

THE CHAMBER OF DEATH.

It is the body—I have orders given
That here it should be laid.   *De Montfort.*

THE recess upon which the panel opened had been a small oratory, and, though entirely disused, still retained its cushions and its crucifix. There were two other entrances to this place of prayer, the one communicating with a further bedchamber, the other leading to the gallery. Through the latter, after closing the aperture, without relinquishing his grasp, Luke passed.

It was growing rapidly dark, and at the brightest seasons this gloomy corridor was but imperfectly lighted from narrow, painted, and wire-protected windows, that looked into the old quadrangular court-yard below; and as they issued from the oratory a dazzling flash of lightning (a storm having suddenly arisen) momentarily illumined the whole length of the passage, disclosing the retreating figure of a man, wrapped in a large sable cloak, at the other extremity of the gallery. Lady Rookwood uttered an outcry for assistance; but the man, whoever he might be, disappeared in the instantaneously succeeding gloom, leaving her in doubt whether or not her situation had been perceived. Luke had seen this dark figure at the same instant; and, not without apprehensions lest his plans should be defeated, he griped Lady Rookwood's arm still more strictly, and placing the muzzle of the pistol to her breast, hurried her rapidly forwards.

All was now in total obscurity; the countenance of neither could be perceived as they trod the dark passage; but Luke's unrelaxed grasp indicated no change in his purposes, nor did the slow, dignified march of the lady betray any apprehension on her part. Descending a spiral staircase, which led from the gallery to a lower story, their way now lay beneath the entrance-hall, a means of communication little used. Their tread sounded hollowly on the flagged floor; no other sound was heard. Mounting a staircase, similar to the one they had just descended, they arrived at another passage. A few paces brought them to a door. Luke turned the handle, and they stood within the chamber of the dead.

The room which contained the remains of poor Sir Piers was arrayed in all that mockery of state, which, vainly attempting to deride death, is itself a bitter derision of the living. It was the one devoted to the principal meals of the day; a strange choice, but convenience had dictated its adoption by those with whom this part of the ceremonial had originated, and long custom had rendered its usage, for this purpose, almost prescriptive. This room, which was of some size, had originally formed part of the great hall, from which it was divided by a thick screen of black lustrously varnished oak, enriched with fanciful figures carved in bold relief. The walls were paneled with the same embrowned material, and sustained sundry portraits of the members of the family, in every possible costume, from the steely gear of Sir Ranulph, down to the flowing attire of Sir Reginald. Most of the race were ranged around the room; and, seen in the yellow light shed upon their features by the flambeaux, they looked like an array of stern and silent witnesses, gazing upon their departed descendant. The sides of the chamber were hung with black cloth, and upon a bier in the middle of the room rested the body. Broad escutcheons, decked out in glowing colours, pompously set forth the heraldic honours of the departed. Tall lights burnt at the head and feet, and fragrant perfumes diffused their odours from silver censers.

The entrance of Luke and his unwilling companion had been abrupt. The transition from darkness to the glare of light was almost blinding, and they had advanced far into the room ere Lady Rookwood perceived a man, whom she took to be one of the mutes, leaning over the bier. The coffin lid was entirely removed, and the person whose back was towards them, appeared to be wrapt in mournful contemplation of the sad spectacle before him. Suddenly bursting from Luke's hold, Lady Rookwood rushed forward with a scream, and touched the man's shoulder. He started at the summons, and disclosed the features of her son!

Rapidly as her own act, Luke followed. He levelled a pistol at her head, but his hand dropped to his side, as he encountered the glance of Ranulph. All three seemed paralyzed by surprise. Ranulph, in astonishment, extended his arm to his mother, who, placing one arm over his shoulder, pointed with the other to Luke; the latter stared sternly and inquiringly at both—yet none spoke.

XIII.

THE BROTHERS.

> We're sorry
> His violent act has e'en drawn blood of honour,
> And stained our honours;
> Thrown ink upon the forehead of our fame,
> Which envious spirit will dip their pens into
> After our death, and blot us in our tombs;
> For that which would seem treason in our lives,
> Is laughter when we're dead. Who dares now whisper,
> That dares not then speak out; and even proclaim,
> With loud words, and broad pens, our closest shame?
> *The Revenger's Tragedy.*

WITH that quickness of perception, which at once supplies information on such an emergency, Luke instantly conjectured who was before him. Startled as he was, he yet retained his composure, abiding the result with his arms folded upon his breast.

"Seize him," cried Lady Rookwood, as soon as she could command her speech.

"He rushes on his death if he stirs," exclaimed Luke, pointing his pistol.

"Bethink you where you are, villain," cried Ranulph; "you are entrapped in your own toils. Submit yourself to our mercy—resistance is vain, and will not secure your safety, while it will aggravate your offence. Surrender yourself——"

"Never!" answered Luke. "Know you whom you ask to yield?"

"How should I?" answered Ranulph.

"By that instinct which tells me who *you* are. Ask Lady Rookwood—she can inform you, if she will."

"Parley not with him—seize him," cried Lady Rookwood. "He is a robber, a murderer, who has assailed my life."

"Beware," said Luke to Ranulph, who was preparing to

obey his mother's commands; "I am no robber—no murderer. Do not you make me a fratricide."

"Fratricide!" echoed Ranulph.

"Heed him not," ejaculated Lady Rookwood. "It is false—he dares not harm thee, for his soul. I will call assistance."

"Hold, mother!" exclaimed Ranulph, detaining Lady Rookwood; "this man may be what he represents himself. Before we proceed to extremities I would question him. I would not have mentioned it in your hearing could it have been avoided, but my father had another son."

"Lady Rookwood frowned. She would have checked him, but Luke rejoined—

"You have spoken the truth; he had a son—I am he. I——"

"Be silent, I command you," said Lady Rookwood.

"Death!" cried Luke, in a loud voice. "Why should I be silent at your bidding—at *yours*—who regard no laws, human or divine; who pursue your own fell purposes, without fear of God or man? Waste not your frowns on me—I heed them not. Do you think I am like a tame hound, to be cowed to silence? I *will* speak. Ranulph Rookwood, the name you bear is mine, and by a right as good as is your own. From his loins, who lies a corpse before us, I sprang. No brand of shame is on my birth. I am your father's son—his first-born—your *elder* brother. Hear me!" cried he, rushing to the bier. "By this body, I swear that I have avouched the truth—and though to me the dead Sir Piers Rookwood hath never been what a father should be to a son—though I have never known his smile, felt his caresses, or received his blessing, yet now be all forgiven, all forgotten." And he cast himself with frantic violence upon the coffin.

It is difficult to describe the feelings with which Ranulph heard Luke's avowal. Amazement and dread predominated. Unable to stir, he stood gazing on in silence. Not so Lady Rookwood. The moment for action was arrived. Addressing her son in a low tone, she said, "Your prey is within your power. Secure him."

"Wherefore?" rejoined Ranulph; "if he be my brother, shall I raise my hand against him?"

"Wherefore not?" returned Lady Rookwood.

"'Twere an accursed deed," replied Ranulph. "The mystery is resolved. 'Twas for this that I was summoned home."

Ha! what say you? summoned! by whom?"

"My father!"

"Your father?" echoed Lady Rookwood, in great surprise.

"Ay, my dead father! He has appeared to me since his decease."

"Ranulph, you rave—you are distracted with grief—with astonishment."

"No, mother; but I will not struggle against my destiny."

"Pshaw! your destiny is Rookwood, its manors, its land, its rent-roll, and its title; nor shall you yield it to a base-born churl like this. Let him prove his rights. Let the law adjudge them to him, and we will yield—but not till then. I tell thee he has *not* the right, nor can he maintain it. He is a deluded dreamer, who, having heard some idle tale of his birth, believes it, because it chimes with his wishes. I treated him with the scorn he deserved. I would have driven him from my presence, but he was armed, as you see, and forced me hither, perhaps to murder me; a deed he might have accomplished, had it not been for your intervention. His life is already forfeit, for an attempt of the same sort last night. Why else came he hither? for what else did he drag me to this spot? Let him answer that!"

"I *will* answer it," replied Luke, raising himself from the bier. His face was of an ashy paleness, and ghastly as the corpse over which he leaned. "I had a deed to do, which I wished you to witness. It was a wild conception. But the means by which I have acquired the information of my rights were wild. Ranulph, we are both the slaves of fate. You have received your summons hither—I have had mine. Your father's ghost called you; my mother's spectral hand beckoned me. Both are arrived. One thing more remains, and my mission is completed." Saying which, he drew forth the skeleton hand; and having first taken the wedding-ring from the finger, he placed the withered limb upon the left breast of his father's body. "Rest there," he cried, "for ever."

"Will you suffer that?" said Lady Rookwood, tauntingly, to her son.

"No," replied Ranulph; "such profanation of the dead shall not be endured, were he ten times my brother. Stand aside," added he, advancing towards the bier, and motioning Luke away. "Withdraw your hand from my father's body, and remove what you have placed upon it."

"I will neither remove it nor suffer it to be removed," returned Luke. "'Twas for that purpose I came hither. 'Twas to that hand he was united in life, in death he shall not be divided from it."

"Such irreverence shall not be," exclaimed Ranulph, seizing Luke with one hand, and snatching at the cereclothes with the other. "Remove it, or by Heaven——"

"Leave go your hold," said Luke, in a voice of thunder; "you strive in vain."

Ranulph ineffectually attempted to push him backwards; and shaking away the grasp that was fixed upon his collar, seized his brother's wrist, so as to prevent the accomplishment of his purpose. In this unnatural and indecorous strife, the corpse of their father was reft of its covering, and the hand discovered lying upon the pallid breast.

And as if the wanton impiety of their conduct called forth an immediate rebuke, even from the dead, a frown seemed to pass over Sir Piers's features, as their angry glances fell in that direction. This startling effect was occasioned by the approach of Lady Rookwood, whose shadow, falling over the brow and visage of the deceased, produced the appearance we have described. Simultaneously quitting each other, with a deep sense of shame, mingled with remorse, both remained, their eyes fixed upon the dead, whose repose they had violated.

Folding the graveclothes decently over the body, Luke prepared to depart.

"Hold," cried Lady Rookwood; "you go not hence."

"My brother Ranulph will not oppose my departure," returned Luke; "who else shall prevent it?"

"That will I," cried a sharp voice behind him; and, ere he could turn to ascertain from whom the exclamation proceeded, Luke felt himself grappled by two nervous assailants, who, snatching the pistol from his hold, fast pinioned his arms. This was scarcely the work of a moment, and he was a prisoner before he could offer any resistance. A strong smile of exultation evinced Lady Rookwood's satisfaction.

"Bravo, my lads, bravo!" cried Coates, stepping forward, for he it was under whose skilful superintendence the seizure had been effected: "famously managed; my father the thief-taker's runners couldn't have done it better—hand me that pistol—loaded, I see—slugs, no doubt—oh, he's a precious rascal—search him—turn his pockets inside out while I speak to her ladyship." Saying which, the brisk attorney, enchanted

with the feat he had performed, approached Lady Rookwood
with a profound bow, and an amazing smirk of self-satisfac-
tion. "Just in time to prevent mischief," said he; "hope
your ladyship does not suffer any inconvenience from the
alarm—beg pardon, annoyance I meant to say—which this
horrible outrage must have occasioned; excessively disagreeable this sort of thing to a lady at any time, but at a period
like this more than usually provoking. However, we have
the villain safe enough. Very lucky I happened to be in the
way. Perhaps your ladyship would like to know how I discovered——"

"Not now," replied Lady Rookwood, checking the volu-
bility of the man of law. "I thank you, Mr. Coates, for the
service you have rendered me; you will now add materially
to the obligation by removing the prisoner with all convenient
despatch."

"Certainly, if your ladyship wishes it. Shall I detain him
a close prisoner in the hall for the night, or remove him at
once to the lock-up house in the village?"

"Where you please, so you do it quickly," replied Lady
Rookwood, noticing, with great uneasiness, the agitated
manner of her son, and apprehensive lest, in the presence
of so many witnesses, he might say or do something pre-
judicial to their interests. Nor were her fears groundless.
As Coates was about to return to the prisoner, he was
arrested by the voice of Ranulph, commanding him to stay.

"Mr. Coates," said he, "however appearances may be
against this man, he is no robber—you must, therefore, release him."

"Eh day, what's that? release him, Sir Ranulph?"

"Yes, sir; I tell you he came here neither with the intent
to rob nor to offer violence."

"That is false, Ranulph," replied Lady Rookwood. "I
was dragged hither by him, at the peril of my life. He is
Mr. Coates's prisoner on another charge."

"Unquestionably, your ladyship is perfectly right; I have
a warrant against him for assaulting Hugh Badger, the
keeper, and for other misdemeanours."

"I will myself be responsible for his appearance to that
charge," replied Ranulph. "Now, sir, at once release him."

"At your peril!" exclaimed Lady Rookwood.

"Well, really," muttered the astonished attorney, "this is
the most perplexing proceeding I ever witnessed."

"Ranulph," said Lady Rookwood, sternly, to her son,
"beware how you thwart me!"

"Yes, Sir Ranulph, let me venture to advise you, as a friend, not to thwart her ladyship," whispered the attorney; "indeed, she is in the right." But, seeing his advice unheeded, Coates withdrew to a little distance.

"I will not see injustice done to my father's son," replied Ranulph, in a low tone. "Why would you detain him?"

"Why?" returned she, "our safety demands it—our honour."

"Our honour demands his instant liberation; each moment he remains in those bonds sullies its purity. I will free him myself from his fetters."

"And brave my curse, foolish boy? You incurred your miserable father's anathema for a lighter cause than this. Our honour cries aloud for his destruction. Have I not been injured in the nicest point a woman can be injured? Shall I lend my name to mockery and scorn, by base acknowledgment of such deceit, or will you? Where would be my honour, then, stripped of my fair estates—my son—myself—beggars—dependent on the bounty of an upstart? Does honour ask you to bear this? It is a phantom sense of honour, unsubstantial as your father's shade, of which you just now spoke, that would prompt you to do otherwise."

"Do not evoke his awful spirit, mother," cried Ranulph, with a shudder; "do not arouse his wrath."

"Do not arouse *my* wrath," returned Lady Rookwood. "I am the more to be feared. Think of Eleanor Mowbray; the bar betwen your nuptials is removed. Would you raise up a greater impediment?"

"Enough, mother; more than enough. You have decided, though not convinced me. Detain him within the house, if you will, until the morrow; in the mean time, I will consider over my line of conduct."

"Is this, then, your resolve?"

"It is. Mr. Coates," said Ranulph, calling the attorney, who had been an inquisitive spectator, though, luckily, not an auditor of this interview, "unbind the prisoner, and bring him hither."

"Is it your ladyship's pleasure?" asked Mr. Coates, who regretted exceedingly that he could not please both parties.

Lady Rookwood signified her assent by a slight gesture in the affirmative.

"Your bidding shall be done, Sir Ranulph," said Coates, bowing and departing.

"*Sir Ranulph!*" echoed Lady Rookwood, with strong emphasis; "marked you that?"

"Body o' me," muttered the attorney, "this is the most extraordinary family to be sure. Make way, gentlemen, if you please," added he, pushing through the crowd, toward the prisoner.

Having described what took place between Lady Rookwood and her son in one part of the room, we must now briefly narrate some incidental occurrences in the other. The alarm of a robber having been taken, spread with great celerity through the house, and almost all its inmates rushed into the room, including Doctor Small, Titus Tyrconnel, and Jack Palmer.

"Odsbodikins! are you there, honey?" said Titus, who discovered his ally; "the bird's caught, you see."

"Caught be d—d," replied Jack, bluffly; "so I see; all his own fault; infernal folly to come here, at such a time as this. However, it can't be helped now; he must make the best of it. And as to that sneaking, gimlet-eyed, parchment-skinned quill-driver, if I don't serve him out for his officiousness, one of these days, my name's not Jack Palmer."

"Och! cushlamacree! did I ever; why, what the devil's the boy to you, Jack? Fair play's a jewel, and surely Mr. Coates only did his duty. I'm sorry he's captured, for his relationship to Sir Piers, and because I think he'll be tucked up for his pains; and, moreover, I could forgive the poaching; but as to the breaking into a house, on such an occasion as this, och! it's a plaguy bad look. I'm afraid he's worse than I thought him."

A group of the tenantry, many of whom were in a state of intoxication, had, in the mean time, formed themselves round the prisoner. Whatever might be the nature of his thoughts, no apprehension was visible in Luke's countenance. He stood erect amidst the assemblage, his tall form towering above them all, and his eyes fixed upon the movements of Lady Rookwood and her son. He had perceived the anguish of the latter, and the vehemence of the former, attributing both to their real causes. The taunts and jeers, threats and insolent inquiries, of the hinds who thronged around him, passed unheeded; yet one voice in his ear, sharp as the sting of a serpent, made him start. It was that of the sexton.

"You have done well," said Peter, "have you not? Your fetters are, I hope, to your liking. Well! a wilful man must have his own way, and perhaps the next time you will be content to follow my advice. You must now free yourself, the best way you can, from these Moabites, and I promise you it will be no easy matter. Ha, ha!"

Peter withdrew into the crowd; and Luke, vainly endeavouring to discover his retreating figure, caught the eye of Jack Palmer fixed upon himself, with a peculiar and very significant expression.

At this moment Mr. Coates made his appearance.

"Bring forward the prisoner," said the man of law to his two assistants; and Luke was accordingly hurried along, Mr. Coates using his best efforts to keep back the crowd. It was during the pressure that Luke heard a voice whisper in his ear, "Never fear, all's right;" and turning his head, he became aware of the propinquity of Jack Palmer. The latter elevated his eyebrows with a gesture of silence, and Luke passed on as if nothing had occurred. He was presently confronted with Lady Rookwood and her son; and, notwithstanding the efforts of Mr. Coates, seconded by some few others, the crowd grew dense around them.

"Remove his fetters," said Ranulph. And his manacles were removed.

"You will consent to remain here a prisoner till to-morrow?"

"I consent to nothing," replied Luke; "I am in your hands."

"He does not deserve your clemency, Sir Ranulph," interposed Coates.

"Let him take his own course," said Lady Rookwood; "he will reap the benefit of it anon."

"Will you pledge yourself not to depart?" asked Ranulph.

"Of course," cried the attorney; "to be sure he will. Ha, ha!"

"No," returned Luke, haughtily, "I will not—and you will detain me at your proper peril."

"Better and better," exclaimed the attorney. "This is the highest joke I ever heard."

"I shall detain you, then, in custody, until proper inquiries can be made," said Ranulph. "To your care, Mr. Coates, and to that of Mr. Tyrconnel, whom I must request to lend you his assistance, I commit the charge; and I must further request, that you will show him every attention which his situation will permit. Remove him. We have a sacred duty to the dead to fulfil, to which even justice to the living must give way. Disperse this crowd, and let instant preparations be made for the completion of the ceremonial. You understand me, sir."

"Ranulph Rookwood," said Luke, sternly, as he departed,

"you have another—a more sacred office, to perform. Fulfil your duty to your father's son."

"Away with him," cried Lady Rookwood. "I am out of all patience with this trifling. Follow me to my chamber," added she to her son, passing towards the door. The concourse of spectators, who had listened to this extraordinary scene in astonishment, made way for her instantly, and she left the room, accompanied by Ranulph. The prisoner was led out by the other door.

"Botheration!" cried Titus to Mr. Coates, as they followed in the wake, "why did he choose out me? I lose the funeral entirely by his arrangement."

"That you will," replied Palmer. "Shall I be your deputy?"

"No, no," returned Coates. "I will have no other than Mr. Tyrconnel. It was Sir Ranulph's express wish."

"That's the devil of it," returned Titus; "and I who was to have been chief mourner, and have made all the preparations, am to be omitted. I wish Sir Ranulph had stayed till to-morrow—what could bring him here, to spoil all?—it's cursedly provoking!"

"Cursed provoking!" echoed Jack.

"But then there's no help, so I must make the best of it," returned the good-humoured Irishman.

"Body o' me," said Coates, "there's something in all this that I can't fathom. As to keeping the prisoner *here*, that's all moonshine. But I suppose we shall know the whole drift of it to-morrow."

"Ay," replied Jack, with a meaning smile, "to-morrow!"

Book the Second.

THE SEXTON.

Duchess. Thou art very plain.
Bosola. My trade is to flatter the dead—not the living—
I am a tomb-maker. WEBSTER.

I.

THE STORM.

Come, list, and hark! the bell doth towle
For some but now departing sowle ;
And was not that some ominous fowle?
The bat, the night-crow, or screech-owle?
To these I hear the wild wolfe howle,
In this dark night that seems to scowlo ;—
All these my blacke booke shall enrowle,
For hark! still hark! the bell doth towle
For some but now-departed sowle!—HAYWOOD.—*Rape of Lucrece.*

THE night was wild and stormy. The day had been sultry,
with a lurid, metallic-looking sky, hanging like a vast galvanic plate over the face of nature. As evening drew on,
everything betokened the coming tempest. Unerring indications of its approach were noted by the weatherwise at the
hall. The swallow was seen to skim the surface of the pool
so closely, that he ruffled its placid mirror as he passed ;
and then sharply darting round and round, with twittering
scream, he winged his rapid flight to his clay-built home
beneath the barn eaves. The kine that had herded to the
margin of the water, and sought, by splashing, to relieve
themselves from the keen persecution of their myriad insect
tormentors, wended stallwards, undriven, and deeply lowing.
The deer, that at twilight had trooped thither also for refreshment, suddenly, "with expanded nostrils, snuffed the air," and
bounded off to their coverts, amidst the sheltering fernbrake.
The rooks, "obstreperous of wing, in crowds combined,"
cawed in a way that, as plainly as words could have done,
bespoke their apprehension ; and were seen, some hovering
and beating the air with flapping pinion, others shooting
upwards in mid space, as if to reconnoitre the weather ; while
others, again, were croaking to their mates, in loud discordant
tone, from the highest branches of the lime-trees ; all,

seemingly, as anxious and as busy as mariners before a gale
of wind. At sunset, the hazy vapours, which had obscured
the horizon through the day, rose up in spiral volumes,
like smoke from a burning forest, and, becoming gradually
condensed, assumed the form of huge, billowy masses, which,
reflecting the sun's light, changed, as the sinking orb declined, from purple to flame colour, and thence to ashy, angry
grey. Night rushed onwards, like a sable steed. There was
a dead calm. The stillness was undisturbed, save by an
intermittent, sighing wind, which, hollow as a murmur from
the grave, died as it rose. At once the grey clouds turned
to an inky blackness. A single, sharp, intensely vivid flash
shot from the bosom of the rack, sheer downwards, and
struck the earth with a report like that of a piece of ord-
nance. In ten minutes it was dunnest night, and a rattling
thunderstorm.

The progress of the storm was watched with infinite apprehension by the crowd of tenantry assembled in the great
hall; and loud and frequent were the ejaculations uttered, as
each succeeding peal burst over their heads. There was,
however, one amongst the assemblage who seemed to enjoy
the uproar. A kindred excitement appeared to blaze in his
glances as he looked upon the storm without. This was Peter
Bradley. He stood close by the window, and shaded not his
eyes even before the fiercest flashes. A grin of unnatural
exhilaration played upon his features, and he seemed to exult
in, and to court, the tempestuous horrors, which affected the
most hardy amongst his companions with consternation, and
made all shrink trembling into the recesses of the room.
Peter's conduct was not unobserved, nor his reputation for
unholy dealing forgotten. To some he was almost as much
an object of dread as the storm itself.

"Didst ever see the like o' that?" said Farmer Burtenshaw
(one of the guests, whose round, honest face, good wine had
recently empurpled, but fear had now mottled white), addressing a neighbour. "Didst ever hear of any man that
were a Christian laughing in the very face o' a thunderstorm,
with the lightnin' fit to put out his eyes, and the rattle above
ready to break the drums o' his ears? I always thought
Peter Bradley was not exactly what he ought to be, and now
I am sure on it."

"For my part, I think, neighbour Burtenshaw," returned
the other, "that this great burst of weather's all of his
raising, for in all my born days I never see'd such a hurly-

burly, and hope never to see the like of it again. I've heard
my grandfather tell of folk as could command wind and rain;
and, mayhap, Peter may have the power—we all know he
can do more nor any other man."

"We know, at all events," replied Burtenshaw, "that he
lives like no other man; that he spends night after night by
himself in that dreary churchyard; that he keeps no living
thing, except an old terrier dog, in his crazy cottage; and
that he never asks a body into his house from one year's end
to another. I've never crossed his threshold these twenty
years. But," continued he, mysteriously, "I happened to
pass the house one dark dismal night, and there what dost
think I see'd through the window?"

"What—what didst see?"

"Peter Bradley sitting with a great book open on his
knees; it were a Bible, I think, and he crying like a child."

"Art sure o' that?"

"The tears were falling fast upon the leaves," returned
Burtenshaw; "but when I knocked at the door, he hastily
shut up the book, and ordered me to be gone, in a surly tone,
as if he were ashamed of being caught in the fact."

"I thought no tear had ever dropped from his eye," said
the other. "Why, he laughed when his daughter Susan
went off at the ball; and when she died, folks said he received hush-money to say nought about it. *That* were a bad
business anyhow; and now that his grandson Luke be taken
in the fact of housebreaking, he minds it no more, not he,
than if nothing had happened."

"Don't be too sure of that," replied Burtenshaw; "he
may be scheming summat all this time. Well, I've known
Peter Bradley now these two-and-fifty years, and, excepting
that night, I never saw any good about him, and never
heard of nobody who could tell who he be, or where he do
come from."

"One thing's certain, at least," replied the other farmer—
"he were never born at Rookwood. How he came here the
devil only knows. Save us! what a crash!—this storm be
all of his raising, I tell 'ee."

"He be—what he certainly will be," interposed another
speaker, in a louder tone and with less of apprehension in
his manner than his comrade, probably from his nerves being
better fortified with strong liquor. "Dost thou think,
Sammul Plant, as how Providence would intrust the like o'
him with the command of the elements? No—no, it's rank

blasphemy to suppose such a thing, and I've too much of the true Catholic and apostate church about me, to stand by and hear that said."

"Maybe, then, he gets his power from the Prince of Darkness," replied Plant; "no man else could go on as he does —only look at him. He seems to be watching for the thunderbowt."

"I wish he may catch it, then," returned the other.

"That's an evil wish, Simon Toft, and thou mayst repent it."

"Not I," replied Toft; "it would be a good clearance to the neighbourhood to get rid o' th' old croaking curmudgeon."

Whether or not Peter overheard the conversation we pretend not to say, but at that moment a blaze of lightning showed him staring fiercely at the group.

"As I live, he's overheard you, Simon," exclaimed Plant. "I wouldn't be in your skin for a trifle."

"Nor I," added Burtenshaw.

"Let him overhear me," answered Toft; "who cares? he shall hear summat worth listening to. I'm not afraid o' him or his arts, were they as black as Beelzebuth's own; and to show you I'm not, I'll go and have a crack with him on the spot."

"Thou'rt a fool for thy pains, if thou dost, friend Toft," returned Plant, "that's all I can say."

"Be advised by me, and stay here," seconded Burtenshaw, endeavouring to hold him back.

But Toft would not be advised—

> Kings may be blest, but he was glorious,
> O'er all the ills of life victorious.

Staggering up to Peter, he laid a hard grasp upon his shoulder, and, thus forcibly soliciting his attention, burst into a loud horse-laugh.

But Peter was, or affected to be, too much occupied to look at him.

"What dost see, man, that thou starest so?"

"It comes, it comes—the rain—the rain—a torrent—a deluge—ha, ha! Blessed is the corpse the rain rains on. Sir Piers may be drenched through his leaden covering by such a downfall as that—splash, splash—fire and water and thunder, all together—is not that fine?—ha, ha! The heavens will weep for him, though friends shed not a tear. When did a great man's heir feel sympathy for his sire's decease? When did his widow mourn? When doth any man regret his fellow? Never! He rejoiceth—he maketh glad in his inmost heart—he cannot help it—it is his nature. We all pray for, we all delight in each other's destruction. We were created to do so; or why else should we act thus? I never wept for any man's death, but I have often laughed. Natural sympathy!—out on the phrase. The distant heavens—the senseless trees—the impenetrable stones—shall regret you more than man—shall bewail your death with more sincerity. Ay, 'tis well—rain on—splash, splash; it will cool the hell-fever. Down, down—buckets and pails—ha, ha!"

There was a pause, during which the sexton, almost exhausted by the frenzy in which he had suffered himself to be involved, seemed insensible to all around him.

"I tell you what," said Burtenshaw to Plant; "I have always thought there was more in Peter Bradley nor appears on the outside. He is not what he seems to be, take my word on it. Lord love you! do you think a man such as he pretends to be could talk in that sort of way—about nat'ral simpering?—no such thing."

When Peter recovered, his insane merriment broke out afresh, having only acquired fury by the pause.

"Look out, look out," cried he; "hark to the thunder—list to the rain. Marked ye that flash—marked ye the clock-house —and the bird upon the roof? 'tis the rook—the great bird of the house, that hath borne away the soul of the departed. There, there—can you not see it? it sits and croaks through storm and rain, and never heeds at all—and wherefore should it heed? See, it flaps its broad black wings—it croaks —ha! ha! It comes—it comes."

And driven, it might be, by the terror of the storm, from more secure quarters, a bird, at this instant, was dashed against the window, and fell to the ground.

"That's a call," continued Peter; "it will be over soon, and we must set out. The dead will not need to tarry. Look at that trail of fire along the avenue; dost see yon line of sparkles, like a rocket's tail? That's the path the corpse will take. St. Hermes' flickering fire, Robin Goodfellow's dancing light, or the blue flame of the corpse-candle, which I saw flitting to the churchyard last week, was not so pretty a sight—ha, ha! You asked me for a song a moment ago— you shall have one now without asking."

And without waiting to consult the inclinations of his com-

rades, Peter broke into the following wild strain with all the
fervour of a half-crazed improvisatore.

THE CORPSE-CANDLE.

Lambere flamma ταφος et circum funera pasci.

Through the midnight gloom did a pale blue light
To the churchyard mirk wing its lonesome flight :—
Thrice it floated those old walls round—
Thrice it paused—till the grave it found.
Over the grass-green sod it glanced,
Over the fresh-turned earth it danced,
Like a torch in the night-breeze quivering—
Never was seen so gay a thing !
Never was seen so blithe a sight
As the midnight dance of that pale blue light !

Now what of that pale blue flame dost know ?
Canst tell where it comes from, or where it will go ?
Is it the soul, released from clay,
Over the earth that takes its way,
And tarries a moment in mirth and glee
Where the corse it hath quitted interr'd shall be ?
Or is it the trick of some fanciful sprite,
That taketh in mortal mischance delight,
And marketh the road the coffin shall go,
And the spot where the dead shall be soon laid low ?
Ask him who can answer these questions aright ;
I know not the cause of that pale blue light !

"I can't say I like thy song, Master Peter," said Toft, as
the sexton finished his stave, "but if thou *didst* see a corpse-
candle, as thou call'st thy pale blue flame, whose death doth
it betoken ?—eh !"

"Thy own," returned Peter, sharply.

"Mine ! thou lying old cheat—dost dare to say that to my
face ? Why, I'm as hale and hearty as ever a man in the
house. Dost think there's no life and vigour in this arm,
thou drivelling old dotard ?"

Upon which, Toft seized Peter by the throat, with an
energy that, but for the timely intervention of the company,
who rushed to his assistance, the prophet might himself have
anticipated the doom he prognosticated.

Released from the grasp of Toft, who was held back by the
bystanders, Peter again broke forth into his eldritch laugh ;
and staring right into the face of his adversary, with eyes
glistening, and hands uplifted, as if in the act of calling down
an imprecation on his head, he screamed, in a shrill and discordant voice, "Soh ! you will not take warning ? you revile
me—you flout me ! 'Tis well ! your fate shall prove a warning to all unbelievers—*they* shall remember this night, though
you will not. Fool ! fool ! your doom has long been sealed !

I saw your wraith choose out its last lodgment on Halloween; I know the spot. Your grave is dug already—ha, ha!" And, with renewed laughter, Peter rushed out of the room.

"Did I not caution thee not to provoke him, friend Toft?" said Plant; "it's ill playing with edge tools; but don't let him fly off in that tantrum—one of ye go after him."

"That will I," replied Burtenshaw; and he departed in search of the sexton.

"I'd advise thee to make it up with Peter so soon as thou canst, neighbour," continued Plant; "he's a bad friend, but a worse enemy."

"Why, what harm can he do me?" returned Toft, who, however, was not without some misgivings. "If I must die, I can't help it—I shall go none the sooner for him, even if he speak the truth, which I don't think he do; and if I must, I shan't go unprepared; only I think as how, if it pleased Providence, I could have wished to keep my old missis company some few years longer, and see those bits of lasses of mine grow up into women, and respectably provided for. But His will be done. I shan't leave 'em quite penniless, and there's one eye at least, I'm sure, won't be dry at my departure." Here the stout heart of Toft gave way, and he shed some few "natural tears;" which, however, he speedily brushed away. "I tell you what, neighbours," continued he, "I think we may all as well be thinking of going to our own homes, for, to my mind, we shall never reach the churchyard to-night."

"That *you* never will," exclaimed a voice behind him; and Toft turning round, again met the glance of Peter.

"Come, come, Master Peter," cried the good-natured farmer, "this be ugly jesting—ax pardon for my share of it—sorry for what I did; so give us thy hand, man, and think no more about it."

Peter extended his claw, and the parties were, apparently, once more upon terms of friendship.

II.

THE FUNERAL ORATION.

In northern customs duty was exprest
To friends departed by their funeral feast;
Though I've consulted Holingshead and Stow,
I find it very difficult to know,
Who, to refresh the attendants to the grave,
Burnt claret first, or Naples' biscuit gave.

KING.—*Art of Cookery.*

Ceterum priusquam corpus humo injectâ contegatur, defunctus oratione funebri laudabatur.—DURAND.

A SUPPLY of spirits was here introduced; lights were brought at the same time, and placed upon a long oak table. The party gathering round it, ill-humour was speedily dissipated, and even the storm disregarded, in the copious libations that ensued. At this juncture, a loiterer appeared in the hall. His movements were unnoticed by all excepting the sexton, who watched his proceedings with some curiosity. The person walked to the window, appearing, so far as could be discovered, to eye the storm with great impatience. He then paced the hall rapidly backwards and forwards, and Peter fancied he could detect sounds of disappointment, in his muttered exclamations. Again he returned to the window, as if to ascertain the probable duration of the shower. It was a hopeless endeavour; all was pitch dark without; the lightning was now only seen at long intervals, but the rain still audibly descended in torrents. Apparently, seeing the impossibility of controlling the elements, the person approached the table.

"What think you of the night, Mr. Palmer?" asked the sexton of Jack, for he was the anxious investigator of the weather.

"Don't know—can't say—set in, I think; cursed unlucky —for the funeral, I mean; we shall be drowned if we go."

"And drunk if we stay," rejoined Peter. "But never fear, it will hold up, depend upon it, long before we can start. Where have they put the prisoner?" asked he, with a sudden change of manner.

"I know the room, but can't describe it; it's two or three doors down the lower corridor of the eastern gallery."

"Good. Who are on guard?"

"Titus Tyrconnel, and that swivel-eyed quill-driver, Coates."

"Enough."

"Come, come. Master Peter," roared Toft, "let's have another stave. Give us one of your old snatches. No more corpse-candles, or that sort of thing. Something lively—something jolly—ha, ha!"

"A good move," shouted Jack. "A lively song from *you*—lillibullero from a death's head—ha, ha!"

"My songs are all of a sort," returned Peter; "I am seldom asked to sing a second time. However, you are welcome to the merriest I have." And preparing himself, like certain other accomplished vocalists, with a few preliminary hems and haws, he struck forth the following doleful ditty:

THE OLD OAK COFFIN.

Sic ego componi versus in ossa velim.—TIBULLUS.

In a churchyard, upon the sward, a coffin there was laid,
And leaning stood, beside the wood, a sexton on his spade.
A coffin old and black it was, and fashioned curiously,
With quaint device of carved oak, in hideous fantasie.

For here was wrought the sculptured thought of a tormented face,
With serpents lithe that round it writhe, in folded strict embrace.
Grim visages of grinning fiends were at each corner set,
And emblematic scrolls, mort-heads, and bones together met.

"Ah, well-a-day!" that sexton grey unto himself did cry,
"Beneath that lid much lieth hid—much awful mysterie.
It is an ancient coffin from the abbey that stood here;
Perchance it holds an abbot's bones, perchance those of a frere.

"In digging deep, where monks do sleep, beneath yon cloister shrined,
That coffin old, within the mould, it was my chance to find;
The costly carvings of the lid I scraped full carefully,
In hope to get at name or date, yet nothing could I see.

"With pick and spade I've plied my trade for sixty years and more,
Yet never found, beneath the ground, shell strange as that before;
Full many coffins have I seen—have seen them deep or flat,
Fantastical in fashion—none fantastical as that."

And saying so, with heavy blow, the lid he shattered wide,
And, pale with fright, a ghastly sight that sexton grey espied;
A miserable sight it was, that loathsome corpse to see,
The last, last, dreary, darksome stage of fall'n humanity.

Though all was gone, save reeky bone, a green and grisly heap,
With scarce a trace of fleshy face, strange posture did it keep.
The hands were clench'd, the teeth were wrench'd, as if the wretch had risen,
E'en after death had ta'en his breath, to strive and burst his prison.

The neck was bent, the nails were rent, no limb or joint was straight;
Together glued, with blood imbued, black and coagulate.
And, as the sexton stooped him down to lift the coffin plank,
His fingers were defiled all o'er with slimy substance dank.

"Ah, well-a-day!" that sexton grey unto himself did cry,
"Full well I see how Fate's decree foredoomed this wretch to die;
A living man, a breathing man, within the coffin thrust,
Alack! alack! the agony ere he returned to dust."

A vision drear did then appear unto that sexton's eyes:
Like that poor wight before him straight he in a coffin lies.
He lieth in a trance within that coffin close and fast;
Yet though he sleepeth now, he feels he shall awake at last.

The coffin then, by reverend men, is borne with footsteps slow,
Where tapers shine before the shrine, where breathes the requiem **low**;
And for the dead the prayer is said, for the soul that is *not* flown—
Then all is drown'd in hollow sound, the earth is o'er him thrown!

He draweth breath—he wakes from death to life more horrible;
To agony! such agony! no living tongue may tell.
Die! die he must, that wretched one! he struggles—strives in vain!
No more heaven's light, nor sunshine bright, shall he behold again.

"Gramercy, Lord!" the sexton roar'd, awakening suddenly,
"If this be dream, yet doth it seem most dreadful so to die.
Oh, cast my body in the sea! or hurl it on the shore!
But nail me not in coffin fast—no grave will I dig more."

It was not difficult to discover the effect produced by this
song, in the lengthened faces of the greater part of the
audience. Jack Palmer, however, laughed loud and long.

"Bravo, bravo!" cried he; "that suits my humour exactly. I can't abide the thoughts of a coffin. No deal box
for me."

"A gibbet might, perhaps, serve your turn as well," muttered the sexton; adding aloud, "I am now entitled to call
upon you;—a song!—a song!"

"Ay, a song, Mr. Palmer, a song," reiterated the hinds.
"Yours will be the right sort of thing."

"Say no more," replied Jack. "I'll give you a chant composed upon Dick Turpin, the highwayman. It's no great
shakes, to be sure, but it's the best I have." And with a
knowing wink at the sexton, he commenced in the true nasal
whine the following strain:

ONE FOOT IN THE STIRRUP;

OR, TURPIN'S FIRST FLING.

"Cum esset proposita *Turpi*(n)*s*."—CICERO.

"One foot in the stirrup, one hand in the rein
And the noose be my portion, or freedom I'll gain!
Oh! give me a seat in my saddle once more,
And these bloodhounds shall find that the chase is not o'er!"
Thus muttered Dick Turpin, who found, while he slept,
That the Philistines old on his slumbers had crept,
Had entrapped him as puss on her form you'd ensnare,
And that gone were his *snappers*—and gone was his mare. *Hilloah!*

How Dick had been captured is readily told,
The pursuit had been hot, though the night had been cold:
So at daybreak, exhausted, he sought brief repose
Mid the thick of a cornfield, away from his foes.

But in vain was his caution—in vain did his steed,
Ever watchful and wakeful in moments of need,
With lip and with hoof on her master's cheek press—
He slept on, nor heeded the warning of Bess.   *Hilloah!*

"Zounds! gem'men!" cried Turpin, "you've found me at fault,
And the highflying highwayman's come to a halt;
You have turned up a trump (for I weigh well my weight),
And the *forty is yours*, though the halter's *my* fate.
Well, come on't what will, you shall own when all's past,
That Dick Turpin, the Dauntless, was game to the last.
But, before we go further, I'll hold you a bet,
That one foot in my stirrup you won't let me set.   *Hilloah!*

"A hundred to one is the odds *I* will stand,
A hundred to one is the odds *you* command;
Here's a handful of goldfinches ready to fly!
May I venture a foot in my stirrup to try?"
As he carelessly spoke, Dick directed a glance
At his courser, and motioned her slyly askance:—
You might tell by the singular toss of her head,
And the prick of her ears, that his meaning she read.   *Hilloah!*

With derision at first was Dick's wager received,
And his error at starting as yet unretrieved;
But when from his pocket the *shiners* he drew,
And offered to "make up the hundred to two,"
There were *havers* in plenty, and each whispered each,
The same thing, though varied in figure of speech,
"Let the fool act his folly—the stirrup of Bess!
He has put his foot *in it* already we guess!"   *Hilloah!*

Bess was brought to her master—Dick steadfastly gazed
At the eye of his mare, then his foot quick upraised:
His toe touched the stirrup, his hand grasped the rein—
He was safe on the back of his courser again!
As the clarion, fray-sounding and shrill, was the neigh
Of Black Bess, as she answered his cry "hark-away!"
"Beset me, ye bloodhounds! in rear and in van;
My foot's in the stirrup, now catch me who can?"   *Hilloah!*

There was riding and gibing mid rabble and rout,
And the old woods re-echoed the Philistines' shout!
There was hurling and whirling o'er brake and o'er brier,
But the course of Dick Turpin was swift as heaven's fire.
Whipping, spurring, and straining, would nothing avail,
Dick laughed at their curses, and scoffed at their wail;
"My foot's in the stirrup!"—thus rang his last cry;
"Bess has answered my call; now her mettle we'll try!"   *Hilloah!*

Uproarious applause followed Jack's song, when the joviality of the mourners was interrupted by a summons to attend in the state room. Silence was at once completely restored; and, in the best order they could assume, they followed their leader, Peter Bradley. Jack Palmer was amongst the last to enter, and remained a not incurious spectator of a by no means common scene.

Preparations had been made to give due solemnity to the

ceremonial. The leaden coffin was fastened down, and enclosed in an outer case of oak, upon the lid of which stood a richly-chased massive silver flagon, filled with burnt claret, called the grace-cup. All the lights were removed, save two lofty wax flambeaux, which were placed to the back, and threw a lurid glare upon the group immediately about the body, consisting of Ranulph Rookwood and some other friends of the deceased. Doctor Small stood in front of the bier; and, under the directions of Peter Bradley, the tenantry and household were formed into a wide half-moon across the chamber. There was a hush of expectation, as Doctor Small looked gravely round; and even Jack Palmer, who was as little likely as any man to yield to an impression of the kind, felt himself moved by the scene.

The very orthodox Small, as is well known to our readers, held everything savouring of the superstitions of the Scarlet Lady in supreme abomination; and, entertaining such opinions, it can scarcely be supposed that a funeral oration would find much favour in his eyes, accompanied, as it was, with the accessories of censer, candle, and cup; all evidently derived from that period when, under the three-crowned pontiff's sway, the shaven priest pronounced his benediction o'er the dead, and released the penitent's soul from purgatorial flames, while he heavily mulcted the price of his redemption from the possessions of his successor. Small resented the idea of treading in such steps, as an insult to himself and his cloth. Was he, the intolerant of Papistry, to tolerate this? Was he, who could not endure the odour of Catholicism, to have his nostrils thus polluted, his garments thus defiled by actual contact with it. It was not to be thought of: and he had formally signified his declination to Mr. Coates, when a little conversation with that gentleman, and certain weighty considerations therein held forth (the advowson of the church of Rookwood residing with the family), and represented by him, as well as the placing in juxtaposition of penalties to be incurred by refusal, that the scruples of Small gave way; and, with the best grace he could muster, very reluctantly promised compliance.

With these feelings, it will be readily conceived that the doctor was not in the best possible frame of mind for the delivery of his exhortation. His temper had been ruffled by a variety of petty annoyances, amongst the greatest of which was the condition to which the good cheer had reduced his clerk, Zachariah Trundletext, whose reeling eye, pendulous position and open mouth, proclaimed him absolutely incapable of office. Zachariah was, in consequence, dismissed, and Small commenced his discourse unsupported. But as our recording it would not probably conduce to the amusement of our readers, whatever it might be to their edification, we shall pass it over with very brief mention. Suffice it to say, that the oration was so thickly interstrewn with lengthy quotations from the fathers — Chrysostomus, Hieronimus, Ambrosius, Basilius, Bernardus, and the rest with whose recondite Latinity, notwithstanding the clashing of their opinions with his own, the doctor was intimately acquainted, and which he moreover delighted to quote, that his auditors were absolutely mystified and perplexed, and probably not without design. Countenances of such amazement were turned towards him, that Small, who had a keen sense of the ludicrous, could scarcely forbear smiling as he proceeded; and if we could suspect so grave a personage of waggery, we should almost think that, by way of retaliation, he had palmed some abstruse monkish epicedium upon his astounded auditors.

The oration concluded, biscuits and confectionery were, according to old observance, handed to such of the tenantry as chose to partake of them. The serving of the grace-cup, which ought to have formed part of the duties of Zachariah, had he been capable of office, fell to the share of the sexton. The bowl was kissed, first by Ranulph, with lips that trembled with emotion, and afterwards by his surrounding friends; but no drop was tasted—a circumstance which did not escape Peter's observation. Proceeding to the tenantry, the first in order happened to be farmer Toft. Peter presented the cup, and as Toft was about to drain a deep draught of the wine, Peter whispered in his ear, "Take my advice for once, friend Toft, and don't let a bubble of the liquid pass your lips. For every drop of the wine you drain, Sir Piers will have one sin the less, and you a load the heavier on your conscience. Didst never hear of sin swallowing? For what else was this custom adopted? Seest thou not the cup's brim hath not yet been moistened? Well, as you will —ha, ha!" And the sexton passed onwards.

His work being nearly completed, he looked round for Jack Palmer, whom he had remarked during the oration, but could nowhere discover him. Peter was about to place the flagon, now almost drained of its contents, upon its former resting-place, when Small took it from his hands.

"'*In poculi fundo residuum non relinque*,' admonisheth Pythagoras," said he, returning the cup drained of its contents to the sexton.

"My task here is ended," muttered Peter, "but not elsewhere. Foul weather or fine, thunder or rain, I must to the church."

Bequeathing his final instructions to certain of the household who were to form part of the procession, in case it set out, he opened the hall door, and, the pelting shower dashing heavily in his face, took his way up the avenue, screaming, as he strode along, the following congenial rhymes:

EPHIALTES.

I am the hag who ride by night
Through the moonless air on a courser white!
Over the dreaming earth I fly,
Here and there—at my phantasy!
My frame is withered, my visage old,
My locks are frore, and my bones ice-cold.
The wolf will howl as I pass his lair,
The ban-dog moan, and the screech-owl stare.
For breath, at my coming, the sleeper strains,
And the freezing current forsakes his veins!
Vainly for pity the wretch may sue—
Merciless Mara no prayers subdue!

> *To his couch I flit—*
> *On his breast I sit!*
> *Astride! astride! astride!*
> *And one charm alone*
> *(A hollow stone!*)*
> *Can scare me from his side!*

A thousand antic shapes I take;
The stoutest heart at my touch will quake.
The miser dreams of a bag of gold,
Or a ponderous chest on his bosom roll'd.
The drunkard groans 'neath a cask of wine;
The reveller swelts 'neath a weighty chine.
The recreant turns, by his foes assailed,
To flee!—but his feet to the ground are nailed.
The goatherd dreams of his mountain-tops,
And, dizzily reeling, downward drops.
The murderer feels at his throat a knife,
And gasps, as his victim gasp'd, for life!

---

* In reference to this imaginary charm, Sir Thomas Browne observes, in his *Vulgar Errors*, " What natural effects can reasonably be expected, when, to prevent the Ephialtes, or Nightmare, we hang a hollow stone in our stables?" Grose also states, " that a stone with a hole in it, hung at the bed's head, will prevent the nightmare, and is therefore called a hag-stone." The belief in this charm still lingers in some districts, and maintains, like the horse-shoe affixed to the barn-door, a feeble stand against the superstition-destroying " march of intellect."

The thief recoils from the scorching brand ;
The mariner drowns in sight of land !
—Thus sinful man have I power to fray,
Torture and rack—but not to slay !
But ever the couch of purity,
With shuddering glance I hurry by.
>   *Then mount ! away !*
>   *To horse ! I say,*
>   *To horse ! astride ! astride !*
>   *The fire-drake shoots—*
>   *The screech-owl hoots—*
>   *As through the air I glide !*

III.

THE CHURCHYARD.

> Methought I walked, about the mid of night,
> Into a churchyard.   WEBSTER.—*The White Devil.*

LIGHTS streamed through the chancel window as the sexton
entered the churchyard, darkly defining all the ramified
tracery of the noble Gothic arch, and illumining the gorgeous dyes of its richly-stained glass, profusely decorated
with the armorial bearings of the founder of the fane, and
the many alliances of his descendants. The sheen of their
blazonry gleamed bright in the darkness, as if to herald to
his last home another of the line whose achievements it displayed. Glowing colourings, chequered like rainbow tints,
were shed upon the broken leaves of the adjoining yew-trees,
and upon the rounded grassy tombs.

Opening the gate, as he looked in that direction, Peter
became aware of a dark figure, enveloped in a large black
cloak, and covered with a slouched hat, standing at some
distance, between the window and the tree, and so intervening as to receive the full influence of the stream of radiance
which served to dilate its almost superhuman stature. The
sexton stopped. The figure remained stationary. There
was something singular both in the costume and situation of
the person. Peter's curiosity was speedily aroused, and,
familiar with every inch of the churchyard, he determined to
take the nearest cut, and to ascertain to whom the mysterious
cloak and hat belonged. Making his way over the undulating graves, and instinctively rounding the headstones that
intercepted his path, he quickly drew near the object of his
inquiry. From the moveless posture it maintained, the

I

figure appeared to be unconscious of Peter's approach. To
his eyes it seemed to expand as he advanced. He was now
almost close upon it, when his progress was arrested by a
violent grasp laid on his shoulder. He started, and uttered
an exclamation of alarm. At this moment a vivid flash of
lightning illuminated the whole churchyard, and Peter then
thought he beheld, at some distance from him, two other
figures, bearing upon their shoulders a huge chest, or, it
might be, a coffin. The garb of these figures, so far as it could
be discerned through the drenching rain, was fantastical in
the extreme. The foremost seemed to have a long white
beard descending to his girdle. Little leisure, however, was
allowed Peter for observation. The vision no sooner met his
glance than it disappeared, and nothing was seen but the
glimmering tombstones, nothing heard but the whistling
wind and the heavily-descending shower. He rubbed his eyes.
The muffled figure had vanished, and not a trace could be
discovered of the mysterious coffin-bearers, if such they were.

"What have I seen?" mentally ejaculated Peter: "is this
sorcery or treachery, or both? No body-snatchers would
visit this place on a night like this, when the whole neighbourhood is aroused. Can it be a vision I have seen. Pshaw!
shall I juggle myself as I deceive these hinds? It was no
bearded demon that I beheld, but the gipsy patrico, Balthazar. I knew him at once. But what meant that muffled
figure; and whose arm could it have been that griped my
shoulder? Ha! what if Lady Rookwood should have given
orders for the removal of Susan's body. No, no; that
cannot be. Besides, I have the keys of the vault; and there
are hundreds now in the church who would permit no such
desecration. I am perplexed to think what it can mean.
But I will to the vault." Saying which, he hastened to the
church porch, and after wringing the wet from his clothes,
as a water-dog might shake the moisture from his curly hide,
and doffing his broad felt hat, he entered the holy edifice.
The interior seemed one blaze of light to the sexton, in his
sudden transition from outer darkness. Some few persons
were assembled, probably such as were engaged in the preparations; but there was one group which immediately
attracted his attention.

Near the communion table stood three persons, habited in
deep mourning, apparently occupied in examining the various
monumental carvings that enriched the walls. Peter's office
led him to that part of the church. About to descend into

the vaults, to make the last preparations for the reception of the dead, with lantern in hand, keys, and a crowbar, he approached the party. Little attention was paid to the sexton's proceedings, till the harsh grating of the lock attracted their notice.

Peter started as he beheld the face of one of the three, and relaxing his hold upon the key, the strong bolt shot back in the lock. There was a whisper amongst the party. A light step was heard advancing towards him; and ere the sexton could sufficiently recover his surprise, or force open the door, a female figure stood by his side.

The keen, inquiring stare which Peter bestowed upon the countenance of the young lady so much abashed her, that she hesitated in her purpose of addressing him, and hastily retired.

"She here," muttered Peter; "nay, then, I must no longer withhold the dreaded secret from Luke, or Ranulph may, indeed, wrest his possessions from him."

Reinforced by her companions, an elderly lady and a tall handsome man, whose bearing and deportment bespoke him to be a soldier, the fair stranger again ventured towards Peter.

"You are the sexton," said she, addressing him in a voice sweet and musical.

"I am," returned Peter. It was harmony succeeded by dissonance.

"You, perhaps, can tell us, then," said the elderly lady, "whether the funeral is likely to take place to-night? we thought it possible that the storm might altogether prevent it."

"The storm is over, as nearly as may be," replied Peter. "The body will soon be on its way. I am but now arrived from the hall."

"Indeed!" exclaimed the lady. "None of the family will be present, I suppose. Who is the chief mourner?"

"Young Sir Ranulph!" answered the sexton. "There will be more of the family than were expected.'"

"Is Sir Ranulph returned?" asked the young lady, with great agitation of manner. "I thought he was abroad; that he was not expected. Are you sure you are rightly informed?"

"I parted with him at the hall not ten minutes since," replied Peter. "He returned from France to-night most unexpectedly."

"Oh, mother!" exclaimed the younger lady, "that this should be—that I should meet him here. Why did we come?—let us depart."

"Impossible," replied her mother; "the storm forbids it. This man's information is so strange, I scarce can credit it. Are you sure you have asserted the truth?" said she, addressing Peter.

"I am not accustomed to be doubted," answered he. "Other things as strange have happened at the hall."

"What mean you?" asked the gentleman, noticing this last remark.

"You would not need to ask the question of me had you been there, amongst the other guests," retorted Peter. "Odd things, I tell you, have been done there this night, and stranger things may occur before the morning."

"You are insolent, sirrah. I comprehend you not."

"Enough! I can comprehend *you*," replied Peter, significantly; "I know the count of the mourners invited to this ceremonial, and I am aware that there are three too many."

"Know you this saucy knave, mother?"

"I cannot call him to mind, though I fancy I have seen him before."

"My recollection serves me better, lady," interposed Peter. "I remember one, who was once the proud heiress of Rookwood—ay, proud and beautiful. Then the house was filled with her gallant suitors. Swords were crossed for her. Hearts bled for her. Yet she favoured none, until one hapless hour. Sir Reginald Rookwood *had* a daughter; Sir Reginald *lost* a daughter. Ha!—I see I am right. Well, he is dead and buried; and Reginald, his son, is dead likewise; and Piers is on his road hither; and you are the last, as in the course of nature you might have been the first. And, now that they are all gone, you do rightly to bury your grievances with them."

"Silence, sirrah," exclaimed the gentleman, "or I will beat your brains out with your own spade."

"No; let him speak, Vavasour," said the lady, with an expression of anguish; "he has awakened thoughts of other days."

"I have done," said Peter, "and must to work. Will you descend with me, madam, into the sepulchre of your ancestry? All your family lie within—ay, and the Lady Eleanor, your mother, amongst the number."

Mrs. Mowbray signified her assent, and the party prepared to follow him.

The sexton held the lantern, so as to throw its light upon the steps as they entered the gloomy receptacle of the departed. Eleanor half repented having ventured within its dreary limits, so much did the appearance of the yawning catacombs, surcharged with mortality, and, above all, the ghostly figure of the grim knight, affect her with dread, as she looked wistfully around. She required all the support her brother's arm could afford her; nor was Mrs. Mowbray altogether unmoved.

"And all the family are here interred, you say?" inquired the latter.

"All," replied the sexton.

"Where, then, lies Sir Reginald's younger brother?"

"Who?" exclaimed Peter, starting.

"Alan Rookwood."

"What of him?"

"Nothing of moment. But I thought you could, perhaps, inform me. He died young."

"He did," replied Peter, in an altered tone—"very young; but not before he had lived to an old age of wretchedness. Do you know his story, madam?"

"I have heard it."

"From your father's lips?"

"From Sir Reginald Rookwood's—never. Call him not my father, sirrah; even *here* I will not have him named so to me."

"Your pardon, madam," returned the sexton. "Great cruelty was shown to the Lady Eleanor, and may well call forth implacable resentment in her child; yet methinks the wrong he did his brother Alan was the foulest stain with which Sir Reginald's black soul was dyed."

"With what particular wrong dost thou charge Sir Reginald?" demanded Major Mowbray. "What injury did he inflict upon his brother Alan?"

"He wronged his brother's honour," replied the sexton; "he robbed him of his wife, poisoned his existence, and hurried him to an untimely grave."

Eleanor shudderingly held back during this horrible narration, the hearing of which she would willingly have shunned, had it been possible.

"Can this be true?" asked the major.

"Too true, my son," replied Mrs. Mowbray, sorrowfully.

"And where lies the unfortunate Alan?" asked Major Mowbray.

" 'Twixt two cross roads. Where else should the suicide lie?"

Evading any further question, Peter hastily traversed the vault, elevating the light, so as to reveal the contents of each cell. One circumstance filled him with surprise and dismay —he could nowhere perceive the coffin of his daughter. In vain he peered into every catacomb—they were apparently undisturbed; and, with much internal marvelling and misgiving, Peter gave up the search. "That vision is now explained," muttered he; "the body is removed, but by whom? Death! can I doubt? It must be Lady Rookwood—who else can have any interest in its removal. She has acted boldly. But she shall yet have reason to repent her temerity." As he continued his search, his companions silently followed. Suddenly he stopped, and signifying that all was finished, they not unwillingly quitted this abode of horror, leaving him behind them.

" It is a dreadful place," whispered Eleanor to her mother; " nor would I have visited it, had I conceived anything of its horrors. And that strange man! who or what is he?"

"Ay, who is he?" repeated Major Mowbray.

"I recollect him now," replied Mrs. Mowbray; "he is one who has ever been connected with the family. He had a daughter, whose beauty was her ruin: it is a sad tale; I cannot tell it now: you have heard enough of misery and guilt: but that may account for his bitterness of speech. He was a dependent upon my poor brother."

"Poor man!" replied Eleanor; "if he has been unfortunate, I pity him. I am sorry we have been into that dreadful place. I am very faint: and I tremble more than ever at the thought of meeting Ranulph Rookwood again. I can scarcely support myself; I am sure I shall not venture to look upon him."

"Had I dreamed of the likelihood of his attending the ceremony, rest assured, dear Eleanor, we should not have been here: but I was informed there was no possibility of his return. Compose yourself, my child. It will be a trying time to both of us; but it is now inevitable."

At this moment the bell began to toll. "The procession has started," said Peter, as he passed the Mowbrays. "That bell announces the setting out."

"See yonder persons hurrying to the door," exclaimed Eleanor, with eagerness, and trembling violently. "They are coming. Oh! I shall never be able to go through with it, dear mother."

Peter hastened to the church door, where he stationed himself, in company with a host of others equally curious. Flickering lights in the distance, shining like stars through the trees, showed them that the procession was collecting in front of the hall. The rain had now entirely ceased; the thunder muttered from afar, and the lightning seemed only to lick the moisture from the trees. The bell continued to toll, and its loud booming awoke the drowsy echoes of the valley. On the sudden, a solitary, startling concussion of thunder was heard; and presently a man rushed down from the belfry, with the tidings that he had seen a ball of fire fall from a cloud right over the hall. Every ear was on the alert for the next sound: none was heard. It was the crisis of the storm. Still the funeral procession advanced not. The strong sheen of the torchlight was still visible from the bottom of the avenue, now disappearing, now brightly glimmering, as if the bearers were hurrying to and fro amongst the trees. It was evident that much confusion prevailed, and that some misadventure had occurred. Each man muttered to his neighbour, and few were there who had not in a measure surmised the cause of the delay. At this juncture, a person without his hat, breathless with haste, and almost palsied with fright, rushed through the midst of them, and, stumbling over the threshold, fell headlong into the church.

"What's the matter, Master Plant? What has happened? Tell us! Tell us!" exclaimed several voices simultaneously.

"Lord have mercy upon us!" cried Plant, gasping for utterance, and not attempting to raise himself. "It's horrible! dreadful! oh!—oh!"

"What has happened?" inquired Peter, approaching the fallen man.

"And dost *thou* need to ask, Peter Bradley? thou, who foretold it all? but I will not say what I think, though my tongue itches to tell thee the truth. Be satisfied, thy wizard's lore has served thee right—he is dead."

"Who? Ranulph Rookwood! Has anything befallen him, or the prisoner, Luke Bradley?" asked the sexton, with eagerness.

A scream here burst forth from one who was standing behind the group; and, in spite of the efforts of her mother to withhold her, Eleanor Mowbray rushed forward.

"Has aught happened to Sir Ranulph?" asked she.

"Noa—noa—not to Sir Ranulph—he be with the body."

"Heaven be thanked for that!" exclaimed Eleanor. And then, as ashamed of her own vehemence, and, it might seem, apparent indifference to another's fate, she inquired who was hurt?

"It be poor neighbour Toft, that be killed by a thunder-bolt, ma'am," replied Plant.

Exclamations of horror burst from all around.

No one was more surprised at this intelligence than the sexton. Like many other seers, he had not, in all probability, calculated upon the fulfilment of his predictions, and he now stared aghast at the extent of his own foreknowledge.

"I tell'ee what, Master Peter," said Plant, shaking his bullet-head, "it be well for thee thou didn't live in my grandfather's time, or thou'dst ha' been ducked in a blanket; or maybe burnt at the stake, like Ridley and Latimer, as we read on; but however that may be, ye shall hear how poor Toft's death came to pass, and nobody can tell'ee better nor I, seeing I were near to him, poor fellow, at the time. Well, we thought as how the storm were all over, and had all got into order of march, and were just beginning to step up the avenue, the coffin-bearers pushing lustily along, and the torches shining grandly, when poor Simon Toft, who could never travel well in liquor in his life, reeled to one side, and staggering against the first huge lime-tree, sat himself down beneath it—thou knowest the tree I mean."

"The tree of fate," returned Peter. "I ought, methinks, to know it."

"Well, I were just stepping aside, to pick him up, when all at once there comes such a crack of thunder, and whizzing through the trees, flashed a great globe of red fire, so bright and dazzlin', it nearly blinded me; and when I opened my eyes, winkin' and waterin', I see'd that which blinded me more even than the flash—that which had just afore been poor Simon, but which was now a mass o' black smouldering ashes, clean consumed and destroyed—his clothes rent to a thousand tatters—the earth and stones tossed up, and scattered all about, and a great splinter of the tree lying beside him."

"God's will be done!" said the sexton; "this is an awful judgment."

"And Sathan cast down; for this is a spice o' his handi-work," muttered Plant; adding, as he slunk away, "If ever Peter Bradley do come to the blanket, dang me if I don't lend a helpin' hand."

IV.

THE FUNERAL.

How like a silent stream, shaded by night,
And gliding softly with our windy sighs,
Moves the whole frame of this solemnity !
Tears, sighs, and blacks, filling the simile !
Whilst I, the only murmur in this grove
Of death, thus hollowly break forth.   *The Fatal Dowry.*

WORD being given that the funeral train was fast approaching, the church door was thrown open, and the assemblage divided in two lines to allow it admission.

Meanwhile, a striking change had taken place, even in this brief period, in the appearance of the night. The sky, heretofore curtained with darkness, was now illumined by a serene, soft moon, which, floating in a watery halo, tinged with silvery radiance the edges of a few ghostly clouds that hurried along the deep and starlit skies. The suddenness of the change could not fail to excite surprise and admiration, mingled with regret that the procession had not been delayed until the present time.

Slowly and mournfully the train was seen to approach the churchyard, winding, two by two, with melancholy step, around the corner of the road. First came Doctor Small; then the mutes, with their sable panoply; next, the torch-bearers; next, those who sustained the coffin, bending beneath their ponderous burden, followed by Sir Ranulph, and a long line of attendants, all plainly to be distinguished by the flashing torchlight. There was a slight halt at the gate, and the coffin changed supporters.

"Ill luck betide them!" ejaculated Peter; "could they find no other place except that to halt at? Must Sir Piers be gatekeeper till next Yule? No," added he, seeing what followed; "it will be poor Toft, after all."

Following close upon the coffin came a rude shell, containing, as Peter rightly conjectured, the miserable remains of Simon Toft, who had met his fate in the manner described by Plant. The bolt of death glanced from the tree which it first struck, and reduced the unfortunate farmer to a heap of dust. Universal consternation prevailed, and doubts were entertained as to what course should be pursued. It was judged best by Doctor Small to remove the remains at once to the charnel-house. Thus, "unanointed, unaneled, with all his imperfections on his head," was poor Simon Toft, in one brief second, in the twinkling of an eye, plunged from the height of festivity to the darkness of the grave, and so horribly disfigured, that scarce a vestige of humanity was discernible in the mutilated mass that remained of him. Truly may we be said to walk in blindness, and amidst deep pitfalls!

The churchyard was thronged by the mournful train. The long array of dusky figures—the waving torchlight, gleaming ruddily in the white moonshine—now glistening upon the sombre habiliments of the bearers, and on their shrouded load, now reflected upon the jagged branches of the yew-trees, or falling upon the ivied buttresses of the ancient church, constituted no unimpressive picture. Over all, like a lamp hung in the still sky, shone the moon, shedding a soothing, spiritual lustre over the scene.

The organ broke into a solemn strain, as the coffin was borne along the mid-aisle—the mourners following, with reverent step, and slow. It was deposited near the mouth of the vault, the whole assemblage circling around it. Doctor Small proceeded with the performance of that magnificent service appointed for the burial of the dead, in a tone as remarkable for its sadness, as for its force and fervour. There was a tear in every eye—a cloud on every brow.

Brightly illumined as was the whole building, there were still some recesses which, owing to the intervention of heavy pillars, were thrown into shade; and in one of these, supported by her mother and brother, stood Eleanor, a weeping witness of the scene. She beheld the coffin silently borne along; she saw one dark figure slowly following; she knew those pale features—oh, how pale they were! A year had wrought a fearful alteration; she could scarce credit what she beheld. He must, indeed, have suffered—deeply suffered; and her heart told her that his sorrows had been for her.

Many a wistful look, besides, was directed to the principal figure in this ceremonial, Ranulph Rookwood. He was a prey to unutterable anguish of soul; his heart bled inwardly for the father he had lost. Mechanically following the body down the aisle, he had taken his station near it, gazing with confused vision upon the bystanders; had listened, with a sad composure, to the expressive delivery of Small, until he read —"*For man walketh in a vain shadow and disquieteth himself in vain; he heapeth up riches, and cannot tell who shall gather them.*"

" Verily !" exclaimed a deep voice ; and Ranulph looking round, met the eyes of Peter Bradley fixed full upon him. But it was evidently not the sexton who had spoken.

Small continued the service. He arrived at this verse :— " *Thou hast set our misdeeds before thee ; and our secret sins in the light of Thy countenance.*"

" Even so !" exclaimed the voice ; and as Ranulph raised his eyes in the direction of the sound, he thought he saw a dark figure, muffled in a cloak, disappear behind one of the pillars. He bestowed, however, at the moment, little thought upon this incident. His heart melted within him ; and leaning his face upon his hand, he wept aloud.

" Command yourself, I entreat of you, my dear Sir Ranulph," said Doctor Small, as soon as the service was finished, " and suffer this melancholy ceremonial to be completed." Saying which, he gently withdrew Ranulph from his support, and the coffin was lowered into the vault.

Ranulph remained for some time in the extremity of sorrow. When he in part recovered, the crowd had dispersed, and few persons were remaining within the church ; yet near him stood three apparent loiterers. They advanced towards him. An exclamation of surprise and joy burst from his lips.

" Eleanor !"

" Ranulph !"

" Is it possible ? Do I indeed behold you, Eleanor !"

No other word was spoken. They rushed into each other's arms. Oh ! sad—sad is the lover's parting—no pang so keen ; but if life hath a zest more exquisite than others—if felicity hath one drop more racy than the rest in her honeyed cup, it is the happiness enjoyed in such a union as the present. To say that he was as one raised from the depths of misery, by some angel comforter, were a feeble comparison of the transport of Ranulph. To paint the thrilling delight of Eleanor— the trembling tenderness—the fond abandonment which vanquished all her maiden scruples, would be impossible. Reluctantly yielding—fearing, yet complying, her lips were sealed in one long, loving kiss, the sanctifying pledge of their tried affection.

" Eleanor, dear Eleanor," exclaimed Ranulph, " though I hold you within my arms—though each nerve within my frame assures me of your presence—though I look into those eyes, which seem fraught with greater endearment than ever I have known them wear—though I see and feel, and know all this, so sudden, so unlooked for is the happiness, that I could almost doubt its reality. Say to what blessed circumstance I am indebted for this unlooked-for happiness."

"We are staying not far hence, with friends, dear Ranulph; and my mother, hearing of Sir Piers Rookwood's death, and wishing to bury all animosity with him, resolved to be present at the sad ceremony. We were told you could not be here."

"And would my presence have prevented your attendance, Eleanor?"

"Not that, dear Ranulph; but——"

"But what?"

At this moment the advance of Mrs. Mowbray offered an interruption to their further discourse.

"My son and I appear to be secondary in your regards, Sir Ranulph," said she, gravely.

"*Sir* Ranulph!" mentally echoed the young man. "What will *she* think, when she knows that that title is not mine? I dread to tell her." He then added aloud, with a melancholy smile, "I crave your pardon, madam; the delight of a meeting, so unexpected, with your daughter must plead my apology."

"None is wanting, Sir Ranulph," said Major Mowbray. "I, who have known what separation from my sister is, can readily excuse your feelings. But you look ill."

"I have, indeed, experienced much mental anxiety," said Ranulph, looking at Eleanor; "it *is* now past, and I would fain hope that a brighter day is dawning." His heart answered, 'twas but a hope.

"You were unlooked for here to-night, Sir Ranulph," said Mrs. Mowbray; "by us, at least: we were told you were abroad."

"You were rightly informed, madam," replied Ranulph. "I only arrived this evening from Bordeaux."

"I am glad you are returned. We are at present on a visit with your neighbours, the Davenhams, at Braybrook, and t ust we shall see you there."

"I will ride over to-morrow," replied Ranulph; "there is much on which I would consult you all. I would have ventured to request the favour of your company at Rookwood, had the occasion been other than the present."

"And I would willingly have accepted your invitation," returned Mrs. Mowbray; "I should like to see the old house once mor . During your father's lifetime I could not approach it. You are lord of broad lands, Sir Ranulph—a goodly inheritance."

"Madam!"

"And a proud title, which you will grace well, I doubt not. The first, the noblest of our house, was he from whom you derive your name. You are the third Sir Ranulph; the first founded the house of Rookwood; the next advanced it; 'tis for you to raise its glory to its height."

"Alas! madam, I have no such thought."

"Wherefore not? You are young, wealthy, powerful. With such domains as those of Rookwood—with such a title as its lord can claim, nought should be too high for your aspirations."

"I aspire to nothing, madam, but your daughter's hand; and even that I will not venture to solicit until you are acquainted with——" And he hesitated.

"With what?" asked Mrs. Mowbray, in surprise.

"A singular, and to me most perplexing event has occurred to-night," replied Ranulph, "which may materially affect my future fortunes."

"Indeed!" exclaimed Mrs. Mowbray. "Does it relate to your mother?"

"Excuse my answering the question now, madam," replied Ranulph; "you shall know all to-morrow."

"Ay, to-morrow, dear Ranulph," said Eleanor; "and whatever that morrow may bring forth, it will bring happiness to me, if you are bearer of the tidings."

"I shall expect your coming with impatience," said Mrs. Mowbray.

"And I," added Major Mowbray, who had listened thus far in silence, "would offer you my services in any way you think they would be useful. Command me as you think fitting."

"I thank you heartily," returned Ranulph. "To-morrow you shall learn all. Meanwhile, it shall be my business to investigate the truth or falsehood of the statement I have heard, ere I report it to you. Till then, farewell!"

As they issued from the church it was grey dawn. Mrs. Mowbray's carriage stood at the door. The party entered it; and, accompanied by Doctor Small, whom he found within, in the vestry, Ranulph walked towards the hall, where a fresh surprise awaited him

V.

THE CAPTIVE.

Black Will. Which is the place where we're to be concealed?
Green.   This inner room.
Black Will. 'Tis well. The word is, " Now I take you."
                                    Arden of Feversham.

GUARDED by the two young farmers who had displayed so
much address in seizing him, Luke, meanwhile, had been
conveyed in safety to the small chamber in the eastern wing,
destined by Mr. Coates to be his place of confinement for the
night. The room, or rather closet, opening from another
room, was extremely well adapted for the purpose, having no
perceptible outlet; being defended, on either side, by thick
partition walls of the hardest oak, and at the extremity by
the solid masonry of the mansion. It was, in fact, a remnant
of the building anterior to the first Sir Ranulph's day; and
the narrow limits of Luke's cell had been erected long before
the date of his earliest progenitor. Having seen their prisoner
safely bestowed, the room was carefully examined, every board
sounded, every crevice and corner peered into, by the curious
eye of the little lawyer; and nothing being found insecure,
the light was removed, the door locked, the rustic constables
dismissed, and a brace of pistols having been loaded and laid
on the table, Mr. Coates pronounced himself thoroughly satisfied, and quite comfortable.

   "Comfortable!" Titus heaved a sigh as he echoed the
word. He felt anything but comfortable. His heart was
with the body all the while. He thought of the splendour
of the funeral, the torches, the illumined church, his own
dignified march down the aisle, and the effect he expected to
produce amongst the bewildered rustics. He thought of all
these things, and cursed Luke by all the saints in the calendar.
The sight of the musty old apartment, hung round with faded
arras, which, as he said, " smelt of nothing but rats and
ghosts, and such like varmint," did not serve to inspirit him;
and the proper equilibrium of his temper was not completely
restored until the appearance of the butler, with all the
requisites for the manufacture of punch, afforded him some
prospective solace.

   "And what are they about now, Tim?" asked Titus.

   "All as jolly as can be," answered the domestic; " Doctor
Small is just about about to pronounce the funeral 'ration.''

"Devil take it," ejaculated Titus, "there's another miss. Couldn't I just slip out and hear that?"

"On no account," said Coates. "Consider, Sir Ranulph is there."

"Well, well," rejoined Titus, heaving a deep sigh, and squeezing a lemon; "are you sure this is *biling* water, Tim? You know, I'm mighty particular."

"Perfectly aware of it, sir."

"Ah, Tim, do you recollect the way I used to brew for poor Sir Piers, with a bunch of red currants at the bottom of the glass? And then to think that, after all, I should be left out of his funeral—it's the height of barbarity. Tim, this rum of yours is poor stuff — there's no punch worth the trouble of drinking, except whisky punch. A glass of right potheen, straw-colour, peat-flavour, ten degrees over proof, would be the only thing to drown my cares. Any such thing in the cellar? There used to be an odd bottle or so, Tim— in the left bin, near the door."

"I've a notion there be," returned Timothy. "I'll try the bin your honour mentions, and if I can lay hands upon a bottle, you shall have it, you may depend."

The butler departed, and Titus, emulating Mr. Coates, who had already enveloped himself, like Juno at the approach of Ixion, in a cloud, proceeded to light his pipe.

Luke, meanwhile, had been left alone, without light. He had much to meditate upon, and with nought to check the current of his thoughts, he pensively revolved his present situation and future prospects. The future was gloomy enough — the present fraught with danger. And now that the fever of excitement was passed, he severely reproached himself for his precipitancy.

His mind, by degrees, assumed a more tranquil state; and, exhausted with his great previous fatigue, he threw himself upon the floor of his prison-house, and addressed himself to slumber. The noise he made induced Coates to enter the room, which he did with a pistol in each hand, followed by Titus, with a pipe and candle; but finding all safe the sentinels retired.

"One may see, with half an eye, that you're not used to a feather bed, my friend," said Titus, as the door was locked. "By the powers, he's a tall chap, any how—why his feet almost touch the door. I should say that room was a matter of six feet long, Mr. Coates."

"Exactly six feet, sir."

"Well, that's a good guess. Curse that ugly rascal, Tim; he's never brought the whisky. But I'll be even with him to-morrow. Couldn't you just see to the prisoner for ten minutes, Mr. Coates?"

"Not ten seconds. I shall report you, if you stir from your post."

Here the door was opened, and Tim entered with the whisky.

"Arrah! by my soul, Tim, and here you are at last—uncork it, man, and give us a thimbleful—blob! there goes the stopper—here's a glass"—smacking his lips—"whist, Tim, another drop—stuff like this will never hurt a body. Mr. Coates, try it—no—I thought you'd be a man of more taste."

"I must limit you to a certain quantity," replied Coates, "or you will not be fit to keep guard—another glass must be the extent of your allowance."

"Another glass! and do you think I'll submit to any such iniquitous proposition?"

"Beg pardon, gentlemen," said Tim; "but her ladyship desires me to tell you both, that she trusts you will keep the strictest watch upon the prisoner. I have the same message also from Sir Ranulph."

"Do you hear that?" said Coates.

"And what are they all about now, Tim?" groaned Titus.

"Just starting, sir," returned Tim; "and, indeed, I must not lose my time gossiping here, for I be wanted below. You must be pleased to take care of yourselves, gentlemen, for an hour or so, for there will be only a few women-kind left in the house. The storm's just over, and the men are all lighting their torches. Oh, it's a grand sight!" And off set Tim.

"Bad luck to myself, anyhow," ejaculated Titus; "this is more than I can bear—I've had enough of this watch and ward business—if the prisoner stirs, shoot him, if you think proper—I'll be back in an hour."

"I tell you what, Mr. Tyrconnel," said Coates, coolly, taking up the pistol from the table, "I'm a man of few words, but those few are, I hope, to the purpose, and I'd have you to know, if you stir from that chair, or attempt to leave the room, damme but I'll send a brace of bullets after you. I'm serious, I assure you. Saying which, he cocked the pistol.

By way of reply to this menace, Titus deliberately filled a stiff glass of whisky and water.

"That's your last glass," said the inexorable Coates.

To return once more to Luke. He slept uneasily for some short space, and was awakened by a sound which reached his dreaming ears, and connected itself with the visions that slumber was weaving around him. It was some moments before he could distinctly remember where he was. He would not venture to sleep again, though he felt overwhelmed by drowsiness—there was a fixed pain at his heart, as if circulation were suspended. Changing his posture, he raised himself upon one arm; he then became aware of a scratching noise, somewhat similar to the sound he had heard in his dream, and perceived a light gleaming through a crevice in the oaken partition. His attention was immediately arrested, and placing his eye close to the chink, distinctly saw a dark lantern burning; and by its light, a man filing some implements of house-breaking. The light fell before the hard features of the man, with whose countenance Luke was familiar; and although only one person came within the scope of his view, Luke could make out, from a muttered conversation that was carried on, that he had a companion. The parties were near to him, and though speaking in a low tone, Luke's quick ear caught the following:

"What keeps Jack Palmer, I wonder?" said he of the file. "We're all ready for the fakement—pops primed—and I tell you what, Rob Rust, I've made my clasp-knife as sharp as a razor, and dammee, if Lady Rookwood offers any resistance, I'll spoil her talking in future, I promise you."

Suppressed laughter, from Rust, followed this speech. That laugh made Luke's blood run cold within his veins.

"Harkee, Dick Wilder, you're a reg'lar out-and-outer, and stops at nothing, and curse me if I'd think any more of it than yourself. But Jack's as squeamish of bloodshed as young miss that cries at her cut finger. It's the safer plan. Say what you will, nothing but *that* will stop a woman's tongue."

"I shall make short work with her ladyship to-night, any how. Hist! here Jack comes."

A footstep crossed in the room, and, presently afterwards, exclamations of surprise and smothered laughter were heard from the parties.

"Bravo, Jack! famous! That disguise would deceive the devil himself."

"And now, my lads," said the new comer, "is all right?"

"Right and tight."

K

"Nothing forgotten?"

"Nothing."

"Then off with your stamps, and on with your list slippers; not a word. Follow me, and for your lives, don't move a step, but as I direct you. The word must be, '*Sir Piers Rookwood calls.*' We'll overhaul the swag here, when the speak is spoken over. This crack may make us all for life; and if you'll follow my directions implicitly, we'll do the trick in style. This slum must be our rendezvous, when all's over; for hark ye, my lads, I'll not budge an inch till Luke Bradley be set free. He's an old friend, and I always stick by old friends. I'd do the same for one of you if you were in the same scrape, so damn you, no flinching; besides, I owe that spider-shank'd, snivelling, split-cause Coates, who stands sentry, a grudge, and I'll pay him off, as Paul did the Ephesians. You may crop his ears, or slit his tongue as you would a magpie's, or any other chattering varmint; make him sign his own testament, or treat him with a touch of your *Habeas Corpus* Act, if you think proper, or give him a taste of blue plumb. One thing only I stipulate, that you don't hurt that fat, mutton-headed Brogaueer, whatever he may say or do; he's a devilish good fellow. And now to business."

Saying which, they noiselessly departed. But carefully as the door was closed, Luke's ear could detect the sound. His blood boiled with indignation; and he experienced what all must have felt, who have been similarly situated, with the will, but not the power, to assist another—a sensation almost approaching to torture. At this moment a distant scream burst upon his ears—another—he hesitated no longer. With all his force, he thundered at the door.

"What do you want, rascal?" cried Coates from without.

"There are robbers in the house."

"Thank you for the information. There is one I know of already."

"Fool, they are in Lady Rookwood's room; run to her assistance."

"A likely story, and leave you here."

"Do you hear that scream?"

"Eh, what's that? I do hear something."

Here Luke dashed with all his force against the door. It yielded to the blow, and he stood before the astonished attorney.

"Advance a footstep, villain," exclaimed Coates, presenting both his pistols, "and I lodge a brace of balls in your head."

"Listen to me," said Luke; "the robbers are in Lady Rookwood's chamber—they will plunder the place of everything—perhaps murder her. Fly to her assistance, I will accompany you—assist you—it is your only chance."

"*My* only chance—*your* only chance. Do you take me for a greenhorn? This is a poor subterfuge; could you not have vamped up something better? Get back to your own room, or I shall make no more of shooting you than I would of snuffing that candle."

"Be advised, sir," continued Luke. "There are three of them—give me a pistol, and fear nothing."

"Give *you* a pistol! Ha, ha!—to be its mark myself. You are an amusing rascal, I will say."

"Sir, I tell you not a moment is to be lost. Is life nothing? Lady Rookwood may be murdered."

"I tell *you*, once for all, it won't do. Go back to your room, or take the consequences."

"By the powers! but it shall do, anyhow," exclaimed Titus, flinging himself upon the attorney, and holding both his arms; "you have bullied me long enough. I'm sure the lad's in the right."

Luke snatched the pistols from the hands of Coates.

"Very well, Mr. Tyrconnel; very well, sir," cried the attorney, boiling with wrath, and spluttering out his words. "Extremely well, sir; you are not perhaps aware, sir, what you have done; but you will repent this, sir—repent, I say—repent was my word, Mr. Tyrconnel."

"Repent be d—d," replied Titus. "I shall never repent a good-natured action."

"Follow me," cried Luke; "settle your disputes hereafter. Quick, or we shall be too late."

Coates bustled after him, and Titus, putting the neck of the forbidden whisky bottle to his lips, and gulping down a hasty mouthful, snatched up a rusty poker, and followed the party with more alacrity than might have been expected from so portly a personage.

VI.

THE APPARITION.

Gibbet. Well, gentlemen, 'tis a fine night for our enterprise.
Hounslow. Dark as hell.
Bagshot. And blows like the devil.
Boniface. You'll have no creature to deal with but the ladies.
Gibbet. And I can assure you, friend, there's a great deal of address, **and good manners**, in robbing a lady. I am the most of a gentleman, that way, that ever travelled the road.   *Beaux Stratagem.*

ACCOMPANIED by her son, Lady Rookwood, on quitting the chamber of the dead, returned to her own room. She then renewed all her arguments; had recourse to passionate supplications—to violent threats; but without effect. Ranulph maintained profound silence. Passion, as it ever doth, defeated its own ends; and Lady Rookwood, seeing the ill effect her anger would probably produce, gradually softened the asperity of her manner, and suffered him to depart.

Left to herself, and to the communings of her own troubled spirit, her fortitude, in a measure, forsook her, under the pressure of the difficulties by which she was environed. There was no plan she could devise—no scheme adopt, unattended with peril. She must act alone—with promptitude, and secrecy. To win her son over was her chief desire, and that, at all hazards, she was resolved to do. But how? She knew of only one point on which he was vulnerable—his love for Eleanor Mowbray. By raising doubts in his mind, and placing fresh difficulties in his path, she might compel him to acquiesce in her machinations, as a necessary means of accomplishing his own object. This she hoped to effect. Still there was a depth of resolution in the placid stream of Ranulph's character, which she had often noticed with apprehension. Aware of his firmness, she dreaded lest his sense of justice should be stronger than his passion.

As she wove these webs of darkness, fear hitherto unknown, took possession of her soul. She listened to the howling of the wind—to the vibration of the rafters—to the thunder's roar, and to the hissing rain; till she, who never trembled at the thought of danger, became filled with vague uneasiness. Lights were ordered; and when her old attendant returned, Lady Rookwood fixed a look so wistful upon her, that Agnes ventured to address her.

"Bless you, my lady," said the ancient handmaiden, trem-

bling, " you look very pale, and no wonder. I feel sick at
heart, too. Oh ! I shall be glad when they return from the
church, and happier still when the morning dawns. I can't
sleep a wink—can't close my eyes, but I think of him."

" Of *him ?*"

" Of Sir Piers, my lady; for though he's dead, I don't
think he's gone."

" How ?"

" Why, my lady, the corruptible part of him's gone, sure
enough. But the incorruptible, as Doctor Small calls it—the
sperrit, my lady. It might be my fancy, your ladyship; but
as I am standing here, when I went back into the room just
now for the lights, as I hope to live, I thought I saw Sir
Piers in the room."

" You are crazed, Agnes."

" No, my lady, I'm not crazed; it was mere fancy, no
doubt. Oh, it's a blessed thing to live with an easy conscience—a thrice blessed thing to *die* with an easy one, and
that's what I never shall, I'm afeard. Poor Sir Piers! I'd
mumble a prayer for him, if I durst."

" Leave me," said Lady Rookwood, impatiently.

And Agnes quitted the room.

" What if the dead can return ?" thought Lady Rookwood.
" All men doubt it, yet all men believe it. *I* would not
believe it, were there not a creeping horror that overmasters
me, when I think of the state beyond the grave—that inter-
mediate state, for such it must be, betwixt heaven or hell,
when the body lieth mouldering in the ground, and the soul
survives, to wander, unconfined, until the hour of doom. And
doth the soul survive when disenthralled ? Is it dependent
on the body ? Does it perish with the body ? These are
doubts I cannot resolve. But if I deemed there was no
future state, this hand should at once liberate me from my
own weaknesses—my fears—my life. There is but one path to
acquire that knowledge, which once taken can never be re-
traced. I am content to live—while living to be feared—it
may be, hated; when dead, to be contemned—yet still remembered. Ha! what sound was that ? A stifled scream !
Agnes!—without there ! She is full of fears. I am not free
from them myself, but I will shake them off. This will divert
their channel," continued she, drawing from her bosom the
marriage certificate. " This will arouse the torpid current
of my blood—' *Piers Rookwood to Susan Bradley.*' And by
whom was it solemnized ? The name is Checkley—Richard

Checkley.   Ha! I bethink me, a Papist priest—a recusant—
who was for some time an inmate of the hall. I have heard
of this man—he was afterwards imprisoned, but escaped—he
is either dead, or in a foreign land. No witnesses—'tis well!
Methinks Sir Piers Rookwood did well to preserve this.   It
shall light his funeral pyre.   Would he could now behold me,
as I consume it!"

She held the paper in the direction of the candle; but, ere
it could touch the flame, it dropped from her hand. As if her
horrible wish had been granted, before her stood the figure
of her husband!   Lady Rookwood started not.   No sign of
trepidation or alarm, save the sudden stiffening of her form,
was betrayed.   Her bosom ceased to palpitate—her respiration stopped—her eyes were fixed upon the apparition.

The figure appeared to regard her sternly.   It was at some
little distance, within the shade cast by the lofty bedstead.
Still she could distinctly discern it.   There was no ocular deception; it was attired in the costume Sir Piers was wont to
wear—a hunting dress.   All that her son had told her rushed
to her recollection.   The phantom advanced.   Its countenance
was pale, and wore a gloomy frown.

" What would you destroy ?" demanded the apparition, in
a hollow tone.

" The evidence of——"

" What ?"

" Your marriage."

" With yourself, accursed woman ?"

" With Susan Bradley."

" Blood and thunder," shouted the figure, in an altered
tone.   " Married to her! then Luke *is* legitimate, and heir
to this estate !"   Whereupon the apparition rushed to the
table, and laid a very substantial grasp upon the document.
" A marriage certificate !" ejaculated the spectre; " here's a
piece of luck! It ain't often in our lottery life we draw a
prize like this.   One way or the other, it must turn up a few
cool thousands."

" Restore that paper, villain," exclaimed Lady Rookwood,
recovering all the audacity natural to her character, the instant she discovered the earthly nature of the intruder;
" restore it, or, by Heaven, you shall rue your temerity."

" Softly, softly," replied the pseudo-phantom, with one
hand pushing back the lady, while the other conveyed the
precious document to the custody of his nether man—
" softly," said he, giving the buckskin pocket a slap—" two

words to that, my lady. I know its value as well as yourself, and *must* make my market. The highest offer has me, your ladyship; he's but a poor auctioneer that knocks down his ware when only one bidder is present. Luke Bradley, or, as I find he now is, Sir Luke Rookwood, may come down more handsomely."

"Who are you, ruffian, and to what end is this masquerade assumed? If for the purpose of terrifying me into compliance with the schemes of that madman, Luke Bradley, whom I presume to be your confederate, your labour is misspent—*your* stolen disguise has no more weight with me than *his* forged claims."

"Forged claims. Egad, he must be a clever hand to have forged that certificate. Your ladyship, however, is in error. Sir Luke Rookwood is no associate of mine; I am his late father's friend. But I have no time to bandy talk. What money have you in the house? Be alive."

"You *are* a robber, then?"

"Not I. I'm a tax-gatherer—a collector of *Rich-Rates*—ha! ha! What plate have you got? Nay, don't be alarmed—take it quietly—these things can't be helped—better make up your mind to it without more ado—much the best plan—no screaming, it may injure your lungs, and can alarm nobody. Your maids have done as much before—it's beneath *your* dignity to make so much noise. So, you will not heed me? As you will." Saying which, he deliberately cut the bell-cord, and drew out a brace of pistols at the same time.

"Agnes!" shrieked Lady Rookwood, now seriously alarmed.

"I must caution your ladyship to be silent," said the robber, who, as our readers will no doubt have already conjectured, was no other than the redoubted Jack Palmer. "Agnes is already disposed of," said he, cocking a pistol. "However, like your deceased 'lord and master,' I may appear, you will find you have got a very different *spirit* from that of Sir Piers to deal with. I am naturally the politest man breathing—have been accounted the best-bred man on the road, by every lady whom I have had the honour of addressing; and I should be sorry to sully my well-earned reputation by anything like rudeness. I must use a little force of the gentlest kind. Perhaps you will permit me to hand you to a chair. Bless me! what a wrist your ladyship has got. Excuse me, if I hurt you, but you are so devilish strong. What ho! 'Sir Piers Rookwood calls——'"

"Ready," cried a voice.

"That's the word," rejoined another; "ready," and immediately two men, their features entirely hidden by a shroud of black crape, accoutred in rough attire, and each armed with pistols, rushed into the room.

"Lend a hand," said Jack.

Even in this perilous extremity, Lady Rookwood's courage did not desert her. Anticipating their purpose, ere her assailants could reach her, she extricated herself from Palmer's grasp, and rushed upon the foremost so unexpectedly, that, before the man could seize her, she snatched a pistol from his hand, and presented it at the group with an aspect like that of a tigress at bay—her eye wandering from one to the other, as if selecting a mark.

There was a pause of a few seconds, in which the men glanced at the lady, and then at their leader. Jack looked blank.

"Hem!" said he, coolly; "this is something new—disarmed—defied by a petticoat. Hark ye, Rob Rust; the disgrace rests with you. Clear your character by securing her at once. What! afraid of a woman?"

"A woman?" repeated Rust, in a surly tone; "devilish like a woman, indeed. Few men could do what she has done. Give the word, and I fire. As to seizing her, that's more than I'll engage to do."

"Then damn you for a coward," said Jack. "I will steer clear of blood—if I can help it. Come, madam, surrender, like the more sensible part of your sex, at discretion. You will find resistance of no avail." And he stepped boldly towards her.

Lady Rookwood pulled the trigger. The pistol flashed in the pan. She flung away the useless weapon, without a word.

"Ha, ha!" said Jack, as he leisurely stooped to pick up the pistol, and approached her ladyship; "the bullet is not yet cast that is to be my billet. Here," added he, dealing Rust a heavy thump upon the shoulder with the butt-end of the piece, "take back your snapper, and look you, prick the touch-hole, or your barking-iron will never bite for you. And now, madam, I must take the liberty of again handing you to a seat. Dick Wilder, the cord—quick. It distresses me to proceed to such lengths with your ladyship—but safe bind, safe find, as Mr. Coates would say."

"You will not bind me, ruffian."

"Your ladyship is very much mistaken—I have no alternative—your ladyship's wrist is far too dexterous to be at liberty. I must furthermore request of your ladyship to be less vociferous—you interrupt business, which should be transacted with silence and deliberation."

Lady Rookwood's rage and vexation at this indignity were beyond all bounds. Resistance, however, was useless, and she submitted in silence. The cord was passed tightly round her arms, when it flashed upon her recollection, for the first time, that Coates and Tyrconnel, who were in charge of her captive in the lower corridor, might be summoned to her assistance. This idea no sooner crossed her mind than she uttered a loud and prolonged scream.

"Damnation!" cried Jack; "civility is wasted here. Give me the gag, Bob!"

"Better slit her squeaking-pipe at once," replied Rust, drawing his clasped knife; "she'll thwart everything."

"The gag, I say, not *that*."

"I can't find the gag," exclaimed Wilder, savagely. "Leave Rob Rust to manage her—he'll silence her, I warrant you, while you and I rummage the room."

"Ay, leave her to me," said the other miscreant. "Go about your business, and take no heed. Her hands are fast—she can't scratch—I'll do it with a single gash—send her to join her lord, whom she loved so well, before he's under ground. They'll have something to see when they come home from the master's funeral—their mistress *cut and dry* for another. Ho, ho!"

"Mercy, mercy!" shrieked Lady Rookwood.

"Ay, ay, I'll be merciful," said Rust, brandishing his knife before her eyes. "I'll not be long about it. Leave her to me—I'll give her a taste of Sir Sidney."

"No, no, Rust; no bloodshed," said Jack, authoritatively; "I'll find some other way to gag the jade."

At this moment, a noise of rapid footsteps was heard within the passage.

"Assistance comes," screamed Lady Rookwood. "Help! help!"

"To the door," cried Jack. The words were scarcely out of his mouth before Luke dashed into the room, followed by Coates and Tyrconnel.

Palmer and his companions levelled their pistols at the intruders, and the latter would have fired; but Jack's keen eye having discerned Luke amongst the foremost, checked

further hostilities for the present. Lady Rookwood, meanwhile, finding herself free from restraint, rushed towards her
deliverers, and crouched beneath Luke's protecting arms,
which were extended, pistol in hand, over her head. Behind
them stood Titus Tyrconnel, flourishing the poker, and Mr.
Coates, who, upon the sight of so much warlike preparation,
began somewhat to repent having rushed so precipitately
into the lion's den.

"Luke Bradley!" exclaimed Palmer, stepping forward.

"Luke Bradley!" echoed Lady Rookwood, recoiling, and
staring into his face.

"Fear nothing, madam," cried Luke. "I am here to assist
you—I will defend you with my life."

"*You* defend *me*?" exclaimed Lady Rookwood, doubtfully.

"Even *I*," cried Luke, "strange as it may sound."

"Holy powers protect me!" ejaculated Titus. "As I live
it is Sir Piers himself."

"Sir Piers!" echoed Coates, catching the infection of
terror, as he perceived Palmer more distinctly. "What! is
the dead come to life again? A ghost! a ghost!"

"By my soul," cried Titus, "it's the first ghost I ever
heard of that committed a burglary in its own house, and on
the night of the body's burial, too. But who the devil are
these? maybe they're ghosts likewise."

"They are," said Palmer, in a hollow tone, mimicking the
voice of Sir Piers, "attendant spirits. We are come for this
woman; her time is out; so no more palavering, Titus.
Lend a hand to take her to the churchyard, and be d—d
to you."

"Upon my conscience, Mr. Coates," cried Titus, "it's
either the devil or Sir Piers. We'll only be in the way here.
He's only just settling his old scores with his lady. I
thought it would come to this long ago. We'd best beat a
retreat."

Jack took advantage of the momentary confusion created
by this incidental alarm at his disguise, to direct Rust towards the door by which the new comers had entered; and,
this being accomplished, he burst into a loud laugh.

"What! not know me?" cried he; "not know your old
friend with a new face, Luke? Nor you, Titus? Nor you,
who can see through a millstone, lawyer Coates, don't you
recognise——"

"Jack Palmer, as I'm a sinner!" cried Titus. "Why,
this beats Banaghan. Arrah! Jack, honey, what does this

mean? Is it yourself I see in such company? You're not robbing in earnest?"

"Indeed but I am, friend Titus," exclaimed Jack; "and *it is* my own self you see. I just took the liberty of borrowing Sir Piers's old hunting-coat from the justice-room. You said my toggery wouldn't do for the funeral. I'm no other than plain Jack Palmer, after all."

"With half-a-dozen aliases at your back, I dare say," cried Coates. "*I* suspected you all along. All your praise of highwaymen was not lost upon me. No, no; I *can* see into a millstone, be it ever so thick."

"Well," replied Jack, "I'm sorry to see you here, friend Titus. Keep quiet, and you shall come to no harm. As to you, Luke Bradley, you have anticipated my intention by half an hour; I meant to set you free. For you, Mr. Coates, you may commit all future care of your affairs to your exe-cutors, administrators, and assigns. You will have no further need to trouble yourself with worldly concerns," added he, levelling a pistol at the attorney, who, however, shielded himself, in an agony of apprehension, behind Luke's person. "Stand aside, Luke."

"I stir not," replied Luke. "I thank you for your good intention, and will not injure you—that is, if you do not force me to do so. I am here to defend her ladyship."

"What's that you say?" returned Jack, in surprise— "*defend* her ladyship?"

"With my life," replied Luke. "Let me counsel you to depart."

"Are you mad? Defend *her!*—Lady Rookwood—your enemy—who would hang you? Tut, tut! Stand aside, I say, Luke Bradley, or look to yourself."

"You had better consider well ere you proceed," said Luke. "You know me of old. I have taken odds as great, and not come off the vanquished."

"The odds are even," cried Titus, "if Mr. Coates will but show fight. I'll stand by you to the last, my dear joy. You're the right son of your father, though on the wrong side. Och! Jack Palmer, my jewel, no wonder you resemble Dick Turpin."

"You hear this?" cried Luke.

"Hot-headed fool!" muttered Jack.

"Why don't you shoot him on the spot?" said Wilder.

"And mar my own chance," thought Jack. "No, that will never do; his life is not to be thrown away. "Be quiet," said he, in a whisper to Wilder; "I've another card to play, which shall serve us better than all the plunder here. No harm must come to that youngster; his life is worth thousands to us." Then, turning to Luke, he continued, "I'm loth to hurt you; yet what can I do? You must have the worst of it if we come to a pitched battle. I therefore advise you, as a friend, to draw off your forces. We are three to three, it is true; but two of *your* party are unarmed."

"Unarmed!" interrupted Titus. "Devil burn me! this iron shillelah shall convince you to the contrary, Jack, or any of your friends."

"Make ready then, my lads," cried Palmer.

"Stop a minute," exclaimed Coates; "this gets serious; it will end in homicide—in murder. We shall all have our throats cut to a certainty; and though these rascals will as certainly be hanged for it, that will be poor satisfaction to the sufferers. Had we not better refer the matter to arbitration?"

"I'm for fighting it out," said Titus, whisking the poker round his head, like a flail in action. "My blood's up. Come on, Jack Palmer, I'm for you."

"I should vote for retreating," chattered the attorney, "if that cursed fellow had not placed a *ne exeat* at the door."

"Give the word, captain," cried Rust, impatiently.

"Ay, ay," echoed Wilder.

"A skilful general always parleys," said Jack. "A word in your ear, Luke, ere that be done which cannot be undone."

"You mean me no treachery?" returned Luke.

Jack made no answer, but uncocking his pistols, deposited them within his pockets.

"Shoot him as he advances," whispered Coates; "he is in your power now."

"Scoundrel!" replied Luke, "do you think me as base as yourself?"

"Hush, hush! for God's sake don't expose me," said Coates.

Lady Rookwood had apparently listened to this singular conference with sullen composure, though in reality she was racked with anxiety as to its results; and, now apprehending that Palmer was about to make an immediate disclosure to Luke, she accosted him as he passed her.

"Unbind me!" cried she, "and what you wish shall be yours—money—jewels——"

"Ha! may I depend?"

"I pledge my word."

Palmer untied the cord, and Lady Rookwood, approaching

a table whereon stood the escritoir, touched a spring, and a secret drawer flew open.

"You do this of your own free will?" asked Luke. "Speak, if it be otherwise."

"I do," returned the lady, hastily.

Palmer's eyes glistened at the treasures exposed to his view.

"They are jewels of countless price. Take them, and rid me," she added in a whisper, "of *him*."

"Luke Bradley?"

"Ay."

"Give them to me."

"They are yours freely on those terms."

"You hear that, Luke," cried he aloud; "you hear it, Titus; this is no robbery, Mr. Coates—'Know all men by these *presents*'—I call you to witness, Lady Rookwood gives me these pretty things."

"I do," returned she; adding, in a whisper, "on the terms which I proposed."

"Must it be done at once?"

"Without an instant's delay."

"Before your own eyes?"

"I fear not to look on. Each moment is precious. He is off his guard now. You do it, you know, in self-defence."

"And you?"

"For the same cause."

"Yet he came here to aid you?"

"What of that?"

"He would have risked his life for yours?"

"I cannot pay back the obligation. He must die!"

"The document?"

"Will be useless then."

"Will not that suffice; why aim at life?"

"You trifle with me. You fear to do it."

"*Fear!*"

"About it, then; you shall have more gold."

"I will about it," cried Jack, throwing the casket to Wilder, and seizing Lady Rookwood's hands. I am no Italian bravo, madam—no assassin—no remorseless cut-throat. What are you—devil or woman—who ask me to do this? Luke Bradley, I say."

"Would you betray me?" cried Lady Rookwood.

"You have betrayed yourself, madam. Nay, nay, Luke, hands off. See, Lady Rookwood, how you would treat a friend. This strange fellow would blow out my brains for laying a finger upon your ladyship."

"I will suffer no injury to be done to her," said Luke; "release her."

"Your ladyship hears him," said Jack. "And you, Luke, shall learn the value set upon your generosity. You will not have *her* injured. This instant she has proposed, nay, paid for *your* assassination."

"How?" exclaimed Luke, recoiling.

"A lie, as black as hell," cried Lady Rookwood.

"A truth, as clear as heaven," returned Jack. "I will speedily convince you of the fact." Then turning to Lady Rookwood, he whispered, "Shall I give him the marriage document?"

"Beware!" said Lady Rookwood.

"Do I avouch the truth, then?"

She was silent.

"I am answered," said Luke.

"Then leave her to her fate," cried Jack.

"No," replied Luke; "she is still a woman, and I will not abandon her to ruffianly violence. Set her free."

"You are a fool," said Jack.

"Hurrah, hurrah!" vociferated Coates, who had rushed to the window. "Rescue, rescue! they are returning from the church; I see the torchlight in the avenue; we are saved!"

"Hell and the devil!" cried Jack; "not an instant is to be lost. Alive lads; bring off all the plunder you can; be handy!"

"Lady Rookwood, I bid you farewell," said Luke, in a tone in which scorn and sorrow were blended. "We shall meet again."

"We have not parted yet," returned she; "will you let this man pass? A thousand pounds for his life."

"Upon the nail?" asked Rust.

"By the living God, if any of you attempt to touch him, I will blow his brains out upon the spot, be he friend or foe," cried Jack. "Luke Bradley, *we* shall meet again. You shall hear from me."

"Lady Rookwood," said Luke, as he departed, "I shall not forget this night."

"Is all ready?" asked Palmer of his comrades.

"All."

"Then budge."

"Stay," said Lady Rookwood, in a whisper to him. "What will purchase that document?"

"Hem!"

"A thousand pounds?"

"Double it."

"It *shall* be doubled."

"I will turn it over."

"Resolve me now."

"You shall hear from me."

"In what manner?"

"I will find speedy means."

"Your name is Palmer?"

"Palmer is the name he goes by, your ladyship," replied Coates; "but it is a fashion with these rascals to have an alias."

"Ha! ha!" said Jack, thrusting the ramrod into his pistol-barrel, as if to ascertain there was a ball within it; "are you there Mr. Coates? Pay your wager, sir."

"What wager?"

"The hundred we bet you would take me if ever you had the chance."

"Take *you!*—it was Dick Turpin I betted to take."

"*I* am DICK TURPIN—that's my alias!" replied Jack.

"Dick Turpin! then I'll have a snap at you at all hazards," cried Coates, springing suddenly towards him.

"And I at you," said Turpin, discharging his pistol right in the face of the rash attorney; "there's a quittance in full."

Book the Third.

THE GIPSY.

Lay a garland on my hearse
  Of the dismal yew;
Maidens, willow branches bear,
  Say I died true.
My love was false, but I was firm
  From my hour of birth;
Upon my buried body lie
  Lightly, gentle earth. BEAUMONT AND FLETCHER.

I.

A MORNING RIDE.

I had a sister, who among the race
Of gipsies was the fairest. Fair she was
In gentle blood, and gesture to her beauty. BROME.

ON quitting Lady Rookwood's chamber, Luke speeded along the gloomy corridor, descended the spiral stairs, and,

swiftly traversing sundry other dark passages, issued from a
door at the back of the house. Day was just beginning to
break. His first object had been to furnish himself with
means to expedite his flight; and perceiving no one in the
yard, he directed his hasty steps towards the stable. The
door was fortunately unfastened; and, entering, he found a
strong roan horse, which he knew, from description, had been
his father's favourite hunter, and to the use of which he now
considered himself fully entitled. The animal roused himself as he approached, shook his glossy coat, and neighed, as
if he recognised the footsteps and voice.

"Thou art mistaken, old fellow," said Luke; "I am not
he thou thinkest; nevertheless, I am glad thy instinct would
have it so. If thou bearest my father's son as thou hast
borne thy old master, o'er many a field for many a day, he
need not fear the best mounted of his pursuers. Soho! come
hither, Rook."

The noble steed turned at the call. Luke hastily saddled
him, vaulted upon his back, and, disregarding every impediment in the shape of fence or ditch, shaped his course across
the field towards the sexton's cottage, which he reached just
as its owner was in the act of unlocking the door. Peter
testified his delight and surprise at the escape of his grandson by a greeting of chuckling laughter.

"How?—escaped!" exclaimed he. "Who has delivered
you from the hands of the Moabites? Ha, ha! But why do
I ask? Who could it have been but Jack Palmer?"

"My own hands have set me free," returned Luke. "I
am indebted to no man for liberty; still less to *him*. But I
cannot tarry here; each moment is precious. I came to
request you to accompany me to the gipsy encampment.
Will you go, or not?"

"And mount behind you?" replied Peter: "I like not the
manner of conveyance."

"Farewell, then," and Luke turned to depart.

"Stay; that is Sir Piers's horse, old Rook. I care not if I
do ride him."

"Quick, then; mount."

"I will not delay you a moment," rejoined the sexton,
opening his door and throwing his implements into the
cottage. "Back, Mole; back, sir," cried he as the dog rushed
out to greet him. "Bring your steed nigh this stone, grandson Luke—there—a little nearer—all's right. And away
they galloped.

The sexton's first inquiries were directed to ascertain how Luke had accomplished his escape; and, having satisfied himself in this particular, he was content to remain silent; musing, it might be, on the incidents detailed to him.

The road Luke chose was a rough, unfrequented lane, that skirted, for nearly a mile, the moss-grown palings of the park. It then diverged to the right, and seemed to bear towards a range of hills rising in the distance. High edges impeded the view on either hand; but there were occasional gaps, affording glimpses of the tract of country through which he was riding. Meadows were seen steaming with heavy dews, intersected by a deep channelled stream, whose course was marked by a hanging cloud of vapour, as well as by a row of melancholy pollard-willows, that stood like stripped, shivering urchins by the river side. Other fields succeeded, yellow with golden grain, or bright with flowering clover (the autumnal crop), coloured with every shade, from the light green of the turnip to the darker verdure of the bean, the various products of the teeming land. The whole was backed by round drowsy masses of trees.

Luke spoke not, nor abated his furious course, till the road began to climb a steep ascent. He then drew in the rein, and from the heights of the acclivity surveyed the plain over which he had passed.

It was a rich agricultural district, with little picturesque beauty, but much of true English endearing loveliness to recommend it. Such a quiet, pleasing landscape, in short, as one views, at such a season of the year, from every eminence in every county of our merry isle. The picture was made up of a tract of land, filled with corn ripe for the sickle, or studded with sheaves of the same golden produce, enlivened with green meadows, so deeply luxuriant as to claim the scythe for the second time; each divided from the other by thick hedgerows, the uniformity of which was broken ever and anon by some towering elm, tall poplar, or wide-branching oak. Many old farmhouses, with their broad barns and crowded haystacks (forming little villages in themselves), ornamented the landscape at different points, and by their substantial look evidenced the fertility of the soil, and the thriving condition of its inhabitants. Some three miles distant might be seen the scattered hamlet of Rookwood; the dark russet thatch of its houses scarcely perceptible amidst the embrowned foliage of the surrounding timber. The site of the village was, however, pointed out by the square tower of

the antique church, that crested the summit of the adjoining
hill; and although the hall was entirely hidden from view,
Luke readily traced out its locality amidst the depths of the
dark grove in which it was embosomed.

This goodly prospect had other claims to attention in
Luke's eyes besides its agricultural or pictorial merit.   It
was, or he deemed it was, his own.   Far as his eye ranged,
yea, even beyond the line of vision, the estates of Rookwood
extended.

"Do you see that house below us in the valley?" asked
Peter of his companion.

"I do," replied Luke; "a snug old house—a model of a
farm.   Everything looks comfortable and well to do about it.
There are a dozen lusty haystacks, or thereabouts; and the
great barn, with its roof yellowed like gold, looks built for a
granary; and there are stables, kine-houses, orchards, dove-
cots, and fishponds, and an old circular garden, with wall-
fruit in abundance.   He should be a happy man, and a
wealthy one, who dwells therein."

"He dwells therein no longer," returned Peter; "he died
last night."

"How know you that?   None are stirring in the house as
yet."

"The owner of that house, Simon Toft," replied Peter,
"was last night struck by a thunderbolt.   He was one of the
coffin-bearers at your father's funeral.   They are sleeping
within the house, you say.   'Tis well.   Let them sleep on—
they will awaken too soon, wake when they may—ha, ha!"

"Peace," cried Luke; "you blight everything—even this
smiling landscape you would turn to gloom.   Does not this
morn awaken a happier train of thoughts within your mind?
With me it makes amends for want of sleep, effaces resentment, and banishes every black misgiving.   'Tis a joyous
thing, thus to scour the country at earliest dawn; to catch
all the spirit and freshness of the morning; to be abroad
before the lazy world is half awake; to make the most of
brief existence; and to have spent a day of keen enjoyment,
almost before the day begins with some.   I like to anticipate
the rising of the glorious luminary; to watch every line of
light changing, as at this moment, from shuddering grey
to blushing rose!   See how the heavens are dyed!   Who
would exchange yon gorgeous spectacle," continued he,
pointing towards the east, and again urging his horse to full
speed down the hill, endangering the sexton's seat, and
threatening to impale him upon the crupper of the saddle—

"who would exchange that sight, and the exhilarating feeling of this fresh morn, for a couch of eiderdown, and a headache in reversion?"

"I for one," returned the sexton, sharply, "would willingly exchange it for that, or any other couch, provided it rid me of this accursed crupper, which galls me sorely. Moderate your pace, grandson Luke, or I must throw myself off the horse in self-defence."

Luke slackened his charger's pace, in compliance with the sexton's wish.

"Ah! well," continued Peter, restored in a measure to comfort; "now I can contemplate the sunrise, which you laud, somewhat at mine ease. 'Tis a fine sight, I doubt not, to the eyes of youth; and, to the sanguine soul of him upon whom life itself is dawning, is, I dare say, inspiriting: but when the heyday of existence is past; when the blood flows sluggishly in the veins; when one has known the desolating storms which the brightest sunrise has preceded, the scared heart refuses to trust its false glitter; and, like the experienced sailor, sees oft in the brightest skies a forecast of the tempest. To such a one, there can be no new dawn of the heart; no sun can gild its cold and cheerless horizon; no breeze can revive pulses that have long since ceased to throb with any chance emotion. I am too old to feel freshness in this nipping air. It chills me more than the damps of night, to which I am accustomed. Night—midnight! is my season of delight. Nature is instinct then with secrets dark and dread. There is a language which he who sleepeth not, but will wake, and watch, may haply learn. Strange organs of speech hath the invisible world; strange language doth it talk; strange communion hold with him who would pry into its mysteries. It talks by bat and owl—by the graveworm, and by each crawling thing—by the dust of graves, as well as by those that rot therein—but ever doth it discourse by night, and 'specially when the moon is at the full. 'Tis the lore I have then learnt that makes that season dear to me. Like your cat, mine eye expands in darkness. I blink at the sunshine, like your owl."

"Cease this forbidding strain," returned Luke; "it sounds as harshly as your own screech-owl's cry. Let your thoughts take a more sprightly turn, more in unison with my own and the fair aspect of nature."

"Shall I direct them to the gipsies' camp, then?" said Peter, with a sneer. "Do your own thoughts tend thither?"

" You are not altogether in the wrong," replied Luke. "I *was* thinking of the gipsies' camp, and of one who dwells amongst its tents."

" I knew it," replied Peter. " Did you hope to deceive me, by attributing all your joyousness of heart to the dawn? Your thoughts have been wandering all this while upon one who hath, I will engage, a pair of sloe-black eyes, an olive skin, and yet withal a clear one—'black, yet comely, as the tents of Kedar, as the curtains of Solomon'—a mesh of jetty hair, that hath entangled you in its network—ripe lips, and a cunning tongue—one of the plagues of Egypt. Ha, ha!"

" You have guessed shrewdly," replied Luke; "I care not to own that my thoughts were so occupied."

" I was assured of it," replied the sexton. "And what may be the name of her towards whom your imagination was straying?"

" Sibila Perez," replied Luke. Her father was a Spanish Gitano. She is known amongst her people by her mother's name of Lovel."

" She is beautiful, of course?"

" Ay, very beautiful!—but no matter! You shall judge of her charms anon."

" I will take your word for them," returned the sexton; " and you love her?"

" Passionately."

" You are not married?" asked Peter, hastily.

"Not as yet," replied Luke; " but my faith is plighted."

" Heaven be praised! The mischief is not then irreparable. I would have you married—though not to a gipsy girl."

" And whom would you select?"

" One before whom Sybil's beauty would pale as stars at day's approach."

" There lives not such a one."

"Trust me there does. Eleanor Mowbray is lovely beyond parallel. I was merely speculating upon a possibility, when I wished her yours—it is scarcely likely she would cast her eyes upon you."

" I shall not heed her neglect. Graced with my title, I doubt not, were it my pleasure to seek a bride amongst those of gentle blood, I should not find all indifferent to my suit."

" Possibly not. Yet what might weigh with others, would not weigh with her. There are qualities you lack which she has discovered in another."

" In whom ?"

" In Ranulph Rookwood."

" Is *he* her suitor ?"

" I have reason to think so."

" And you would have me abandon my own betrothed love, to beguile from my brother his destined bride ? That were to imitate the conduct of my grandsire, the terrible Sir Reginald, towards *his* brother Alan."

The sexton answered not, and Luke fancied he could perceive a quivering in the hands that grasped his body for support. There was a brief pause in their conversation.

" And who is Eleanor Mowbray ?" asked Luke, breaking the silence.

" Your cousin. On the mother's side a Rookwood. 'Tis therefore I would urge your union with her. There is a prophecy relating to your house, which seems as though it would be fulfilled in your person and in hers :

> 𝔚𝔥𝔢𝔫 𝔱𝔥𝔢 𝔰𝔱𝔯𝔞𝔶 𝔑𝔬𝔬𝔨 𝔰𝔥𝔞𝔩𝔩 𝔭𝔢𝔯𝔠𝔥 𝔬𝔫 𝔱𝔥𝔢 𝔱𝔬𝔭𝔪𝔬𝔰𝔱 𝔟𝔬𝔲𝔤𝔥,
> 𝔗𝔥𝔢𝔯𝔢 𝔰𝔥𝔞𝔩𝔩 𝔟𝔢 𝔠𝔩𝔞𝔪𝔬𝔲𝔯 𝔞𝔫𝔡 𝔰𝔠𝔯𝔢𝔞𝔪𝔦𝔫𝔤, 𝔍 𝔱𝔯𝔬𝔴 ;
> 𝔅𝔲𝔱 𝔬𝔣 𝔯𝔦𝔤𝔥𝔱, 𝔞𝔫𝔡 𝔬𝔣 𝔯𝔲𝔩𝔢, 𝔬𝔣 𝔱𝔥𝔢 𝔞𝔫𝔠𝔦𝔢𝔫𝔱 𝔫𝔢𝔰𝔱,
> 𝔗𝔥𝔢 𝔑𝔬𝔬𝔨 𝔱𝔥𝔞𝔱 𝔴𝔦𝔱𝔥 𝔑𝔬𝔬𝔨 𝔪𝔞𝔱𝔢𝔰 𝔰𝔥𝔞𝔩𝔩 𝔥𝔬𝔩𝔡 𝔥𝔦𝔪 𝔭𝔬𝔰𝔰𝔢𝔰𝔱.

" I place no faith in such fantasies," replied Luke ; " and yet the lines bear strangely upon my present situation."

" Their application to yourself and Eleanor Mowbray is unquestionable," replied the sexton.

" It would seem so, indeed," rejoined Luke ; and he again sank into abstraction, from which the sexton did not care to arouse him.

The aspect of the country had materially changed since their descent of the hill. In place of the richly-cultivated district which lay on the other side, a broad brown tract of waste land spread out before them, covered with scattered patches of gorse, stunted fern, and low brushwood, presenting an unvaried surface of unbaked turf. The shallow coat of sod was manifested by the stones that clattered under the horse's hoofs as he rapidly traversed the arid soil, clearing with ease to himself, though not without discomfort to the sexton, every gravelly trench, natural chasm, or other inequality of ground that occurred in his course. Clinging to his grandson with the tenacity of a bird of prey, Peter for some time kept his station in security ; but, unluckily, at one dike rather wider than the rest, the horse, owing possibly to the mismanagement, intentional or otherwise, of Luke, swerved, and the sexton dislodged from his "high estate," fell at the edge of the trench, and rolled incontinently to the bottom.

Luke drew in the rein to inquire if any bones were broken; and Peter presently upreared his dusty person from the abyss, and without condescending to make any reply, yet muttering curses, "not loud, but deep," accepted his grandson's proffered hand, and remounted.

While thus occupied, Luke fancied he heard a distant shout, and noting whence the sound proceeded—the same quarter by which he had approached the heath—he beheld a single horseman, spurring in their direction, at the top of his speed; and to judge from the rate at which he advanced, it was evident he was anything but indifferently mounted. Apprehensive of pursuit, Luke expedited the sexton's ascent; and that accomplished, without bestowing further regard upon the object of his solicitude, he resumed his headlong flight. He now thought it necessary to bestow more attention to his choice of road, and, perfectly acquainted with the heath, avoided all unnecessary hazardous passes. In spite of his knowledge of the ground, and the excellence of his horse, the stranger sensibly gained upon him. The danger, however, was no longer imminent.

"We are safe," cried Luke; "the limits of Hardchase are past. In a few seconds we shall enter Davenham Wood. I will turn the horse loose, and we will betake ourselves to flight amongst the trees. I will show you a place of concealment. He cannot follow us on horseback, and on foot I defy him."

"Stay," cried the sexton. "He is not in pursuit; he takes another course; he wheels to the right. By Heaven! it is the fiend himself upon a black horse, come for Bow-legged Ben. See, he is there already."

The horseman had turned, as the sexton stated, careering towards a revolting object, at some little distance on the right hand. It was a gibbet, with its grisly burden. He rode swiftly towards it, and, reining in his horse, took off his hat, bowing profoundly to the carcase that swung in the morning breeze. Just at that moment a gust of air catching the flesh-less skeleton, its arms seemed to be waved in reply to the salutation. A solitary crow winged its flight over the horseman's head as he paused. After a moment's halt, he wheeled about, and again shouted to Luke, waving his hat.

"As I live," said the latter, "it is Jack Palmer."

"Dick Turpin, you mean," rejoined the sexton. "He has

been paying his respects to a brother blade. Ha, ha! Dick will never have the honour of a gibbet; he is too tender of the knife. Did you mark the crow? But here he comes." And in another instant Turpin was by their side.

II.

A GIPSY ENCAMPMENT.

I see a column of slow-rising smoke
O'ertop the lofty wood, that skirts the wild.
COWPER.—*The Task.*

"THE top of the morning to you, gem'men," said Turpin, as he rode up at an easy canter. "Did you not hear my halloo? I caught a glimpse of you on the hill yonder. I knew you both, two miles off; and so, having a word or two to say to you, Luke Bradley, before I leave this part of the country, I put Bess to it, and she soon brought me within hail. Bless her black skin," added he, affectionately patting his horse's neck, "there's not her match in these parts, or in any other; she wants no coaxing to do her work—no bleeders for her. I should have been up with you before this had I not taken a cross-cut to look at poor Ben.

One night, when mounted on my mare,
To Bagshot Heath I did repair,
And saw Will Davies hanging there,
Upon the gibbet bleak and bare,
　　With a rustified, justified, mustified air.

Excuse my singing. The sight of a gibbet always puts me in mind of the Golden Farmer. May I ask whither you are bound, comrades?"

"Comrades!" whispered the sexton to Luke; "you see *he* does not so easily forget his old friends."

"I have business that will not admit of delay," rejoined Luke; "and, to speak plainly——"

"You want not my society," returned Turpin; "I guessed as much. Natural enough! You have got an inkling of your good fortune. You have found out you are a rich man's heir, not a poor wench's bastard. No offence, I'm a plain-spoken man, as you will find, if you know it not already. I have no objection to your playing these fine tricks on others, though it won't answer your turn to do so with me."

"Sir!" exclaimed Luke, sharply.

"Sir to you," replied Turpin. "Sir Luke—as I suppose you would now choose to be addressed. I am aware of all. A nod is as good as a wink to me. Last night I learnt the fact of Sir Piers's marriage from Lady Rookwood—ay, from her ladyship. You stare, and old Peter, there, opens his ogles now. She let it out by accident; and I am in possession of what can alone substantiate your father's first marriage, and establish your claims to the property."

"The devil!" cried the sexton; adding, in a whisper to Luke, "You had better not be precipitate in dropping so obliging an acquaintance."

"You are jesting," said Luke to Turpin.

"It is ill jesting before breakfast," returned Dick: "I am seldom in the mood for a joke so early. What if a certain marriage certificate had fallen into my hand?"

"A marriage certificate!" echoed Luke and the sexton simultaneously.

"The only existing proof of the union of Sir Piers Rookwood with Susan Bradley," continued Turpin. "What if I had stumbled upon such a document—nay more, if I knew where to direct you to it?"

"Peace!" cried Luke to his tormentor; and then addressing Turpin, "If what you say be true, my quest is at an end. All that I need you appear to possess. Other proofs are secondary to this. I know with whom I have to deal. What do you demand for that certificate?"

"We will talk about the matter after breakfast," said Turpin. "I wish to treat with you as friend with friend. Meet me on those terms, and I am your man; reject my offer, and I turn my mare's head, and ride back to Rookwood. With me now rest all your hopes. I have dealt fairly with you, and I expect to be fairly dealt with in return. It were idle to say, now I have an opportunity, that I should not turn this luck to my account. I were a fool to do otherwise. You cannot expect it. And then I have Rust and Wilder to settle with. Though I have left them behind, they know my destination. We have been old associates. I like your spirit—I care not for your haughtiness; but I will not help you up the ladder to be kicked down myself. Now you understand me. Whither are you bound?"

"To Davenham Priory, the gipsy camp."

"The gipsies are your friends?"

"They are."

"I am alone."

"You are safe."

"You pledge your word that all shall be on the square. You will not mention to one of that canting crew what I have told you?"

"With one exception, you may rely upon my secrecy."

"Whom do you except?"

"A woman."

"Bad! never trust a petticoat."

"I will answer for her with my life."

"And for your granddad there?"

"He will answer for himself," said Peter. "You need not fear treachery in me. Honour among thieves, you know."

"Or where else should you seek it?" rejoined Turpin; "for it has left all other classes of society. Your highwayman is your only man of honour. I will trust you both; and you shall find you may trust me. After breakfast, as I said before, we will bring the matter to a conclusion. Tip us your daddle, Sir Luke, and I am satisfied. You shall rule in Rookwood, I'll engage, ere a week be flown; and then—but so much parleying is dull work; let's make the best of our way to breakfast."

And away they cantered.

A narrow bridle-road conducted them singly through the defiles of a thick wood. Their route lay in the shade, and the air felt chilly amidst the trees, the sun not having attained sufficient altitude to penetrate its depths, while overhead all was warmth and light. Quivering on the tops of the timber, the horizontal sunbeams created, in their refraction, brilliant prismatic colourings, and filled the air with motes like golden dust. Our horsemen heeded not the sunshine or the shade. Occupied each with his own train of thought, they silently rode on.

Davenham Wood, through which they urged their course, had, in the olden time, been a forest of some extent. It was then an appendage to the domains of Rookwood, but had passed from the hands of that family to those of a wealthy adjoining landowner and lawyer, Sir Edward Davenham, in the keeping of whose descendants it had ever after continued. A noble wood it was, and numbered many patriarchal trees. Ancient oaks, with broad gnarled limbs, which the storms of five hundred years had vainly striven to uproot, and which were now sternly decaying; gigantic beech-trees, with silvery stems shooting smoothly upwards, sustaining branches of such size, that each, dissevered, would in itself have formed a tree, populous with leaves, and variegated with rich autumnal tints; the sprightly sycamore, the dark chestnut, the weird wych-elm, the majestic elm itself, festooned with ivy, every variety of wood, dark, dense, and intricate, composed the forest through which they rode; and so multitudinous was the timber, so closely planted, so entirely filled up with a thick matted vegetation, which had been allowed to collect beneath, that little view was afforded, had any been desired by the parties, into the labyrinth of the grove. Tree after tree, clad in the glowing livery of the season, was passed, and as rapidly succeeded by others. Occasionally a bough projected over their path, compelling the riders to incline their heads as they passed; but, heedless of such difficulties, they pressed on.

Now the road grew lighter, and they became at once sensible of the genial influence of the sun. The transition was as agreeable as instantaneous. They had opened upon an extensive plantation of full-grown pines, whose tall, branchless stems grew up like a forest of masts, and freely admitted the pleasant sunshine. Beneath those trees, the soil was sandy and destitute of all undergrowth, though covered with brown, hair-like fibres and dry cones, shed by the pines. The agile squirrel, that freest denizen of the grove, starting from the ground as the horsemen galloped on, sprang up the nearest tree, and might be seen angrily gazing at the disturbers of his haunts, beating the branches with his fore-feet, in expression of displeasure; the rabbit darted across their path; the jays flew screaming amongst the foliage; the blue cushat, scared at the clatter of the horses' hoofs, sped on swift wing into quarters secure from their approach; while the parti-coloured pies, like curious village gossips, congregated to peer at the strangers, expressing their astonishment by loud and continuous chattering. Though so gentle of ascent as to be almost imperceptible, it was still evident that the path they were pursuing gradually mounted a hill-side; and when at length they reached an opening, the view disclosed the eminence they had insensibly won. Pausing for a moment upon the brow of the hill, Luke pointed to a stream that wound through the valley, and, tracing its course, indicated a particular spot amongst the trees. There was no appearance of a dwelling house; no cottage roof, no white canvas shed, to point out the tents of the wandering tribe whose abode they were seeking. The only circumstance betokening that it had once been the haunt of man, were a few grey monastic ruins, scarce distinguishable from the stony barrier by which they were surrounded; and the sole evidence that it was still frequented by human beings was a thin column of pale blue smoke, that arose in curling wreaths from out the brake, the light-coloured vapour beautifully contrasting with the green umbrage whence it issued.

"Our destination is yonder," exclaimed Luke, pointing in the direction of the vapour.

"I am glad to hear it," cried Turpin, "as well as to perceive there is some one awake. That smoke holds out a prospect of breakfast. No smoke without fire, as old Lady Scanmag said; and I'll wager a trifle that fire was not lighted for the fayter fellows to count their fingers by. We shall find three sticks, and a black pot with a kid seething in it, I'll engage. These gipsies have picked out a prettyish spot to quarter in—quite picturesque, as one may say—and but for that tell-tale smoke, which looks for all the world like a Dutch skipper blowing his morning cloud, no one need know of their vicinity. A pretty place, upon my soul."

The spot, in sooth, merited Turpin's eulogium. It was a little valley, in the midst of wooded hills, so secluded, that not a single habitation appeared in view. Clothed with timber to the very summits, excepting on the side where the party stood, which verged upon the declivity, these mountainous ridges presented a broken outline of foliage, variegated with tinted masses of bright orange, umber, and deepest green. Four hills hemmed in the valley. Here and there, a grey slab of rock might be discerned amongst the wood, and a mountain-ash figured conspicuously upon a jutting crag immediately below them. Deep sunken in the ravine, and concealed in part from view by the wild herbage and dwarf shrubs, ran a range of precipitous rocks, severed, it would seem, by some diluvial convulsion, from the opposite mountain side, as a corresponding rift was there visible, in which the same dip of strata might be observed, together with certain ribbed cavities, matching huge bolts of rocks which had once locked these stony walls together. Washing this cliff, swept a clear stream, well known and well regarded, as it waxed in width, by the honest brethren of the angle, who seldom, however, tracked it to its rise amongst these hills. The stream found its way into the valley through a chasm far to the left, and rushed thundering down the mountain

side in a boiling cascade. The valley was approached in this
direction from Rookwood by an unfrequented carriage-road,
which Luke had, from prudential reasons, avoided. All
seemed consecrated to silence—to solitude—to the hush of
nature; yet this quiet scene was the chosen retreat of lawless
depredators, and had erstwhile been the theatre of feudal
oppression. We have said that no habitation was visible;
that no dwelling tenanted by man could be seen; but following the spur of the furthest mountain hill, some traces of a
stone wall might be discovered; and upon a natural platform
of rock stood a stern square tower, which had once been the
donjon of the castle, the lords of which had called the four
hills their own. A watch-tower then had crowned each eminence, every vestige of which had, however, long since disappeared. Sequestered in the vale, stood the priory before
alluded to (a monastery of Grey Friars, of the order of St.
Francis), some of the venerable walls of which were still
remaining; and if they had not reverted to the bat and owl,
as is wont to be the fate of such sacred structures, their
cloistered shrines were devoted to beings whose nature partook, in some measure, of the instincts of those creatures of
the night—a people whose deeds were of darkness, and whose
eyes shunned the light. Here the gipsies had pitched their
tent; and though the place was often, in part, deserted by
the vagrant horde, yet certain of the tribe, who had grown
into years (over whom Barbara Lovel held queenly sway),
made it their haunt, and were suffered, by the authorities of
the neighbourhood, to remain unmolested—a lenient piece of
policy, which, in our infinite regard for the weal of the tawny
tribe, we recommend to the adoption of all other justices and
knights of the shire.

Bidding his grandsire have regard to his seat, Luke leaped
a high bank; and, followed by Turpin, began to descend the
hill. Peter, however, took care to provide for himself. The
descent was so perilous, and the footing so insecure, that he
chose rather to trust to such conveyance as nature had furnished him with, than to hazard his neck by any false step of
the horse. He contrived, therefore, to slide off from behind,
shaping his own course in a more secure direction.

He who has wandered amidst the Alps must have often had
occasion to witness the wonderful surefootedness of that
mountain pilot, the mule. He must have remarked how,
with tenacious hoof, he will claw the rock, and drag himself
from one impending fragment to another, with perfect security

to his rider; how he will breast the roaring currents of air, and stand unshrinking at the verge of almost unfathomable ravines. But it is not so with the horse: fleet on the plain, careful over rugged ground, he is timid and uncertain on the hill-side, and the risk incurred by Luke and Turpin, in their descent of the almost perpendicular sides of the cliff, was tremendous. Peter watched them in their descent, with some admiration, and with much contempt.

"He will break his neck, of a surety," said he; "but what matters it? As well now as hereafter."

So saying, he approached the verge of the precipice, where he could see them more distinctly.

The passage along which Luke rode had never before been traversed by horse's hoof. Cut in the rock, it presented a steep zigzag path amongst the cliffs, without any defence for the foot traveller, except such as was afforded by a casual clinging shrub, and no protection whatever existed for a horseman; the possibility of any one attempting the passage not having, in all probability, entered into the calculation of those who framed it. Added to this, the steps were of such unequal heights, and withal so narrow, that the danger was proportionately increased.

"Ten thousand devils!" cried Turpin, staring downwards, "is this the best road you have got?"

"You will find one more easy," replied Luke, "if you ride for a quarter of a mile down the wood, and then return by the brook side. You will meet me at the priory."

"No," answered the highwayman, boldly; "if you go, I go too. It shall never be said that Dick Turpin was afraid to follow where another would lead. Proceed."

Luke gave his horse the bridle, and the animal slowly and steadily commenced the descent, fixing his forelegs upon the steps, and drawing his hinder limbs carefully after him. Here it was that the lightness and steadiness of Turpin's mare was completely shown. No Alpine mule could have borne its rider with more apparent ease and safety. Turpin encouraged her by hand and word; but she needed it not. The sexton saw them, and, tracking their giddy descent, he became more interested than he anticipated. His attention was suddenly drawn towards Luke.

"He is gone," cried Peter. "He falls—he sinks—my plans are all defeated—the last link is snapped. No," added he, recovering his wonted composure, "his end is not so fated."

Rook had missed his footing. He rolled stumbling down the precipice a few yards. Luke's fate seemed inevitable. His feet were entangled in the stirrup, he could not free himself. A birch-tree, growing in a chink of the precipice, arrested his further fall. But for this timely aid all had been over. Here Luke was enabled to extricate himself from the stirrup, and to regain his feet; seizing the bridle, he dragged his faulty steed back again to the road.

"You have had a narrow escape, by Jove," said Turpin, who had been thunderstruck with the whole proceeding. "Those big cattle are always clumsy; devilish lucky it's no worse."

It was now comparatively smooth travelling; but they had not as yet reached the valley, and it seemed to be Luke's object to take a circuitous path. This was so evident, that Turpin could not help commenting upon it.

Luke evaded the question. "The crag is steep there," said he; "besides, to tell you the truth, I want to surprise them."

"Ho, ho!" laughed Dick. "Surprise them, eh? What a pity the birch-tree was in the way; you would have done it properly then. Egad, here's another surprise."

Dick's last exclamation was caused by his having suddenly come upon a wide gully in the rock, through which dashed a headlong torrent, crossed by a single plank.

"You must be mad to have taken this road," cried Turpin, gazing down into the roaring depths in which the waterfall raged, and measuring the distance of the pass with his eye. "So, so, Bess!—Ay, look at it, wench. Curse me, Luke, if I think your horse will do it; and, therefore, turn him loose."

But Dick might as well have bidden the cataract to flow backwards. Luke struck his heels into his horse's sides. The steed galloped to the brink, snorted, and refused to leap.

"I told you so—he can't do it," said Turpin. "Well, if you are obstinate, a wilful man must have his way. Stand aside, while I try it for you." Patting Bess, he put her to a gallop. She cleared the gulf bravely, landing her rider safely upon the opposite rock.

"Now then," cried Turpin, from the other side of the chasm.

Luke again urged his steed. Encouraged by what he had seen, this time the horse sprang across without hesitation. The next instant they were in the valley.

For some time they rode along the banks of the stream

in silence. A sound at length caught the quick ears of the highwayman.

"Hist!" cried he; "some one sings. Do you hear it?"

"I do," replied Luke, the blood rushing to his cheeks.

"And could give a guess at the singer, no doubt," said Turpin, with a knowing look. "Was it to hear yon woodlark that you nearly broke your own neck, and put mine in jeopardy?"

"Prithee, be silent," whispered Luke.

"I am dumb," replied Turpin; "I like a sweet voice as well as another."

Clear as the note of a bird, yet melancholy as the distant dole of a vesper-bell, arose the sound of that sweet voice from the wood. A fragment of a Spanish gipsy song it warbled: Luke knew it well. Thus ran the romance:

LA GITANILLA.*

By the Guadalquivir,
　Ere the sun be flown,
By that glorious river
　Sits a maid alone.
Like the sunset splendour
　Of that current bright,
Shone her dark eyes tender
　As its witching light;
Like the ripple flowing,
　Tinged with purple sheen,
Darkly, richly glowing,
　Is her warm cheek seen.
　　'Tis the Gitanilla
　　　By the stream doth linger,
　　In the hope that eve
　　　Will her lover bring her.

See, the sun is sinking;
　All grows dim, and dies;
See, the waves are drinking
　Glories of the skies.
Day's last lustre playeth
　On that current dark;
Yet no speck betrayeth
　His long looked-for bark.
'Tis the hour of meeting!
　Nay, the hour is past;
Swift the time is fleeting!
　Fleeteth hope as fast?
　　Still the Gitanilla
　　　By the stream doth linger,
　　In the hope that night
　　　Will her lover bring her.

The tender trembling of a guitar was heard in accompaniment of the ravishing melodist.

The song ceased.

"Where is the bird?" asked Turpin.

"Move on in silence, and you shall see," said Luke; and, keeping upon the turf, so that his horse's tread became inaudible, he presently arrived at a spot where, through the boughs, the object of his investigation could plainly be distinguished, though he himself was concealed from view.

Upon a platform of rock, rising to the height of the trees, nearly perpendicularly from the river's bed, appeared the figure of the gipsy maid. Her footstep rested on the extreme edge of the abrupt cliff, at whose base the water boiled in a

---

* Set to music by Mr. F. Romer.

deep whirlpool, and the bounding chamois could not have
been more lightly poised. One small hand rested upon her
guitar, the other pressed her brow. Braided hair, of the
jettest die and sleekest texture, was twined around her brow,
in endless twisted folds:

> Rowled it was in many a curious fret,
> Much like a rich and curious coronet,
> Upon whose arches twenty Cupids lay,
> And were as tied, or loth to fly away.

And so exuberant was this rarest feminine ornament, that,
after encompassing her brow, it was passed behind, and hung
down in long thick plaits almost to her feet. Sparkling as
the sunbeams that played upon her dark yet radiant features,
were the large black, Oriental eyes of the maiden, and shaded
with lashes long and silken. Hers was a Moorish countenance, in which the magnificence of the eyes eclipses the face,
be it ever so beautiful (an effect to be observed in many of
the paintings of Murillo), and the lovely contour is scarcely
noticed in the gaze which those long, languid, luminous orbs
attract. Sybil's features were exquisite, yet you looked only
at her eyes—they were the loadstars of her countenance.
Her costume was singular, and partook, like herself, of other
climes. Like the Andalusian dame, her choice of colour inclined towards black, as the material of most of her dress
was of that sombre hue. A bodice of embroidered velvet
restrained her delicate bosom's swell; a rich girdle, from
which depended a silver chain, sustaining a short poniard,
bound her waist; around her slender throat was twined a
costly kerchief; and the rest of her dress was calculated to
display her slight, yet faultless, figure to the fullest advantage.

Unconscious that she was the object of regard, she raised
her guitar, and essayed to touch the chords. She struck a
few notes, and resumed her romance:

> Swift that stream flows on,
> Swift the night is wearing,—
> Yet she is not gone,
> Though with heart despairing.

Her song died away. Her hand was needed to brush off
the tears that were gathering in her large dark eyes. At
once her attitude was changed. The hare could not have
started more suddenly from her form. She heard accents
well known concluding the melody:

Dips an oar-plash—hark !—
 Gently on the river ;
'Tis her lover's bark,
 On the Guadalquivir.
Hark ! a song she hears !
 Every note she snatches.
As the singer nears,
 Her own name she catches.
  Now the Gitanilla
   Stays not by the water,
  For the midnight hour
   Hath her lover brought her.

It was her lover's voice. She caught the sound at once, and, starting, as the roe would arouse herself at the hunter's approach, bounded down the crag, and ere he had finished the refrain, was by his side.

Flinging the bridle to Turpin, Luke sprang to her, and caught her in his arms. Disengaging herself from his ardent embrace, Sybil drew back, abashed at the sight of the highwayman.

"Heed him not," said Luke ; "it is a friend."

"He is welcome here, then," replied Sybil. "But where have you tarried so long, dear Luke ?" continued she, as they walked to a little distance from the highwayman. "What hath detained you ? The hours have passed wearily since you departed. You bring good news ?"

"Good news, my girl ; so good, that I falter even in the telling of it. You shall know all anon. And see, our friend yonder grows impatient. Are there any stirring ? We must bestow a meal upon him, and that forthwith : he is one of those who brook not much delay."

"I came not to spoil a love meeting," said Turpin, who had good-humouredly witnessed the scene ; "but, in sober seriousness, if there is a stray capon to be met with in the land of Egypt, I shall be glad to make his acquaintance. Methinks I scent a stew afar off."

"Follow me," said Sybil ; "your wants shall be supplied."

"Stay," said Luke ; "there is one other of our party, whose coming we must abide."

"He is here," said Sybil, observing the sexton at a distance. "Who is that old man ?"

"My grandsire, Peter Bradley."

"Is that Peter Bradley ?" asked Sybil.

"Ay, you may well ask whether that old dried-up otomy, who ought to grin in a glass case for folks to stare at, be kith and kin of such a bang-up cove as your fancy man, Luke," said Turpin, laughing—"but i'faith he is."

M

"Though he is your grandsire, Luke," said Sybil, "I like him not. His glance resembles that of the Evil Eye."

And, in fact, the look which Peter fixed upon her was such as the rattlesnake casts upon its victim, and Sybil felt like a poor fluttering bird under the fascination of that venomous reptile. She could not remove her eyes from his, though she trembled as she gazed. We have said that Peter's orbs were like those of the toad. Age had not dimmed their brilliancy. In his harsh features you could only read bitter scorn or withering hate; but in his eyes resided a magnetic influence of attraction or repulsion. Sybil underwent the former feeling in a disagreeable degree. She was drawn to him as by the motion of a whirlpool, and involuntarily clung to her lover.

"It is the Evil Eye," dear Luke.

"Tut, tut, dear Sybil; I tell you it is my grandsire."

"The girl says rightly, however," rejoined Turpin; "Peter has a confounded ugly look about the ogles, and stares enough to put a modest wench out of countenance. Come, come, my old earthworm, crawl along; we have waited for you long enough. Is this the first time you have seen a pretty lass, eh?"

"It is the first time I have seen one so beautiful," said Peter; "and I crave your pardon if my freedom has offended her. I wonder not at your enchantment, grandson Luke, now I behold the object of it. But there is one piece of council I would give to this fair maid. The next time she trusts you from her sight, I would advise her to await you at the hill-top, otherwise the chances are shrewdly against your reaching the ground with neck unbroken."

There was something, notwithstanding the satirical manner in which Peter delivered this speech, calculated to make a more favourable impression upon Sybil than his previous conduct had inspired her with; and, having ascertained from Luke to what his speech referred, she extended her hand to him, yet not without a shudder, as it was enclosed in his skinny grasp. It was like the fingers of Venus in the grasp of a skeleton.

"This is a little hand," said Peter, "and I have some skill myself in palmistry. Shall I peruse its lines?"

"Not now, in the devil's name!" said Turpin, stamping impatiently. "We shall have Old Ruffin himself amongst us presently, if Peter Bradley grows gallant."

Leading their horses, the party took their way through the

trees. A few minutes' walking brought them in sight of the
gipsy encampment, the spot selected for which might be
termed the Eden of the valley. It was a small green plain,
smooth as a well-shorn lawn, kept ever verdant (save in such
places as the frequent fires had scorched its surface) by the
flowing stream that rushed past it, and surrounded by an
amphitheatre of wooded hills. Here might be seen the
canvas tent with its patches of varied colouring; the rude-
fashioned hut of primitive construction; the kettle slung

> Between two poles, upon a stick transverse;

the tethered beasts of burden, the horses, asses, dogs, carts,
caravans, wains, blocks, and other movables and immovables
belonging to the wandering tribe. Glimmering through the
trees, at the extremity of the plain, appeared the ivy-mantled
walls of Davenham Priory. Though much had gone to
decay, enough remained to recal the pristine state of this
once majestic pile, and the long, though broken line of Saxon
arches, that still marked the cloister wall; the piers that yet
supported the dormitory; the enormous horse-shoe arch that
spanned the court; and, above all, the great marigold, or
circular window, which terminated the chapel, and which,
though now despoiled of its painted honours, retained, like
the skeleton leaf, its fibrous intricacies entire,—all eloquently
spoke of the glories of the past, while they awakened reverence and admiration for the still-enduring beauty of the
present.

Towards these ruins Sybil conducted the party.

"Do you dwell therein?" asked Peter, pointing towards
the priory.

"That is my dwelling," said Sybil.

"It is one I should covet more than a modern mansion,"
returned the sexton.

"I love those old walls better than any house that was
ever fashioned," replied Sybil.

As they entered the Prior's Close, as it was called, several
swarthy figures made their appearance from the tents. Many
a greeting was bestowed upon Luke, in the wild jargon of the
tribe. At length an uncouth dwarfish figure, with a shock
head of black hair, hopped towards them. He seemed to
acknowledge Luke as his master.

"What, ho! Grasshopper," said Luke; "take these horses,
and see that they lack neither dressing nor provender."

"And hark ye, Grasshopper," added Turpin; "I give you

a special charge about this mare. Neither dress nor feed her till I see both done myself. Just walk her for ten minutes, and if you have a glass of ale in the place, let her sip it."

"Your bidding shall be done," chirped the human insect, as he fluttered away with his charges.

A motley assemblage of tawny-skinned varlets, dark-eyed women and children, whose dusky limbs betrayed their lineage, in strange costume, and of wild deportment, checked the path, muttering welcome upon welcome into the ear of Luke as he passed. As it was evident he was in no mood for converse, Sybil, who seemed to exercise considerable authority over the crew, with a word dispersed them, and they herded back to their respective habitations.

A low door admitted Luke and his companions into what had once been the garden, in which some old moss-encrusted apple and walnut trees were still standing, bearing a look of antiquity almost as venerable as that of the adjoining fabric.

Another open door gave them entrance to a spacious chamber, formerly the eating-room, or refectory of the holy brotherhood; and a goodly room it had been, though now its slender lancolated windows were stuffed with hay, to keep out the air. Large holes told where huge oaken rafters had once crossed the roof, and a yawning aperture marked the place where a cheering fire had formerly blazed. As regarded this latter spot, the good old custom was not even now totally abrogated. An iron plate, covered with crackling wood, sustained a ponderous black caldron, the rich steam from which gratefully affected the olfactory organs of the highwayman.

"That augurs well," said he, rubbing his hands.

"Still hungering after the fleshpots of Egypt," said the sexton, with a ghastly smile.

"We will see what that kettle contains," said Luke.

"Handassah—Grace!" exclaimed Sybil, calling.

Her summons was answered by two maidens, habited, not unbecomingly, in gipsy gear.

"Bring the best our larder can furnish," said Sybil, "and use despatch. You have appetites to provide for sharpened by a long ride in the open air."

"And by a night's fasting," said Luke, "and solitary confinement to boot."

"And a night of business," added Turpin, "and plaguing, perplexing business into the bargain."

"And the night of a funeral, too," doled Peter; "and that funeral a father's. Let us have breakfast speedily, by all means. We have rare appetites."

An old oaken table (it might have been the self-same upon which the holy friars had broken their morning fast) stood in the middle of the room. The ample board soon groaned beneath the weight of the savoury caldron, the unctuous contents of which proved to be a couple of dismembered pheasants, an equal proportion of poultry, great gouts of ham, mushrooms, onions, and other piquant condiments, so satisfactory to Dick Turpin, that, upon tasting a mouthful, he absolutely shed tears of delight. The dish was indeed the triumph of gipsy cookery; and so sedulously did Dick apply himself to his mess, and so complete was his abstraction, that he perceived not he was left alone. It was only when about to wash down the last drumstick of the last fowl with a can of excellent ale that he made this discovery.

"What! all gone? And Peter Bradley, too? What the devil does this mean?" mused he. "I must not muddle my brain with any more Pharaoh, though I have feasted like a king of Egypt. That will never do. Caution, Dick, caution. Suppose I shift yon brick from the wall, and place this precious document beneath it. Pshaw! Luke would never play me false. And now for Bess! Bless her black skin! she'll wonder where I've been so long. It's not my way to leave her to shift for herself, though she can do that on a pinch."

Soliloquizing thus, he arose and walked towards the door.

III.

SYBIL.

The waving vine, that round the friendly elm
Twines her soft limbs, and weaves a leafy mantle
For her supporting lover, dares not venture
To mix her humble boughs with the embraces
Of the more lofty cedar.
        ALBERTUS WALLENSTEIN.—*Glapthorne.*

BENEATH a mouldering wall, whither they had strayed, to be free from interruption, and upon a carpet of the greenest moss, sat Sybil and her lover.

With eager curiosity she listened to his tale. He recounted all that had befallen him since his departure. He told her

of the awful revelations of the tomb ; of the ring that, like a
talisman, had conjured up a thousand brilliant prospects ; of
his subsequent perils ; his escapes ; his rencontre with Lady
Rookwood ; his visit to his father's body ; and his meeting
with his brother. All this she heard with a cheek now
flushed with expectation, now made pale with apprehension ;
with palpitating bosom, and suppressed breath. But when
taking a softer tone, love, affection, happiness, inspired the
theme, and Luke sought to paint the bliss that should be
theirs in his new estate ; when he would throw his fortune
into her lap, his titles at her feet, and bid her wear them
with him ; when, with ennobled hand and unchanged heart,
he would fulfil the troth plighted in his outcast days ; in lieu
of tender, grateful acquiescence, the features of Sybil became
overcast, the soft smile faded away, and, as spring sunshine
is succeeded by the sudden shower, the light that dwelt in
her sunny orbs grew dim with tears.

"Why—why is this, dear Sybil?" said Luke, gazing upon
her in astonishment, not unmingled with displeasure. "To
what am I to attribute these tears? You do not, surely,
regret my good fortune?"

"Not on your own account, dear Luke," returned she,
sadly. "The tears I shed were for myself—the first, the only
tears that I have ever shed for such cause ; and," added she,
raising her head like a flower surcharged with moisture,
"they shall be the last."

"This is inexplicable, dear Sybil. Why should you lament
for yourself, if not for me? Does not the sunshine of prosperity that now shines upon me gild you with the same
beam? Did I not even now affirm that the day that saw
me enter the hall of my forefathers should dawn upon our
espousals?"

"True ; but the sun that shines upon you, to me wears a
threatening aspect. The day of those espousals will never
dawn. You cannot make me the lady of Rookwood."

"What do I hear?" exclaimed Luke, surprised at this
avowal of his mistress, sadly and deliberately delivered.
"Not wed you! And wherefore not? Is it the rank I have
acquired, or hope to acquire, that displeases you? Speak,
that I may waste no further time in thus pursuing the shadows of happiness, while the reality fleets from me."

"And *are* they shadows ; and *is* this the reality, dear
Luke? Question your secret soul, and you will find it other-

wise. You could not forego your triumph; it is not likely. You have dwelt too much upon the proud title which will be yours to yield it to another, when it may be won so easily. And, above all, when your mother's reputation, and your own stained name, may be cleared by one word, breathed aloud, would you fail to utter it? No, dear Luke, I read your heart; you would not."

"And if I could *not* forego this, wherefore is it that you refuse to be a sharer in my triumph? Why will you render my honours valueless when I have acquired them? You love me not."

"Not love you, Luke?"

"Approve it, then."

"I do approve it. Bear witness the sacrifice I am about to make of all my hopes, at the shrine of my idolatry to you. Bear witness the agony of this hour. Bear witness the horror of the avowal, that I never can be yours. As Luke Bradley, I would joyfully—oh, how joyfully!—have been your bride. As Sir Luke Rookwood"—and she shuddered as she pronounced the name—"I never can be so."

"Then, by Heaven! Luke Bradley will I remain. But wherefore—wherefore not as Sir Luke Rookwood?"

"Because," replied Sybil, with reluctance—"because I am no longer your equal. The gipsy's low-born daughter is no mate for Sir Luke Rookwood. Love cannot blind me, dear Luke. It cannot make me other than I am; it cannot exalt me in my own esteem, nor in that of the world, with which you, alas! too soon will mingle, and which will regard even me as—no matter what!—it shall not scorn me as your bride. I will not bring shame and reproach upon you. Oh! if for me, dear Luke, the proud ones of the earth were to treat you with contumely, this heart would break with agony. For myself, I have pride sufficient—perchance too much. Perchance 'tis pride that actuates me now. I know not. But for you I am all weakness. As you were heretofore, I would have been to you the tenderest and truest wife that ever breathed; as you are now——"

"Hear me, Sybil."

"Hear *me* out, dear Luke. One other motive there is that determines my present conduct, which, were all else surmounted, would in itself suffice. Ask me not what that is. I cannot explain it. For your own sake, I implore you, be satisfied with my refusal."

"What a destiny is mine!" exclaimed Luke, striking his forehead with his clenched hand. "No choice is left me. Either way I destroy my own happiness. On the one hand stands love—on the other ambition; yet neither will conjoin."

"Pursue, then, ambition," said Sybil, energetically, "if you can hesitate. Forget that I have ever existed; forget you have ever loved; forget that such a passion dwells within the human heart, and you may still be happy, though you are great."

"And do you deem," replied Luke, with frantic impatience, "that I can accomplish this; that I can forget that I have loved you; that I can forget you? Cost what it will the effort shall be made. Yet by our former love, I charge you tell me what has wrought this change in you? Why do you now refuse me?"

"I have said you are Sir Luke Rookwood," returned Sybil, with painful emotion. "Does that name import nothing?"

"Imports it aught of ill?"

"To me, everything of ill. It is a fated house. Its line are all predestined."

"To what?" demanded Luke.

"To murder!" replied Sybil, with solemn emphasis. "To the murder of their wives. Forgive me, Luke, if I have dared to utter this. Yourself compelled me to it."

Amazement, horror, wrath, kept Luke silent for a few moments. Starting to his feet, he cried:

"And can you suspect me of a crime so foul? Think you, because I shall assume the name, that I shall put on the nature likewise of my race? Do you believe me capable of aught so horrible?"

"Oh, no, I believe it not. I am sure you would not do it. Your soul would reject with horror such a deed. But if Fate should guide your hand, if the avenging spirit of your murdered ancestress should point the steel, you could not shun it then."

"In Heaven's name! to what do you allude?"

"To a tradition of your house," replied Sybil. "Listen to me, and you shall hear the legend." And with a pathos that produced a thrilling effect upon Luke, she sang the following ballad:

THE LEGEND OF THE LADY OF ROOKWOOD.

Grim Ranulph home hath at midnight come, from the long wars of the Roses,
And the squire, who waits at his ancient gates, a secret dark discloses;
To that varlet's words no response accords his lord, but his visage stern
Grows ghastly white in the wan moonlight, and his eyes like the lean wolf's
    burn.

To his lady's bower, at that lonesome hour, unannounced, is Sir Ranulph
    gone:
Through the dim corridor, through the hidden door he glides—she is all
    alone!
Full of holy zeal doth this young dame kneel at the meek Madonna's feet,
Her hands are pressed on her gentle breast, and upturned is her aspect sweet.

Beats Ranulph's heart with a joyful start, as he looks on her guiltless face;
And the raging fire of his jealous ire is subdued by the words of grace;
His own name shares her murmured prayers—more freely can he breathe;
But ah! that look! Why doth he pluck his poniard from its sheath?

On a footstool thrown lies a costly gown of saye and of minevere
(A mantle fair for the dainty wear of a migniard cavalier),
And on it flung, to a bracelet hung, a picture meets his eye;
"By my father's head," grim Ranulph said, "false wife, thy end draws
    nigh."

From off its chain hath the fierce knight ta'en that fond and fatal pledge;
His dark eyes blaze, no word he says, thrice gleams his dagger's edge!
Her blood it drinks, and, as she sinks, his victim hears his cry,
"For kiss impure of paramour, adult'ress, dost thou die."

Silent he stood, with hands embrued in gore, and glance of flame,
As thus her plaint, in accents faint, made his ill-fated dame:
"Kind Heaven can tell, that all too well, I've loved thee, cruel lord;
But now with hate commensurate, assassin, thou'rt abhorred.

"I've loved thee long, through doubt and wrong; I've loved thee, and no
    other;
And my love was pure for my paramour, for alas! he was my brother!
The Red, Red Rose, on thy banner glows, on his pennon gleams the White,
And the bitter feud, that ye both have rued, forbids ye to unite.

"My bower he sought, what time he thought thy jealous vassals slept,
Of joy we dreamed, and never deemed that watch those vassals kept;
An hour flew by, too speedily!—that picture was his boon:
Ah! little thrift to me that gift: he left me all too soon!

"Wo worth the hour! dark fates did lower, when our hands were first
    united,
For my heart's firm truth, 'mid tears and ruth, with death hast thou
    requited:
In prayer sincere, full many a year of my wretched life I've spent;
But to hell's control would I give my soul, to work thy chastisement!"

These wild words said, low drooped her head, and Ranulph's life-blood froze,
For the earth did gape, as an awful shape from out its depths arose:
"Thy prayer is heard, Hell hath concurred," cried the fiend, "thy soul is
    mine!
Like fate may dread each dame shall wed with Ranulph or his line!"

Within the tomb to await her doom is that hapless lady sleeping,
And another bride by Ranulph's side through the livelong night is weeping.
This dame declines—a third repines, and fades, like the rest, away;
Her lot she rues, whom a Rookwood woos—cursed is her Wedding Day!

"And this is the legend of my ancestress?" said Luke, as Sybil's strains were ended.

"It is," replied she.

"An idle tale," observed Luke, moodily.

"Not so," answered Sybil. "Has not the curse of blood clung to all your line? Has it not attached to your father—to Sir Reginald—Sir Ralph—Sir Ranulph—to all? Which of them has escaped it? And when I tell you this, dear Luke; when I find you bear the name of this accursed race, can you wonder if I shudder at adding to the list of the victims of that ruthless spirit, and that I tremble for you? I would die *for* you willingly—but not by your hand. I would not that my blood, which I would now pour out for you as freely as water, should rise up in judgment against you. For myself I have no fears—for *you* a thousand. My mother, upon her deathbed, told me I should never be yours. I believed her not, for I was happy then. She said that we never should be united; or, if united——"

"What, in Heaven's name?"

"That you would be my destroyer; that your love should turn to hatred; that you would slay me. How could I credit her words then? How can I doubt them now, when I find you are a Rookwood? And think not, dear Luke, that I am ruled by selfish fears in this resolution. To renounce you may cost me my life; but the deed will be my own. You may call me superstitious, credulous; I have been nurtured in credulity. It is the faith of my fathers. There are those, methinks, who have an insight into futurity; and such boding words have been spoken, that, be they true or false, I will not risk their fulfilment in my person. I may be credulous; I may be weak; I may be erring; but I am steadfast in this. Bid me perish at your feet, and I will do it. I will not be your Fate. I will not be the wretched instrument of your perdition. I will love, worship, watch, serve, perish for you —but I will not wed you."

Exhausted by the vehemence of her emotion, she would have sunk upon the ground, had not Luke caught her in his arms. Pressing her to his bosom, he renewed his passionate protestations. Every argument was unavailing. Sybil appeared inflexible.

"You love me as you have ever loved me?" said she, at length

"A thousand-fold more fervently," replied Luke; "put it to the test."

"How if I dared to do so? Consider well: I may ask too much."

"Name it. If it be not to surrender you, by my mother's body I will obey you."

"I would propose an oath."

"Ha!"

"A solemn, binding oath, that, if you wed me not, you will not wed another. Ha! do you start? Have I appalled you?"

"I start? I will take it. Hear me—by——"

"Hold!" exclaimed a voice behind them. "Do not forswear yourself." And immediately afterwards the sexton made his appearance. There was a malignant smile upon his countenance. The lovers started at the ominous interruption.

"Begone!" cried Luke.

"Take not that oath," said Peter, "and I leave you. Remember the counsel I gave you on our way hither."

"What counsel did he give you, Luke?" inquired Sybil, eagerly, of her lover.

"We spoke of you, fond girl," replied Peter. "I cautioned him against the match. I knew not your sentiments, or I had spared myself the trouble. You have judged wisely. Were he to wed you, ill would come of it. But he *must* wed another."

"*Must!*" cried Sybil, her eyes absolutely emitting sparkles of indignation from their night-like depths; and, unsheathing as she spoke the short poniard which she wore at her girdle, she rushed towards Peter, raising her hand to strike. "*Must* wed another! And dare you counsel this?"

"Put up your dagger, fair maiden," said Peter, calmly. "Had I been younger, your eyes might have had more terrors for me than your weapon; as it is I am proof against both. You would not strike an old man like myself, and of your lover's kin?"

Sybil's uplifted hand fell to her side.

"'Tis true," continued the sexton, "I dared to give him this advice; and when you have heard me out, you will not, I am persuaded, think me so unreasonable as, at first, I may appear to be. I have been an unseen listener to your converse; not that I desire to pry into your secrets, far from it; I overheard you by accident. I applaud your resolution; but if you are inclined to sacrifice all for your lover's weal, do not let the work be incomplete. Bind him not by oaths

which he will regard as spiders' webs, to be burst through at
pleasure. You see, as well as I do, that he is bent on being
lord of Rookwood; and, in truth, to an aspiring mind, such
a desire is natural—is praiseworthy. It will be pleasant, as
well as honourable, to efface the stain cast upon his birth.
It will be an act of filial duty in him to restore his mother's
good name; and I, her father, laud his anxiety on that score;
though, to speak truth, fair maid, I am not so rigid as your
nice moralists in my view of human nature, and can allow a
latitude to love, which their nicer scruples will not admit.
It will be a proud thing to triumph over his implacable
foe; and this he may accomplish——"

"Without marriage," interrupted Sybil, angrily.

"True," returned Peter; "yet not maintain it. May win
it, but not wear it. You have said truly, the house of Rookwood is a fated house; and it hath been said likewise, that
if he wed not one of his own kindred—that if Rook mate not
with Rook, his possessions shall pass away from his hands.
Listen to this prophetic quatrain:

When the stray Rook shall perch on the topmost bough,
There shall be clamour and screeching. I trow;
But of right to. and rule of the ancient nest.
The Rock that with Rook mates shall hold him possest.

You hear what these quaint rhymes say. Luke, is, doubtless,
the stray rook, and a fledgling hath flown hither from a distant
country. He must take her to his mate, or relinquish her
and 'the ancient nest' to his brother. For my own part, I
disregard such sayings. I have little faith in prophecy and
divination. I know not what Eleanor Mowbray, for so she is
called, can have to do with the tenure of the estates of Rookwood. But if Luke Rookwood, after he has lorded it for a
while in splendour, be cast forth again in rags and wretchedness, let him not blame his grandsire for his own want of
caution."

"Luke, I implore you, tell me," said Sybil, who had listened, horror-stricken, to the sexton, shuddering, as it were,
beneath the chilly influence of his malevolent glance, "is
this true? Does your fate depend upon Eleanor Mowbray?
Who is she? What has she to do with Rookwood? Have
you seen her? Do you love her?"

"I have never seen her," replied Luke.

"Thank Heaven for that!" cried Sybil. "Then you love
her not?"

"How were that possible?" returned Luke. "Do I not say I have not seen her?"

"Who is she, then?"

"This old man tells me she is my cousin. She is betrothed to my brother, Ranulph."

"How?" ejaculated Sybil. "And would you snatch his betrothed from your brother's arms? Would you do him this grievous wrong? Is it not enough that you must wrest from him that which he has long deemed his own? And if he has falsely deemed it so, it will not make his loss the less bitter. If you do thus wrong your brother, do not look for happiness; do not look for respect; for neither will be your portion. Even this stony-hearted old man shrinks aghast at such a deed. His snake-like eyes are buried on the ground. See, I have moved even *him*."

And in truth Peter did appear, for an instant, strangely moved.

"'Tis nothing," returned he, mastering his emotion by strong effort. "What is all this to me? I never had a brother. I never had aught—wife, child, or relative, that loved me. And I love not the world, nor the things of the world, nor those that inhabit the world. But I know what sways the world and its inhabitants; and that is, SELF! AND SELF-INTEREST. Let Luke reflect on this. The key to Rookwood is Eleanor Mowbray. The hand that grasps hers, grasps those lands: thus saith the prophecy."

"It is a lying prophecy."

"It was uttered by one of your race."

"By whom?"

"By Barbara Lovel," said Peter, with a sneer of triumph.

"Ha!"

"Heed him not," exclaimed Luke, as Sybil recoiled at this intelligence. "I am yours."

"Not mine! not mine!" shrieked she; "but, oh! not *hers!*"

"Whither go you?" cried Luke, as Sybil, half-bewildered, tore herself from him.

"To Barbara Lovel."

"I will go with you."

"No! let me go alone. I have much to ask her; yet tarry not with this old man, dear Luke, or close your ears to his crafty talk. Avoid him. Oh, I am sick at heart. Follow me not; I implore you, follow me not."

And with distracted air she darted amongst the mouldering

cloisters, leaving Luke stupefied with anguish and surprise. The sexton maintained a stern and stoical composure.

"She is a woman, after all," muttered he; "all her high-flown resolves melt like snow in the sunshine, at the thought of a rival. I congratulate you, grandson Luke; you are free from your fetters."

"Free!" echoed Luke. "Quit my sight; I loathe to look upon you. You have broken the truest heart that ever beat in woman's bosom."

"Tut, tut," returned Peter; "it is not broken yet. Wait till we hear what old Barbara has got to say; and, meanwhile, we must arrange with Dick Turpin the price of that certificate. The knave knows its value well. Come, be a man. This is worse than womanish."

And at length he succeeded, half by force and half by persuasion, in dragging Luke away with him.

IV.

BARBARA LOVEL.

Los Gitanos son encantadores, adivinos, magos, chyromanticos, que dicen por las rayas de las manos lo Futuro, que ellos llaman Buenaventura, y generalmente son dados à toda superticion. DOCTOR SANCHO DE MONCADA.
Discurso sobre Expulsion de los Gitanos.

LIKE a dove escaped from the talons of the falcon, Sybil fled from the clutches of the sexton. Her brain was in a whirl, her blood on fire. She had no distinct perception of external objects; no definite notion of what she herself was about to do, and glided more like a flitting spirit than a living woman along the ruined ambulatory. Her hair had fallen in disorder over her face. She stayed not to adjust it, but tossed aside the blinding locks with frantic impatience. She felt as one may feel who tries to strain his nerves, shattered by illness, to the endurance of some dreadful, yet necessary pain.

Sybil loved her granddame, old Barbara; but it was with a love tempered by fear. Barbara was not a person to inspire esteem or to claim affection. She was regarded by the wild tribe which she ruled as their queen-elect, with some such feeling of inexplicable awe as is entertained by the African slave for the Obeah woman. They acknowledged her power, unhesitatingly obeyed her commands, and shrank with terror from her anathema, which was indeed seldom pronounced; but when uttered, was considered as doom. Her tribe she looked upon as her flock, and stretched her maternal hand over all, ready alike to cherish or chastise; and having already survived a generation, that which succeeded, having from infancy imbibed a superstitious veneration for the "cunning woman," as she was called, the sentiment could never be wholly effaced.

Winding her way, she knew not how, through roofless halls, over disjointed fragments of fallen pillars, Sybil reached a flight of steps. A door, studded with iron nails, stayed her progress; it was an old strong oaken frame, surmounted by a Gothic arch, in the keystone of which leered one of those grotesque demoniacal faces with which the fathers of the church delighted to adorn their shrines. Sybil looked up—her glance encountered the fantastical visage. It recalled the features of the sexton, and seemed to mock her—to revile her. Her fortitude at once deserted her. Her fingers were upon the handle of the door. She hesitated: she even drew back, with the intention of departing, for she felt then that she dare not face Barbara. It was too late—she had moved the handle. A deep voice from within called to her by name. She dared not disobey that call—she entered.

The room in which Sybil found herself was the only entire apartment now existing in the priory. It had survived the ravages of time; it had escaped the devastation of man, whose ravages outstrip those of time. Octagonal, lofty, yet narrow, you saw at once that it formed the interior of a turret. It was lighted by a small oriel window commanding a lovely view of the scenery around, and panelled with oak, richly wrought in ribs and groins; and from overhead depended a moulded ceiling of honeycomb plaster-work. This room had something, even now, in the days of its desecration, of monastic beauty about it. Where the odour of sanctity had breathed forth, the fumes of idolatry prevailed; but imagination, ever on the wing, flew back to that period (and a tradition to that effect warranted the supposition) when, perchance, it had been the sanctuary and the privacy of the prior's self.

Wrapped in a cloak composed of the skins of various animals, upon a low pallet, covered with stained scarlet cloth, sat Barbara. Around her head was coiffed, in folds like those of an Asiatic turban, a rich, though faded shawl, and her waist was encircled with the magic zodiacal zone—proper to the sorceress—the *Mago Cinco* of the Cingara (whence the name Zingaro, according to Moncada), which Barbara had brought from Spain. From her ears depended long golden drops, of curious antique fashioning; and upon her withered fingers, which looked like a coil of lizards, were hooped a multitude of silver rings, of the purest and simplest manufacture. They seemed almost of massive unwrought metal, Her skin was yellow as the body of a toad; corrugated as its back. She might have been steeped in saffron from her finger tips, the nails of which were of the same hue, to such portions of her neck as were visible, and which was puckered up like the throat of a turtle. To look at her, one might have thought the embalmer had experimented her art upon herself. So dead, so bloodless, so blackened seemed the flesh, where flesh remained, leather could scarce be tougher than her skin. She seemed like an animated mummy. A frame, so tanned, appeared calculated to endure for ages; and, perhaps, might have done so. But, alas! the soul cannot be embalmed. No oil can reillumine that precious lamp! And that Barbara's vital spark was fast waning, was evident from her heavy, bloodshot eyes, once of a swimming black, and lengthy as a witch's, which were now sinister and sunken.

The atmosphere of the room was as strongly impregnated as a museum with volatile odours emitted from the stores of drugs with which the shelves were loaded, as well as from various stuffed specimens of birds and wild animals. Barbara's only living companion was a monstrous owl, which, perched over the old gipsy's head, hissed a token of recognition as Sybil advanced. From a hook, placed in the plaster roof, was suspended a globe of crystal glass, about the size and shape of a large gourd, filled with a pure pellucid liquid, in which a small snake, the Egyptian aspic, described perpetual gyrations.

Dim were the eyes of Barbara, yet not altogether sightless. The troubled demeanour of her grandchild struck her as she entered. She felt the hot drops upon her hand as Sybil stooped to kiss it; she heard her vainly-stifled sobs.

"What ails you, child?" said Barbara, in a voice that rattled in her throat, and hollow as the articulation of a phantom. "Have you heard tidings of Luke Bradley? Has any ill befallen him? I told you thou wouldst either hear of him or see him this morning. He is not returned, I see. What have you heard?"

"He *is* returned," replied Sybil, faintly; "and no ill hath happened to him."

"He *is* returned, and you are here," echoed Barbara. "No ill hath happened to *him*, thou sayest—am I to understand there is ill to *you?*"

Sybil answered not. She could not answer.

"I see, I see," said Barbara, more gently, her head and hand shaking with paralytic affection: "a quarrel, a lovers' quarrel. Old as I am, I have not forgotten my feelings as a girl. What woman ever does, if she be woman? and you, like your poor mother, are a true-hearted wench. She loved her husband, as a husband should be loved, Sybil; and though she loved me well, she loved him better, as was right. Ah! it was a bitter day when she left me for Spain; for though, to one of our wandering race, all countries are alike, yet the soil of our birth is dear to us, and the presence of our kindred dearer. Well, well, I will not think of that. She is gone. Nay, take it not so to heart, wench. Luke has a hasty temper. 'Tis not the first time I have told you so. He will not bear rebuke, and you have questioned him too shrewdly touching his absence. Is it not so? Heed it not. Trust me, you will have him seek your forgiveness ere the shadows shorten 'neath the noontide sun."

"Alas! alas!" said Sybil, sadly; "this is no lovers' quarrel, which may, at once, be forgotten and forgiven—would it were so!"

"What is it, then?" asked Barbara; and, without waiting Sybil's answer, she continued, with vehemence, "has he wronged you? Tell me, girl, in what way? Speak, that I may avenge you, if your wrong requires revenge. Are you blood of mine, and think I will not do this for you, girl? None of the blood of Barbara Lovel were ever unrevenged. When Richard Cooper stabbed my first-born, Francis, he fled to Flanders, to escape my wrath. But he did not escape it. I pursued him thither. I hunted him out; drove him back to his own country, and brought him to the gallows. It took a power of gold? What matter? Revenge is dearer than gold. And as it was with Richard Cooper, so it shall be with Luke Bradley. I will catch him, though he run. I will trip him, though he leap. I will reach him, though he flee afar. I will drag him hither by the hair of his head," added she, with a livid smile, and clutching at the air with her hands, as if in the act of pulling some one towards her. "He shall wed you within the hour, if you will have it, or if your honour

N

need that it should be so. My power is not departed from
me. My people are yet at my command. I am still their
queen, and woe to him that offendeth me!"

"Mother! mother!" cried Sybil, affrighted at the storm
she had unwittingly aroused, "he has not injured me. 'Tis
I alone who am to blame, not Luke."

"You speak in mysteries," said Barbara.

"Sir Piers Rookwood is dead."

"Dead!" echoed Barbara, letting fall her hazel rod. "Sir
Piers dead!"

"And Luke Bradley——"

"Ha!"

"Is his successor."

"Who told you that?" asked Barbara, with increased
astonishment.

"Luke himself. All is disclosed." And Sybil hastily
recounted Luke's adventures. "He is now Sir Luke Rookwood."

"This is news, in truth," said Barbara; "yet not news to
weep for. You should rejoice, not lament. Well, well; I
foresaw it. I shall live to see all accomplished; to see my
Agatha's child ennobled; to see her wedded; ay, to see her
well wedded."

"Dearest mother!"

"I can endow you, and I will do it. You shall bring your
husband not alone beauty, you shall bring him wealth."

"But, mother——"

"My Agatha's daughter shall be Lady Rookwood."

"Never! It cannot be."

"What cannot be?"

"The match you now propose."

"What mean you, silly wench? Ha! I perceive the
meaning of those tears. The truth flashes upon me. He has
discarded you."

"No, by the Heaven of Heavens, he is still the same—un-
altered in affection."

"If so, your tears are out of place."

"Mother, it is not fitting that I, a gipsy born, should wed
with him."

"Not fitting! Ha! and you my child! Not fitting! Get
up, or I will spurn you. Not fitting! This from you to me!
I tell you it *is* fitting; you shall have a dower as ample as
that of any lady in the land. Not fitting! Do you say so,
because you think that he derives himself from a proud and

ancient line?—ancient and proud—ha, ha! I tell you, girl, that for his one ancestor I can number twenty; for the years in which his lineage hath flourished my race can boast centuries and was a people—a kingdom!—ere the land in which he dwells was known. What! if by the curse of Heaven we were driven forth, the curse of hell rests upon his house."

"I know it," said Sybil; "a dreadful curse, which, if I wed him, will alight on me."

"No; not on you; you shall avoid that curse. I know a means to satisfy the avenger. Leave that to me."

"I dare not, as it never can be; yet, tell me—you saw the body of Luke's ill-fated mother. Was she poisoned? Nay, you may speak. Sir Piers's death releases you from your oath. How died she?"

"By strangulation," said the old gipsy, raising her palsied hand to her throat.

"Oh!" cried Sybil, gasping with horror. "Was there a ring upon her finger when you embalmed the body?"

"A ring—a wedding-ring! The finger was crookened. Listen, girl. I could have told Luke the secret of his birth long ago, but the oath imposed by Sir Piers sealed fast my lips. His mother was wedded to Sir Piers; his mother was murdered by Sir Piers. Luke was intrusted to my care by his father. I have brought him up with you. I have affianced you together; and I shall live to see you united. He is now Sir Luke. He is your husband."

"Do not deceive yourself, mother," said Sybil, with a fearful earnestness. "He is not yet Sir Luke Rookwood; would he had no claim to be so! The fortune that has hitherto been so propitious may yet desert him. Bethink you of a prophecy you uttered."

"A prophecy? Ha!"

And with slow enunciation Sybil pronounced the mystic words which she had heard repeated by the sexton.

As she spoke, a gloom, like that of a thundercloud, began to gather over the brow of the old gipsy. The orbs of her sunken eyes expanded, and wrath supplied her frame with vigour. She arose.

"Who told you that?" cried Barbara.

"Luke's grandsire, Peter Bradley."

"How learnt he it?" said Barbara. "It was to one who hath long been in his grave I told it; so long ago, it had passed from my memory. 'Tis strange! Old Sir Reginald had a brother, I know. But there is no other of the house."

"There is a cousin, Eleanor Mowbray."

"Ha! I see; a daughter of that Eleanor Rookwood who fled from her father's roof. Fool, fool. Am I caught in my own toils? Those words were words of truth and power, and compel the future and 'the will be' as with chains of brass. They must be fulfilled, yet not by Ranulph. He shall never wed Eleanor."

"Whom, then, shall she wed?"

"His elder brother."

"Mother!" shrieked Sybil. "Do you say so? Oh! recall your words."

"I may not; it is spoken. Luke shall wed her."

"Oh God, support me!" exclaimed Sybil.

"Silly wench, be firm. It must be as I say. He shall wed her; yet shall he wed her not. The nuptial torch shall be quenched as soon as lighted; the curse of the avenger shall fall—yet not on thee."

"Mother," said Sybil, "if sin must fall upon some innocent head, let it be on mine—not upon hers. I love him. I would gladly die for him. She is young, unoffending, perhaps happy. Oh! do not let her perish."

"Peace, I say!" cried Barbara, "and mark me. This is your birthday. Eighteen summers have flown over your young head; eighty winters have sown their snows on mine. *You* have yet to learn. Years have brought wrinkles; they have brought wisdom likewise. To struggle with Fate, I tell you, is to wrestle with Omnipotence. We may foresee, but not avert our destiny. What will be, shall be. This is your eighteenth birthday, Sybil: it is a day of fate to you; in it occurs your planetary hour—an hour of good or ill, according to your actions. I have cast your horoscope. I have watched your natal star; it is under the baneful influence of Scorpion, and fiery Saturn sheds his lurid glance upon it. Let me see your hand. The line of life is drawn out distinct and clear; it runs—ha! what means that intersection? Beware—beware, my Sybil. Act as I tell you, and you are safe. I will make another trial, by the crystal bowl. Attend."

Muttering some strange words, sounding like a spell, Barbara, with the bifurcate hazel staff which she used as a divining-rod, described a circle upon the floor. Within this circle she drew other lines, from angle to angle, forming seven triangles, the basis of which constituted the sides of a septilateral figure. This figure she studied intently for a few moments. She then raised her wand and touched the owl with it. The bird unfolded its wings, and arose in flight; then slowly circled round the pendulous globe. Each time it drew nearer, until at length it touched the glassy bowl with its flapping pinions.

"Enough!" ejaculated Barbara. And at another motion from her rod the bird stayed its flight and returned to its perch.

Barbara arose. She struck the globe with her staff. The pure lymph became instantly tinged with crimson, as if blood had been commingled with it. The little serpent could be seen within, coiled up and knotted, as in the struggles of death.

"Again I say, beware!" ejaculated Barbara, solemnly. "This is ominous of ill."

Sybil had sunk, from faintness, on the pallet. A knock was heard at the door.

"Who is without?" cried Barbara.

"'Tis I, Balthazar," replied a voice.

"Thou mayst enter," answered Barbara; and an old man with a long beard, white as snow, reaching to his girdle, and a costume which might be said to resemble the raiment of a Jewish high-priest, made his appearance. This venerable personage was no other than the patrico (from *Pattercove*), or hierophant of the canting crew.

"I come to tell you that there are strangers—ladies— within the priory," said the patrico, gravely. "I have searched for you in vain," continued he, addressing Sybil; "the younger of them seems to need your assistance."

"Whence come they?" exclaimed Barbara.

"They have ridden, I understand, from Rookwood," answered the patrico. "They were on their way to Davenham, when they were prevented."

"From Rookwood?" echoed Sybil. "Their names—did you hear their names?"

"Mowbray is the name of both; they are a mother and a daughter; the younger is called——"

"Eleanor?" asked Sybil, with an acute foreboding of calamity.

"Eleanor is the name, assuredly," replied the patrico, somewhat surprised. "I heard the elder, whom I guess to be her mother, so address her."

"Gracious God! She here!" exclaimed Sybil.

"Here! Eleanor Mowbray here," cried Barbara; "within my power. Not a moment is to be lost. Balthazar, hasten

round the tents—not a man must leave his place—above
all, Luke Bradley. See that these Mowbrays are detained
within the abbey. Let the bell be sounded. Quick, quick;
leave this wench to me; she is not well. I have much to
do. Away with thee, man, and let me know when thou hast
done it." And as Balthazar departed on his mission, with a
glance of triumph in her eyes, Barbara exclaimed, "Soh, no
sooner hath the thought possessed me, than the means of
accomplishment appear. It shall be done at once. I will tie
the knot. I will untie, and then retie it. This weak wench
must be nerved to the task," added she, regarding the senseless form of Sybil. "Here is that will stimulate her," opening the cupboard, and taking a small phial; "this will fortify
her; and this," continued she, with a ghastly smile, laying her
hand upon another vessel, "this shall remove her rival when
all is fulfilled; this liquid shall constrain her lover to be her
titled, landed husband. Ha, ha!"

V.

THE INAUGURATION.

Beggar. Concert, sir! we have musicians, too, among us. True, merry
beggars, indeed, that, being within the reach of the lash for singing libellous
songs at London, were fain to fly into one covey, and here they sing all our
poet's ditties. They can sing anything, most tuneably, sir, but psalms.
What they may do hereafter, under a triple tree, is much expected; but they
live very civilly and genteelly among us.
Spring. But, what is here—that solemn old fellow, that neither speaks of
himself, or any for him?
Beggar. O, sir, the rarest man of all: he is a prophet. See how he holds
up his prognosticating nose. He is divining now.
Spring. How, a prophet?
Beggar. Yes, sir; a cunning man, and a fortune-teller; a very ancient
stroller all the world over, and has travelled with gipsies? and is a patrico.
                                            The Merry Beggars.

In consequence of some few words which the sexton let
fall, in the presence of the attendants, during breakfast, more
perhaps by design than accident, it was speedily rumoured
throughout the camp that the redoubted Richard Turpin was
for the time its inmate. This intelligence produced some
such sensation as is experienced by the inhabitants of a petty
town on the sudden arrival of a prince of the blood, a com-
mander-in-chief, or other illustrious and distinguished per-

sonage, whose fame has been vaunted abroad amongst his fellow-men by Rumour, " and her thousand tongues ;" and who, like our highwayman, has rendered himself sufficiently notorious to be an object of admiration and emulation amongst his contemporaries.

All started up at the news. The upright man, the chief of the crew, arose from his chair, donned his gown of state, a very ancient brocade dressing-gown, filched, most probably, from the wardrobe of some strolling-player, grasped his bâton of office, a stout oaken truncheon, and sallied forth. The ruffler, who found his representative in a very magnificently equipped, and by no means ill-favoured knave, whose chin was decorated with a beard as lengthy and as black as Sultan Mahmoud's, together with the dexterous hooker, issued forth from the hovel which they termed their boozing-ken, eager to catch a glimpse of the prince of the high-tobygloaks. The limping palliard tore the bandages from his mock wounds, shouldered his crutch, and trudged hastily after them. The whip-jack unbuckled his strap, threw away his timber leg, and " leapt exulting, like the bounding roe." " With such a sail in sight," he said, " he must heave to, like the rest." The dummerar, whose tongue had been cut out by the Algerines, suddenly found the use of it, and made the welkin ring with his shouts. Wonderful were the miracles Dick's advent wrought. The lame became suddenly active, the blind saw, the dumb spoke ; nay, if truth must be told, absolutely gave utterance to " most vernacular execrations." Morts, autem morts, walking morts, dells, doxies, kinching morts, and their coes, with all the shades and grades of the canting crew, were assembled. There were, to use the words of Brome—

——Stark, errant, downright beggars. Ay,
Without equivocation, statute beggars,
Couchant and passant, guardant, rampant beggars ;
Current and vagrant, stockant, whippant beggars !*

Each sunburnt varlet started from his shed ; each dusky dame, with her brown, half-naked urchins, followed at his heels ; each " ripe young maiden, with the glossy eye," lingered but to sleek her raven tresses, and to arrange her straw bonnet, and then overtook the others ; each wrinkled beldame hobbled as quickly after as her stiffened joints would permit ; while the ancient patrico, the priest of the crew (who joined the couples together by the hedge-side, " with the nice cus-

* The Merry Beggars.

tom of a dead horse between,"*) brought up the rear; all
bent on one grand object, that of having a peep at the "foremost man of all this prigging world!"

Dick Turpin, at the period of which we treat, was in the
zenith of his reputation. His deeds were full blown; his
exploits were in every man's mouth; and a heavy price was
set upon his head. That he should show himself thus openly,
where he might be so easily betrayed, excited no little surprise amongst the craftiest of the crew, and augured an excess
of temerity on his part. Rash daring was the main feature
of Turpin's character. Like our great Nelson, he knew fear
only by name; and when he thus trusted himself into the
hands of strangers, confident in himself and in his own resources, he felt perfectly easy as to the result. He relied
also in the continuance of his good fortune, which had as yet
never deserted him. Possessed of the belief that his hour
was not yet come, he cared little or nothing for any risk he
might incur; and though he might, undoubtedly, have some
presentiment of the probable termination of his career, he
never suffered it to militate against his present enjoyment,
which proved that he was no despicable philosopher.

Turpin was the *ultimus Romanorum*, the last of a race,
which (we were almost about to say, we regret) is now altogether extinct. Several successors he had, it is true, but no
name worthy to be recorded after his own. With him expired the chivalrous spirit which animated successively the
bosoms of so many knights of the road; with him died away
that passionate love of enterprise, that high spirit of devotion
to the fair sex, which was first breathed upon the highway by
the gay, gallant Claude Du-Val, the Bayard of the road—
le filou sans peur et sans reproche—but which was extinguished
at last by the cord that tied the heroic Turpin to the remorseless tree. It were a subject well worthy of inquiry, to trace
this decline and fall of the empire of the tobymen to its
remoter causes; to ascertain the why and the wherefore,
that—with so many half-pay captains; so many poor curates;
so many lieutenants of both services, without hopes of promotion; so many penny-a-liners and fashionable novelists; so
many damned dramatists, and damning critics; so many

* The parties to be wedded find out a dead horse, or any other beast, and
standing one on the one side, and the other on the other, the patrico bids
them live together till death do them part; and so shaking hands, the wedding dinner is kept at the next alehouse they stumble into, where the union
is nothing but knocking of cannes, and the sauce, none but drunken brawles.
—DEKKAR.

Edinburgh and Quarterly Reviewers; so many detrimental
brothers and younger sons; when there are horses to be
hired, pistols to be borrowed, purses to be taken, and mails
are as plentiful as partridges—it were worth serious investigation, we repeat, to ascertain why, with the best material
imaginable for a new race of highwaymen, we have none, not
so much as an amateur. Why do not some of these choice
spirits quit the *salons* of Pall Mall, and take to the road? the
air of the heath is more bracing and wholesome, we should
conceive, than that of any "hell" whatever, and the chances
of success incomparably greater. We throw out this hint,
without a doubt of seeing it followed up. Probably the solution of our inquiry may be, that the supply is greater than
the demand; that, in the present state of things, embryo
highwaymen may be more abundant than purses; and then,
have we not the horse-patrol? With such an admirably-
organised system of conservation, it is vain to anticipate a
change. The highwaymen, we fear, like their Irish brothers,
the Rapparees, went out with the Tories. They were averse
to reform, and eschewed emancipation.

Lest any one should think we have overrated the pleasures
of the highwayman's existence, they shall hear what "the
right villanous" Jack Hall, a celebrated tobyman of his day,
has got to say on the subject. "His life (the highwayman's)
has, generally, the most mirth and the least care in it of any
man's breathing, and all he deals for is clear profit: he has
that point of good conscience, that he always sells as he buys,
a good pennyworth, which is something rare, since he trades
with so small a stock. The *fence** and he are like the devil
and the doctor, they live by one another; and, like traitors,
'tis best to keep each other's counsel. He has this point of
honesty, that he never robs the house he frequents" (Turpin had the same scruples respecting the Hall of Rookwood
in Sir Piers's lifetime); "and perhaps pays his debts better
than some others, for he holds it below the dignity of his
employment to commit so ungenteel a crime as insolvency,
and loves to pay nobly. He has another quality, not much
amiss, that he takes no more than he has occasion for"
(Jack, we think, was a little mistaken here); "which he
verifies this way; he craves no more while that lasts. He
is a less nuisance in a commonwealth than a miser, because
the money he engrosses all circulates again, which the other
hoards as though 'twere only to be found again at the day of

* Receiver.

judgment. He is the tithe-pig of his family, which the gallows, instead of the parson, claims as its due. He has reason enough to be bold in his undertakings, for, though all the world threaten him, he stands in fear of but one man in it, and that's the hangman; and with him, too, he is generally in fee: however, I cannot affirm he is so valiant that he dares look any man in the face, for in that point he is now and then a little modest. Newgate may be said to be his country-house, where he frequently lives so many months in the year, and he is not so much concerned to be carried thither for a small matter, if 'twere only for the benefit of renewing his acquaintance there. He holds a petit larceny as light as a nun does auricular confession, though the priest has a more compassionate character than the hangman. Every man in this community is esteemed according to his particular quality, of which there are several degrees, though it is contrary often to public government; for here a man shall be valued purely for his merit, and rise by it too, though it be but to a halter, in which there is a great deal of glory in dying like a hero, and making a decent figure in the cart to the two last staves of the fifty-first psalm."*

This, we repeat, is the plain statement of a practical man, and again we throw out the hint for adoption. All we regret is, that we are now degenerated from the grand tobyman to the cracksman and the sneak, about whom there are no redeeming features. How much lower the next generation of thieves will dive it boots not to conjecture:

> Ætas parentum pejor avis tulit,
> Nos nequiores; mox daturos,
> Progeniem vitiosiorem.

"Cervantes laughed Spain's chivalry away," sang Byron; and if Gay did not extinguish the failing flame of our *night* errantry (unlike the "Robbers" of Schiller, which is said to have inflamed the Saxon youth with an irrepressible mania for brigandage), the "Beggar's Opera" helped not to fan the dying fire. That laugh was fatal, as laughs generally are. Macheath gave the highwayman his *coup de grace*.

The last of this race (for we must persist in maintaining that he *was* the last), Turpin, like the setting sun, threw up some parting rays of glory, and tinged the far highways with a lustre that may yet be traced like a cloud of dust raised by his horse's retreating heels. Unequalled in the command of

* Memoirs of the right villanous John Hall, the famous and notorious Robber, penned from his Mouth some Time before his Death, 1708.

his steed, the most singular feat that the whole race of the annals of horsemanship has to record, and of which we may have more to say hereafter, was achieved by him. So perfect was his jockeyship, so clever his management of the animal he mounted, so intimately acquainted was he with every cross-road in the neighbourhood of the metropolis (a book of which he constructed, and carried constantly about his person), as well as with many other parts of England, particularly the counties of Chester, York, and Lancaster, that he outstripped every pursuer, and baffled all attempts at capture. His reckless daring, his restless rapidity (for so suddenly did he change his ground, and renew his attacks in other quarters, that he seemed to be endowed with ubiquity), his bravery, his resolution, and, above all, his generosity, won for him a high reputation amongst his compatriots, and even elicited applauses from those upon whom he levied his contributions.

Beyond dispute he ruled as master of the road. His hands were, as yet, unstained with blood; he was ever prompt to check the disposition to outrage, and to prevent, as much as lay in his power, the commission of violence by his associates. Of late, since he had possessed himself of his favourite mare, Black Bess, his robberies had been perpetrated with a suddenness of succession, and at distances so apparently impracticable, that the idea of all having been executed by one man, was rejected as an impossibility; and the only way of reconciling the description of the horse and rider, which tallied in each instance, was the supposition that these attacks were performed by confederates similarly mounted and similarly accoutred.

There was, in all this, as much of the "*famœ sacra fames*" as of the "*auri;*" of the hungering after distinction, as well as of the appetite of gain. Enamoured of his vocation, Turpin delighted to hear himself designated as the Flying Highwayman; and it was with rapturous triumph that he found his single-handed feats attributed to a band of marauders. But this state of things could not long endure: his secret was blown; the vigilance of the police was aroused; he was tracked to his haunts; and after a number of hairbreadth 'scapes, which he only effected by miracle, or by the aid of his wonder-working mare, he reluctantly quitted the heathy hills of Bagshot, the Pampas plains of Hounslow (over which, like an archetype of the galloping Sir Francis Head, he had so often scoured), the gorsy commons of Highgate, Hampstead, and Finchley, the marshy fields of Batter-

sea, almost all of which he had been known to visit in a
single night, and, leaving these beaten tracks to the occupation of younger and less practised hands, he bequeathed to
them, at the same time, his own reversionary interest in
the gibbets thereupon erected, and betook himself to the
country.

After a journey of more or less success, our adventurer
found himself at Rookwood, whither he had been invited
after a grand field-day by its hospitable and by no means
inquisitive owner.   Breach of faith and good fellowship
formed no part of Turpin's character; he had his lights as
well as his shades; and as long as Sir Piers lived, his purse
and coffers would have been free from molestation, except
"so far," Dick said, "as a cog or two of dice went.   My
dice, you know, are longs for odd and even, a bale of bar'd
cinque deuces," a pattern of which he always carried with
him; beyond this, excepting a take-in at a steeple-chase,
Rookwood church being the mark, a "do" at a leap, or some
such trifle, to which the most scrupulous could not raise an
objection, Dick was all fair and aboveboard.   But when poor
Sir Piers had "put on his wooden surtout," to use Dick's
own expressive metaphor, his conscientious scruples evapo-
rated into thin air.   Lady Rookwood was nothing to him;
there was excellent booty to be appropriated—

> " The wise *convey* it call."

He began to look about for hands; and having accidentally
encountered his old comrades, Rust and Wilder, they were
let into the business, which was imperfectly accomplished in
the manner heretofore described.

To return from this digression.   When Turpin presented
himself at the threshold of the door, on his way to inquire
after his mare, to his astonishment he found it closely invested.   A cheering shout from the tawny throng, succeeded
by a general clapping of hands, and attended by a buzzing
susurration of applause, such as welcomes the entrance of a
popular actor upon the stage, greeted the appearance of the
highwayman.   At the first sight of the crowd he was a little
startled, and involuntarily sought for his pistols.   But the
demonstrations of admiration were too unequivocal to be for
a moment mistaken; his hand was drawn from his pocket to
raise his hat from his brow.

Thunders of applause.

Turpin's external man, we have before said, was singularly prepossessing. It was especially so in the eyes of *the* sex (fair we certainly cannot say upon the present occasion), amongst whom not a single dissentient voice was to be heard. All concurred in thinking him a fine fellow; could plainly read his high courage in his bearing; his good breeding in his *débonnaire* deportment; and his manly beauty in his extravagant red whiskers. Dick saw the effect that he produced. He was at home in a moment. Your true highwayman has ever a passion for effect. This does not desert him at the gallows; it rises superior to death itself, and has been known to influence the manner of his dangling from the gibbet! To hear some one cry, "There goes a proper handsome man," saith our previously-quoted authority, Jack Hall, " somewhat ameliorates the terrible thoughts of the meagre tyrant Death ; and to go in a dirty shirt, were enough to save the hangman a labour, and make a man die with grief and shame at being in that deplorable condition." With a gracious smile of condescension, like a popular orator—with a look of blarney like that of O'Connell, and of assurance like that of Hume—he surveyed the male portion of the spectators, tipped a knowing wink at the prettiest brunettes he could select, and finally cut a sort of fling with his well-booted legs, that brought down another peal of rapturous applause.

" A rank scamp !"* cried the upright man, and this exclamation, however equivocal it may sound, was intended, on his part, to be highly complimentary.

" I believe ye," returned the ruffler, stroking his chin— " one may see that he's no half swell by the care with which he cultivates the best gifts of nature, his whiskers. He's a rank nib."†

" Togged out to the ruffian, no doubt," said the palliard, who was incomparably the shabbiest rascal in the corps. " Though a needy mizzler mysel, I likes to see a cove vot's vel dressed. Jist twig his swell kickseys and pipes ;‡ if they ain't the thing, I'm done. Lame Harry can't dance better nor he—no, nor Jerry Juniper neither."

" I'm dumfounded," roared the dummerar, " if he can't patter Romany§ as vel as the best on us ! He looks like a rum 'un."

---

* A famous highwayman.   † A real gentleman.
‡ Breeches and boots.   § Gipsy flash.

"And a rum 'un he be, take my word for it," returned the whip-jack, or sham sailor. "Look at his rigging—see how he flashes his sticks*—those are the tools to rake a three-decker. He's as clever a craft as I've seen this many a day, or I'm no judge."

The women were equally enchanted—equally eloquent in the expression of their admiration.

"What ogles!" cried a mort.

"What pins!" said an autem mort, or married woman.

"Sharp as needles," said a dark-eyed dell, who had encountered one of the free and frolicsome glances which our highwayman distributed so liberally amongst the petti-coats.

It was at this crisis Dick took off his hat. Cæsar betrayed his baldness.

"A thousand pities!" cried the men, compassionating his thinly-covered skull, and twisting their own ringlets, glossy and luxuriant, though unconscious of Macassar. "A thousand pities that so fine a fellow should have a sconce like a cocoa-nut!"

"But then his red whiskers," rejoined the women, tired of the uniformity of thick black heads of hair; "what a warmth of colouring they impart to his face, and then only look how beautifully bushy they make his cheeks appear!"

La Fosseuse and the court of the queen of Navarre were not more smitten with the Sieur de Croix's jolly pair of whiskers.

The hawk's eye of Turpin ranged over the whole assem-blage. Amidst that throng of dark faces there was not one familiar to him.

Before him stood the upright man, Zoroaster (so was he called), a sturdy, stalwart rogue, whose superior strength and stature (as has not unfrequently been the case in the infancy of governments that have risen to more importance than is likely to be the case with that of Lesser Egypt) had been the means of his elevation to his present dignified position. Zoroaster literally *fought* his way upwards, and had at first to maintain his situation by the strong arm; but he now was enabled to repose upon his hard-won laurels, to smoke "the calumet of peace," and quaff his tipple with impunity. For one of gipsy blood, he presented an unusually jovial, liquor-loving countenance; his eye was mirthful; his lip moist, as

---

* How he exposes his pistols

if from oft potations; his cheek mellow as an Orleans plum, which fruit, in colour and texture, it mightily resembled. Strange to say, also, for one of that lithe race, his person was heavy and hebetudinous; the consequence, no doubt, of habitual intemperance. Like Cribb, he waxed obese upon the championship. There was a kind of mock state in his carriage as he placed himself before Turpin, and with his left hand twisted up the tail of his dressing-gown, while the right thrust his truncheon into his hip, which was infinitely diverting to the highwayman.

Turpin's attention, however, was chiefly directed towards his neighbour, the ruffler, in whom he recognised a famous impostor of the day, with whose history he was sufficiently well acquainted to be able at once to identify the individual. We have before stated, that a magnificent coal-black beard decorated the chin of this worthy; but this was not all—his costume was in perfect keeping with his beard, and consisted of a very theatrical-looking tunic, upon the breast of which was embroidered, in golden wire, the Maltese cross; while over his shoulders were thrown the ample folds of a cloak of Tyrian hue. To his side was girt a long and doughty sword, which he termed, in his knightly phrase, Excalibur; and upon his profuse hair rested a hat as broad in the brim as a Spanish sombrero.

Exaggerated as this description may appear, we can assure our readers that it is not overdrawn; and that a counterpart of the sketch we have given of the ruffler certainly "strutted his hour" upon the stage of human life, and that the very ancient and discriminating city of Canterbury (to which be all honour) was his theatre of action. His history is so far curious, that it exemplifies, more strongly than a thousand discourses could do, how prone we are to be governed by appearances, and how easily we may be made the dupes of a plausible imposter. Be it remembered, however, that we treat of the eighteenth century, before the march of intellect had commenced; we are much too knowing to be similarly practised upon in these enlightened times. But we will let the knight of Malta, for such was the title assumed by the ruffler, tell his own story in his own way hereafter; contenting ourselves with the moral precepts we have already deduced from it.

Next to the knight of Malta stood the whip-jack, habited in his sailor gear—striped shirt and dirty canvas trousers; and adjoining him was the palliard, a loathsome tatterde-

mallion, his dress one heap of rags, and his discoloured skin
one mass of artificial leprosy and imposthumes.

As Turpin's eye shifted from one to another of these
figures, he chanced upon an individual who had been long
endeavouring to arrest his attention. This personage was
completely in the back-ground. All that Dick could discern
of him was a brown curly head of hair, carelessly arranged
in the modern mode; a handsome, impudent, sun-freckled
face, with one eye closed, and the other occupied by a broken
bottle neck, through which, as a substitute for a lorgnette,
the individual reconnoitred him. A cocked hat was placed in
a very *dégagée* manner under his arm, and he held an ebony
cane in his hand, very much in the style of a "*fassionable,*"
as the French have it, of the present day. This glimpse was
sufficient to satisfy Turpin. He recognised in this whimsical
personage an acquaintance.

Jerry Juniper was what the classical Captain Grose would
designate a "gentleman with three outs;" and, although he
was not entirely without wit, nor his associates avouched,
without money, nor, certainly, in his own opinion, had that
been asked, without manners; yet was he assuredly without
shoes, without stockings, without shirt. This latter deficiency
was made up by a voluminous cravat, tied with proportionately large bows. A jaunty pair of yellow breeches, somewhat faded; a waistcoat of silver brocade, richly embroidered,
somewhat tarnished and lack-lustre, a murrey-coloured velvet
coat, somewhat chafed, completed the costume of this beggar
Brummell, this mendicant maccorani!

Jerry Juniper was a character well known at the time as
a constant frequenter of all races, fairs, regattas, ship-
launches, bull-baits, and prize-fights, all of which he attended, and to which he transported himself with an expedition little less remarkable than that of Turpin. You met
him at Epsom, at Ascot, at Newmarket, at Doncaster, at the
Roodee of Chester, at the Curragh of Kildare. The most
remote as well as the most adjacent meeting attracted him.
The cock-pit was his constant haunt, and in more senses than
one was he a *leg*. No opera-dancer could be more agile,
more nimble; scarcely, indeed, more graceful than was Jerry,
with his shoeless and stockingless feet; and the manner in
which he executed a pirouette, or a pas, before a line of
carriages, seldom failed to procure him "golden opinions
from all sorts of dames." With the ladies, it must be

owned, Jerry was rather upon too easy terms; but then, perhaps, the ladies were upon too easy terms with Jerry; and if a bright-eyed fair one condescended to jest with him, what marvel if he should sometimes slightly transgress the laws of decorum? These aberrations, however, were trifling; altogether he was so well known, and knew everbody else so well, that he seldom committed himself; and, singular to say, could on occasions even be serious. In addition to his other faculties, no one cut a sly joke, or trolled a merry ditty, better than Jerry. His peculiarities, in short, were on the pleasant side, and he was a general favourite in consequence.

No sooner did Jerry perceive that he was recognised, than, after kissing his hand, with the air of a *petit-maître*, to the highwayman, he strove to edge his way through the crowd. All his efforts were fruitless; and, tired of a situation in the rear rank, so inconsistent, he conceived, with his own importance, he had recourse to an expedient often practised with success in harlequinades, and not unfrequently in real life, where a flying leap is occasionally taken over our heads. He ran back a few yards to give himself an impetus, returned, and, placing his hands upon the shoulders of a stalwart vagabond near to him, threw a summerset upon the broad cap of a palliard, who was so jammed in the midst that he could not have stirred to avoid the shock; thence, without pausing, he vaulted forwards, and dropped lightly upon the ground in front of Zoroaster, and immediately before the highwayman.

Dick laughed immoderately at Jerry's manœuvre. He shook his old chum cordially by the hand, saying, in a whisper, "What the devil brings you here, Jerry?"

"I might retort, and ask you that question, Captain Turpin," replied Jerry, *sotto voce.* "It is odd to see me here, certainly—quite out of my element—lost amongst this *canaille*—this canting crew—all the fault of a pair of gipsy eyes, bright as a diamond, dark as a sloe. You comprehend —a little affair, ha! Liable to these things. Bring your ear closer, my boy; be upon your guard; keep a sharp lookout; there's a devil of a reward upon your head; I won't answer for all these rascals."

"Thank you for the hint, Jerry," replied Dick, in the same tone. "I calculated my chances pretty nicely when I came here. But if I should perceive any symptoms of foul play— any attempt to snitch or nose, amongst this pack of pedlars —I have a friend or two at hand, who won't be silent upon the occasion. Rest assured I shall have my eye upon the gnarling scoundrels. I won't be sold for nothing."

"Trust you for that," returned Juniper, with a wink. "Stay," added he; "a thought strikes me. "I have a scheme *in petto* which, may, perhaps, afford you some fun, and will at all events, insure your safety during your stay."

"What is it?" asked Dick.

"Just amuse yourself with a flirtation for a moment or two with that pretty damsel, who has been casting her ogles at you for the last five minutes without success, while I effect a master-stroke."

And, as Turpin, nothing loth, followed his advice, Jerry addressed himself to Zoroaster. After a little conference, accompanied by that worthy and the knight of Malta, the trio stepped forward from the line and approached Dick, when Juniper, assuming some such attitude as our admirable Jones, the comedian, is wont to display, delivered himself of the following address. Turpin listened with the gravity of one of the distinguished persons alluded to, at the commencement of the present chapter, upon their receiving the freedom of a city at the hands of a mayor and corporation. Thus spoke Jerry :

"Highest of High-Tobymen; rummest of rum Padders, and most scampish of Scampsmen! We, in the name of Barbara, our most tawny queen; in the name of Zoroaster, our Upright Man, Dimber Damber, or Olli Campolli, by all which titles his excellency is distinguished; in our own respective names, as High Pads and Low Pads, Rum Gills and Queer Gills, Patricos, Palliards, Priggers, Whip-Jacks, and Jarkmen, from the Arch Rogue to the needy Mizzler, fully sensible of the honour you have conferred upon us in gracing Stop-Hole Abbey with your presence; and conceiving that we can in no way evince our sense of your condescension so entirely as by offering you the freedom of our crew, together with the privileges of an Upright Man,* which you may be aware are considerable, and by creating you an honorary member of the Vagrant Club, which we have recently established; and in so doing, we would fain express the sentiments of gratification and pride which we experience in enrolling among our members one who has extended the glory of roguery so widely over the land, and who has kicked up such a dust upon the highways of England, as most effectually

* For an account of these, see Grose. They are much too *gross* to be set down here.

to blind the natives ; one who is in himself a legion—of highwaymen ! Awaiting, with respectful deference, the acquiescence of Captain Richard Turpin, we beg to tender him the
freedom of our crew."

"Really, gentlemen," said Turpin, who did not exactly see
the drift of this harangue, " you do me a vast deal of honour.
I am quite at a loss to conceive how I can possibly have
merited so much attention at your hands ! and, indeed, I feel
myself so unworthy——" Here Dick received an expressive
wink from Juniper, and therefore thought it prudent to alter
his expression. "Could I suppose myself at all deserving
of so much distinction," continued the modest speaker, "I
should at once accept your very obliging offer ; but——"

" None so worthy," said the upright man.

" Can't hear of a refusal," said the knight of Malta.

" Refusal—impossible !" reiterated Juniper.

"No ; no refusal," exclaimed a chorus of voices. "Dick
Turpin must be one of us. He shall be our dimber damber."

"Well, gentlemen, since you are so pressing," replied
Turpin, " even so be it. I *will* be your dimber damber."

"Bravo ! bravo !" cried the mob, *not* " of gentlemen."

"About it, pals, at once," said the knight of Malta,
flourishing excalibur. "By Saint Thomas à Becket, we'll
have as fine a scene as I myself ever furnished to the Canterbury lieges."

"About what ?" asked Dick.

"Your matriculation'" replied Jerry. "There are certain
forms to be gone through, with an oath to be taken ; merely
a trifle. We'll have a jolly boose when all's over. Come,
bing avast, my merry pals ; to the green, to the green ; a
Turpin ! a Turpin ! a new brother !"

"A Turpin ! a Turpin ! a new brother !" echoed the crew.

"I've brought you through," said Jerry, taking advantage
of the uproar that ensued, to whisper to his chum ; "none of
them will dare to lift a finger against you now. They are all
your friends for life."

"Nevertheless," returned Turpin, "I should be glad to
know what has become of Bess."

"If it's your prancer you are wanting," chirped a fluttering creature, whom Turpin recognised as Luke's groom,
Grasshopper, "I gave her a fresh loaf and a stoup of stingo,
as you bade me ; and there she be under yon tree, as quiet
as a lamb."

"I see her," replied Turpin ; "just tighten her girths,

Grasshopper, and bring her after me, and thou shalt have wherewithal to chirp over thy cups at supper."

Away bounded the elfin dwarf, to execute his behest.

A loud shout now rent the skies, and presently afterwards was heard the vile scraping of a fiddle, accompanied by the tattoo of a drum. Approaching Turpin, a host of gipsies elevated the highwayman upon their shoulders; and in this way he was carried to the centre of the green, where the long oaken table, which had once served the Franciscans for refection, was now destined for the stage of the pageant.

Upon this table three drums were placed; and Turpin was requested to seat himself on the central one. A solemn prelude, more unearthly than the incantation in the Freischutz, was played by the orchestra of the band, conducted by the Paganini of the place, who elicited the most marvellous notes from his shell. A couple of shawms* emitted sepulchral sounds, while the hollow rolling of the drum broke ever and anon upon the ear. The effect was prodigiously fine. During this overture, the patrico and the upright man had ascended the rostrum, each taking their places; the former on the right hand of Turpin, the latter upon his left. Below them stood the knight of Malta, with excalibur drawn in his hand, and gleaming in the sunshine. On the whole, Dick was amused with what he saw, and with the novel situation in which he found himself placed. Around the table were congregated a compact mass of heads; so compact, indeed, that they looked like one creature—an Argus, with each eye up-turned upon the highwayman. The idea struck Turpin that the restless mass of parti-coloured shreds and patches, of vivid hues and varied tintings, singularly, though accidentally, disposed to produce such an effect, resembled an immense tiger-moth, or it might be a Turkey carpet, spread out upon the grass!

This scene was a joyous one. It was a brilliant sunshiny morning. Freshened and purified by the storm of the preceding night, the air breathed a balm upon the nerves and senses of the robber. The wooded hills were glittering in light; the brook was flowing swiftly past the edge of the verdant slope, glancing like a wreathed snake in the sunshine —its "quiet song" lost in the rude harmony of the mummers, as were the thousand twitterings of the rejoicing birds; the rocks bared their bosoms to the sun, or were buried

* "The shalm, or shawm, was a wind instrument, like a pipe, with a swelling protuberance in the middle."—*Earl of Northumberland's Household Book.*

in deep-cast gloom ; the shadows of the pillars and arches
of the old walls of the priory were projected afar, while
the rose-like ramifications of the magnificent marigold window were traced, as if by a pencil, upon the verdant tablet
of the sod.

The overture was finished. With the appearance of the
principal figures in this strange picture the reader is already
familiar. It remains only to give him some idea of the
patrico. Imagine, then, an old superannuated goat, reared
upon its hind legs, and clad in a white sheet, disposed in
folds like those of a simar about its limbs, and you will have
some idea of Balthazar, the patrico. This resemblance to the
animal before mentioned was rendered the more striking
by his huge, hanging, goat-like under-lip, his lengthy white
beard, and a sort of cap, covering his head, which was ornamented with a pair of horns, such as are to be seen in
Michael Angelo's tremendous statue of Moses. Balthazar,
besides being the patrico of the tribe, was its principal
professor of divination, and had been the long-tried and
faithful minister of Barbara Lovel, from whose secret instructions he was supposed to have derived much of his
magical skill.

Placing a pair of spectacles upon his " prognosticating
nose," and unrolling a vellum skin, upon which strange characters were written, Balthazar, turning to Turpin, thus
commenced, in a solemn voice :

> Thou who wouldst our brother be,
> Say how we shall enter thee?
> Name the name that thou wilt bear
> Ere our livery thou wear.

" I see no reason why I should alter my designation," replied the novitiate; "but as popes change their titles on
their creation, there can be no objection to a scampsman following so excellent an example. Let me be known as the
Night Hawk."

" The Night Hawk—good," returned the hierophant, proceeding to register the name upon the parchment. " Kneel
down," continued he.

After some hesitation, Turpin complied.

" You must repeat the 'salamon,' or oath of our creed,
after my dictation," said the patrico ; and Turpin, signifying
his asssnt by a nod, Balthazar propounded the following
abjuration :

OATH OF THE CANTING CREW.

I, Crank-Cuffin, swear to be
True to this fraternity;
That I will in all obey
Rule and order of the lay.
Never blow the gab, or squeak;
Never snitch to bum or beak;
But religiously maintain
Authority of those who reign
Over Stop Hole Abbey Green,
Be their tawny king, or queen.
In their cause alone will fight;
Think what they think, wrong or
    right;
Serve them truly, and no other,
And be faithful to my brother;
Suffer none, from far or near,
With their rights to interfere;
No strange Abram, ruffler crack,
Hooker of another pack,
Rogue or rascal, frater, maunderer,
Irish toyle, or other wanderer;
No dimber damber, angler, dancer,
Prig of cackler; prig of prancer;
No swigman, swaddler, clapper-
    dudgeon;
Cadge-gloak, curtal, or curmudgeon;
No whip-jack, palliard, patrico;
No jarkman, be he high or low;
No dummerar, or romany;
No member of "_the Family;_"
No balladbasket, bouncing buffer,
Nor any other, will I suffer;
But stall-off now and for ever,
All outliers whatsoever:
And as I keep to the fore-gone,
So may help me Salamon!*

"So help me Salamon!" repeated Turpin, with emphasis.

"Zoroaster," said the patrico to the upright man, "do thy part of this ceremonial."

Zoroaster obeyed; and, taking excalibur from the knight of Malta, bestowed a hearty thwack with the blade upon the shoulders of the kneeling highwayman, assisting him afterwards to arise.

The inauguration was complete.

"Well," exclaimed Dick, "I'm glad its all over. My leg

---

* Perhaps the most whimsical laws that were ever prescribed to a gang of thieves were those framed by William Holliday, one of the prigging community, who was hanged in 1695:

Art. I. directs—That none of his company should presume to wear shirts, upon pain of being cashiered.

II.—That none should lie in any other places than stables, empty houses, or other bulks.

III.—That they should eat nothing but what they begged, and that they should give away all the money they got by cleaning boots among one another, for the good of the fraternity.

IV.—That they should neither learn to read nor write, that he may have them the better under command.

V.—That they should appear every morning by nine, on the parade, to receive necessary orders.

VI.—That none should presume to follow the scent but such as he ordered on that party.

VII.—That if any one gave them shoes or stockings, he should convert them into money to play.

VIII.—That they should steal nothing they could not come at, for fear of bringing a scandal upon the company.

IX.—That they should not endeavour to clear themselves of vermin by killing or eating them.

X.—That they should cant better than the Newgate birds, pick pockets without bungling, outlie a Quaker, outswear a lord at a gaming-table, and brazen out all their villanies beyond an Irishman.

feels a little stiffish. I'm not much given to kneeling. I must
dance it off ;" saying which, he began to shuffle upon the
boards. "I tell you what," continued he, "most reverend
patrico, that same 'salmon' of yours has a cursed long tail.
I could scarce swallow it all, and it's strange if it don't give
me an indigestion. As to you, sage Zory, from the dexterity
with which you flourish your sword, I should say you had
practised at court. His majesty could scarce do the thing
better, when, slapping some fat alderman upon the shoulder,
he bids him arise Sir Richard. And now, pals," added he,
glancing round, "as I am one of you, let's have a boose
together ere I depart, for I don't think my stay will be long
in the land of Egypt."

This suggestion of Turpin was so entirely consonant to the
wishes of the assemblage, that it met with universal approbation ; and upon a sign from Zoroaster, some of his followers departed in search of supplies for the carousal. Zoroaster leaped from the table, and his example was followed by
Turpin, and more leisurely by the patrico.

It was rather early in the day for a drinking-bout. But
the canting crew were not remarkably particular. The chairs
were removed, and the jingling of glasses announced the
arrival of the preliminaries of the matutine *symposion*. Poles,
canvas, and cords were next brought ; and in almost as short
space of time as one scene is substituted for another in a
theatrical representation, a tent was erected. Benches, stools,
and chairs appeared with equal celerity, and the interior soon
presented an appearance like that of a booth at a fair. A keg
of brandy was broached, and the health of the new brother
quaffed in brimmers.

Our highwayman returned thanks. Zoroaster was in the
chair, the knight of Malta acting as croupier. A second toast
was proposed—the tawny queen. This was drunk with a like
enthusiasm, and with a like allowance of the potent spirit ;
but as bumpers of brandy are not to be repeated with impunity, it became evident to the president of the board that
he must not repeat his toasts quite so expeditiously. To
create a temporary diversion, therefore, he called for a song.

The dulcet notes of the fiddle now broke through the
clamour ; and, in answer to the call, Jerry Juniper volun-
teered the following :

JERRY JUNIPER'S CHANT.

In a box (1) of the stone jug (2) I was born,
Of a hempen widow (3) the kid forlorn,
   Fake away.
And my father, as I've heard say,
   Fake away.
Was a merchant of capers (4) gay,
Who cut his last fling with great applause,
   (5) *Nix my doll pals, fake away.*

Who cut his last fling with great applause, (6)
To the tune of a " hearty choke with caper sauce."
   Fake away.
The knucks in quod (7) did my schoolmen play,
   Fake away,
And put me up to the time of day ;
Until at last there was none so knowing,
   Nix my doll pals, fake away.

Until at last there was none so knowing,
No such sneaksman (8) or buzgloak (9) going.
   Fake away.
Fogles (10) and fawnies (11) soon went their way,
   Fake away,
To the spout (12) with the sneezers (13) in grand array.
No dummy hunter (14) had forks (15) so fly ;
   Nix my doll pals, fake away.

No dummy hunter had forks so fly.
No knuckler (16) so deftly could fake a cly, (17)
   Fake away.
No slour'd hoxter (18) my snipes (19) could stay,
   Fake away.
None knap a reader (20) like me in the lay.
Soon then I mounted in swell-street high.
   Nix my doll pals, fake away.

Soon then I mounted in swell-street high,
And sported my flashest toggery, (21)
   Fake away.
Firmly resolved I would make my hay,
   Fake away,

---

(1) Cell.   (2) Newgate.   (3) A woman whose husband has been hanged.
(4) A dancing-master.
(5) " Nothing, comrades ; on, on," supposed to be addressed by a thief to his confederates.
(6) Thus Victor Hugo, in " Le Dernier Jour d'un Condamné," makes an imprisoned felon sing :

  " J'le ferai danser une danse
   Où il n'y a pas de plancher."

(7) Thieves in prison.   (8) Shoplifter.   (9) Pickpocket.
(10) Handkerchiefs.   (11) Rings.   (12) To the pawnbroker.
(13) Snuff-boxes.   (14) Pickpocket.
(15) The two fore-fingers used in picking a pocket.
(16) Pickpocket.   (17) Pick a pocket.
(18) No inside coat-pocket, buttoned up.   (19) Scissors.
(20) Steal a pocket-book.   (21) Best-made clothes.

While Mercury's star shed a single ray;
And ne'er was there seen such a dashing prig, (22)
   Nix my doll pals, fake away.

And ne'er was there seen such a dashing prig,
With my strummel faked in the newest twig. (23)
   Fake away.
With my fawnied famms, (24) and my onions gay, (25)
   Fake away;
My thimble of ridge, (26) and my driz kemesa ; (27)
All my togs were so niblike (28) and splash,
   Nix my doll pals, fake away

All my togs were so niblike and splash,
Readily the queer screens I then could smash ; (29)
   Fake away.
But my nuttiest blowen, (30) one fine day,
   Fake away,
To the beaks (31) did her fancy man betray,
And thus I was bowled out at last. (32)
   Nix my doll pals, fake away.

And thus I was bowled out at last
And into the jug for a lag was cast ; (33)
   Fake away.
But I slipped my darbies (34) one morn in May,
   Fake away.
And I gave to the dubsman (35) a holiday.
And here I am, pals, merry and free,
A regular rollicking romany. (36)
   Nix my doll pals, fake away.

Much laughter and applause rewarded Jerry's attempt to
please ; and though the meaning of his chant, even with the
aid of the numerous notes appended to it, may not be quite
obvious to our readers, we can assure them that it was perfectly intelligible to the canting crew. Jerry was now
entitled to a call ; and happening, at the moment, to meet
the fine dark eyes of a sentimental gipsy, one of that better
class of mendicants who wandered about the country with a
guitar at his back, his election fell upon him. The youth,
without prelude, struck up a

GIPSY SERENADE.*

Merry maid, merry maid, wilt thou wander with me?
We will roam through the forest, the meadow, and lea ;

---

(22) Thief.   (23) With my hair dressed in the first fashion.
(24) With several rings on my hands.   (25) Seals.
(26) Gold watch.   (27) Laced shirt.
(28) Gentlemanlike.   (29) Easily then forged notes could I pass.
(30) Favourite mistress.   (31) Police.
(32) Taken at length.   (33) Cast for transportation.
(34) Fetters.   (35) Turnkey.   (36) Gipsy.
* Set to music by Mr. Alexander Roche.

We will haunt the sunny bowers, and when day begins to flee,
Our couch shall be the ferny brake, our canopy the tree,
    Merry maid, merry maid, come and wander with me!
    No life like the gipsy's, so joyous and free!

Merry maid, merry maid, though a roving life be ours,
We will laugh away the laughing and quickly fleeting hours;
Our hearts are free, as is the free and open sky above,
And we know what tamer souls know not, how lovers *ought* to love,
    Merry maid, merry maid, come and wander with me!
    No life like the gipsy's, so joyous and free!

Zoroaster now removed the pipe from his upright lips to intimate his intention of proposing a toast.

A universal knocking of knuckles by the knucklers* was followed by profound silence. The sage spoke:

"The city of Canterbury, pals," said he, "and may it never want a knight of Malta."

The toast was pledged with much laughter, and in many bumpers.

The knight, upon whom all eyes were turned, rose, "with stately bearing and majestic motion," to return thanks.

"I return you an infinitude of thanks, brother pals," said he, glancing round the assemblage; and bowing to the president, "and to you, most upright Zory, for the honour you have done me in associating my name with that city. Believe me, I sincerely appreciate the compliment, and echo the sentiment from the bottom of my soul. I trust it never *will* want a knight of Malta. In return for your consideration, but a poor one you will say, you shall have a ditty, which I composed upon the occasion of my pilgrimage to that city, and which I have thought proper to name after myself:"

THE KNIGHT OF MALTA:

A Canterbury Tale.†

Come list to me, and you shall have, without a hem or haw, sirs,
A Canterbury pilgrimage, much better than old Chaucer's.
'Tis of a hoax I once played off, upon that city clever,
The memory of which I hope, will stick to it for ever.
    With my coal-black beard, and purple cloak,
    jack-boots, and broad-brimmed castor.
    Hey-ho! for the Knight of Malta!

---

* Pickpockets.

† This song describes pretty accurately the career of an extraordinary individual, who in the lucid intervals of a half-crazed understanding, imposed himself upon the credulous inhabitants of Canterbury, in the year 1832, as a certain "SIR WILLIAM PERCY HONEYWOOD COURTENAY, KNIGHT OF MALTA;" and contrived—for there was considerable "method in his madness"—to support the deception during a long period. The anachronism of

To execute my purpose, in the first place, you must know, sirs,
My locks I let hang down my neck—my beard and whiskers grow, sirs;
A purple cloak I next clapped on, a sword tagged to my side, sirs,
And mounted on a charger black, I to the town did ride, sirs.

With my coal-black beard, &c.

---

his character in a tale (the date of which is nearly a century back), will perhaps be overlooked, when it is considered of how much value, in the illustration of "wise saws," are "*modern instances.*" Imposture and credulity are of all ages; and the Courtenays of the nineteenth are rivalled by the Tofts and Andrés of the eighteenth century. The subjoined account of the *soi-disant* SIR WILLIAM COURTENAY is extracted from "An Essay on his Character, and Reflections on his Trial," published at the theatre of his exploits: "About Michaelmas last it was rumoured that an extraordinary man was staying at the Rose Inn of this city (Canterbury), who passed under the name of Count Rothschild, but had been recently known in London by the name of Thompson! This would have been sufficient to excite attention, had not other incidents materially added to the excitement. His costume and countenance denoted foreign extraction, while his language and conversation showed that he was well acquainted with almost every part of this kingdom. He was said to live with singular frugality, notwithstanding abundant samples of wealth, and professions of an almost unlimited command of money. He appeared to study retirement, if not concealment, although subsequent events have proved that society of every grade, beneath the middle class, is the element in which he most freely breathes. He often decked his person with a fine suit of Italian clothing, and sometimes with the more gay and imposing costume of the Eastern nations, yet these foreign habits were for months scarcely visible beyond the limits of the inn of his abode, and the chapel not far from it, in which he was accustomed to offer his Sabbath devotions. This place was the first to which he made a public and frequent resort; and though he did not always attempt to advance towards the uppermost seat in the synagogue, he attracted attention from the mere singularity of his appearance.

"Such was the eccentric, incongruous individual who surprised our city by proposing himself as a third candidate for its representation, and who created an entertaining contest for the honour, long after the sitting candidates had composed themselves to the delightful vision of an unexpensive and unopposed return. The notion of representing the city originated beyond all doubt in the fertile brain of the man himself. It would seem to have been almost as sudden a thought in his mind, as it was a sudden and surprising movement in the view of the city; nor have we been able to ascertain whether his sojourn at the Rose was the cause or the effect of his offering to advocate our interests in parliament—whether he came to the city with that high-minded purpose, or subsequently formed the notion, when he saw, or thought he saw, an opening for a stranger of enterprise like himself.

* * * * * * *

"As the county election drew on, we believe between the nomination on Barham Downs and the voting in the cattle market of the city, the draught of a certain handbill was sent to a printer of this city, with a request that he would publish it without delay. Our readers will not be surprised that he instantly declined the task; but as we have obtained possession of the copy, and its publication can now do no injury to any one, we entertain them with a sight of this delectable sample of Courtenay prudence and politeness.

"'O yes! O yes! O yes! I, Lord Viscount William Courtenay, of Powderham Castle, Devon, do hereby proclaim Sir Thomas Tylden, Sir Brook Brydges, Sir Edward Knatchbull, and Sir William Cosway, four cowards, unfit to represent, or to assist in returning members of parliament to serve the brave men of Kent.

Two pages were there by my side, upon two little ponies,
Decked out in scarlet uniform as spruce as macaronies;
Caparisoned my charger was, as grandly as his master.
And o'er my long and curly locks I wore a broad-brimmed castor.
                        With my coal-black beard, &c.

The people all flocked forth, amazed to see a man so hairy,
Oh! such a sight had ne'er before been seen in Canterbury!
My flowing robe, my flowing beard, my horse with flowing mane, sirs!
They stared—the days of chivalry, they thought, were come again, sirs!
                        With my coal-black beard, &c.

I told them a long rigmarole romance, that did not halt a
Jot, that they beheld in me a real Knight of Malta!
Tom à Becket had I sworn I was, that saint and martyr hallowed,
I doubt not just as readily the bait they would have swallowed.
                        With my coal-black beard, &c.

I rode about, and speechified, and everybody gullied,
The tavern-keepers diddled, and the magistracy bullied;
Like puppets were the townsfolk led in that show they call a raree;
The Gotham sages were a joke to those of Canterbury.
                        With my coal-black beard, &c.

The theatre I next engaged, where I addressed the crowd, sirs,
And on retrenchment, and reform, I spouted long and loud, sirs;
On tithes, and on taxation, I enlarged with skill and zeal, sirs,
Who so able as a Malta knight, the malt tax to repeal, sirs?
                        With my coal-black beard, &c.

As a candidate I then stepped forth to represent their city,
And my non-election to that place was certainly a pity;
For surely I the fittest was, and very proper, very,
To represent the wisdom and the wit of Canterbury.
                        With my coal-black beard, &c.

At the trial of some smugglers next, one thing I rather queer did,
And the justices upon the bench I literally *bearded*;
For I swore that I some casks did see, though proved as clear as day, sirs,
That I happened at the time to be some fifty miles away, sirs.
                        With my coal-black beard, &c.

This last assertion, I must own, was somewhat of a blunder,
And for perjury indicted they compelled me to knock under;
To my prosperous career this slight error put a stop, sirs,
And thus *crossed*, the Knight of Malta was at length obliged to *hop*, sirs.
                With his coal-black beard, and purple cloak,
                        jack-boots, and broad-brimmed castor,
                        Good-bye to the Knight of Malta.

"'Percy Honeywood Courtenay, of Hales and Evington Place, Kent, and Knight of Malta.

"'Any gentleman desiring to know the reasons why Lord Courtenay so publicly exposes backbiters, any man of honour shall have satisfaction at his hands, and in a public way, according to the laws of our land—trial by combat; when the Almighty God, the Lord of Hosts is his name, can decide the "truth," whether it is a libel or not. I worship truth as my God, and will die for it—and upon this we will see who is strongest, God or man.'

"It is a coincidence too curious to be overlooked, that this doughty champion of *truth* should soon have removed himself from public life by an act of deliberate and wanton perjury. We never read any of his rhapsodies,

The knight sat down amidst the general plaudits of the company.

The party, meanwhile, had been increased by the arrival of Luke and the sexton. The former, who was in no mood for revelry, refused to comply with his grandsire's solicitation to enter, and remained sullenly at the door, with his arms folded, and his eyes fixed upon Turpin, whose movements he commanded through the canvas aperture. The sexton walked

---

periodical or occasional, till the publication of this essay imposed the self-denying task upon us; but now we find that they abound in strong and solemn appeals to the *truth*; in bold proclamations that *truth* is his palladium; in evidences that he writes and raves, that he draws his sword and clenches his fist, that he expends his property and the property of others committed to his hands, in no cause but that of *truth!* His famous periodical contains much vehement declamation in defence of certain doctrines of religion, which he terms the truth of the sublime system of Christianity, and for which alone he is content to live and also willing to die. All who deviate from his standard of truth, whether theological or moral, philosophical or political, he appears to consider as neither fit for life or death. Now it is a little strange, his warmest followers being witnesses, that such an advocate of truth should have become the willing victim of falsehood, the ready and eager martyr of the worst form of falsehood—perjury.

"The decline of his influence between the city and county elections has been partly attributed, and not without reason, to the sudden change in his appearance from comparative youth to advancing, if not extreme age. On the hustings of the city he shone forth in all the dazzling lustre of an oriental chief; and such was the effect of gay clothing on the meridian of life, that his admirers, especially of the weaker sex, would insist upon it that he had not passed the beautiful spring-time of May. There were, indeed, some suspicious appearances of a near approach to forty, if not two or three years beyond it; but these were fondly ascribed to his foreign travels in distant and insalubrious climes; he had acquired his duskiness of complexion, and his strength of feature and violence of gesture, and his profusion of beard in Egypt and Syria, in exploring the catacombs of the one country, and bowing at the shrines of the other. On the other hand, the brilliancy of his eye, the melody of his voice, and the elasticity of his muscles and limbs, were sufficient arguments in favour of his having scarcely passed the limit that separates manhood from youth.

"All doubts on these points were removed, when the crowd of his fair admirers visited him at the retirement of his inn, and the intervals of his polling. These *sub Rosâ* interviews—we allude to the name of the inn, and not to anything like privacy there, which the very place and number of the visitors altogether precluded—convinced them that he was even a younger and lovelier man than his rather boisterous behaviour in the hall would allow them to hope. In fact, he was now installed by acclamation *Knight of Canterbury as well as Malta, and King of Kent as well as Jerusalem!* It became dangerous then to whisper a syllable of suspicion against his wealth or rank, his wisdom or beauty; and all who would not bow down before this golden image were deemed worthy of no better fate than Shadrach, Meshech, and Abednego—to be cast into a burning fiery furnace."

As a sequel to the above story, it may be added, that the Knight of Malta became the inmate of a lunatic asylum; and on his liberation was shot at the head of a band of Kentish hinds whom he had persuaded that he was the Messiah!

up to Dick, who was seated at the post of honour, and clapping him upon the shoulder, congratulated him upon the
comfortable position in which he found him.

"Ha, ha! Are you there, my old death's head on a mop-
stick?" said Turpin, with a laugh. "Ain't we merry mum-
pers, eh? Keeping it up in style. Sit down, old Noah;
make yourself comfortable, Methusalem."

"What say you to a drop of as fine Nantz as you ever
tasted in your life, old cove?" said Zoroaster.

"I have no sort of objection to it," returned Peter, "provided you will all pledge my toast."

"That I will, were it Old Ruffin himself," shouted Turpin.

"Here's to the three-legged mare," cried Peter. "To the
tree that bears fruit all the year round, and yet has neither
bark nor branch. You won't refuse that toast, Captain
Turpin?"

"Not I," answered Dick; "I owe the gallows no grudge.
If, as Jerry's song says, I must have a hearty choke and
caper sauce for my breakfast one of these fine mornings, it
shall never be said that I fell to my meal without appetite, or
neglected saying grace before it. Gentlemen, here's Peter
Bradley's toast, 'The scragging-post; the three-legged mare,'
with three times three."

Appropriate as this sentiment was, it did not appear to be
so inviting to the party as might have been anticipated, and
the shouts soon died away.

"They like not the thoughts of the gallows," said Turpin
to Peter. "More fools they. A mere bugbear to frighten
children, believe me; and never yet alarmed a brave man.
The gallows, pshaw! One can but die once, and what signifies it how, so that it be over quickly. I think no more of
the last leap into eternity than clearing a five-barred gate. A
rope's-end for it! So let us be merry, and make the most
of our time, and that's true philosophy. I know you can
throw off a rum chant," added he, turning to Peter. "I
heard you sing last night at the hall. Troll us a stave, my
antediluvian file, and, in the mean time, tip me a gage of
fogus,* Jerry; and if that's a bowl of huckle-my-butt† you
are brewing, Sir William," added he, addressing the knight
of Malta, "you may send me a jorum at your convenience."

Jerry handed the highwayman a pipe, together with a
tumbler of the beverage which the knight had prepared,

---

* A pipe of tobacco.
† A drink composed of beer, eggs, and brandy.

which he pronounced excellent; and while the huge bowl
was passed round to the company, a prelude of shawms
announced that Peter was ready to break into song.

Accordingly, after the symphony was ended, accompanied
at intervals by a single instrument, Peter began his melody,
in a key so high, that the utmost exertion of the shawm-
blower failed to approach its altitudes. The burden of his
ministrelsy was:

THE MANDRAKE.*

Μῶλυ δέ μιν καλέουσι θεοί, χαλεπὸν δέ τ᾽ ὀρύσσειν
Ἀνδράσι γε θνητοῖσι, θεοὶ δέ τε πάντα δύνανται.

HOMERUS.

The mandrake grows 'neath the gallows-tree,
And rank and green are its leaves to see;
Green and rank, as the grass that waves
Over the unctuous earth of graves;
And though all around it be bleak and bare,
Freely the mandrake flourisheth there.
        Maranatha—Anathema!
    Dread is the curse of mandragora!
            Euthanasy!

At the foot of the gibbet the mandrake springs,
Just where the creaking carcase swings;
Some have thought it engendered
From the fat that drops from the bones of the dead;
Some have thought it a human thing;
But this is a vain imagining.
        Maranatha—Anathema!
    Dread is the curse of mandragora!
            Euthanasy!

A charnel leaf doth the mandrake wear,
A charnel fruit doth the mandrake bear;

---

* The supposed malignant influence of this plant is frequently alluded to
by our elder dramatists; and with one of the greatest of them, Webster (as
might be expected from a muse revelling like a ghoul in graves and sepulchres),
it is an especial favourite. But none have plunged so deeply into the subject
as Sir Thomas Browne. He tears up the fable root and branch. Concerning
the danger ensuing from eradication of the mandrake, he thus writes:—" The
last assertion is, that there follows a hazard of life to them that pull it up,
that some evil fate pursues them, and that they live not very long hereafter.
Therefore the attempt hereof among the ancients was not in ordinary way;
but, as Pliny informeth, when they intended to take up the root of this plant,
they took the wind thereof, and with a sword describing three circles about
it, they digged it up, looking toward the west. A conceit not only injurious
unto truth and confutable by daily experience, but somewhat derogatory unto
the providence of God; that is, not only to impose so destructive a quality on
any plant, but to conceive a vegetable whose parts are so useful unto many,
should, in the only taking up, prove mortal unto any. This were to introduce
a second forbidden fruit, and enhance the first malediction, making it not
only mortal for Adam to taste the one, but capital for his posterity to eradicate, or dig up the other."—*Vulgar Errors*, book ii. c. vi.

Yet none like the mandrake hath such great power,
Such virtue resides not in herb or flower;
Aconite, hemlock, or moonshade I ween,
None hath a poison so subtle and keen.
              Maranatha—Anathema!
          Dread is the curse of mandragora!
                  Euthanasy!

And whether the mandrake be create
Flesh with the flower incorporate,
I know not; yet, if from the earth 'tis rent,
Shrieks and groans from the root are sent;
Shrieks and groans, and a sweat like gore,
Oozes and drops from the clammy core.
              Maranatha—Anathema!
          Dread is the curse of mandragora!
                  Euthanasy!

Whoso gathereth the mandrake shall surely die;
Blood for blood is his destiny.
Some who have plucked it have died with groans,
Like to the mandrake's expiring moans;
Some have died raving, and some beside,
With penitent prayers—but *all* have died.
          Jesu! save us by night and by day!
          From the terrible death of mandragora!
                  Euthanasy.

"A queer chant that," said Zoroaster, coughing loudly, i.
token of disapprobation.

"Not much to my taste," quoth the knight of Malta. "We
like something more sprightly in Canterbury."

"Nor to mine," added Jerry; "don't think it's likely to
have an encore. 'Pon my soul, Dick, you must give us something yourself, or we shall never cry Euthanasy at the Triple
Tree."

"With all my heart," replied Turpin. "You shall have
—but what do I see, my friend, Sir Luke? Devil take my
tongue, Luke Bradley, I mean. What, ho! Luke—nay, nay,
man, no shrinking—stand forward; I've a word or two to say
to you. We must have a nob-a-nob glass together, for old
acquaintance sake. Nay, no airs, man; dammee you're not
a lord yet, nor a baronet either, though I do hold your title in
my pocket; never look glum at me. It won't pay. I'm one
of the canting crew now; no man shall sneer at me with impunity, eh, Zory? Ha, ha! here's a glass of Nantz; we'll
have a bottle of black strap when you are master of your
own. Make ready there, you gut-scrapers, you shawm-
shavers; I'll put your lungs in play for you presently. In
the mean time—charge, pals, charge—a toast, a toast!
Health and prosperity to Sir Luke Rookwood! I see you
are surprised—this, gem'men, is Sir Luke Rookwood, some-

while Luke Bradley, heir to the house of that name, not ten miles distant from this. Say, shall we not drink a bumper to his health?"

Astonishment prevailed amongst the crew. Luke himself had been taken by surprise. When Turpin discovered him at the door of the tent, and summoned him to appear, he reluctantly complied with the request; but when, in a half-bantering vein Dick began to rally him upon his pretensions, he would most gladly have retreated, had it been in his power. It was then too late. He felt he must stand the ordeal. Every eye was fixed upon him with a look of inquiry.

Zoroaster took his everlasting pipe from his mouth.

"This ain't true, sure*ly?*" asked the perplexed Magus.

"He has said it," replied Luke; "I may not deny it."

This was sufficient. There was a wild hubbub of delight amongst the crew, for Luke was a favourite with all.

"Sir Luke Rookwood!" cried Jerry Juniper, who liked a title as much as Tommy Moore is said to dote upon a lord. "Upon my soul I sincerely congratulate you; devilish fortunate fellow. Always cursed unlucky myself. I could never find out my own father, unless it were one Monsieur des Capriolles, a French dancing-master, and *he* never left anything behind him that I could hear of, except a broken kit and a hempen widow. Sir Luke Rookwood, we shall do ourselves the pleasure of drinking your health and prosperity."

Fresh bumpers, and immense cheering.

Silence being in a measure restored, Zoroaster claimed Turpin's promise of a song.

"True, true," replied Dick; "I have not forgotten it. Stand to your bows, my hearties."

THE GAME OF HIGH TOBY.

Now Oliver (1) puts his black nightcap on,
    And every star its glim (2) is hiding,
And forth to the heath is the scampsman (3) gone,
    His matchless cherry-black (4) prancer riding;
Merrily over the common he flies,
    Fast and free as the rush of rocket,
His crape-covered vizard drawn over his eyes.
    His tol (5) by his side, and his pops (6) in his pocket.

CHORUS.
*Then who can name
So merry a game.
As the game of all games—high toby? (7)*

---

(1) The moon. (2) Light. (3) Highwayman.
(4) "Cherry-coloured—black; there being black cherries as well as red."— GROSE. (5) Sword. (6) Pistols. (7) Highway-robbery.

P

The traveller hears him, away! away!
  Over the wide wide heath he scurries;
He heeds not the thunderbolt summons to stay,
  But ever the faster and faster he hurries.
But what daisy-cutter can match that black tit?
  He is caught—he must "stand and deliver;"
Then out with the dummy, (8) and off with the bit, (9)
  Oh! the game of high toby for ever!

      CHORUS.
    Then who can name
    So merry a game,
    As the game of all games—high toby!

Believe me, there is not a game, my brave boys,
  To compare with the game of high toby;
No rapture can equal the tobyman's joys,
  To blue devils, blue plumbs (10) give the go-by;
And what if, at length, boys, he come to the crap! (11)
  Even rack punch has *some* bitter in it,
For the mare-with-three-legs, (12) boys, I care not a rap,
  'Twill be over in less than a minute!

      GRAND CHORUS.
    Then hip, hurrah!
    Fling care away!
    Hurrah for the game of high toby!

"And now, pals," said Dick, who began to feel the influence of these morning cups, "I vote that we adjourn.
Believe me I shall always bear in mind that I am a brother
of your band. Sir Luke and I must have a little chat together ere I take my leave. Adieu!"

And taking Luke by the arm, he walked out of the tent.
Peter Bradley rose, and followed them.

At the door they found the dwarfish Grasshopper, with
Black Bess. Rewarding the urchin for his trouble, and slipping the bridle of his mare over his hand, Turpin continued
his walk over the green. For a few minutes he seemed to be
lost in rumination.

"I tell you what, Sir Luke," said he; "I should like to do
generous thing, and make you a present of this bit of paper.
But one ought not to throw away one's luck, you know—
there is a tide in the affairs of thieves, as the player coves say,
which must be taken at the flood, or else—no matter! Your
old dad, Sir Piers (God help him!) had the gingerbread, *that*
I know; he was, as we say, a regular rhino-cerical cull. You
won't feel a few thousands, especially at starting; and besides,
there are two others, Rust and Wilder, who row in the same
boat with me, and must therefore come in for their share of
the reg'lars. All this considered, you can't complain, I think,

(8) Pocket-book.   (9) Money.   (10) Bullets.
      (11) The gallows.   (12) Ditto.

if I ask five thousand for it. That old harridan, Lady Rook-wood, offered me nearly as much."

"I will not talk to you of fairness," said Luke; "I will not say that document belongs of right to me. It fell by accident into your hands. Having possessed yourself of it, I blame you not that you dispose of it to the best advantage. I must, perforce, agree to your terms."

"Oh, no," replied Dick, "it's quite optional; Lady Rook-wood will give as much and make no mouths about it. Soho, lass! What makes Bess prick her ears in that fashion?— Ha! carriage-wheels in the distance! that jade knows the sound as well as I do. I'll just see what it's like!—you will have ten minutes for reflection. Who knows if I may not have come in for a good thing here?"

At that instant a carriage passed the angle of rock some three hundred yards distant, and was seen slowly ascending the hill-side. Eager as a hawk after his quarry, Turpin dashed after it.

In vain the sexton, whom he nearly overthrew in his career, called after him to halt. He sped like a bolt from the bow.

"May the devil break his neck!" cried Peter, as he saw him dash through the brook; "could he not let them alone?"

"This must not be," said Luke; "know you whose carriage it is?"

"It is a shrine that holds the jewel that should be dearest in your eyes," returned Peter; "haste, and arrest the spoiler's hand."

"Whom do you mean?" asked Luke.

"Eleanor Mowbray," replied Peter. "She is there. To the rescue—away."

"Eleanor Mowbray," echoed Luke—"and Sybil!——"

At this instant a pistol-shot was heard.

"Will you let murder be done, and upon your cousin?" cried Peter, with a bitter look. "You are not what I took u for."

Luke answered not, but, swift as the hound freed from the leash, darted in the direction of the carriage.

VI.

ELEANOR MOWBRAY.

—— Mischiefs
Are like the visits of Franciscan friars,
They never come to prey upon us single.—*Devil's Law Case.*

THE course of our tale returns now to Eleanor Mowbray.
After she had parted from Ranulph Rookwood, and had
watched him disappear beneath the arches of the church
porch, her heart sank, and, drawing herself back within the
carriage, she became a prey to the most poignant affliction.
In vain she endeavoured to shake off this feeling of desolation. It would not be. Despair had taken possession of
her; the magic fabric of delight melted away, or only gleamed
to tantalize, at an unreachable distance. A presentiment
that Ranulph would never be hers had taken root in her imagination, and overshadowed all the rest.

While Eleanor pursued this train of reflection, the time insensibly wore away, until the sudden stoppage of the carriage
aroused the party from their meditation. Major Mowbray
perceived that the occasion of the halt was the rapid advance
of a horseman, who was nearing them at full speed. The appearance of the rider was somewhat singular, and might have
created some uneasiness as to the nature of his approach, had
not the major immediately recognized a friend; he was,
nevertheless, greatly surprised to see him, and turned to Mrs.
Mowbray to inform her that Father Ambrose, to his infinite
astonishment, was coming to meet them, and appeared, from
his manner, to be the bearer of unwelcome tidings.

Father Ambrose was, perhaps, the only being whom Eleanor
disliked. She had felt an unaccountable antipathy towards
him, which she could neither extirpate nor control, during
their long and close intimacy. It may be necessary to mention that her religious culture had been in accordance with
the tenets of the Romish Church, in whose faith (the faith of
her ancestry) her mother had continued; and that Father
Ambrose, with whom she had first become acquainted during
the residence of the family near Bordeaux, was her ghostly
adviser and confessor. An Englishman by birth, he had
been appointed pastor to the diocese in which they dwelt,
and was, consequently, a frequent visitor, almost a constant
inmate, of the château; yet, though duty and respect would
have prompted her to regard the father with affection, Eleanor

could never conquer the feelings of dislike and distrust which she had at first entertained towards him; a dislike which was increased by the strange control in which he seemed to hold her mother, who regarded him with a veneration approaching to infatuation. It was, therefore, with satisfaction that she bade him adieu. He had, however, followed his friends to England under a feigned name (as, being a recusant Romish priest, and supposed to have been engaged in certain Jesuitical plots, his return to his own country was attended with considerable risk), and had now remained domesticated with them for some months. That he had been in some way, early in life, connected with a branch of the house of Rookwood, Eleanor was aware (she fancied he might have been engaged in political intrigue with Sir Reginald, which would have well accorded with his ardent ambitious temperament), and the knowledge of this circumstance made her doubly apprehensive lest the nature of his present communication should have reference to her lover, towards whose cause the father had never been favourable, and respecting whose situation he might have made some discovery, which she feared he might use to Ranulph's disadvantage.

Wrapped in a long black cloak, with a broad-brimmed hat drawn closely over his brows, it was impossible to distinguish further of the priest's figure and features beyond the circumstance of his height, which was remarkable, until he had reached the carriage-window, when, raising his hat, he disclosed a head that Titian might have painted, and which, arising from the dark drapery, looked not unlike the visage of some grave and saturnine Venetian. There was a venerable expanse of forehead, thinly scattered with hair, towering over black pent-house-like brows, which, in their turn, shadowed keen penetrating eyes; the temples were hollow, and blue veins might be traced beneath the sallow skin; the cheek-bones were high, and there was something in the face that spoke of self-mortification; while the thin livid lips closely compressed, and the austere and sinister expression of his countenance, showed that his self-abasement, if he had ever practised it, had scarcely prostrated the demon of pride, whose dominion might still be traced in the lines and furrows of his haughty physiognomy. The father looked at Mrs. Mowbray, and then glanced suspiciously at Eleanor. The former appeared to understand him.

"You would say a word to me in private," said Mrs. Mowbray; "shall I descend?"

The priest bowed assent.

"It is not to you alone that my mission extends," said he, gravely; "you are all in part concerned; your son had better alight with you."

"Instantly," replied the major. "If you will give your horse in charge to the postilion, we will attend you at once."

With a feeling of renewed apprehension, connected, she knew not why, with Ranulph, Eleanor beheld her relatives descend from the carriage; and, in the hope of gaining some clue from their gestures to the subject of their conversation, she watched their motions as narrowly as her situation permitted. From the earnest manner of the priest, and the interest his narrative seemed to excite in his hearers, it was evident that his communication was of importance.

Presently, accompanied by Father Ambrose, Mrs. Mowbray returned to the carriage, while the major, mounting the priest's horse, after bidding a hasty adieu to his sister, adding, with a look that belied the consolation intended to be conveyed by his words, that "all was well," but without staying to offer her any explanation of the cause of his sudden departure, rode back the way they had just traversed, and in the direction of Rookwood. Bereft of the only person to whom she could have applied for information, though dying with curiosity and anxiety to know the meaning of this singular interview, and of the sudden change of plans which she felt so intimately concerned herself, Eleanor was constrained to preserve silence, as, after their entrance into the carriage, her mother again seemed lost in painful reflection, and heeded her not; and the father, drawing from his pocket a small volume, appeared intently occupied in its perusal.

"Dear mother," said Eleanor, at length, turning to Mrs. Mowbray, "my brother is gone——"

"To Rookwood," said Mrs. Mowbray, in a tone calculated to check further inquiry; but Eleanor was too anxious to notice it.

"And wherefore, mother?" said she. "May I not be informed?"

"Not as yet, my child—not as yet," replied Mrs. Mowbray. "You will learn all sufficiently early."

The priest raised his cat-like eyes from the book to watch the effect of this speech, and dropped them instantly, as Eleanor turned towards him. She had been about to appeal to him, but having witnessed this look, she relinquished her scarce-formed purpose, and endeavoured to divert her tristful thoughts by gazing through the glimmering medium of her tears upon the soothing aspect of external nature—that aspect which, in sunshine or in storm, has ever relief in store for a heart embittered by the stony coldness of the world.

The road, meanwhile, led them through a long woody valley, and was now climbing the sides of a steep hill. They were soon in the vicinity of the priory, and of the gipsies' encampment. The priest leaned forward, and whispered something in Mrs. Mowbray's ear, who looked towards the ruined shrine, part of the mouldering walls being visible from the road.

At this moment the clatter of a horse's hoofs, and the sound of a loud voice commanding the postilion, in a menacing tone, to stop, accompanied by a volley of imprecations, interrupted the conference, and bespoke the approach of an unwelcome intruder, and one whom all, too truly, feared would not be readily dismissed. The postilion did his best to rid them of the assailant. Perceiving a masked horseman behind him, approaching at a furious rate, he had little doubt as to his intentions, and Turpin, for it was our highwayman, soon made his doubts certainties. He halloo'd to him to stop; but the fellow paid no attention to his command, and disregarded even the pistol which he saw, in a casual glimpse over his near side, presented at his person. Clapping spurs into his horse's flanks, he sought succour in flight. Turpin was by his side in an instant. As the highwayman endeavoured to catch his reins, the lad suddenly wheeled the carriage right upon him, and but for the dexterity of Turpin, and the clever conduct of his mare, would inevitably have crushed him against the roadside. As it was, his left leg was slightly grazed. Irritated at this, Turpin fired over the man's head, and with the butt-end of his pistol felled him from his seat. Startled by the sound, and no longer under the governance of their rider, the horses rushed with frantic violence towards a ditch that bounded the other side of the highway, down which the carriage was precipitated, and at once overturned. Turpin's first act, after he had ascertained that no mischief had been occasioned to those within, beyond the alarm incident to the shock, was to compel the postilion, who had by this time gained his legs, to release the horses from their traces. This done, with the best grace he could assume, and, adjusting his mask, he opened the carriage, and proceeded to liberate the captives.

"Beg pardon, ma'am," said he, so soon as he had released

Mrs. Mowbray; "excessively sorry, upon my soul, to have
been the cause of so much unnecessary alarm to you—all
the fault, I assure you, of that rascal of a postilion; had the
fellow only pulled up when I commanded him, this botheration
might have been avoided. You will remember that
when you pay him—all his fault, I assure you, ma'am."

Receiving no reply, he proceeded to extricate Eleanor,
with whose beauty the inflammable highwayman was instantly
smitten. Leaving the father to shift for himself, he turned
to address some observation of coarse gallantry to her : but
she eluded his grasp, and flew to her mother's side.

"It is useless, sir," said Mrs. Mowbray, as Turpin drew
near them, "to affect ignorance of your intentions. You
have already occasioned us serious alarm, much delay, and
inconvenience. I trust, therefore, that beyond our purses,
to which, though scantily supplied, you are welcome, we
shall sustain no molestation. You seem to have less of the
ruffian about you than the rest of your lawless race, and are
not, I should hope, destitute of common humanity."

"Common humanity!" replied Turpin : "bless you, ma'am,
I'm the most humane creature breathing—would not hurt a
fly, much less a lady. Incivility was never laid to my charge.
This business may be managed in a few seconds ; and as soon
as we have settled the matter, I'll lend your stupid jack-boy
a hand to put the horses to the carriage again, and get the
wheels out of the ditch. You have a banker, ma'am, I suppose in town—perhaps in the country; but I don't like
country bankers ; besides, I want a little ready cash in Rum-
ville—beg pardon, ma'am, London, I mean. My ears have
been so stunned with those Romany patterers, I almost *think*
in flash. Just draw me a cheque; I've pen and ink always
ready ; a cheque for fifty pounds, ma'am—only fifty. What's
your banker's name? I've blank cheques of all the best
houses in my pocket ; that and a kiss from the pretty lips of
that cherry-cheek'd maid," winking to Eleanor, "will fully
content me. You see you have neither an exorbitant nor
uncivil personage to deal with."

Eleanor shrank closer to her mother. Exhausted by previous agitation of the night, greatly frightened by the shock
which she had just sustained, and still more alarmed by the
words and gestures of the highwayman, she felt that she was
momentarily in danger of fainting, and with difficulty prevented herself from falling. The priest, who had succeeded
in freeing himself from the carriage, now placed himself between Turpin and the ladies.

"Be satisfied, misguided man," said the father, in a stern voice, offering a purse, which Mrs. Mowbray hastily extended towards him, "with the crime you have already committed, and seek not to peril your soul by deeper guilt; be content with the plunder you now obtain, and depart; for, by my holy calling, I affirm to you, that if you advance one footstep towards the further molestation of these ladies, it shall be at the hazard of your life."

"Bravo!" exclaimed Turpin. "Now this is what I like; who would have thought the old autem-bawler had so much pluck in him? Sir, I commend you for your courage, but you are mistaken. I am the quietest man breathing, and never harm a human being; in proof of which, only look at your rascal of a postilion, whom any one of my friends would have sent post-haste to the devil for half the trouble he gave me. Easy as I am, I never choose to be balked in my humours. I must have the fifty and the buss, and then I'm off, as soon as you like; and I may as well have the kiss while the old lady signs the cheque, and then we shall have the seal as well as the signature. Poh—poh—no nonsense! Many a pretty lass has thought it an honour to be kissed by Turpin."

Eleanor recoiled with deepest disgust, as she saw the highwayman thrust aside the useless opposition of the priest, and approach her. He had removed his mask; his face, flushed with insolent triumph, was turned towards her. Despite the loathing which curdled the blood within her veins, she could not avert her eyes. He drew near her; she uttered a shrill scream. At that moment a powerful grasp was laid upon Turpin's shoulder; he turned and beheld Luke.

"Save me! save me!" cried Eleanor, addressing the new comer.

"Damnation!" said the highwayman, "what has brought *you* here? One would think you were turned assistant to all distressed damsels. Quit your hold, or, by the God above us, you will repent it."

"Fool!" exclaimed Luke, "talk thus to one who heeds you." And as he spoke he hurled Turpin backwards with so much force that, staggering a few yards, the highwayman fell to the ground.

The priest stood like one stunned with surprise at Luke's sudden appearance and subsequent daring action.

Luke, meanwhile, approached Eleanor. He gazed upon her with curiosity mixed with admiration, for his heart told him she was very fair. A death-like paleness had spread over her cheeks; yet still, despite the want of colour, she looked exquisitely beautiful, and her large blue eyes eloquently thanked her deliverer for her rescue. The words she wanted were supplied by Mrs. Mowbray, who thanked him in appropriate terms, when they were interrupted by Turpin, who had by this time picked himself up, and was drawing near them. His countenance wore a fierce expression.

"I tell you what," said he, "Luke Bradley, or Luke Rookwood, or whatever else you may call yourself, you have taken a damned unfair advantage of me in this matter, and deserve nothing better at my hands than that I should call you to instant account for it; and curse me! if I don't too."

"Luke Bradley!" interrupted Mrs. Mowbray; "are you that individual?"

"I have been so called, madam," replied Luke.

"Father Ambrose, is this the person of whom you spoke?" eagerly asked the lady.

"So I conclude," returned the priest, evasively.

"Did he not call you Luke Rookwood?" eagerly demanded Eleanor. "Is that also your name?"

"Rookwood is my name, fair cousin," replied Luke, "if I may venture to call you so."

"And Ranulph Rookwood is——"

"My brother."

"I never heard he had a brother," rejoined Eleanor, with some agitation. "How can that be?"

"I am his brother, nevertheless," replied Luke, moodily— "his ELDER BROTHER!"

Eleanor turned to her mother and the priest with a look of imploring anguish: she saw a confirmation of the truth of this statement in their glances. No contradiction was offered by either to his statement; both, indeed, appeared in some mysterious manner prepared for it. This, then, was the dreaded secret. This was the cause of her brother's sudden departure. The truth flashed with lightning swiftness across her brain.

Chagrined and mortified, Luke remarked that glance of inquiry. His pride was hurt at the preference thus naturally shown towards his brother. He had been struck, deeply struck, with her beauty. He acknowledged the truth of Peter's words. Eleanor's loveliness was without parallel. He had seen nought so fair, and the instant he beheld her, he felt that for *her* alone could he cancel his vows to Sybil.

The spirit of rivalry and jealousy was instantly aroused by Eleanor's exclamations.

"His elder brother!" echoed Eleanor, dwelling upon his words, and addressing Luke—"then you must be—but no, you are not, you cannot be—it is Ranulph's title—it is not yours—you are not——"

"I am Sir Luke Rookwood," replied Luke, proudly.

Ere the words were uttered Eleanor had fainted.

"Assistance is at hand, madam, if you will accept it, and follow me," said Luke, raising the insensible girl in his arms, and bearing her down the hill towards the encampment, whither he was followed by Mrs. Mowbray and the priest, between whom, during the hurried dialogue we have detailed, very significant glances had been exchanged. Turpin, who, as it may be supposed, had not been an incurious observer of the scene passing, burst into his usual loud laugh on seeing Luke bear away his lovely burden.

"Cousin! Ha, ha!" said he. "So the wench is his cousin. Damme, I half suspect he has fallen in love with his new-found cousin; and if so, Miss Sybil, or I'm mistaken, will look as yellow as a guinea. If that little Spanish devil gets it into her pretty jealous pate that he is about to bring home a new mistress, we shall have a tragedy scene in the twinkling of a bed-post. However, I shan't lose sight of Sir Luke until I have settled my accounts with him. Hark ye, boy," continued he, addressing the postilion; "remain where you are; you won't be wanted yet awhile, I imagine. There's a guinea for you, to drink Dick Turpin's health."

Upon which he mounted his mare, and walked her easily down the hill.

"And so that be Dick Turpin, folks talk so much about," soliloquized the lad, looking curiously after him; "well, he's as civil speaking a chap as need be, blow my boots if he ain't! and if I'd had a notion it were he, I'd have pulled up at first call, without more ado. Nothing like experience; I shall know better another time," added he, pocketing the douceur.

Rushing swiftly down the hill, Luke tarried at the river's brink, to sprinkle some of the cool element upon the pale brow of Eleanor. As he held her in his arms, thoughts which he fain would have stifled in their birth took possession of his heart. "Would she were mine?" murmured he. "Yet no! the wish is unworthy." But that wish returned unbidden.

Eleanor opened her eyes. She was still too weak to walk without support, and Luke, raising her once more in his arms, and motioning Mrs. Mowbray to follow, crossed the brook by means of stepping-stones, and conducting his charge along a by-path towards the priory, so as to avoid meeting with the crew assembled upon the green.

They had gained one of the roofless halls, when he encountered Balthazar. Astonished at the sight of the party, the patrico was about to address the priest as an acquaintance, when his more orthodox brother raised his finger to his lips, in token of caution. The action passed unobserved.

"Hie thee to Sybil," said Luke to the patrico. "Bid her haste hither. Say that this maiden—that Miss Mowbray is here, and requires her aid. Fly! I will bear her to the refectory."

As Balthazar passed the priest, he pointed with a significant glance towards a chasm in the wall, which seemed to be an opening to some subterraneous chamber. The father again made a gesture of silence, and Balthazar hastened upon his mission.

Luke led them to the refectory. He brought a chair for Eleanor's support; but so far from reviving, after such attention as could be afforded her, she appeared to become weaker.

He was about to issue forth in search of Sybil, when to his surprise he found the door fastened.

"You cannot pass this way," said a voice, which Luke instantly recognised as that of the knight of Malta.

"Not pass!" echoed Luke. "What does this mean?"

"Our orders are from the queen," returned the knight.

At this instant the low tolling of a muffled bell was heard.

"Ha!" exclaimed Luke; "some danger is at hand."

His heart smote him as he thought of Sybil, and he looked anxiously towards Eleanor.

Balthazar rushed into the room.

"Where is Sybil?" cried Luke. "Will she not come?"

"She will be here anon," answered the patrico.

"I will seek her myself, then," said Luke. "The door by which you entered is free."

"It is *not* free," replied Balthazar. "Remain where you are."

"Who will prevent my going forth?" demanded Luke, sternly.

"I will," said Barbara Lovel, as she suddenly appeared in

the doorway. "You stir not, excepting at my pleasure. Where is the maiden?" continued she, looking around with a grim smile of satisfaction at the consternation produced by her appearance. "Ha! I see; she faints. Here is a cordial that shall revive her. Mrs. Mowbray, you are welcome to the gipsies' dwelling—you and your daughter. And you, Sir Luke Rookwood, I congratulate you upon your accession of dignity." Turning to the priest, who was evidently overwhelmed with confusion, she exclaimed, "And you too, sir, think you I recognise you not? We have met ere this, at Rookwood. Know you not, Barbara Lovel? Ha, ha! It is long since my poor dwelling has been so highly honoured. But I must not delay the remedy. "Let her drink of this," said she, handing a phial to Mrs. Mowbray. "It will instantly restore her."

"It is poison!" cried Luke. "She shall not drink it."

"Poison!" reiterated Barbara. "Behold!" and she drank off the liquid. "I would not poison your bride," added she, turning to Luke.

"My bride," echoed Luke.

"Ay, your bride," repeated Barbara.

Luke recoiled in amazement. Mrs. Mowbray almost felt inclined to believe she was a dreamer, so visionary did the whole scene appear. A dense crowd of witnesses stood at the entrance. Foremost amongst them was the sexton. Suddenly a shriek was heard, and the crowd opening to allow her passage, Sybil rushed forward.

VII.

MRS. MOWBRAY.

Well, go thy ways, old Nick Machiavel, there will never be the peer of thee for wholesome policy and good counsel; thou took'st pains to chalk men out the dark paths and hidden plots of murther and deceit, and no man has the grace to follow thee. The age is unthankful, thy principles are quite forsaken, and worn out of memory.—SHAKERLEY MARMION's *Antiquary*.

SYBIL's sudden entrance filled the group that surrounded Miss Mowbray with new dismay. But she saw them not. Her soul seemed rivetted by Eleanor, towards whom she rushed; and while her eye wandered over her beauty, she raised the braided hair from her brow, revealing the clear, polished forehead. Wonder, awe, devotion, pity, usurped the place of hatred. The fierce expression that had lit up her dark orbs was succeeded by tender commiseration. She looked an imploring appeal at Barbara.

"Ay, ay," returned the old gipsy, extending at the same time the phial; "I understand. Here is that will bring the blood once more into her pallid cheeks, and kindle the fire within her eyes. Give her of this."

The effect of the potion was almost instantaneous, amply attesting Barbara's skill in its concoction. Stifled respiration first proclaimed Eleanor's recovery. She opened her large and languid eyes; her bosom heaved almost to bursting; her pulses throbbed quickly and feverishly: and as the stimulant operated, the wild lustre of excitement blazed in her eyes.

Sybil took her hand to chafe it. The eyes of the two maidens met. They gazed upon each other steadfastly and in silence. Eleanor knew not whom she regarded, but she could not mistake that look of sympathy; she could not mistake the tremulous pressure of her hand; she felt the silent trickling tears. She returned the sympathising glance, and gazed with equal wonder upon the ministering fairy, for such she almost seemed that knelt before her. As her looks wandered from the kindly glance of Sybil to the withered and inauspicious aspect of the gipsy queen, and shifted thence to the dusky figures of her attendants, filled with renewed apprehension, she exclaimed, "Who are these, and where am I?"

"You are in safety," replied Luke. "This is the ruined priory of St. Francis; and those strange personages are a horde of gipsies. You need fear no injury from them."

"My deliverer!" murmured Eleanor; when all at once the recollection that he had avowed himself a Rookwood, and the elder brother of Ranulph, flashed across her memory. "Gipsies; did you not say these people were gipsies? Your own attire is the same as theirs. You are not, cannot be the brother of Ranulph."

"I do not boast the same mother," returned Luke, proudly; "but my father was Sir Piers Rookwood, and I am his elder born."

He turned away. Dark thoughts swept across his brain. Maddened by the beauty of Eleanor, stung by her slights, and insensible to the silent agony of Sybil, who sought in vain to catch his eye, he thought of nothing but of revenge, and the accomplishment of his purposes. All within was a wild and fearful turmoil. His better principles were stifled by the promptings of evil. "Methinks," cried he, half aloud, "if the Tempter were near to offer that maiden to me, even at the peril of my soul's welfare, I could not resist it."

The Tempter *was* at hand. He is seldom absent on occasions like the present. The sexton stood beside his grandson. Luke started. He eyed Peter from head to foot, almost expecting to find the cloven foot, supposed to be proper to the fiend. Peter grinned in ghastly derision.

"Soh! you would summon hell to your aid; and lo! the devil is at your elbow. Well, she is yours."

"Make good your words," cried Luke, impatiently.

"Softly—softly," returned Peter. "Moderate yourself, and your wishes shall be accomplished. Your own desires chime with those of others; nay, with those of Barbara. *She* would wed you to Miss Mowbray. You stare. But it is so. This is a cover for some deeper plot; no matter. It shall go hard, despite her cunning, if I foil her not at her own weapons. There is more mischief in that old woman's brain than was ever hatched within the crocodile's egg; yet she shall find her match. Do not thwart her; leave all to me. She is about it now," added he, noticing Barbara and Mrs. Mowbray in conference together. "Be patient—I will watch her." And he quitted his grandson for the purpose of scanning more closely the manœuvres of the old gipsy.

Barbara, meanwhile, had not remained inactive.

"You need fear no relapse in your daughter; I will answer for that," said the old gipsy to Mrs. Mowbray; "Sybil will tend her. Quit not the maiden's side," continued she, addressing her grandchild, adding in a whisper, "Be cautious —alarm her not—mine eye will be upon you—drop not a word."

So saying, she shuffled to a little distance with Mrs. Mowbray, keeping Sybil in view, and watching every motion, as the panther watches the gambols of a fawn.

"Know you who speaks to you?" said the old crone, in the peculiar low and confidential tone assumed by her tribe to strangers. "Have you forgotten the name of Barbara Lovel?"

"I have no distinct remembrance of it," returned Mrs. Mowbray.

"Think again," said Barbara; "and though years are

flown, you may perchance recall the black gipsy woman, **who,**
when you were surrounded with gay gallants, with dancing
plumes, perused your palm, and whispered in your ear the
favoured suitor's name. Bide with me a moment, madam,"
said Barbara, seeing that Mrs. Mowbray shrank from the
recollection thus conjured up; " I am old—very old; I have
survived the shows of flattery, and being vested with a power
over my people, am apt, perchance, to take too much upon
myself with others." The old gipsy paused here, and then,
assuming a more familiar tone, exclaimed, "The estates of
Rookwood are ample——"

" Woman, what mean you ?"

"They should have been yours, lady, and would have been,
but for that marriage. You would have beseemed them
bravely. Sir Reginald was wilful, and erased the daughter's
name to substitute that of his son. Pity it is that so fair a
creature as Miss Mowbray should lack the dower her beauty
and her birth entitle her to expect. Pity that Ranulph
Rookwood should lose his title, at the moment when he
deemed it was dropping into his possession. Pity that those
broad lands should pass away from you and your children, as
they will do, if Ranulph and Eleanor are united."

"They never shall be united," replied Mrs. Mowbray,
hastily.

"'Twere indeed to wed your child to beggary," said Barbara.

Mrs. Mowbray sighed deeply.

"There is a way," continued the old crone, in a deep
whisper, "by which the estates might still be hers and
yours."

" Indeed!" said Mrs. Mowbray, eagerly.

" Sir Piers Rookwood had two sons."

" Hah!"

" The elder is here."

" Luke—Sir Luke. He brought us hither."

" He loves your daughter. I saw his gaze of passion just
now. I am old now, but I have some skill in lovers' glances.
Why not wed her to him ? I read hands—read hearts, you
know. They were born for each other. Now, madam, do
you understand me ?"

" But," returned Mrs. Mowbray, with hesitation, "though
I might wish for—though I might sanction this, Eleanor is
betrothed to Ranulph—she loves him."

" Think not of *her*, if *you* are satisfied. She cannot **judge** so well for herself as you can for her. She is a child, and knows not what she loves. Her affection will soon be Luke's. He is a noble youth—the image of his grandfather, your father, Sir Reginald; and if your daughter be betrothed to any one, 'twas to the heir of Rookwood. That was an essential part of the contract. Why should the marriage not take place at once, and here?"

"Here! How were that possible?"

"You are within sacred walls. I will take you where an altar stands. There is no lack of holy priest to join their hands together. Your companion, Father Ambrose as you call him, will do the office fittingly. He has essayed his clerkly skill already on others of your house."

"To what do you allude, mysterious woman?" asked Mrs. Mowbray, with anxiety.

"To Sir Piers and Susan Bradley," returned Barbara. "That priest united them."

"Indeed! He never told me this."

"He dared not do so; he had an oath which bound him to concealment. The time is coming when greater mysteries will be revealed."

"'Tis strange I should not have heard of this before," said Mrs. Mowbray, musingly; "and yet I might have guessed as much from his obscure hints respecting Ranulph. I see it all now. I see the gulf into which I might have plunged; but I am warned in time. Father Ambrose," continued she, to the priest, who was pacing the chamber at some little distance from them, "is it true that my brother was wedded by you to Susan Bradley?"

Ere the priest could reply the sexton presented himself.

"Ha, the very father of the girl!" said Mrs. Mowbray, "whom I met within our family vault, and who was so strangely moved when I spoke to him of Alan Rookwood. Is he here likewise?"

"Alan Rookwood!" echoed Barbara, upon whom a light seemed suddenly to break; "ha! what said he of him?"

"Ill-boding raven," interposed Peter, fiercely; "be content with what thou knowest of the living, and trouble not the repose of the dead. Let them rest in their infamy."

"The dead!" echoed Barbara, with a chuckling laugh; "ha! ha! he is dead, then; and what became of his fair wife—his brother's minion? 'Twas a foul deed, I grant; and yet there was expiation. Blood flowed—blood——"

"Silence, thou night-hag," thundered Peter, "or I will

Q

have thee burned at the stake for the sorcery thou practisest.
Beware," added he, in a deep tone, "I am thy friend."

Barbara's withered countenance exhibited for an instant
the deepest indignation at the sexton's threat. The malediction trembled on her tongue; she raised her staff to smite
him, but she checked the action. In the same tone, and with
a sharp, suspicious look, she replied, "My *friend*, sayest
thou? See that it prove so, or beware of *me*."

And, with a malignant scowl, the gipsy queen slowly
shuffled towards her satellites, who were stationed at the
door.

VIII.

THE PARTING.

No marriage I esteem it, where the friends
Force love upon their children ; where the virgin
Is not so truly given as betrayed.
I would not have betrothed people (for
I can by no means call them lovers) make
Their rites no wedlock, but a sacrifice.
                    Combat of Love and Friendship.

ELEANOR MOWBRAY had witnessed her mother's with-
drawal from her side with much uneasiness, and was with
difficulty prevented by Sybil from breaking upon her conference with the gipsy queen. Barbara's dark eye was fixed
upon them during the whole of the interview, and communicated an indefinite sense of dread to Eleanor.

"Who—who is that old woman?" asked Eleanor, under
her breath. "Never, even in my wildest dreams, have I seen
aught so terrible. Why does she look so at us? She terrifies
me ; and yet she cannot mean me ill, or my mother ; we have
never injured her."

"Alas!" sighed Sybil.

"You sigh!" exclaimed Eleanor, in alarm. "Is there any
real danger, then? Help us to avoid it. Quick, warn my
mother ; she seems agitated. Oh, let me go to her."

"Hush!" whispered Sybil, maintaining an unmoved demeanour under the lynx-like gaze of Barbara. "Stir not, as
you value your life ; you know not where you are, or what
may befall you. Your safety depends upon your composure.
Your life is not in danger ; but what is dearer than life, your

love, is threatened with a fatal blow. There is a dark design to wed you to another."

"Heavens!" ejaculated Eleanor, "and to whom?"

"To Sir Luke Rookwood."

"I would die sooner! Marry *him?* They shall kill me ere they force me to it!"

"Could you not love him?"

"Love him! I have only seen him within this hour. I knew not of his existence. He rescued me from peril. I would thank him. I would love him, if I could, for Ranulph's sake; and yet for Ranulph's sake I hate him."

"Speak not of him thus to me," said Sybil, angrily. "If *you* love him not *I* love him. Oh! forgive me, lady; pardon my impatience—my heart is breaking, yet it has not ceased to beat for him. You say you will die sooner than consent to this forced union. Your faith shall not be so cruelly attested. If there must be a victim, I will be the sacrifice. God grant I may be the only one. Be happy! as happy as I am wretched! You shall see what the love of a gipsy can do."

As she spoke, Sybil burst into a flood of passionate tears. Eleanor regarded her with the deepest commiseration; but the feeling was transient; for Barbara, now advancing, exclaimed, "Hence to your mother. The bridegroom is waiting: to your mother girl!" And she motioned Eleanor fiercely away. "What means this? continued the old gipsy. What have you said to that girl? Did I not caution you against speech with her? and you have dared to disobey me. You, my grandchild—the daughter of my Agatha, with whom my slightest wish was law. I abandon you! I curse you!"

"Oh, curse me not!" cried Sybil. "Add not to my despair."

"Then follow my advice implicitly. Cast off this weakness; all is in readiness. Luke shall descend into the vaulted chapel; the ceremony shall there take place—there also shall Eleanor *die*—and there again shall you be wedded. Take this phial, place it within the folds of your girdle. When all is over, I will tell you how to use it? Are you prepared? Shall we set out?"

"I am prepared," replied Sybil, in accents hollow as despair; "but let me speak with Luke before we go."

"Be brief then—each moment is precious. Keep a guard upon your tongue. I will to Mrs. Mowbray. You have placed the phial in safety. A drop will free you from your troubles."

"'Tis in that hope I guard it," replied Sybil, as she departed in the direction of Luke. Barbara watched her join him, and then turned shortly towards Mrs. Mowbray and her daughter.

"You are ill, dear Luke," said Sybil, who had silently approached her faithless lover; "very ill."

"Ill!" echoed Luke, breaking into frantic laughter. "Ill! Ha, ha!—upon my wedding-day. No, I am well—well. Your eyes are jaundiced by jealousy."

"Luke, dear Luke, laugh not thus. It terrifies me. I shall think you insane. There, you are calmer—you are more like yourself—more *human*. You looked just now—oh God! that I should say it of you—as if you were possessed by demons."

"And if I were possessed, what then?"

"Horrible! hint not at it. You almost make me credit the dreadful tales I have heard, that on their wedding-day the Rookwoods are subject to the power of the 'Evil One.'"

"Upon their wedding-day—and *I* look thus?"

"You do—you do. Oh! cast this frenzy from you."

"She is mine—she is mine! I care not though fiends possess me, if it is my wedding-day, and Eleanor is my bride. And you say I look like a Rookwood. Ha, ha!"

"That wild laughter again. Luke, I implore you, hear me one word—my last——"

"I will not bear reproaches."

"I mean not to reproach you. I come to bless you—to forgive you—to bid you farewell. Will you not say farewell?"

"Farewell."

"Not so—not so. Mercy! my God! Compassionate him and me! My heart will break with agony. Luke, if you would not kill me, recall that word. Let not the guilt of my death be yours. 'Tis to save you from that remorse that I die!"

"Sybil, you have said rightly, I am not myself. I know not what demons have possession of my soul, that I can behold your agonies without remorse: that your matchless affection should awaken no return. Yet so it is. Since the fatal moment when I beheld yon maid I have loved her."

"No more. *Now* I can part with you. Farewell!"

"Stay, stay! wretch that I am. Stay, Sybil! If we must

part, and that it *must* be so I feel, let me receive your pardon, if you can bestow it. Let me clasp you once more within my arms. May you live to happier days—may you——"

"Oh, to die thus!" sobbed Sybil, disengaging herself from his embrace. "Live to happier days, said you? When have *I* given you reason to doubt, for an instant, the sincerity of *my* love, that you should insult me thus?"

"Then live with me—live for me."

"If you can love me still, I will live as your slave, your minion, your wife; aught you will have me be. You have raised me from wretchedness. Oh!" continued she, in an altered tone, "have I mistaken your meaning? Did you utter those words in false compassion for my sufferings?—Speak, it is not yet too late—all may be well. My fate—my life is in your hands. If you love me yet—if you can forsake Eleanor, speak—if not, be silent."

Luke averted his head.

"Enough!" continued Sybil, in a voice of agony; "I understand. May God forgive you! Fare you well! We shall meet no more."

"Do we part for ever?" asked Luke, without daring to regard her.

"For ever!" answered Sybil.

Before her lover could reply, she shot from his side, and plunging amidst the dark and dense assemblage near the door disappeared from view. An instant after, she emerged into the open air. She stood within the roofless hall. It was filled with sunshine—with the fresh breath of morn. The ivied ruins, the grassy floor, the blue vault of heaven, seemed to greet her with a benignant smile. All was *riant* and rejoicing—all, save her heart. Amid such brightness her sorrow seemed harsh and unnatural; and as she felt the glad influence of day, she was scarcely able to refrain from tears. It was terrible to leave this beautiful world, that blue sky, that sunshine, and all she loved—so young, so soon.

Entering a low arch, that yawned within the wall, she vanished like a ghost at the approach of morn.

IX.

THE PHILTER.

Thou hast practised on her with foul charms—
Abused her delicate youth with drugs and minerals.
SHAKSPEARE.—*Othello.*

To return to Miss Mowbray. In a state of mind bordering upon distraction, Eleanor rushed to her mother, and,
flinging her arms wildly round her neck, besought her to protect her. Mrs. Mowbray gazed anxiously upon the altered
countenance of her daughter, but a few moments relieved her
from much of her uneasiness. The expression of pain gradually subsided, and the look of vacuity was succeeded by one
of frenzied excitement. A film had, for an instant or two,
dimmed her eyes; they now gleamed with unnatural lustre.
She smiled—the smile was singular; it was not the playful,
pleasurable lighting up of the face that it used to be; but it
was a smile, and the mother's heart was satisfied.

Mrs. Mowbray knew not to what circumstance she could
attribute this wondrous change. She looked at the priest.
He was more apt in divining the probable cause of the sudden
alteration in Eleanor's manner.

"What if she has swallowed a love-powder?" said he,
approaching Mrs. Mowbray, and speaking in a whisper. "I
have heard of such abominable mixtures; indeed, the holy
St. Jerome himself relates an instance of similar sorcery, in
his life of Hilarius; and these people are said to compound
them."

"It may be so," replied Mr. Mowbray, in the same tone.
"I think that the peculiar softness in the eye is more than
natural."

"I will at least hazard an experiment, to attest the truth
or fallacy of my supposition," returned the father. "Do you
see your destined bridegroom yonder?" continued he, addressing Eleanor.

She followed with her eyes in the direction which Father
Ambrose pointed. She beheld Luke. We know not how to
describe the sensations which now possessed her. She thought
not of Ranulph; or, if she did, it was with vague indifference.
Wrapped in a kind of mental trance, she yielded to the pleasurable impulse that directed her unsettled fancies towards
Luke. For some moments she did not take her eyes from
him. The priest and Mrs. Mowbray watched her in silence.

Nothing passed between the party until Luke joined them.
Eleanor continued gazing at him, and the seeming tenderness
of her glance emboldened Luke to advance towards her. The
soft fire that dwelt in those orbs was, however, cold as the
shining wing of the luciola.

Luke approached her; he took her hand; she withdrew it
not. He kissed it. Still she withdrew it not; but gazed at
him with gently-glimmering eyes.

" My daughter is yours, Sir Luke Rookwood," exclaimed
Mrs. Mowbray.

" What says the maid herself?" asked Luke.

Eleanor answered not. Her eyes were still fixed on him.

" She will not refuse me her hand," said Luke.

The victim resisted not.

" To the subterranean shrine," cried Barbara. And she
gave the preconcerted signal to the band.

The signal was repeated by the gipsy crew. We may here
casually note that the crew had been by no means uninterested
or silent spectators of passing events, but had, on the contrary, indulged themselves in a variety of conjectures as
to their probable issue. Several bets were pendent, as to
whether it would be a match or not, after all. Zoroaster
took long odds that the match was off; offering a *bean* to
half a quid (in other words, a guinea to a half-guinea) that
Sybil would be the bride. His offer was taken at once by
Jerry Juniper, and backed by the knight of Malta.

" Ha! there's the signal," cried the knight; " I'll trouble
you for the bean."

" And I," added Jerry Juniper, " for another."

" See 'em fairly spliced first," replied Magus; " that's vot
I betted."

" Vell, vell, a few minutes will settle that. Come, pals, to
the autem ken. Avay. Mind and obey orders."

" Ay, ay," answered the crew.

" Here's a torch for the altar of Hymen," said the knight,
flashing his torch in the eyes of the patrico as he passed
him.

" For the halter of Haman, you might say," returned
Balthazar, sulkily. " It's well if some of us don't swing
for it."

" You don't say" rejoined the perplexed Magus, " swing!
Egad, I fear it's a ticklish business. But there's no fighting
shy, I fear, with Barbara present; and then there's that infernal autem-bawler; it will be so cursedly regular. If you

had done the job, Balty, it would not have signified a brass
farden. Luckily, there will be no vitnesses to snitch upon
us. There will be no one in the vault besides ourselves."

"There will be a silent and solemn witness," returned
Balthazar, "and one whom you expect not."

"Eh! Vot's that you say? A spy?"

But the patrico was gone.

"Make way there; make way, pals, for the bride and
bridegroom," cried the knight of Malta, drawing excalibur,
and preparing to lead the way to the vault.

The train began to move. Eleanor leaned upon the arm of
her mother. Beside them stalked Barbara, with an aspect
of triumph. Luke followed, with the priest. One by one the
assemblage quitted the apartment.

The sexton alone lingered. "The moment is at hand,"
said he, musingly, "when all shall be consummated."

A few steps brought him into the court. The crowd was
there still. A brief delay had taken place. The knight of
Malta then entered the mouth of the vault. He held his
torch so as to reveal a broken flight of steps, conducting, it
would seem, to regions of perpetual night. So thought
Eleanor, as she shudderingly gazed into the abyss. She
hesitated; she trembled; she refused. But her mother's
entreaties, and Barbara's threatening looks, induced, in the
end, reluctant compliance. At length the place was empty.
Peter was about to follow, when the sound of a horse's hoofs
broke upon his ear. He tarried for an instant, and the
mounted figure of the highwaymen burst within the limits of
the court.

"Ha, ha! old earthworm," cried Dick, "my Nestor of the
churchyard, alone! Where the devil are all the folks gone?
Where's Sir Luke, and his new-found cousin, eh?"

Peter hastily explained.

"A wedding under ground? famous! the thing of all
others I should like to see. I'll hang Bess to this ivy tod,
and grub my way with you thither, old mole."

"You must stay here, and keep guard," returned Peter.

"May I be hanged if I do, when such fun is going
on."

"Hanged, in all probability, you will be," returned Peter;
"but I should not, were I you, desire to anticipate my
destiny. Stay here you must, and shall; that's peremptory.
You will be the gainer by it. Sir Luke will reward you
nobly. I will answer for him. You can serve him most

effectually. Ranulph Rookwood and Major Mowbray are expected here."

"The devil they are. But how, or why——"

"I have not time to explain. In case of a surprise, discharge a pistol; they must not enter the vault. Have you a whistle? for you must play a double part, and we may need your assistance below."

"Sir Luke may command me. Here's a pipe as shrill as the devil's own cat-call."

"If it will summon you to our assistance below, 'tis all I need. May we rely on you?"

"When did Dick Turpin desert his friends? Anywhere this side the Styx the sound of that whistle will reach me. I'll ride about the court, and stand sentry."

"Enough," replied the sexton, as he dived under ground.

"Take care of your shins," shouted Dick. "That's a cursed ugly turn, but he's used to the dark. A surprise, eh! I'll just give a look to my snappers; flints all safe. Now I'm ready for them, come when they like." And, having made a circuit of the place, he halted near the mouth of the subterranean chapel, to be within hearing of Peter's whistle, and, throwing his right leg lazily over his saddle, proceeded coolly to light a short pipe (the luxury of the cigar being then unknown), humming the while snatches of a ballad, the theme of which was his own calling:

THE SCAMPSMAN.

Quis verè rex?   SENECA.

There is not a king, should you search the world round,
So blithe as the king of the road to be found;
His pistol's his sceptre, his saddle's his throne,
Whence he levies supplies, or enforces a loan.
Derry down.

To this monarch the highway presents a wide field,
Where each passing subject a tribute must yield;
His palace (the tavern!) receives him at night,
Where sweet lips and sound liquor crown all with delight.
Derry down.

The soldier and sailor, both robbers by trade,
Full soon on the shelf, if disabled, are laid;
The one gets a patch, and the other a peg,
But, while luck lasts, the highwayman shakes a loose leg!
Derry down.

Most fowls rise at dawn, but the owl wakes at e'en,
And a jollier bird can there nowhere be seen;
Like the owl, our snug scampsman his snooze takes by day,
And when night draws her curtain, scuds after his prey!
Derry down.

As the highwayman's life is the fullest of zest,
So the highwayman's death is the briefest and best;
He dies not as other men die, by *degrees!*
But AT ONCE! without wincing, and quite at his ease!
Derry down.

And thus for the present we leave him. O rare Dick
Turpin!

X.

ST. CYPRIAN'S CELL.

Lasciate ogni speranza voi ch' entrate.   DANTE.

CYPRIAN DE MULVERTON, fifth prior of the monastery of
Saint Francis, a prelate of singular sanctity, being afflicted,
in his latter days, with a despondency so deep that neither
penance nor fasting could remove it, vowed never again to
behold, with earthly eyes, the blessed light of heaven, nor
to dwell longer with his fellow-men; but, relinquishing his
spiritual dignity, "the world forgetting, by the world forgot,"
to immure himself, while living, within the tomb.

He kept his vow. Out of the living rock that sustained
the saintly structure, beneath the chapel of the monastery,
was another chapel wrought, and thither, after bidding an
eternal farewell to the world, and bestowing his benediction
upon his flock, whom he committed to the care of his successor, the holy man retired.

Never, save at midnight, and then only during the performance of masses for his soul's repose, did he ascend from
his cell; and as the sole light allowed within the dismal dungeon of his choice was that of a sepulchral lamp, as none
spoke with him in his retreat, save in muttered syllables,
what effect must the lustre emanating from a thousand
tapers, the warm and pungent odours of the incense-breathing
shrine, contrasted with the earthy vapours of his prison-
house, and the solemn swell of the Sanctus, have had upon
his excited senses?   Surely they must have seemed like a
foretaste of the heaven he sought to gain!

Ascetic to the severest point to which nature's endurance
could be stretched, Cyprian even denied himself repose. He
sought not sleep, and knew it only when it stole on him unawares. His couch was the flinty rock; and, long afterwards, when the zealous resorted to the sainted prior's cell,

and were shown those sharp and jagged stones, they marvelled how one like unto themselves could rest, or even recline upon their points without anguish, until it was explained to them that, doubtless, He who tempereth the wind to the shorn lamb had made that flinty couch soft to the holy sufferer as a bed of down. His limbs were clothed in a garb of horsehair of the coarsest fabric; his drink was the dank drops that oozed from the porous walls of his cell; and his sustenance, such morsels as were bestowed upon him by the poor—the only strangers permitted to approach him. No fire was suffered, where perpetual winter reigned. None were admitted to his nightly vigils; none witnessed any act of penance; nor were any groans heard to issue from that dreary cave; but the knotted blood-stained thong, discovered near his couch, too plainly betrayed in what manner those long lone nights were spent. Thus did a year roll on. Traces of his sufferings were visible in his failing strength. He could scarcely crawl; but he meekly declined assistance. He appeared not, as had been his wont, at the midnight mass; the door of his cell was thrown open at that hour; the light streamed down like a glory upon his reverend head; he heard the distant reverberations of the deep *Miserere*, and breathed odours as if wafted from Paradise.

One morn it chanced that they who sought his cell found him with his head upon his bosom, kneeling before the image of the virgin patroness of his shrine. Fearing to disturb his devotions, they stood reverentially looking on; and thus silently did they tarry for an hour; but, as in that space he had showed no signs of motion, fearing the worst, they ventured to approach him. He was cold as the marble before which he knelt. In the act of humblest intercession—it may be, in the hope of grace—had Cyprian's spirit fled.

"Blessed are they who die in the Lord," exclaimed his brethren, regarding his remains with deepest awe. On being touched, the body fell to the ground. It was little more than a skeleton.

Under the cloisters of the holy pile were his bones interred, with a degree of pomp and ostentation that little accorded with the lowliness and self-abasement of this man of many sorrows.

This chapel, at the time of which we treat, was pretty much in the same condition as it existed in the days of its holy inmate. Hewn out of the entrails of the rock, the roof, the vaults, the floor, were of solid granite. Three huge cylindrical pillars, carved out of the native rock, rough as the stems of gnarled oak-trees, lent support to the ceiling. Support, however, was unneeded; an earthquake could scarce have shaken down those solid rafters. Only in one corner, where the water welled through a crevice of the rock, in drops that fell like tears, was decay manifest. Here the stone, worn by the constant dripping, had, in some places, given way. In shape, the vault was circular. The interval between each massive pillar formed a pointed arch. Again, from each pillar sprang other arches, which, crossed by diagonal, ogive branches, weaving one into the other, and radiating from the centre, formed those beautifully intricate combinations upon which the eye of the architectural enthusiast loves to linger. Within the ring formed by these triple columns, in which again the pillars had their own web of arches, was placed an altar of stone, and beside it a crucifix of the same rude material. Here also stood the sainted image of her who had filled the prior with holy aspirations, now a shapeless stone. The dim lamp, that like a star struggling with the thick gloom of the wintry cell, had shed its slender radiance over the brow of the Virgin Thecla, was gone. But around the keystone of the central arches, whence a chain had once depended, might be traced in ancient characters, half effaced by time, the inscription:

SCΛ. THECLΛ ORΛ PRO NOBIS.

One outlet only was there from the chapel—that which led by winding steps to the monastery; one only recess—the prior's cell. The former faced the altar; the latter yawned like the mouth of a tomb at its back. Altogether it was a dreary place. Dumb were its walls as when they refused to return the murmured orisons of the anchorite. One uniform sad colouring prevailed throughout. The grey granite was grown hoar with age, and had a ghostly look; the columns were ponderous, and projected heavy shadows. Sorrow and superstition had their tale, and a moral gloom deepened the darkness of the spot. Despair, which had inspired its construction, seemed to brood therein. Hope shunned its inexorable recesses.

Alone, within this dismal sanctuary, with hands outstretched towards the desecrated image of its tutelar saint, knelt Sybil. All was darkness. Neither the heavy vapours that surrounded her, nor the shrine before which she bent, were visible; but familiar with the dreary spot, she knew

that she had placed herself aright. Her touch had satisfied
her that she bowed before the altar of stone; that her be-
nighted vision was turned towards the broken image of the
saint, though now involved in gloom the most profound; and
with clasped hands and streaming eyes, in low and mournful
tones, she addressed herself in the following hymn to the
tutelar saint of the spot:

HYMN TO ST. THECLA.*

In my trouble, in my anguish,
　In the depths of my despair,
As in grief and pain I languish,
　Unto thee I raise my prayer.
Sainted virgin! martyr'd maiden!
　Let thy countenance incline
Upon one with woes o'erladen,
　Kneeling lowly at thy shrine;
That in agony, in terror,
　In her blind perplexity,
Wandering weak in doubt and error,
　Calleth feebly upon thee.
Sinful thoughts, sweet saint, oppress me,
　Thoughts that will not be dismissed;
Temptations dark possess me,
　Which my strength may not resist.
I am full of pain, and weary
　Of my life; I fain would die;
Unto me the world is dreary;
　To the grave for rest I fly.
For rest!—oh! could I borrow
　Thy bright wings, celestial Dove!
They should waft me from my sorrow,
　Where Peace dwells in bowers above.
　　Upon one with woes o'erladen,
　　　Kneeling lowly at thy shrine;
　　Sainted virgin! martyr'd maiden!
　　　Let thy countenance incline!
　　　　Mei miserere Virgo,
　　　　　Requiem æternam dona!

By thy loveliness, thy purity,
　Unpolluted, undefiled,
That in serene security
　Upon earth's temptations smiled;—
By the fetters that constrain'd thee,
　By thy flame-attested faith,
By the fervour that sustain'd thee,
　By thine angel-ushered death;—
By thy soul's divine elation,
　'Mid thine agonies assuring
Of thy sanctified translation
　To beatitude enduring:—
By the mystic interfusion
　Of thy spirit with the rays,

* Set to music by Mr. F. Romer.

That in ever-bright profusion
  Round the Throne Etern l blaze;
By thy portion now partaken,
  With the pain-perfected just;
Look on one of hope forsaken,
  From the gates of mercy thrust.
    Upon one with woes o'erladen,
      Kneeling lowly at thy shrine,
    Sainted virgin! martyr'd maiden!
      Let thy countenance incline!
        Ora pro me mortis horâ!
        Sancta Virgo, oro te!
          Kyrie Eleison!

The sweet sad voice of the singer died faintly away. The
sharpness of her sorrow was assuaged. Seldom, indeed, is it
that fervent supplication fails to call down solace to the
afflicted. Sybil became more composed. She still, however,
trembled at the thoughts of what remained to be done.

"They will be here ere my prayer is finished," murmured
she—"ere the end is accomplished for which I came hither,
alone. Let me, oh! let me make my peace with my Creator,
ere I surrender my being to his hands, and then let them
deal with me as they will." And she bowed her head in
lowly prayer.

Again raising her hands, and casting her eyes towards the
black ceiling, she implored, in song, the intercession of the
saintly man who had bequeathed his name to the cell.

HYMN TO ST. CYPRIAN.

Hear! oh! hear me, sufferer holy,
  Who didst make thine habita-
    tion
'Mid these rocks, devoting wholly
  Life to one long expiation
Of thy guiltiness, and solely
  By severe mortification
Didst deliver thee. Oh! hear me!
  In my dying moments cheer me.
    By thy penance, self-denial,
    Aid me in the hour of trial.

May, through thee, my prayers pre-
    vailing
  On the Majesty of Heaven,
O'er the hosts of hell, assailing
  My soul, in this dark hour be driven!
So my spirit, when exhaling,
  May of sinfulness be shriven,
And His gift unto the Giver
  May be rendered pure as ever!
    By thy own dark, dread possession,
    Aid me with thine intercession!

Scarcely had she concluded this hymn, when the torch of
the knight of Malta in part dissipated the gloom that hung
around the chapel.

XI.

THE BRIDAL.

Cari. I will not die; I must not. I am contracted
   To a young gentleman.
Executioner. Here's your wedding-ring.   *Duchess of Malfy.*

SLOWLY did the train descend; solemnly and in silence, as
if the rites at which they were about to assist had been those
of funereal, and not of nuptial, solemnization. Indeed, to
look upon those wild and fierce faces by the ruddily-flashing
torchlight, which lent to each a stern and savage expression;
to see those scowling visages surrounding a bride from whose
pallid cheeks every vestige of colour, and almost of animation, had fled; and a bridegroom, with a countenance yet
more haggard, and demeanour yet more distracted—the
beholder must have imagined that the spectacle was some
horrible ceremonial, practised by demons rather than human
beings. The arched vault, the pillars, the torchlight, the
deep shadows, and the wild figures, formed a picture worthy
of Rembrandt or Salvator.

"Is Sybil within the chapel?" asked Barbara.

"I am here," returned a voice from the altar.

"Why do we tarry?" said the gipsy queen. "We are all
assembled. To the altar."

"To the altar!" shrieked Eleanor. "Oh! no—no——"

"Remember my threat, and obey," muttered Barbara.
"You are in my power now."

A convulsive sob was all the answer Eleanor could make.

"Our number is not complete," said the priest, who had
looked in vain for the sexton. "Peter Bradley is not with
us."

"Ha!" exclaimed Barbara. "Let him be sought for
instantly."

"Their search need not extend beyond this spot," said
Peter, stepping forward.

The knight of Malta advanced towards the altar. The
torchlight reddened upon the huge stone pillars. It fell upon
the shrine, and upon the ghastly countenance of Sybil, who
stood beside. Suddenly, as the light approached her, an
object, hitherto hidden from view, was revealed. Sybil
uttered a prolonged and fearful shriek; the knight recoiled
likewise in horror; and a simultaneous cry of astonishment
burst from the lips of the foremost of the group. All

crowded forwards, and universal consternation prevailed amongst the assemblage. Each one gazed at his neighbour, anxious to learn the occasion of this tumult, and vague fears were communicated to those behind, from the terrified glances, which were the only answers returned by their comrades in front.

"Who has dared to bring that body here?" demanded Barbara, in a tone in which anger struggled with apprehension, pointing at the same time to the ghastly corpse of a female, with streaming hair, at the altar's feet. "Who has dared to do this, I say? Quick! remove it. What do you stare at? Cravens! is this the first time you have looked upon a corpse, that you shrink aghast—that you tremble before it? It is a clod—ay, less than a clod. Away with it! away, I say."

"Touch it not," cried Luke, lifting a cloud of black hair from off the features: "it is my mother's body."

"My daughter!" exclaimed the sexton.

"What!" vociferated Barbara, "is that your daughter—is that the first Lady Rookwood? Are the dead arisen to do honour to the nuptials? Speak! you can, perchance, explain how she came hither."

"I know not," returned Peter, glancing fiercely at Barbara; "I may, anon, demand that question of you. How came this body here?"

"Ask of Richard Checkley," said Barbara, turning to the priest. "He can, perchance, inform you. Priest," added she, in a low voice, "this is your handiwork."

"Checkley!" screamed Peter. "Is that Richard Checkley? is that——"

"Peace!" thundered Barbara; "will none remove the body? Once more I ask you, do you fear the dead?"

A murmur arose. Balthazar alone ventured to approach the corpse.

Luke started to his feet as he advanced, his eyes glaring with tiger fury.

"Back, old man," cried he, "and dare not, any of you, to lay a sacrilegious finger on her corse, or I will stretch him that advances as lowly as lies my mother's head. When or how it came hither matters not. Here, at the altar, has it been placed, and none shall move it hence. The dead shall witness my nuptials. Fate has ordained it—*my* fate! o'er which the dead preside. Her ring shall link me to my bride. I knew not, when I snatched it from her death-cold finger,

to what end I preserved it. I learn it now. It is here."
And he held forth a ring.

"'Tis a fatal boon, that twice-used ring," cried Sybil;
"such a ring my mother, on her deathbed, said should be
mine. Such a ring she said should wed me——"

"Unto whom?" fiercely demanded Luke.

"Unto Death!" she solemnly rejoined.

Luke's countenance fell. He turned aside, deeply abashed,
unable further to brook her gaze; while, in accents of such
wildly-touching pathos as sank into the hearts of each who
heard her—hearts, few of them framed of penetrable stuff—
the despairing maiden burst into the following strain:

THE TWICE-USED RING.*

" Beware thy bridal day !"
 On her deathbed sighed my mother;
" Beware, beware, I say,
 Death shall wed thee, and no other.
  Cold the hand shall grasp thee,
  Cold the arms shall clasp thee,
 Colder lips thy kiss shall smother!
  Beware thy bridal kiss!

" Thy wedding-ring shall be
 From a clay-cold finger taken
From one that, like to thee,
 Was by her love forsaken.
  For a twice-used ring
  Is a fatal thing;
 Her griefs who wore it are partaken—
  Beware that fatal ring!

" The altar and the grave
 Many steps are not asunder;
Bright banners o'er thee wave,
 Shrouded horror lieth under.
  Blithe may sound the bell,
  Yet 'twill toll thy knell;
 Scathed thy chaplet by the thunder—
  Beware thy blighted wreath !"

Beware my bridal day !
 Dying lips my doom have spoken;
Deep tones call me away;
 From the grave is sent a token.
  Cold, cold fingers bring
  That ill-omened ring;
Soon will a *second* heart be broken!
  This is my bridal day !

There was a deep, profound silence as the last melancholy
cadence died away, and many a rugged heart was melted,
even to tears. Eleanor, meanwhile, remained in a state of

---

* Set to music by Mr. F. Romer.

R

passive stupefaction, vacantly gazing at Sybil, upon whom alone her eyes were fixed, and appearing indistinctly to apprehend the meaning of her song.

"This is my bridal day," murmured she, in a low tone, when Sybil had finished. "Said not that sweet voice so? I know 'tis my bridal day. What a church you have chosen, mother! A tomb—a sepulchre—but 'tis meet for such nuptials as mine. And what wedding guests! Was that pale woman in her shroud-like dress invited here by you? Tell me that, mother."

"My God, her senses are gone!" cried Mrs. Mowbray. "Why did I venture into this horrible place!"

"Ask not *why* now, madam," rejoined the priest. "The hour for consideration is past. We must act. Let the marriage proceed, at all hazards; we will then take means to extricate ourselves from this accursed place."

"Remove that horrible object," said Mrs. Mowbray; "it fascinates the vision of my child."

"Lend me your hand, Richard Checkley," said Peter, sternly regarding the priest.

"No, no," replied the priest, shuddering; "I will not—cannot touch it. Do you alone remove it."

Peter approached Luke. The latter now offered no further opposition, and the body was taken away. The eyes of Eleanor followed it into the dark recesses of the vault; and when she could no longer distinguish the white flutter of the cereclothes, her labouring bosom seemed torn asunder with the profound sigh that burst from it, and her head declined upon her shoulder.

"Let me see that ring," said the priest, addressing Luke, who still held the wedding-ring between his fingers.

"I am not naturally superstitious," said Mrs. Mowbray; "whether my mind be affected with the horrors of this place, I know not; but I have a dread of that ring. She shall not use it."

"Where no other can be found," said the priest, with a significant and peculiar look at Mrs. Mowbray, "I see no reason why this should be rejected. I should not have suspected you, madam, of such weakness. Grant there were evil spell, or charm, attached to it, which, trust me, there is *not*—as how should there be, to a harmless piece of gold?—my benediction, and aspersion with holy lymph, will have sufficient power to exorcise and expel it. To remove your fears, it shall be done at once."

A cup containing water was brought, together with a plate of salt (which condiment the devil is said to abhor, and which is held to be a symbol of immortality and of eternity; in that, being itself incorruptible, it preserves all else from corruption), and, with the customary Romish formula of prayer and exorcism, the priest thrice mingled the crystal particles with the pure fluid: after which, taking the ring in his hand with much solemnity, he sprinkled it with a few drops of the water which he had blessed; made the sign of the cross upon the golden circlet; uttered another and more potent exorcism to eradicate and expel every device of Satan, and delivered it back to Luke.

"She may wear it now in safety," said the sexton, with strong contempt. "Were the snake himself coiled round that consecrated bauble, the prayers of the devout Father Checkley would unclasp his lithest folds. But wherefore do we tarry now? Nought lies between us and the altar. The path is clear. The bridegroom grows impatient."

"And the bride?" asked Barbara.

"Is ready," replied the priest. "Madam, delay not longer. Daughter, your hand."

Eleanor gave her hand. It was clammy and cold. Supported by her mother, she moved slowly towards the altar, which was but a few steps from where they stood. She offered no resistance, but did not raise her head. Luke was by her side. Then, for the first time, did the enormity of the cruel, dishonourable act he was about to commit, strike him with its full force. He saw it in its darkest colours. It was one of those terrible moments when the headlong wheel of passion stands suddenly still.

"There is yet time," groaned he. "Oh! let me not damn myself perpetually! Let me save her; save Sybil; save myself."

They were at the altar—that wild wedding train. High overhead the torch was raised. The red light flashed on bridegroom and on bride, giving to the pale features of each an almost livid look; it fell upon the gaunt aspect of the sexton, and lit up the smile of triumphant malice that played upon his face; it fell upon the fantastical habiliments of Barbara, and upon the haughty but perturbed physiognomy of Mrs. Mowbray; it fell upon the salient points of the Gothic arches; upon one moulded pillar; upon the marble image of the virgin Thecla; and on the scarcely less marble countenance of Sybil, who stood behind the altar, silent, statue-like, immovable. The effect of light and shade on other parts of the scene, upon the wild drapery, and harsh lineaments of many of the group, was also eminently striking.

Just as the priest was about to commence the marriage-service, a yelling chorus, which the gipsies were accustomed to sing at the celebration of the nuptials of one of their own tribe, burst forth. Nothing could be more horribly discordant than their song.

WEDDING CHORUS OF GIPSIES.

Scrape the catgut! pass the liquor!
Let your quick feet move the quicker.
　　　　　Ta-ra-la!

Dance and sing in jolly chorus,
Bride and bridegroom are before us,
And the patrico stands o'er us.
　　　　　Ta-ra-la!

To unite their hands he's ready;
For a moment, pals, be steady;
　　Cease your quaffing,
　　Dancing, laughing;
　　Leave off riot,
　　And be quiet.
　　While 'tis doing.
　　'Tis begun,
　　All is over!
　　　Two are ONE!
The patrico has link'd 'em;
Daddy Hymen's torch has blink'd 'em;
　　Amen!
　　To't again!
　　Now for quaffing,
　　Now for laughing,
　　Stocking-throwing,
　　Liquor flowing;
For our bridals are no bridles, and our altars never alter;
From the flagon never flinch we; in the jig we never falter.
　　No! that's not our way, for we
　　Are stanch lads of Romany.
　　For our wedding, then, hurrah!
　　Hurrah! hurrah! hurrah!

This uncouth chorus ended, the marriage proceeded. Sybil had disappeared. Had she fled? No! she was by the bride. Eleanor mechanically took her place. A faint voice syllabled the responses. You could scarcely have seen Miss Mowbray's lips move. But the answers were given, and the priest was satisfied.

He took the ring, and sprinkled it once again with the holy water, in the form of the cross. He pronounced the prayer: "Benedic, Domine, annulum hunc, quem nos in tuo nomine benedicimus, ut quæ cum gestaverit, fidelitatem integram suo sponso tenens, in pace et voluntate tuâ permaneat atque in mutuâ charitate semper vivat."

He was about to return the ring to Luke, when the torch, held by the knight of Malta, was dashed to the ground by some unseen hand, and instantly extinguished. The wild pageant vanished as suddenly as the figures cast by a magic-lantern upon a wall disappear when the glass is removed. A wild hubbub succeeded. Hoarsely above the clamour arose the voice of Barbara.

"To the door, quickly!—to the door! Let no one pass. I will find out the author of this mishap anon. Away!"

She was obeyed. Several of the crew stationed themselves at the door.

"Proceed now with the ceremony," continued Barbara. "By darkness, or by light, the match shall be completed."

The ring was then placed upon the finger of the bride; and as Luke touched it, he shuddered. It was cold as that of the corpse which he had clasped but now. The prayer was said, the blessing given, the marriage was complete.

Suddenly there issued from the darkness deep dirge-like tones, and a voice solemnly chanted a strain, which all knew to be the death-song of their race, hymned by wailing women over an expiring sister. The music seemed to float in the air.

THE SOUL-BELL.*

Fast the sand of life is failing,
Fast her latest sigh exhaling,
    Fast, fast, is she dying.

With death's chills her limbs are shivering,
With death's gasp the lips are quivering,
    Fast her soul away is flying.

O'er the mountain-top it fleeteth,
And the skyey wonders greeteth,
Singing loud as stars it meeteth
    On its way.

Hark! the sullen Soul-bell tolling,
Hollowly in echoes rolling,
    Seems to say —

"She will ope her eyes—oh, never!
Quenched their dark light—gone for ever!
    She is dead."

The marriage group yet lingered near the altar, awaiting, it would seem, permission from the gipsy queen to quit the cell. Luke stirred not. Clasped in his own, the cold hand of his

---

* Set to music by Mr. F. Romer.

bride detained him; and when he would have moved, her tightened grasp prevented his departure.

Mrs. Mowbray's patience was exhausted by the delay. She was not altogether free from apprehension. "Why do we linger here?" she whispered to the priest. "Do you, father, lead the way."

"The crowd is dense," replied Checkley. "They resist my effort."

"Are we prisoners here?" asked Mrs. Mowbray, in alarm.

"Let me make the attempt," cried Luke, with fiery impatience. "I will force a passage out."

"Quit not your bride," whispered Peter, "as you value her safety. Heed not aught else. She alone is in danger. Suffer her not to be withdrawn from your hand, if you would not lose her. Remain here. I will bring the matter to a speedy issue."

"Enough," cried Luke; "I stir not hence." And he drew his bride closer towards him. He stooped to imprint a kiss upon her lips. A cold shudder ran through her frame as he touched them, but she resisted not his embrace.

Peter's attempt to effect an egress was as unsuccessful as that of the priest. Presenting excalibur at his bosom, the knight of Malta challenged him to stand.

"You cannot pass," exclaimed the knight; "our orders are peremptory."

"What am I to understand by this?" said Peter, angrily. "Why are we detained?"

"You will learn all anon," returned Barbara. "In the mean time, you are my prisoners; or, if you like not the phrase, my wedding guests."

"The wedding is complete," returned the sexton; "the bride and bridegroom are impatient to depart; and we, the guests (albeit, some of us may be no foes to darkness), desire not to hold our nuptial revels here."

"Sybil's wedding has not taken place," said Barbara; "you must tarry for that."

"Ha! now it comes," thought Peter. "And who, may I ask," said he, aloud, "amongst this goodly company is to be her bridegroom?"

"The best amongst them," returned Barbara, "Sir Luke Rookwood."

"He has a bride already," replied Peter.

"She may be *removed*," said Barbara, with bitter and peculiar emphasis. "Dost understand my meaning now?"

"I will not understand it," said Peter. "You cannot mean to destroy her who now stands at the altar?"

"She who now stands at the altar must make way for a successor. She who grasps the bridegroom's hand shall die. I swear it by the oath of my tribe."

"And think you you will be allowed to execute your murderous intention with impunity?" shrieked Mrs. Mowbray, in an agony of terror. "Think you that I will stand by, and see my child slaughtered before my face; that my friends will suffer it? Think you that even your own tribe will dare to execute your horrible purpose? They will not. They will side with us. Even now they murmur. What can you hope to gain by an act so wild and dreadful? What object can you have?"

"The same as your own," reiterated Barbara; "the advancement of my child. Sybil is as dear to me as Eleanor is to you. She is my child's child, the daughter of my best-beloved daughter. I have sworn to marry her to Sir Luke Rookwood. The means are in my power. I will keep my vow; I will wed her to him. You did not hesitate to tear your daughter from the man she loved, to give her to the man she hated; and for what? For gold, for power, for rank. I have the same motive. I love my child, and she loves Sir Luke; has loved him long and truly; therefore shall she have him. What to me is *your* child, or *your* feelings, except they are subservient to my wishes? She stands in my way. I remove her."

"Who placed her in your path?" asked the sexton. "Did you not lend a helping hand to create that obstacle yourself?"

"I did," replied Barbara. "Would you know wherefore? I will tell you. I had a double motive for it. There is a curse upon the house of Rookwood, that kills the first fair bride each generation leads to the altar. Have you never heard of it?

"I have! And did that idle legend sway you?"

"And do you call it idle? *You!* Well, I had another motive—a prophecy."

"By yourself uttered," replied Peter.

"Even so," replied Barbara. "The prophecy is fulfilled. The stray rook is found. The rook hath with rook mated. Luke hath wedded Eleanor. He will hold possession of his lands. The prophecy is fulfilled."

"But *how?*" asked Peter. "Will your art tell you how and why he shall now hold possession? Can you tell me that?"

"My art goes not so far. I have predicted the event. It has come to pass. I am satisfied. He has wedded her. Be it mine to free him from that yoke." And Barbara laughed exultingly.

The sexton approached the old crone, and laid his hand with violence upon her shoulder.

"Hear me," cried he, "and I will tell you that which your juggling art refuses to reveal. Eleanor Mowbray is heir to the lands of Rookwood! The estates are *hers!* They were bequeathed to her by her grandsire, Sir Reginald."

"She was unborn when he died," cried Mrs. Mowbray.

"True," replied Peter; "but the lands were left to your issue *female*, should such issue be born."

"And did Sir Piers, my brother, know of this? did he see this will?" asked Mrs. Mowbray, with trembling impatience.

"He did, and withheld the knowledge of it from you and yours."

"Ah! why knew I not this before? Why did you not tell me ere that was done which cannot be undone? I have sacrificed my child."

"Because it did not chime with my purposes to tell you," returned Peter, coldly.

"It is false; it is false," cried Mrs. Mowbray, her anger and vexation getting the better of her fears. "I will not believe it. Who are you, that pretend to know the secrets of our house?"

"One of that house," replied the sexton.

"Your name?"

"Would you know my name?" answered Peter, **sternly.** "The time is come when I will no longer conceal it. I am Alan Rookwood."

"My father's brother!" exclaimed Mrs. Mowbray.

"Ay, Alan Rookwood. The sworn enemy of your **father,** of you, of all ye; your fate, your destiny, your curse. I am that Alan Rookwood whose name you breathed in the vault. I am he, the avenger, the avenged. I saw your father die. I heard his groans—*his groans!*—ha, ha! I saw his sons die: one fell in battle—I was with him there. The other expired in his bed. I was with Sir Piers when he breathed his last, and listened to his death agonies. 'Twas I who counselled him to keep the lands from you and from your child, and he withheld them. One only amongst the race, whose name I have cast off, have I loved; and him, because," added he, with something like emotion, "because he was **my** daughter's child, Luke Rookwood. And even he shall minister to my vengeance. He will be your curse—your daughter's curse; for he loves her not. Yet he is her husband, and hath her lands; ha, ha!" And he laughed till he became convulsed with the paroxysm of fiendish exultation.

"Mine ears are stunned," cried Mrs. Mowbray.

"The bride is mine; relinquish her to me," said Barbara. "Advance and seize her, my children."

Alan Rookwood (for so we shall henceforth denominate the sexton) suddenly grew calm: he raised the whistle to his lips, and blew a call so loud and shrill, that those who were advancing hung back irresolute.

There was a rush at the door of the vault. The sentinels were struck down; and with pistols in each hand, and followed by two assistants, Dick Turpin sprang into the thick of the crew.

"Here we are," cried he, "ready for action. Where is Sir Luke Rookwood? where my churchyard pal, Peter?"

"Here," cried the sexton and Luke simultaneously.

"Then stand aside," cried Dick, pushing in the direction of the sounds, and bearing down all opposition. "Have a care there, these triggers are ticklish. Friend or foe, he who touches me shall have a bullet in his gizzard. Here I am, pal Peter; and here are my two chums, Rust and Wilder. Cut the whid."

"Have we license to pass scathless now?" asked the sexton, "or shall we make good our way?"

"You shall not pass," cried Barbara, furiously. "Think you to rob me of my prey? What, cowards? do you hesitate? Ha!"

"Kindle the torches," cried several voices. "We fight not in the dark."

A pistol was flashed. The torch again blazed. Its light fell upon a tumultuous group.

"Seize the bride," cried Barbara.

"Hold!" exclaimed a voice from the altar. The voice was that of Sybil.

Her hand was clasped in that of Luke. Eleanor had fainted in the arms of the gipsy girl Handassah.

"Are you my bride?" ejaculated Luke, in dismay.

"Behold the ring upon my finger! Your own hand placed it there."

"Betrayed!" screamed Alan, in a voice of anguish. "My schemes annihilated—myself undone—my enemies triumphant —lost! lost! All is destroyed—all!"

"Joy! joy!" exclaimed Mrs. Mowbray: "my child is saved."

"And *mine* destroyed," groaned Barbara. "I have sworn by the cross to slay the bride—and Sybil is that bride."

XII.

ALAN ROOKWOOD.

The wolf shall find her grave, and scrape it up;
Not to devour the corse, but to discover
The horrid murther.   WEBSTER.

"BRAVO! capital!" cried Turpin, laughing loud and long as an Olympian deity; "has this simple wench outwitted you all; turned the tables upon the whole gang of plotters, eh? Excellent! ha, ha, ha! The next time you wed, Sir Luke, let me advise you not to choose a wife in the dark. A man should have all his senses about him on these occasions. Make love when the liquor's in; marry when it's out, and, above all, with your eyes open. This beats cock-fighting— ha, ha, ha!—you must excuse me; but, upon my soul, I can't help it." And his laughter seemed inextinguishable.

"Take your men without," whispered Alan Rookwood; "keep watch as before, and let the discharge of a pistol bespeak the approach of danger, as agreed upon; much yet remains to be done here."

"How so?" asked Dick: "it seems to me the job's entirely settled—if not to *your* satisfaction. I'm always ready to oblige my friend Sir Luke; but curse me if I'll lend my help to any underhand work. Steer clear of foul play, or Dick Turpin holds no hand with you. As to that poor wench, if you mean her any harm, curse me if I will——"

"No harm is intended her," replied Alan. "I applaud your magnanimity," added he, sarcastically; "such sentiments are, it must be owned, in excellent keeping with your conduct."

"In keeping or not," replied Turpin, gravely, "cold-blooded murder is altogether out of my line, and I wash my hands of it. A shot or two in self-defence is another matter; and when——"

"A truce to this," interrupted Alan; "the girl is safe. Will you mount guard again?"

"If that be the case, certainly," replied Dick: "I shall be glad to get back to Bess. I couldn't bring her with me into this black hole. A couple of shots will tell you 'tis Ranulph Rookwood. But mind, no harm to the gipsy girl—to Lady Rookwood, I should say. She's a jewel, take my word for it, which Sir Luke must be mad to throw away." And calling his companions, he departed.

Alan Rookwood bent his steps towards the gipsy queen. Dark thoughts gathered thickly o'er his brow. He smiled as he drew nigh to Barbara—a smile it was

That wrinkled up his skin even to the hair.

Barbara looked at him at first with distrust; but as he developed his secret purposes, that smile became reflected upon her own features. Their conference took place apart. We willingly leave them to return to the altar.

Mrs. Mowbray and the priest were still there. Both were occupied in ineffectual endeavours to restore Eleanor to consciousness. She recovered from her swoon; but it was evident her senses still wandered; and vainly did Mrs. Mowbray lavish her tenderest caresses upon her child. Eleanor returned them not.

Luke, meanwhile, had given vent to the wildest fury. He shook away Sybil's grasp; he dashed her from him; he regarded her with withering glances: he loaded her with reproaches. She bore his violence with meekest submission; she looked imploringly—but she replied not to his taunts. Again she clung to the hem of his garment when cast aside. Luke appeared unmoved; what passed within we pause not to examine. He grew calmer; his calmness was more terrible to Sybil than his previous wrath had been.

"You are my wife," said he; "what then? By fraud, by stratagem, you have obtained that title, and, perforce, must keep it. But the title *only* shall you retain. No rights of wife shall ever be yours. It will be in your power to call yourself Lady Rookwood—you will be so in name—in nothing else."

"I shall not bear it long," murmured Sybil.

Luke laughed scornfully. "So you said before," replied he; "and yet I see not why you are likely to abandon it. The event will show. Thus far you have deceived me, and I place no further faith in your assertions. My hand was yours; you refused it. When I would give it to another, you grasp it clandestinely. Am I to believe you now? The wind, will change—the vane veer with it."

" It will not veer from you," she meekly answered.

" Why did you step between me and my bride?"

"To save her life; to lay mine down for hers."

" An idle subterfuge. You know well that you run no risk of being called upon to do so. Your life is in no danger. The sacrifice was unnecessary. I could have dispensed with *your* assistance: my own arm would have sufficed to protect Eleanor."

" Your single arm would not have prevailed against numbers : they would have killed you likewise."

" Tush!" said Luke, fiercely. " Not only have you snatched from me my bride, you have robbed me of my fair estates, of all, save of my barren title, and that, even *that*, you have tarnished."

" True, true," sighed Sybil. " I knew not that the lands were hers, else had I never done it."

" False, false," cried Luke; " false as the rest. *They* will be Ranulph's. *She* will be Ranulph's. I shall still be an outcast, while Ranulph will riot in my halls—will press her to his bosom. Cling not to me. Hence! or I will spurn you from me. I am undone, undone by you, accursed one."

" Oh, curse me not! your words cut deep enough."

" Would they could kill you," cried Luke, with savage bitterness. " You have placed a bar between me and my prospects, which nothing can now remove—nothing but— ha!" and his countenance assumed a deadly hue and fearful expression. " By Heaven, you almost rouse the fell spirit which it is said dwells within the breast of my devoted race. I feel as if I could stab thee."

" No, no," shrieked Sybil; "for mercy's sake, for your own sake, do not stab me. It is not too late. I will repair my wrong!"

" Ever deceiving! you would again delude me. You cannot repair it. One way alone remains, and that——"

" I will pursue," responded Sybil, sadly but firmly.

" Never," cried Luke; " you shall not. Ha!" exclaimed he, as he found his arm suddenly pinioned behind him. " What new treachery is this? By whose orders am I thus fettered?"

" By mine," said Alan Rookwood, stepping forward.

" By yours?" echoed Luke. " And wherefore? Release me."

"Be patient," replied Alan. "You will hear all anon. In the mean time you must be content to remain my prisoner. Quit not your hold," added he, addressing the gipsies, who kept charge of Luke.

"Their lives shall answer for their obedience," said Barbara.

Upon a further signal from Alan, Eleanor was torn from her mother's arms, and a bandage passed so suddenly over Mrs. Mowbray's face, that, before she could raise a cry of alarm, all possibility of utterance was effectually prevented. The priest alone was left at liberty.

Barbara snatched the hand of Eleanor. She dragged her to Sybil.

"You are Lady Rookwood," whispered she; "but she has your domains. I give her to you."

"She is the *only bar* between thy husband and his rights," whispered Alan Rookwood, in a tone of horrible irony; "*it is not too late to repair your wrong.*"

"Away, tempter!" cried Sybil, horror-stricken. "I know you well. "Yet," continued she, in an altered tone, "I will risk all for him. I have done him wrong. One mode of atonement remains; and, horrible though it be, I will embrace it. Let me not pause. Give her to me." And she seized upon the unresisting hand of Eleanor.

"Do you need my aid?" asked Barbara.

"No," replied Sybil; "let none approach us. A clapping of hands will let you know when all is over." And she dragged her passive victim deeper into the vault.

"Sybil, Sybil!" cried Luke, struggling with frantic violence to liberate himself; "hurt her not. I was rash. I was mad. I am calmer now. She hears me not—she will not turn. God of heaven! she will murder her. It will be done while I speak. I am the cause of all. Release me, villains! Would that I had died ere I had seen this day."

At a signal from the sexton, Luke also was blindfolded. He ceased to struggle. But his labouring breast told of the strife within.

"Miscreants!" exclaimed the priest, who had hitherto witnessed the proceedings in horror. "Why do not these rocks fall in, and crush you and your iniquities? Save her! oh, save her! Have you no pity for the innocent?"

"Such pity have we," replied Alan Rookwood, "as you showed my daughter. She was as innocent as Eleanor Mowbray, and yet you did not pity *her*."

"Heaven is my witness," exclaimed the priest, "that I never injured her."

"Take not Heaven's name in vain," cried Alan. "Who stood by while it was doing? Whose firmer hand lent aid to the murderer's trembling efforts? Whose pressure stifled her thrilling screams, and choked her cries for mercy? Yours—yours; and now you prate to me of pity—you, the slayer of the sleeping and the innocent!"

"'Tis false!" exclaimed the priest, in extremity of terror.

"False!" echoed Alan. "I had Sir Piers's own confession. He told me all. You had designs upon Sir Piers, which his wife opposed: you hated her; you were in the confidence of both—how did you keep that confidence? He told me *how*, by awakening a spirit of jealousy and pride, that o'ermastered all his better feelings. False! He told me of your hellish machinations; your Jesuitical plots; your schemes. He was too weak, too feeble an instrument to serve you. You left him, but not before *she* had left him. False! ha, I have that shall instantly convict you. The corpse is here, within this cell. Who brought it hither?"

The priest was silent: he seemed confounded by Alan's violence.

"I will answer that question," said Barbara. "It was brought hither by that false priest. His agent, Balthazar, has betrayed him. It was brought hither to prevent the discovery of Sir Luke Rookwood's legitimacy. He meant to make his own terms about it. It has come hither to proclaim his guilt—to be a fearful witness against him." Then, turning to Checkley, she added, "You have called Heaven to witness your innocence: you shall attest it by oath upon that body; and should aught indicate your guilt, I will hang you as I would a dog, and clear off one long score with justice. Do you shrink from this?"

"No," replied the priest, in a voice hollow and broken. "Bring me to the body."

"Seize each an arm," said Barbara, addressing Zoroaster and the knight of Malta, "and lead him to the corse."

"I will administer the oath," said Alan Rookwood, sternly.

"No, not you," stammered the priest.

"And wherefore not?" asked Alan. "If you are innocent, you need fear nothing from her."

"I fear nothing from the *dead*," replied Checkley: "lead on."

We will now return to Sybil. She was alone with her

victim. They were near the mouth of the cell which had been Prior Cyprian's flinty dormitory, and were almost involved in darkness. A broken stream of light glanced through the pillars. Eleanor had not spoken. She suffered herself to be dragged thither without resistance, scarcely conscious, it would seem, of her danger. Sybil gazed upon her for some minutes with sorrow and surprise. "She comprehends not her perilous situation," murmured Sybil. "She knows not that she stands upon the brink of the grave. Oh! would that she could pray. Shall I, her murderess, pray for her? My prayers would not be heard. And yet to kill her unshriven will be a twofold crime. Let me not look on her. My hand trembles. I can scarce grasp the dagger. Let me think on all he has said. I have wronged him. I am his bane, his curse! I have robbed him of all: there is but one remedy—'tis *this!*—Oh, God! she recovers. I cannot do it now."

It was a fearful moment for Eleanor's revival, when the bright steel flashed before her eyes. Terror at once restored her. She cast herself at Sybil's feet.

"Spare, spare me!" cried she. "Oh! what a dream I have had. And to waken thus, with the dagger's point at my breast. You will not kill me—you, gentle maid, who promised to preserve me. Ah, no, I am sure you will not."

"Appeal no more to me," said Sybil, fiercely. "Make your peace with Heaven. Your minutes are numbered."

"I cannot pray," said Eleanor, "while you are near me."

"Will you pray if I retire and leave you?"

"No, no. I dare not—cannot," shrieked Eleanor, in extremity of terror. "Oh! do not leave me, or let me go."

"If you stir," said Sybil, "I stab you to the heart."

"I will not stir. I will kneel here for ever. Stab me as I kneel—as I pray to you. You cannot kill me while I cling to you thus—while I kiss your hands—while I bedew them with my tears. Those tears will not sully them like my blood."

"Maiden," said Sybil, endeavouring to withdraw her hand, "let go your hold—your sand is run."

"Mercy!"

"It is in vain. Close your eyes."

"No, I will fix them on you thus—you cannot strike then. I will cling to you—embrace you. Your nature is not cruel—your soul is full of pity. It melts—those tears—you will be merciful. You cannot deliberately kill me."

"I cannot—I cannot!" said Sybil, with a passionate outburst of grief. "Take you life on one condition."

"Name it."

"That you wed Sir Luke Rookwood."

"Ah!" exclaimed Eleanor, "all rushes back upon me at that name; the whole of that fearful scene passes in review before me."

"Do you reject my proposal?"

"I dare not."

"I must have your oath. Swear by every hope of eternity that you will wed none other than him."

"By every hope, I swear it."

"Handassah, you will bear this maiden's oath in mind, and witness its fulfilment."

"I will," replied the gipsy girl, stepping forward from a recess, in which she had hitherto remained unnoticed.

"Enough. I am satisfied. Tarry with me. Stir not—scream not whatever you may see or hear. Your life depends upon your firmness. When I am no more——"

"No more?" echoed Eleanor, in horror.

"Be calm," said Sybil. "When I am dead, clap your hands together. They will come to seek you—they will find me in your stead. Then rush to him—to Sir Luke Rookwood. He will protect you. Say to him hereafter that I died for the wrong I did him—that I died, and blessed him."

"Can you not live, and save me?" sobbed Eleanor.

"Ask it not. While I live, your life is in danger. When I am gone, none will seek to harm you. Fare you well! Remember your oath, and you, too, remember it, Handassah. Remember, also—ha! that groan!"

All started, as a deep groan knelled in their ears.

"Whence comes that sound?" cried Sybil. "Hist—a voice?"

"It is that of the priest," replied Eleanor. "Hark! he groans. They have murdered him! Kind Heaven, receive his soul!"

"Pray for me," cried Sybil: "pray fervently; avert your face; down on your knees—down—down! Farewell, Handassah!" And breaking from them, she rushed into the darkest recesses of the vault.

We must now quit this painful scene for another scarcely less painful, and return to the unfortunate priest.

Checkley had been brought before the body of Susan Rookwood. Even in the gloom, the shimmer of the white cereclothes, and the pallid features of the corpse, were ghastly enough. The torchlight made them terrible.

"Kneel!" said Alan Rookwood. The priest complied. Alan knelt beside him.

"Do you know these features?" demanded he. "Regard them well. Fix your eyes full upon them. Do you know them?"

"I do."

"Place your hand upon her breast. Does not the flesh creep and shrink beneath your touch? Now raise your hand —make the cross of your faith upon her bosom. By that faith you swear you are innocent?"

"I do," returned the priest; "are you now satisfied?"

"No," replied Alan. "Let the torch be removed. Your innocence must be more deeply attested," continued he, as the light was withdrawn. "This proof will not fail. Entwine your fingers round her throat."

"Have I not done enough?"

"Your hesitation proves your guilt," said Alan.

"That proof is wanting, then," returned the priest; "my hand is upon her throat—what more?"

"As you hope for mercy in your hour of need, swear that you never conspired against her life, or refused her mercy."

"I swear it."

"May the dead convict you of perjury if you have foresworn yourself," said Alan; "you are free. Take away your hand."

"Ha! what is this?" exclaimed the priest. "You have put some jugglery upon me. I cannot withdraw my hand. It sticks to her throat as though 'twere glued by blood. Tear me away. I have not force enough to liberate myself. Why do you grin at me? The corpse grins likewise. It is jugglery. I am innocent. You would take away my life. Tear me away, I say; the veins rise; they blacken; they are filling with new blood. I feel them swell; they coil like living things around my fingers. She is alive."

"And you are innocent?"

"I am—I am. Let not my ravings convict me. For Jesu's sake, release me."

"Blaspheme not, but arise. I hold you not."

"You do," groaned the priest. "Your grasp tightens round my throat; your hard and skinny fingers are there—I strangle—help!"

8

" Your own fears strangle you. My hand is at my side," returned Alan, calmly.

" Villain, you lie. Your grasp is like a vice. The strength of a thousand devils is in your hand. Will none lend help? I never pressed so hard. Your daughter never suffered this torture—never—never. I choke—choke—oh !" And the priest rolled heavily backwards.

There was a deep groan; a convulsive rattle in the throat; and all was still.

" He is dead—strangled," cried several voices, holding down the torch. The face of the priest was blackened and contorted; his eyeballs protruded from their sockets; his tongue was nearly bitten through in the desperate efforts he had made to release himself from Alan's gripe; his hair was erect with horror. It was a ghastly sight.

A murmur arose amongst the gipsies. Barbara deemed it prudent to appease them.

" He was guilty," cried she. " He was the murderer of Susan Rookwood."

" And I, *her father*, have avenged her," said Alan, sternly.

The dreadful silence that followed his speech was broken by the report of a pistol. The sound, though startling, was felt almost as a relief.

" We are beset," cried Alan. " Some of you fly to reconnoitre."

" To your posts !" cried Barbara.

Several of the crew flocked to the entrance.

" Unbind the prisoners," shouted Alan.

Mrs. Mowbray and Luke were accordingly set free.

Two almost simultaneous reports of a pistol were now heard.

" 'Tis Ranulph Rookwood," said Alan; " that was the preconcerted signal."

" Ranulph Rookwood," echoed Eleanor, who caught the exclamation: " he comes to save me."

" Remember your oath," gasped a dying voice. " He is no longer yours."

" Alas ! alas !" sobbed Eleanor, tremblingly.

A moment afterwards a faint clapping of hands reached the ears of Barbara.

" All is over," muttered she.

" Ha !" exclaimed Alan Rookwood, with a frightful look. " Is it done ?"

Barbara motioned him towards the further end of the vault.

XIII.

MR. COATES.

Grimm. Look, captain, here comes one of the bloodhounds of justice.
Schw. Down with him. Don't let him utter a word.
Moor. Silence, I will hear him.   SCHILLER.—*The Robbers.*

GLADLY do we now exchange the dank atmosphere of St.
Cyprian's cell, and the horrors which have detained us there
so long, for balmy air, genial sunshine, and the boon-com-
panionship of Dick Turpin. Upon regaining the verdant
ruins of the ancient priory, all appeared pretty much as our
highwayman had left it. Dick wended towards his mare.
Black Bess uttered an affectionate whinnying sound as he
approached her, and yielded her sleek neck to his caresses.
No Bedouin Arab ever loved his horse more tenderly than
Turpin.

"'Twill be a hard day when thou and I part!" murmured
he, affectionately patting her soft and silky cheeks. Bess
thrust her nose into his hand, biting him playfully, as much
as to say, "That day will never arrive." Turpin, at least,
understood the appeal in that sense; he was skilled in the
language of the Houyhnmns. "I would rather lose my
right hand than *that* should happen," sighed he; "but,
there's no saying: the best of friends must part; and thou
and I may be one day separated : thy destination is the
knacker; mine, perhaps, the gibbet. We are neither of us
cut out for old age, that's certain. Curse me, if I can tell
how it is; since I've been in that vault, I've got some queer
crotchet into my head. I can't help likening thee to that
poor gipsy wench, Sybil; but may I be scragg'd if I'd use
thee as her lover has used her. Ha!" exclaimed he, drawing a pistol with a suddenness that made his companions,
Rust and Wilder, start; "we are watched. See you not how
yon shadow falls from behind the wall?

"I do," replied Rust.

"The varmint shall be speedily unearthed," said Wilder,
rushing to the spot.

In another instant the shadow manifested itself in a substantial little personage, booted, spurred, and mud-be-
spattered. He was brought before our highwayman, who
had, meanwhile, vaulted into his saddle.

"Mr. Coates!" cried Dick, bursting into a loud laugh at

s 2

the ridiculous figure presented to his view, "or the mud de-
ceives me."

"It does not deceive you, Captain Turpin," replied the
attorney; "you do, indeed, behold that twice unfortunate
person."

"What brings you here?" asked Dick. "Ah! I see.
You are come to pay me my wager."

"I thought you gave me a *discharge* for that," rejoined
Coates, unable even in his distress to resist the too-tempting
quibble.

"True, but it was *in blank*," replied Turpin, readily;
"and that don't hold good in law, you know. You have
thrown away a second chance. Play or pay, all the world
over. I sha'nt *let you off* so easily this time, depend upon
it. Come, post the pony, or take your measure on that sod.
No more replications or rejoiners, sir. Down with the
dust. Fake his clies, pals. Let us see what he has about
him."

"In the twinkling of a bed-post," replied Rust. "We'll
turn him inside out. What's here?" cried he, searching the
attorney's pockets. "A brace of barkers," handing a pair
of pistols to Turpin; "a haddock, stuffed with nothing, I'm
thinking; one quid, two coach-wheels, half a bull, three hogs,
and a kick; a d—d dicky concern, captain!"

"Three hogs and a kick," muttered Coates; "the knave
says true enough."

"Is there nothing else?" demanded Dick.

"Only an old snuffy fogle and a pewter sneezer."

"No reader?* Try his hoxter."†

"Here's a pit-man,‡ captain."

"Give it me. Ah! this will do," cried Dick, examining
the contents of the pocket-book. "This is a glorious wind-
fall, indeed; a bill of exchange for 500*l.*, payable *on demand*,
eh, Mr. Coates? Quick! indorse it, sir. Here's pen and
ink. Rascal! if you attempt to tear the bill I'll blow your
brains out. Steady, sir, sign. Good!" added he, as Coates
most reluctantly indorsed the bill. "Good! good! I'll be
off with this bill to London to-night, before you can stop it.
No courier can beat Bess—ha, ha! Eh! what's this?" continued Dick, as, unfolding another leaf of the pocket-book,
he chanced upon a letter; "my Lady Rookwood's superscription! Excuse me, Mr. Coates, I must have a peep at

---

* Pocket-book.   † Inside coat-pocket.   ‡ A small pocket-book.

her ladyship's billet-doux. All's safe with me—man of honour. I must detain your *reader* a moment longer."

"You should take charge of yourself, then," replied Coates, sulkily. "*You* appear to be my reader."

"Bravo!" cried Turpin. "You may jest now with impunity, Mr. Coates. You have paid dear enough for your jokes; and when should a man be allowed to be pleasant, if not at his own expense?—ha, ha! What's this!" exclaimed he, opening the letter. "A ring, as I'm awake! and from her ladyship's own fair finger, I'll be sworn, for it bears her cipher, ineffaceably impressed as your image upon her heart —eh, Coates? Egad! you are a lucky dog, after all, to receive *such* a favour from *such* a lady—ha, ha! Meantime, I'll take care of it for you," continued Dick, slipping the ring on his little finger.

Turpin, we have before remarked, had a turn for mimicry; and it was with an irresistible feeling of deferential awe creeping over him that Coates heard the contents of Lady Rookwood's epistle delivered with an enunciation as peremptory and imperious as that of her ladyship's self. The letter was hastily indited, in a clear, firm hand, and partook of its writer's decision of character. Dick found no difficulty in deciphering it. Thus ran the missive:

"Assured of your devotion and secrecy, I commit my own honour, and that of my son, to your charge. Time will not permit me to see you, or I would not write. But I place myself entirely in your hands. You will not dare to betray my confidence. To the point: A Major Mowbray has just arrived here with intelligence that the body of Susan Bradley (you will know to whom I allude) has been removed from our family vault by a Romish priest and his assistants. How it came there, or why it has been removed, I know not; it is not my present purpose to inquire. Suffice it, that it now lies in a vault beneath the ruins of Davenham Priory. My son, Sir Ranulph, who has lent a credulous ear to the artful tales of the impostor who calls this woman mother, is at present engaged in arming certain of the household, and of the tenantry, to seize upon and bring away this body, as resistance is apprehended from a horde of gipsies who infest the ruins. Now, mark me. THAT BODY MUST NOT BE FOUND! Be it your business to prevent its discovery. Take the fleetest horse you can procure; spare neither whip nor spur. Haste to the priory; procure by any means, and at any expense, the assistance of the gipsies. Find out the body; conceal it, destroy it—do what you will, so my son find it not. Fear not his resentment; I will bear you harmless of the consequences with him. You will act upon my responsibility. I pledge my honour for your safety. Use all despatch, an' calculate upon due requital from

MAUD ROOKWOOD.

"Haste, and God speed you!"

"Good speed you!" echoed Dick, in his own voice, contemptuously. "The devil drive you! would have been a fitter postscript. And it was upon this precious errand you came, Mr. Coates?"

"Precisely," replied the attorney; "but I find the premises preoccupied. Fast as I have ridden, you were here before me."

"And what do you now propose to do?" asked Turpin.

"Bargain with you for the body," replied Coates, in an insinuating tone.

"With *me!*" said Dick; "do you take me for a resurrection cove; for a dealer in dead stock, eh! sirrah?"

"I take you for one sufficiently *alive*, in a general way, to his own interests," returned Coates. "These gentlemen may not, perhaps, be quite so scrupulous, when they hear my proposals."

"Be silent, sir," interrupted Turpin. "Hist! I hear the tramp of horses' hoofs without. Hark! that shout."

"Make your own terms before they come," said Coates. "Leave all to me. I'll put 'em on a wrong scent."

"To the devil with your terms," cried Turpin; "the signal!" And he pulled the trigger of one of Coates's pistols, the shot of which rang in the ears of the astounded attorney as it whizzed past him. "Drag him into the mouth of the vault," thundered Turpin: "he will be a capital cover in case of attack. Look to your sticks, and be on the alert; away!

Vainly did the unfortunate attorney kick and struggle, swear and scream; his hat was pushed over his eyes; his bob-wig thrust into his mouth; and his legs tripped from under him. Thus blind, dumb, and half-suffocated, he was hurried into the entrance of the cell.

Dick, meanwhile, dashed to the arched outlet of the ruin. He there drew in the rein, and Black Bess stood motionless as a statue.

XIV.

DICK TURPIN.

Many a fine fellow, with a genius extensive enough to have effected universal reformation, has been doomed to perish by the halter. But does not such a man's renown extend through centuries, and tens of centuries, while many a prince would be overlooked in history were it not the historian's interest to increase the number of his pages? Nay, when the traveller sees a gibbet, does he not exclaim, "That fellow was no fool!" and lament the hardship of the times?—SCHILLER.—*The Robbers.*

TURPIN's quick eye ranged over the spreading sward in front of the ancient priory, and his brow became contracted. The feeling, however, was transient. The next instant saw him the same easy, reckless being he had been before. There was a little more paleness in his cheek than usual; but his look was keener, and his knees involuntarily clasped the saddle more firmly. No other symptom of anxiety was perceptible. It would be no impeachment to Dick's valour were it necessary to admit that a slight tremor crossed him as he scanned the formidable array of his opponents. The admission is needless. Dick himself would have been the last man to own it; nor shall we do the memory of our undaunted highwayman any such injustice. Turpin was intrepid to a fault. He was rash; apt to run into risks for the mere pleasure of getting out of them: danger was his delight, and the degree of excitement was always in proportion to the peril incurred. After the first glance, he became, to use his own expressive phrase, "as cool as a cucumber;" and continued, as long as they permitted him, like a skilful commander, calmly to calculate the numerical strength of his adversaries, and to arrange his own plan of resistance.

This troop of horsemen, for such it was, might probably amount in the aggregate to twenty men, and presented an appearance like that of a strong muster at a rustic fox-chase, due allowance being made for the various weapons of offence; to wit, naked sabres, fire-locks, and a world of huge horse-pistols, which the present *field* carried along with them. This resemblance was heightened by the presence of an old hunts-man and a gamekeeper or two, in scarlet and green jackets, and a few yelping hounds that had followed after them. The majority of the crew consisted of sturdy yoemen; some of whom, mounted upon wild, unbroken colts, had pretty lives of it to maintain their seats, and curvetted about in "most admired disorder;" others were seated upon more docile, but

quite as provoking specimens of the cart-horse breed, whose
sluggish sides, reckless alike of hobnailed heel or ash sapling,
refused to obey their riders' intimations to move; while
others, again, brought stiff, wrong-headed ponies to the
charge—obstinate, impracticable little brutes, who seemed to
prefer revolving on their own axes, and describing absurd
rotary motions, to proceeding in the direct and proper course
pointed out to them. Dick could scarcely forbear laughing
at these ridiculous manœuvres; but his attention was chiefly
attracted towards three individuals, who were evidently the
leaders of this warlike expedition. In the thin, tall figure of
the first of these, he recognised Ranulph Rookwood. With
the features and person of the second of the group he was
not entirely unacquainted, and fancied (nor incorrectly
fancied) that his military bearing, or, as he would have expressed it, "the soldier-like cut of his jib," could belong to
no other than Major Mowbray, whom he had once eased of a
purse on Finchley Common. In the round rosy countenance
and robustious person of the last of the trio he discovered
his ancient ally, Titus Tyrconnel.

"Ah, Titus, my jewel, are you there?" exclaimed Dick, as
he distinguished the Irishman. "Come, I have *one* friend
among them whom I may welcome. So, they see me now.
Off they come, pell-mell. Back, Bess, back—slowly, wench,
slowly—there—stand!" And Bess again remained motionless.

The report of Turpin's pistol reached the ears of the troop;
and as all were upon the alert, he had scarcely presented himself at the archway, when a loud shout was raised, and the
whole cavalcade galloped towards him, creating, as may be
imagined, the wildest disorder; each horseman yelling, as he
neared the arch, and got involved in the press occasioned by
the unexpected concentration of forces at that point, while
oaths and blows, kicks and cuffs, were reciprocated with such
hearty good-will, that had Turpin ever read Ariosto or Cervantes, or heard of the discord of King Agramante's camp,
this *mêlée* must have struck him as its realization. As it was,
entertaining little apprehension of the result, he shouted
encouragement to them. Scarcely, however, had the foremost horseman disentangled himself from the crowd, and,
struggling to the door, was in the act of levelling his pistol at
Turpin's head, when a well-directed ball pierced the brain of
his charger, and horse and man rolled to the ground. Vowing
vengeance, a second succeeded and was in like manner compelled to bite the dust.

"That will let old Peter know that Ranulph Rookwood is at hand," exclaimed Dick. "I shan't throw away another shot."

The scene at the archway was now one of complete confusion. Terrified by the shots, some of the boors would have drawn back, while others, in mid career, advanced, and propelled them forwards. It was like the meeting of two tides. Here and there, regardless of the bit, and scared by the firing, a wild colt broke all bounds, and, hurling his rider in the air, darted off into the green; or, in another case, rushed forward, and encountering the prostrate cattle cumbering the entrance to the priory hall, stumbled, and precipitated his master neck-over-heels at the very feet of his enemy. During all this tumult, a few shots were fired at the highwayman, which, without doing him a jot of mischief, tended materially to increase their own confusion.

The voice of Turpin was now heard above the din and turmoil to sound a parley; and as he appeared disposed to offer no opposition, some of his antagonists ventured to raise themselves from the ground, and to approach him.

"I demand to be led to Sir Ranulph Rookwood," said Turpin.

"He is here," said Ranulph, riding up. "Villain, you are my prisoner."

"As you list, Sir Ranulph," returned Dick, coolly; "but let me have a word in private with you ere you do aught you may repent hereafter."

"No words, sir; deliver up your arms, or——"

"My pistols are at your service," replied Dick. "I have just discharged them."

"You may have others. We must search you."

"Hold!" cried Dick; "if you will not listen to me, read that paper." And he handed Ranulph his mother's letter to Mr. Coates. It was without the superscription, which he had thrown aside.

"My mother's hand!" exclaimed Ranulph, reddening with anger, as he hastily perused its contents. "And she sent this to you? You lie, villain; 'tis a forgery."

"Let this speak for me," returned Dick, holding out the finger upon which Lady Rookwood's ring was placed. "Know you that cipher?"

"You have stolen it," retorted Ranulph. "My mother," added he, in a deep, stern whisper, articulated only for Turpin's hearing, "would never have intrusted her honour to a highwayman's keeping."

"She has intrusted more—her life," replied Dick, in a careless tone. "She would have bribed me to do murder."

"Murder!" echoed Ranulph, aghast.

"Ay, to murder your brother," returned Dick; "but let that pass. You have read that note. I have acted solely upon your mother's responsibility. Lady Rookwood's *honour* is pledged for my safety. Of course, her son will set me free."

"Never!"

"Well, as you please. Your mother is in my power. Betray me, and you betray her."

"No more!" returned Ranulph, sternly. "Go your ways. You are free."

"Pledge me your word of honour I am safe."

Ranulph had scarcely given his pledge, when Major Mowbray rode furiously up. A deep flush of anger burnt upon his cheeks; his sword was drawn in his hand. He glanced at Turpin, as if he would have felled him from the saddle.

"This is the ruffian," cried the major, fiercely, " by whom I was attacked some months ago, and for whose apprehension the reward of three hundred pounds is offered by his majesty's proclamation, with a free pardon to his accomplices. This is Richard Turpin. He has just added another crime to his many offences. He has robbed my mother and sister. The postboy knew him the moment he came up. Where are they, villain? Whither are they gone? Answer!"

"I know not," replied Turpin, calmly. "Did not the lad tell you they were rescued?"

"Rescued! By whom?" asked Ranulph, with great emotion.

"By one who calls himself Sir Luke Rookwood," answered Turpin, with a meaning smile.

"By him!" ejaculated Ranulph. "Where are they now?"

"I have already answered that question," said Dick. "I repeat, I know not."

"You are my prisoner," cried the major, seizing Turpin's bridle.

"I have Sir Ranulph's word for my safety," rejoined Turpin. "Let go my rein."

"How is this?" asked Major Mowbray, incredulously.

"Ask me not. Release him," replied Ranulph.

"Ranulph," said the major, "you ask an impossibility. My honour—my duty—is implicated in this man's capture."

"The honour of all of us is involved in his deliverance,"

returned Ranulph, in a whisper. "Let him go. I will explain all hereafter. Let us search for them—for Eleanor. Surely, after this, you will help us to find them" added he, addressing Turpin.

"I wish, with all my soul, I could do so," replied the highwayman.

"I see'd the ladies cross the brook, and enter these old ruins," interposed the postboy, who had now joined the party. "I see'd 'em from where I stood on the hill-side; and, as I kept a pretty sharp look-out, and have a tolerably bright eye of my own, I don't think as how they ever comed out again."

"Some one is hidden within yon fissure in the wall," exclaimed Ranulph; "I see a figure move."

And he flung himself from his horse, rushing towards the mouth of the cell. Imitating his example, Major Mowbray followed his friend, sword in hand.

"The game begins now in right earnest," said Dick to himself; "the old fox will soon be unearthed. I must look to my snappers." And he thrust his hand quietly into his pocket in search of a pistol.

Just as Ranulph and the major reached the recess, they were startled by the sudden apparition of the ill-fated attorney.

"Mr. Coates!" exclaimed Ranulph, in surprise. "What do you here, sir?"

"I—I—that is—Sir Ranulph—you must excuse me, sir—particular business—can't say," returned the trembling attorney; for at this instant his eye caught that of Turpin, and the ominous reflection of a polished-steel barrel, held carelessly towards him. He was aware, also, that on the other hand he was, in like manner, the mark of Rust and Wilder; those polite gentlemen having threatened him with a brace of slugs in his brain if he dared to betray their hiding-place. "It is necessary that I should be *guarded* in my answers," murmured he.

"Is there any one within that place beside yourself?" said the major, making a movement thither.

"No, sir; nobody at all," answered Coates, hastily, fancying at the same time that he heard the click of the pistol that was to be his death-warrant.

"How came you here, sir," demanded Ranulph.

"Do you mean in this identical spot?" replied Coates, evasively.

"You can have no difficulty in answering that question," said the major, sternly.

"Pardon me, sir. I find considerable difficulty in answering any question, situated as I am."

"Have you seen Miss Mowbray?" asked Ranulph, eagerly.

"Or my mother?" said the major, in the same breath.

"Neither," replied Coates, rather relieved by these questions.

"I suspect you are deceiving us, sir," said the major. "Your manner is confused. I am convinced you know more of this matter than you choose to explain: and if you do not satisfy me at once, fully and explicitly, I vow to Heaven——" and the major's sword described a glittering circle round his head.

"Are you privy to their concealment?" asked Ranulph. "Have you seen aught of them or of Luke Bradley?"

"Speak, or this moment is your last," said the major.

"If it *is* my last, I *cannot* speak," returned Coates. "I can make neither head nor tail of your questions, gentlemen."

"And you positively assure me you have not seen Mrs. Mowbray and her daughter?" said Ranulph.

Turpin here winked at Coates. The attorney understood him.

"I don't positively assert that," faltered he.

"How! you *have* seen them?" shouted Ranulph.

"Where are they? in safety? Speak!" added the major.

Another expressive gesture from the highwayman communicated to the attorney the nature of his reply.

"Without, sir; without—yonder," he replied. "I will show you myself. Follow, gentlemen, follow." And away scampered Coates, without once venturing to look behind him.

In an instant the ruined hall was deserted, and Turpin alone left behind. In the excitement of the moment, his presence had been forgotten. In an instant afterwards the *arena* was again occupied by a company equally numerous. Rust and Wilder issued from their hiding-places, followed by a throng of the gipsy crew.

"Where is Sir Luke Rookwood?" asked Turpin.

"He remains below," was the answer returned.

"And Peter Bradley?"

"Stays there likewise."

"No matter. Now make ready, pals. Give 'em one shout—Hurrah!"

" Hurrah!" replied the crowd, at the top of their voices.

Ranulph Rookwood and his companions heard this shout. Mr. Coates had already explained the stratagem practised upon them by the wily highwayman, as well as the perilous situation in which he himself had been placed; and they were in the act of returning, to make good his capture, when the loud shouts of the crew arrested them. From the clamour, it was evident that considerable reinforcement must have arrived from some unlooked-for quarter; and, although burning to be avenged upon the audacious highwayman, the major felt it would be a task of difficulty, and that extreme caution could alone insure success. With difficulty restraining the impatience of Ranulph, who could scarcely brook these few minutes of needful delay, Major Mowbray gave particular instructions to each of the men in detail, and caused several of them to dismount. By this arrangement Mr. Coates found himself accommodated with a steed and a pair of pistols, with which latter he vowed to wreak his vengeance upon some of his recent tormentors. After a short space of time occupied in this manner, the troop slowly advanced towards the postern, in much better order than upon the previous occasion; but the stoutest of them quailed as they caught sight of the numerous gipsy gang drawn out in battle array within the abbey walls. Each party scanned the other's movements in silence and wonder, anxiously awaiting, yet in a measure dreading, their leader's signal to begin. That signal was not long delayed. A shot from the ranks of Rookwood did instant and bitter execution. Rob Rust was stretched lifeless upon the ground. Nothing more was needed. The action now became general. Fire-arms were discharged on both sides, without much damage to either party. But a rush being made by a detachment of horse, headed by Major Mowbray, the conflict soon became more serious. The gipsies, after the first fire, threw aside their pistols, and fought with long knives, with which they inflicted desperate gashes, both on men and horses. Major Mowbray was slightly wounded in the thigh, and his steed receiving the blow intended for himself, stumbled, and threw his rider. Luckily for the major, Ranulph Rookwood was at hand, and with the butt-end of a heavy-handled pistol felled the ruffian to the earth, just as he was upon the point of repeating the thrust.

Turpin, meanwhile, had taken comparatively a small share in the conflict. He seemed to content himself with acting upon the defensive, and except in the case af Titus Tyrcon-

nel, whom, espying amidst the crowd, he had considerably
alarmed by sending a bullet through his wig, he did not fire
a single shot. He also succeeded in unhorsing Coates, by
hurling, with great dexterity, the empty pistol at his head.
Though apparently unconcerned in the skirmish, he did not
flinch from it, but kept his ground unyieldingly. "A charmed
life" he seemed to bear; for amid the shower of bullets,
many of which were especially aimed at himself, he came off
unhurt.

"He that's born to be hanged will never be drowned, that's
certain," said Titus. "It's no use trying to bring him down
But by Jasus! he's spoiled my best hat and wig, anyhow.
There's a hole in my beaver as big as a crown piece."

"Your own crown's safe, and that's some satisfaction,"
said Coates; "whereas mine has a bump on it as large as a
swan's egg. Ah! if we could only get behind him."

The strife continued to rage without intermission; and
though there were now several ghastly evidences of its fury,
in the shape of wounded men and slaughtered or disabled
horses, whose gaping wounds flooded the turf with gore, it
was still difficult to see upon which side victory would eventually declare herself. The gipsies, though by far the
greater sufferers of the two, firmly maintained their ground.
Drenched in the blood of the horses they had wounded, and
brandishing their long knives, they presented a formidable
and terrific appearance, the effect of which was not at all
diminished by their wild yells and savage gesticulations. On
the other hand, headed by Major Mowbray and Ranulph,
the troop of yeomen pressed on undauntedly; and where the
sturdy farmers could get a firm gripe of their lithe antagonists, or deliver a blow with their ox-like fists, they seldom
failed to make good the advantages which superior weight
and strength gave them. It will thus be seen that as yet
they were pretty well matched. Numbers were in favour of
the gipsies, but courage was equally distributed, and, perhaps, what is emphatically called "bottom" was in favour of
the rustics. Be this as it may, from what had already
occurred, there was every prospect of a very serious termination to the fray.

From time to time Turpin glanced to the entrance of the
cell, in the expectation of seeing Sir Luke Rookwood make
his appearance; and, as he was constantly disappointed in his
expectation, he could not conceal his chagrin. At length he
resolved to despatch a messenger to him, and one of the crew

accordingly departed upon this errand. He returned presently with a look of blank dismay.

In our hasty narrative of the fight we have not paused to particularize, neither have we enumerated, the list of the combatants. Amongst them, however, were Jerry Juniper, the knight of Malta, and Zoroaster. Excalibur, as may be conceived, had not been idle; but that trenchant blade had been shivered by Ranulph Rookwood in the early stage of the business, and the knight left weaponless. Zoroaster, who was not merely a worshipper of fire, but a thorough milling-cove, had engaged to some purpose in a pugilistic encounter with the rustics; and, having fought several rounds, now "bore his blushing honours thick upon him." Jerry, like Turpin, had remained tolerably quiescent. "The proper moment," he said, "had not arrived." A fatality seemed to attend Turpin's immediate companions. Rust was the first who fell; Wilder also was now among the slain. Things were precisely in this condition when the messenger returned. A marked change was instantly perceptible in Turpin's manner. He no longer looked on with indifference. He seemed angry and distrustful. He gnawed his lip, ever a sign with him of vexation. Addressing a few words to those about him, he then spoke more loudly to the rest of the crew. Being in the jargon of the tawny tribe, his words were not intelligible to the opposite party; but their import was soon made known by the almost instant and total relinquishment of the field by the gipsies. They took to their heels at once, to a man, leaving only a few desperately wounded behind them; and, flying along the intricate ruins of the priory, baffled all pursuits, wherever it was attempted. Jerry Juniper was the last in the retreat; but, upon receiving a hint from Dick, he vaulted like a roe over the heads of his adversaries, and made good his escape. Turpin alone remained. He stood like a lion at bay, quietly regarding the huntsmen hurtling around him. Ranulph Rookwood rode up and bade him surrender.

"Detain me not," cried he, in a voice of thunder. "If you would save her who is dear to you, descend into that vault. Off, I say."

And Turpin shook away, with ease, the grasp that Ranulph had laid upon him.

"Villain, you do not escape me this time," said Major Mowbray, interposing himself between Turpin and the outlet.

"Major Mowbray, I would not have your blood upon my head," said Dick. "Let me pass." And he levelled a pistol.

"Fire, if you dare!" said the major, raising his sword. "You pass not. I will die rather than allow you to escape. Barricade the door. Strike him down if he attempts to pass. Richard Turpin, I arrest you in the king's name. You hear, my lads in his majesty's name. I command you to assist me in this highwayman's capture. Two hundred pounds for his head!"

"Two hundred devils!" exclaimed Dick, with a laugh of disdain. "Go, seek your mother and sister within yon vault, Major Mowbray; you will find employment enough there."

Saying which, he suddenly forced Bess to back a few yards; and then, striking his heels sharply into her sides, ere his purpose could be divined by the spectators, charged, and cleared the lower part of the mouldering priory walls. This feat was apparently accomplished with no great effort by his admirable and unequalled mare.

"By the powers!" cried Titus, "and he's given us the slip after all. And just when we thought to make sure of him, too. Why, Mr. Coates, that wall must be higher than a five-barred gate, or any stone wall in my own country. It's just the most extraordinary *lepp* I ever set eyes on!"

"The devil's in the fellow, certainly, or in his mare," returned Coates: "but if he escapes me, I'll forgive him. I know whither he's bound. He's off to London with my bill of exchange. I'll be up with him. I'll track him like a bloodhound, slowly and surely, as my father, the thief-taker, used to follow up a scent. Recollect the hare and the tortoise. The race is not always to the swift. What say you? 'Tis a match for five hundred pounds; nay, for five thousand: for there is a certain marriage certificate in the way—a glorious golden venture! You shall go halves if we win. We'll have him, dead or alive. What say you for London, Mr. Tyrconnel? Shall we start at once?"

"With all my *soul*," replied Titus. "I'm with you." And away this *par nobile* scoured.

Ranulph, meantime, plunged into the vault. The floor was slippery, and he had nigh stumbled. Loud and deep lamentations and a wailing sound, like that of a lament for the dead, resounded in his ears. A light at the further extremity of the vault attracted his attention. He was filled with terrible forebodings; but the worst reality was not so terrible as suspense. He rushed towards the light. He passed the massive pillars, and there, by the ruddy torch flame discovered two female figures. One was an old woman, fantastically attired, wringing her hands, and moaning, or gibbering wild strains in broken, discordant, yet pathetic tones. The other was Mrs. Mowbray. Both were images of despair. Before them lay some motionless object. He noticed not that old woman; he scarcely saw Mrs. Mowbray; he beheld only that object of horror. It was the lifeless body of a female. The light fell imperfectly upon the face; he could not discern the features, but the veil in which it was swathed: that veil was Eleanor's! He asked no more.

With a wild cry he rushed forward. "Eleanor, my beloved," shrieked he.

Mrs. Mowbray started at his voice, but appeared stunned and helpless.

"She is dead," said Ranulph, stooping towards the body. Dead—dead!"

"Ay," echoed the old woman, in accents of equal anguish —"dead—dead!"

"But this is *not* Eleanor," exclaimed he, as he viewed the features more closely. "This face, though beautiful, is not hers. This dishevelled hair is black. The long lashes that shade her cheek are of the same hue. She is scarce dead. The hand I clasp is yet warm—the fingers are pliant."

"Yet she is dead," said the old woman, in a broken voice. "She is slain."

"Who hath slain her?" asked Ranulph.

"I—I—her mother, slew her."

"You!" exclaimed Ranulph, horror-stricken. "And where is Eleanor?" asked he. "Was she not here?"

"Better she were here now, even though she were as that poor maid," groaned Mrs. Mowbray, "than where she is."

"Where is she then?" asked Ranulph, with frantic eagerness.

"Fled. Whither I know not."

"With whom?"

"With Sir Luke Rookwood—with Alan Rookwood. They have borne her hence. Ranulph, you are too late."

"Gone!" cried Ranulph, fiercely springing to his feet. "How escaped they? There appears to be but one entrance to this vault. I will search each nook and cranny."

"'Tis vain," replied Mrs. Mowbray. "There is another outlet through yon cell. By that passage they escaped."

T

"Too true, too true," shouted Ranulph, who flew to examine the cell. "And wherefore followed you not?"

"The stone rolled to its mouth, and resisted my efforts.   I could not follow."

"Torture and death!   She is lost to me for ever!" cried Ranulph, bitterly.

"No," exclaimed Barbara, clutching his arm.   "Place your trust in me, and I will find her for you."

"You!" ejaculated Ranulph.

"Even I," replied Barbara.   "Your wrongs shall be righted —my Sybil be avenged."

Book the Fourth.

THE RIDE TO YORK.

Then one halloo, boys! one loud cheering halloo!
To the swiftest of coursers, the gallant, the true!
For the sportsman unborn shall the memory bless
Of the horse of the highwayman, bonny Black Bess!
                              RICHARD TURPIN.

I.

THE RENDEZVOUS AT KILBURN.

Hind. Drink deep, my brave boys, of the bastinado;
      Of stramazons, tinctures, and slic passatas;
      Of the carricado, and rare embrocado;
      Of blades, and rapier-hilts of surest guard;
      Of the Vincentio and Burgundian ward.
      Have we not bravely tossed this bombast foil-button?
      Win gold and wear gold, boys, 'tis we that merit it.
                              Prince of Prigs' Revels.
An excellent Comedy, replete with various conceits and Tarltonian mirth.

THE present straggling suburb at the north-west of the metropolis, known as Kilburn, had scarcely been called into existence a century ago, and an ancient hostel with a few detached farmhouses, were the sole habitations to be found in the present populous vicinage.   The place of refreshment for the ruralising cockney of 1737 was a substantial-looking tenement of the good old stamp, with great bay windows, and a balcony in front, bearing as its ensign the jovial visage of the lusty knight, Jack Falstaff.   Shaded by a spreading elm, a circular bench embraced the aged trunk of the tree, sufficiently tempting, no doubt, to incline the wanderer on those dusty ways to "rest and be thankful," and to cry *encore* to a frothing tankard of the best ale to be obtained within the chimes of Bow bells.

Upon a table, green as the privet and holly that formed the walls of the bower in which it was placed, stood a great china bowl, one of those leviathan memorials of bygone wassailry which we may sometimes espy (reversed, in token of its desuetude) perched on the top of an old japanned closet, but seldom, if ever, encounter in its proper position at the genial board. All the appliances of festivity were at hand. Pipes and rummers strewed the board. Perfume, subtle yet mellow, as of pine and lime, exhaled from out of the bowl, and mingling with the scent of a neighbouring bed of mignonette, and the subdued odour of the Indian weed, formed altogether as delectable an atmosphere of sweets as one could wish to inhale on a melting August afternoon. So, at least, thought the inmates of the arbour; nor did they by any means confine themselves to the gratification of a single sense. The ambrosial contents of the china bowl proved as delicious to the taste as its bouquet was grateful to the smell; while the eyesight was soothed by reposing on the smooth sward of a bowling-green spread out immediately before it, or in dwelling upon gently-undulating meads, terminating, at about a mile's distance, in the woody, spire-crowned heights of Hampstead.

At the left of the table was seated, or rather lounged, a slender, elegant-looking young man, with dark languid eyes, sallow complexion, and features wearing that peculiarly pensive expression often communicated by dissipation; an expression which, we regret to say, is sometimes found more pleasing than it ought to be in the eyes of the gentle sex. Habited in a light summer riding-dress, fashioned according to the taste of the time, of plain and unpretending material, and rather under than over-dressed, he had, perhaps, on that very account, perfectly the air of a gentleman. There was, altogether, an absence of pretension about him, which combined with great apparent self-possession, contrasted very forcibly with the vulgar assurance of his showy companions. The figure of the youth was slight, even to fragility, giving little outward manifestation of the vigour of frame he in reality possessed. This spark was a no less distinguished personage than Tom King, a noted high tobygloak of his

time, who obtained, from his appearance and address, the
sobriquet of the "Gentleman Highwayman."

Tom was indeed a pleasant fellow in his day. His career
was brief, but brilliant: your meteors are ever momentary.
He was a younger son of a good family; had good blood in
his veins, though not a groat in his pockets. According to
the old song—

> When he arrived at man's estate,
> It was *all the estate* he had;

and all the estate he was ever likely to have. Nevertheless,
if he had no income, he contrived, as he said, to live as if he
had the mines of Peru at his control—a miracle not solely
confined to himself. For a moneyless man, he had rather
expensive habits. He kept his three nags; and, if fame does
not belie him, a like number of mistresses: nay, if we are to
place any faith in certain scandalous chronicles to which we
have had access, he was for some time the favoured lover of a
celebrated actress, who, for the time, supplied him with the
means of keeping up his showy establishment. But things
could not long hold thus. Tom was a model of infidelity,
and that was the only failing his mistress could not overlook.
She dismissed him at a moment's notice. Unluckily, too, he
had other propensities which contributed to involve him. He
had a taste for the turf—a taste for play—was well known in
the hundreds of Drury, and cut no mean figure at Howell's,
and the faro tables thereanent. He was the glory of the
Smyrna, D'Osyndar's, and other chocolate-houses of the day;
and it was at this time he fell into the hands of certain dexterous sharpers, by whom he was first plucked, and subsequently patronised. Under their tuition he improved
wonderfully. He turned his wit and talent to some account.
He began to open his eyes. His nine days' blindness was
over. The dog saw. But, in spite of his quickness, he was
at length discovered, and ejected from Howell's in a manner
that left him no alternative. He must either have called out
his adversary, or go out himself. He preferred the latter,
and took to the road; and in his new line he was eminently
successful. Fortunately, he had no scruples to get over.
Tom had what Sir Walter Scott happily denominates "an
indistinct notion of *meum* and *tuum*," and became confirmed
in the opinion that everything he could lay hands upon constituted lawful spoil. And, then, even those he robbed
admitted that he was the most gentlemanlike highwayman

they had ever the fortune to meet with, and trusted they might always be so lucky. So popular did he become upon the road, that it was accounted a distinction to be stopped by him; he made a point of robbing none but gentlemen, and —Tom's shade would quarrel with us were we to omit them— ladies. His acquaintance with Turpin was singular, and originated in a rencontre. Struck with his appearance, Dick presented a pistol, and bade King deliver. The latter burst into a laugh, and an explanation immediately ensued. Thenceforward they became sworn brothers—the Pylades and Orestes of the road; and though seldom seen together in public, had many a merry moonlight ride in company.

Tom still maintained three mistresses, his valet, his groom (tiger we should have called him), "and many a change of clothes besides." says his biographer, "with which he appeared more like a lord than a highwayman." And what more, we should like to know, would a lord wish to have? Few younger sons, we believe, can boast so much; and it is chiefly on their account, with some remote view to the benefit of the unemployed youth of all professions, that we have enlarged so much upon Tom King's history. The road, we must beg to repeat, is still open; the chances are greater than they ever were; we fully believe it is *their* only road to preferment, and we are sadly in want of highwaymen!

Fancy Tom lounging at D'Osyndar's, carelessly tapping his boots on the steps; there he stands! Is he not a devilish good-looking gentlemanlike sort of fellow? You could never have taken him for a highwayman but for our information. A waiter appears—supper is ordered at twelve—a broiled chicken and a bottle of Burgundy—his groom brings his nags to the door—he mounts. It is his custom to ride out on an evening—he is less liable to interruption.* At Marylebone Fields (now the Regent's Park) his groom leaves him. He has a mistress in the neighbourhood. He is absent for a couple of hours, and returns gay or dispirited, as his luck may have turned out. At twelve he is at supper, and has the night before him. How very easy all this seems. Can it be possible we have no Tom Kings?

To return to Tom as he was in the arbour. Judging from his manner, he appeared to be almost insensible to the pre-

---

* We have heard of a certain gentleman tobyman, we forget his name, taking the horses from his curricle for a similar purpose; but we own we think King's the simpler plan, and quite practicable still. A cabriolet would be quite out of the question, but particularly easy to *stop*.

sence of his companions, and to be scarcely a partaker in
their revelry. His back was towards his immediate neighbour; his glass sparkled untouched at his elbow; and one
hand, beautifully white and small, a mark of his birth and
breeding (*crede* Byron), rested upon the edge of the table,
while his thin delicate digits, palpably demonstrative of his
faculty of adaptation (*crede* James Hardy Vaux), were employed with a silver toothpick. In other respects, he seemed
to be lost in reverie, and was, in all probability, meditating
new exploits.

Next to King sat our old friend Jerry Juniper; not, however, the Jerry of the gipsies, but a much more showy-looking
personage. Jerry was no longer a gentleman of " three *outs*"
—the difficulty would now have been to say what he was
" without." Snakelike he had cast his slough, and rejoiced
in new and brilliant investiture. His were " speaking garments, speaking pockets too." His linen was of the finest,
his host of the smartest. Gay rings glittered on his fingers;
a crystal snuff-box underwent graceful manipulation; a handsome gold repeater was sometimes drawn from its location
with a monstrous bunch of onions (*anglicé* seals) depending
from its massive chain. Lace adorned his wrists, and shoes
(of which they had been long unconscious), with buckles
nearly as large as themselves, confined his feet. A rich-
powdered peruke and silver-hilted sword completed the gear
of the transmogrified Jerry, or, as he now chose to be designated, Count Albert Conyers. The fact was, that Jerry, after
the *fracas*, apprehensive that the country would be too hot
for him, had, in company with Zoroaster, quitted the ranks
of the canting crew, and made the best of his way to town.
A lucky *spice* on the road set them up; and having some
acquaintance with Tom King, the party on their arrival sought
him out at his customary haunt, D'Osyndar's, and enlisted
unde. his banners.

Tom received them with open arms, gave them unlimited
use of his wardrobe, and only required a little trifling assistance in return. He had a grand scheme *in petto*, in the
execution of which they could mainly assist him. Jerry was
a *Greek* by nature, and could *land* a flat as well as the best
of them. Zoroaster was just the man to *lose* a fight; or, in
the language of the *Fancy* to *play a cross* No two *legs*
could serve Tom's purposes better. He welcomed them with
fraternal affection.

We will now proceed to reconnoitre Jerry's opposite

neighbour, who was, however, no other than that Upright
Man,

The Magus Zoroaster, that great name.

Changed as was Juniper, the Magus was yet more whimsically
metamorphosed. Some traces of Jerry still remained, but
not a vestige was left of the original Dimber Damber. His
tawny mother had not known her son. This alteration, however, was not owing to change of dress : it was the result
of the punishment he had received at the "*set to*" at the
priory. Not a feature was in its place ; his swollen lip tres-
passed upon the precincts of his nose ; his nose trod hard
upon his cheek ; while his cheek again, not to be behind the
rest, rose up like an apple-dumpling under his single eye,—
single we say—for, alas ! there was no speculation in the
other. His dexter daylight was utterly darkened, and, indeed, the orb that remained was as sanguine a luminary as
ever struggled through a London fog at noonday. To borrow
a couplet or so from the laureate of the *Fancy* :

> ————— One of his peepers was put
> On the bankruptcy list, with his shop-windows shut,
> While the other made nearly as tag rag a show,
> All rimmed round with black, like the *Courier* in woe.

One black patch decorated his rainbow-coloured cheek ;
another adorned his chin ; a grinder having been dislodged,
his pipe took possession of the aperture. His toggery was
that of a member of the prize-ring ; what we now call a
"belcher" bound his throat ; a spotted *fogle* bandaged his
jobbernowl, and shaded his right peeper, while a white beaver
crowned the occiput of the Magus. And though, at first
sight, there would appear to be some incongruity in the asso-
ciation of such a battered character as the Upright Man with
his smart companions, the reader's wonder will rapidly dimi-
nish, when he reflects that any distinguished P. C. man can
ever find a ready passport to the most exclusive society,
Viewed in this light, Zoroaster's familiarity with his *swell*
acquaintance occasioned no surprise to old Simon Carr, the
bottle-nosed landlord of the Falstaff, who was a man of dis-
cernment in his way, and knew a thing or two. Despite such
striking evidences to the contrary, the Magus was perfectly
at his ease, and sacrificing as usual to the god of flame. His
mithra, or pipe, the symbol of his faith, was zealously placed
between his lips ; and never did his Chaldean, Bactrian, Per-
sian, Pamphilian, Proconnesian, or Babylonian namesake,
whichever of the six was the true Zoroaster (*vide* Bayle),

respire more fervently at the altar of fire, than our Magus at
the end of his enkindled tube. In his creed we believe Zoroaster was a dualist, and believed in the co-existence and
mystical relation of the principles of good and ill; his pipe
being his Yezdan, or benign influence; his empty pouch his
Ahreman, or the devil. We shall not pause to examine his
tenets; we meddle with no man's religious opinions, and shall
leave the Magus to the enjoyment of his own sentiments, be
they what they may.

One guest alone remains, and him we shall briefly dismiss.
The reader, we imagine, will scarcely need to be told who
was the owner of those keen grey eyes; those exuberant red
whiskers; that airy azure frock. It was—

> Our brave copartner of the roads,
> Skilful surveyor of highways, and hedges;

in a word—Dick Turpin!

Dick had been called upon to act as president of the board,
and an excellent president he made, sedulously devoting
himself to the due administration of the punch-bowl. Not a
rummer was allowed to stand empty for an instant. Toast,
sentiment, and anacreontic song, succeeded each other at
speedy intervals; but there was no speechifying—no politics.
He left church and state to take care of themselves. Whatever his politics might be, Dick never allowed them to interfere with his pleasures. His maxim was to make the most
of the passing moment; the *dum vivimus vivamus* was never
out of his mind; a precautionary measure which we recommend to the adoption of all gentlemen of the like, or any
other precarious profession.

Notwithstanding all Dick's efforts to promote conviviality,
seconded by the excellence of the beverage itself, conversation, somehow or other, began to flag; from being general it
became particular. Tom King, who was no punch-bibber,
especially at that time of day, fell into a deep reverie; your
gamesters often do so; while the Magus, who had smoked
himself drowsy, was composing himself to a doze. Turpin
seized this opportunity of addressing a few words on matters
of business to Jerry Juniper, or, as he now chose to be called,
Count Conyers.

"My dear count," said Dick, in a low and confidential
tone; you are aware that my errand to town is accomplished. I have *smashed* Lawyer Coates's *screen*, pocketed
the *dimmock* (here 'tis," continued he, parenthetically slapping his pockets), "and done t'other trick in prime twig for

Tom King. With a cool thousand in hand, I might, if I choose, rest awhile on my oars. But a quiet life don't suit me. I must be moving. So I shall start to Yorkshire to-night."

"Indeed," said the *soi-disant* count, in a languid tone—"so soon?"

"I have nothing to detain me," replied Dick. "And, to tell you the truth, I want to see how matters stand with Sir Luke Rookwood. I should be sorry if he went to the wall for want of any assistance I can render him."

"True," returned the count; "one would regret such an occurrence, certainly. But I fear your assistance may arrive a little too late. He is pretty well done up, I should imagine, by this time."

"That remains to be seen," said Turpin. "His case is a bad one, to be sure, but I trust not utterly hopeless. With all his impetuosity and pride, I like the fellow, and will help him, if I can. It will be a difficult game to set him on his legs, but I think it may be done. That underground marriage was sheer madness, and turned out as ill as such a scheme might have been expected to do. Poor Sybil! if I could pipe an eye for anything, it should be for her. I can't get her out of my head. Give me a pinch of snuff. Such thoughts unman one. As to the priest, that's a totally different affair. If he strangled his daughter, old Alan did right to take the law into his own hands, and throttle him in return. I'd have done the same myself; and, being a proscribed Jesuit, returned, as I understand, without the king's license for so doing, why Father Checkley's murder (if it must be so called, I can't abide hard terms) won't lie very heavy at Alan's door. That, however, has nothing to do with Sir Luke. He was neither accessory nor principal. Still he will be in danger, at least from Lady Rookwood. The whole county of York, I make no doubt, is up in arms by this time,"

"Then why go thither?" asked the count, somewhat ironically; "for my part I've a strange fancy for keeping out of arm's way as long as possible."

"Every man to his taste," returned Turpin; "I love to confront danger. Run away! pshaw! always meet your foe."

"True," replied the count, *half-way!* but you go the whole distance. What prudent man would beard the lion in his den?"

"I never was a prudent man," rejoined Dick, smiling; "I

have no superfluous caution about me. Come what will, I
shall try to find out this Luke Rookwood, and offer him my
purse, such as it is, and it is now better lined than usual; a
hand free to act as he lists; and a head which, imprudent
though it be, can often think better for others than for its
own master."

"Vastly fine!" exclaimed the count, with an ill-disguised
sneer. "I hope you don't forget that the marriage certificate
which you hold is perfectly valueless now. The estates, you
are aware——"

"Are no longer Sir Luke's. I see what you are driving
at, count," returned Dick, coldly. "But he will need it to
establish his claim to the *title*, and he shall have it. While
he was Sir Luke with ten thousand a year, I drove a hard
bargain, and would have stood out for the last stiver. Now
that he is one of '*us*,' a mere knight of the road, he shall
have it and welcome."

"Perhaps Lady Rookwood, or Mrs. Mowbray, might be
inclined to treat," maliciously insinuated the count; "the
title may be worth something to Ranulph."

"It is worth more to Luke: and if it were *not*, he gets it.
Are you satisfied?"

"Perfectly," replied the count, with affected *bonhommie;*
"and I will now let you into a secret respecting Miss Mowbray, from which you may gather something for your guidance in this matter; and if the word of woman is at all to be
trusted, though individually I cannot say I have much faith
in it, Sir Luke's planetary hour is not yet completely overcast."

"That's exactly what I wish to know, my dear fellow,"
said Turpin, eagerly. "You have already told me you were
witness to a singular interview between Miss Mowbray and
Sir Luke after my departure from the priory. If I mistook
you not, the whole business will hinge upon that. What
occurred? Let me have every particular. The whole history
and mystery."

"You shall have it with pleasure," said the count; "and I
hope it may tend to your benefit. After I had quitted the
scene of action at the priory, and at your desire left the
Rookwood party masters of the field, I fled with the rest of
the crew towards the rocks. There we held a council of war
for a short time. Some were for returning to the fight; but
this was negatived entirely, and in the end it was agreed that
those who had wives, daughters, and sisters, should join

them as speedily as possible at their retreat in the Grange. As I happened to have none of these attractive ties, and had only a troublesome mistress, who I thought could take care of herself, I did not care to follow them, but struck deeper into the wood, and made my way, guided by destiny, I suppose, towards the cave."

"The cave!" cried Dick, rubbing his hands; "I delight in a cave. Tom King and I once had a cave of our own at Epping, and I'll have another one of these fine days. A cave is as proper to a high-tobyman as a castle to a baron. Pray go on."

"The cave I speak of," continued the count, "was seldom used, except upon great emergencies, by any of the Stop Hole Abbey crew. It was a sort of retiring den of our old lioness, Barbara, and, like all belonging to her, respected by her dupes. However, the cave is a good cave for all that; is well concealed by brushwood, and comfortably lighted from a crevice in the rock above; it lies near the brink of the stream, amongst the woods, just above the waterfall, and is somewhat difficult of approach."

"I know something of the situation," said Turpin.

"Well," returned the count, "not to lose time, into this den I crept, and, expecting to find it vacant, you may imagine my surprise on discovering that it was already occupied, and that Sir Luke Rookwood, his granddad old Alan, Miss Mowbray, and, worst of all, the very person I wished most to avoid, my old flame Handassah, constituted the party. Fortunately they did not perceive my entrance, and I took especial care not to introduce myself. Retreat, however, was for the moment impracticable, and I was compelled to be a listener. I cannot tell what had passed between the parties before my arrival, but I heard Miss Mowbray implore Sir Luke to conduct her to her mother. He seemed half inclined to comply with her entreaties; but old Alan shook his head. It was then Handassah put in a word; the minx was ever ready at that. 'Fear not,' said she, 'that she will wed Sir Ranulph. Deliver her to her friends, I beseech you, Sir Luke, and woo her honourably. She will accept you.' Sir Luke stared incredulously, and grim old Alan smiled. 'She has sworn to be yours,' continued Handassah; 'sworn it by every hope of heaven, and the oath has been sealed by blood—by Sybil's blood.'—'Does she speak the truth?' asked Sir Luke, trembling with agitation. Miss Mowbray answered not. 'You will not deny it, lady,' said Handassah. 'I heard that oath proposed. I saw it registered. You cannot deny it.'—'I do not,' replied Miss Mowbray, with much anguish of manner; 'if he claim me, I am his.'—'And he will claim you,' said Alan Rookwood, triumphantly. 'He has your oath, no matter how extorted—you must fulfil your vow.'— 'I am prepared to do so,' said Eleanor. 'But if you would not utterly destroy me, let this maid conduct me to my mother, to my friends.'—'To Ranulph?' asked Sir Luke, bitterly. 'No, no,' returned Miss Mowbray, in accents of deepest despair, 'to my mother—I wish not to behold him again.'—'Be it so,' cried Sir Luke; 'but remember, in love or hate you are mine; I shall claim the fulfilment of your oath. Farewell. Handassah will lead you to your mother.' Miss Mowbray bowed her head but returned no answer, while, followed by old Alan, Sir Luke departed from the cavern."

"Whither went they?" demanded Turpin.

"That I know not," replied Jerry. "I was about to follow, when I was prevented by the abrupt entrance of another party. Scarcely, I think, could the two Rookwoods have made good their retreat, when shouts were heard without, and young Ranulph and Major Mowbray forced their way, sword in hand, into the cave. Here was a situation—for *me*, I mean—to the young lady, I make no doubt, it was pleasant enough. But my neck was in jeopardy. However, you know I am not deficient in strength, and, upon the present occasion, I made the best use of the agility with which nature has endowed me. Amidst the joyous confusion—the sobbings, and embracings, and congratulations that ensued—I contrived, like a wild cat, to climb the rocky sides of the cave, and conceal myself behind a jutting fragment of stone. It was well I did so, for scarcely was I hidden, when in came old Barbara, followed by Mrs. Mowbray, and a dozen others."

"Barbara!" ejaculated Dick. "Was she a prisoner?"

"No," replied Jerry, "the old hell-cat is too deep for that. She had betrayed Sir Luke, and hoped they would seize him and his granddad. But the birds were flown."

"I am glad she was baulked," said Dick. "Was any search made after them?"

"Can't say," replied Jerry. "I could only indistinctly catch the sound of their voices from my lofty retreat. Before they left the cavern, I made out that Mrs. Mowbray resolved to go to Rookwood, and to take her daughter thither; a proceeding to which the latter demurred."

"To Rookwood," said Dick, musingly. "Will she keep her oath, I wonder?"

"That's more than I can say," said Jerry, sipping his punch.

"'Tis a deceitful sex, indeed," echoed Dick, tossing off a tumbler. "For one Sybil we meet with twenty Handassahs, eh, count?"

"Twenty! say rather a hundred," replied Jerry. "'Tis a vile sex!"

II.

TOM KING.

Grimm. How gloriously the sun sets to-night.
Moor. When I was a boy, my favourite thought was, that I should live and die like yonder glorious orb. It was a boyish thought.
Grimm. True, captain.   *The Robbers.*

"PEACE, base calumniators," exclaimed Tom King, aroused from his toothpick reverie by these aspersions of the best part of creation. "Peace, I say. None shall dare to abuse that dear, devoted sex, in the hearing of their champion, without pricking a lance with him in their behalf. What do you, either of you, who abuse women in that wholesale style, know of her? Nothing; less than nothing; and yet you venture, upon your paltry experience, to lift up your voices and decry the sex. Now I *do* know her; and, upon my own experience, avouch that, as a sex, woman, compared with man, is as an angel to a devil. As a sex, woman is faithful, loving, self-sacrificing. *We* 'tis that make her otherwise; *we*, selfish, exacting, neglectful men; we teach her indifference, and then blame her apt scholarship. We spoil our own hand, and then blame the cards. No abuse of woman in my hearing. Give me a glass of grog, Dick. 'The sex! three times three!' and here's a song for you into the bargain." Saying which, in a mellow, plaintive tone, Tom gave the following:

PLEDGE OF THE HIGHWAYMAN.

Come, fill up a bumper to Eve's fairest daughters,
    Who have lavished their smiles on the brave and the free;
Toast the sweethearts of DUDLEY, HIND, WILMOT, and WATERS,*
    Whate'er their attraction, whate'er their degree.

---

* Four celebrated highwaymen, all rejoicing in the honourable distinction of captain.

Pledge! pledge in a bumper, each kind-hearted maiden,
   Whose bright eyes were dimmed at the highwayman's fall;
Who stood by the gallows with sorrow o'erladen,
   Bemoaning the fate of the gallant Du-Val!

Here's to each lovely lass chance of war bringeth near one,
   Who, with manner impassioned, we tenderly stop;
And to whom, like the lover addressing his dear one,
   In terms of entreaty *the question* we pop.

How oft, in such case, rosy lips have proved sweeter
   Than the rosiest book, bright eyes saved a bright ring;
While that *one other* kiss has brought off a *repeater*,
   And a bead as a *favour*—the *favourite* string.

With our hearts ready rifled, each pocket we rifle,
   With the pure flame of chivalry stirring our breasts;
Life's risk for our *mistress's praise* is a trifle;
   And each purse as a *trophy* our *homage* attests.

Then toss off your glasses to all girls of spirit,
   Ne'er with names, or with number, your memories **vex**;
Our toast, boys, embraces each woman of merit,
   And, for fear of omission, we'll drink the **whole sex**.

"Well," replied Dick, replenishing King's rummer, while he laughed heartily at his ditty, "I shan't refuse your toast, though my heart don't respond to your sentiments. Ah, Tom! the sex you praise so much will, I fear, prove your undoing. Do as you please; but curse me if ever I pin my life to a petticoat. I'd as soon think of neglecting the four cautions."

"The four cautions," said King; "What are they?"

"Did you never hear them?" replied Dick. "Attend, then, and be edified."

THE FOUR CAUTIONS.

Pay attention to these cautions four,
And through life you will need little more,
Should you dole out your days to threescore;
Beware of a pistol before!
            Before! before!
Beware of a pistol before!

And when backwards his ears are inclined,
And his tail with his ham is combined,
Caution two you will bear in your mind;
Beware of a prancer behind!
            Behind! behind!
Beware of a prancer behind!

Thirdly, when in the park you may ride,
On your best bit of blood, sir, astride,
Chatting gay to your old friend's young bride;
Beware of a coach at the side!
            At the side! at the side!
Beware of a coach at the side!

> Lastly, whether in purple or grey,
> Canter, ranter, grave, solemn, or gay
> Whate'er he may do or may say,
> Beware of a priest every way!
>   Every way! **every way!**
> Beware of a priest every way!

"Well," said Tom King, "all you can sing or say don't alter my good opinion of the women. Not a secret have I from the girl of my heart. She could have sold me over and over again if she had chosen; but my sweet Sue is not the wench to do that."

"It is not too late," said Dick. "Your Dalilah may yet hand your over to the Philistines."

"Then I shall die in a good cause," said King; "but

> The Tyburn tree
> Has no terrors for me,
> Let better men swing—I'm at liberty.

I shall never come to the scragging-post, unless you turn topsman, Dick Turpin. My nativity has been cast, and the stars have declared I am to die by the hand of my best friend —and that's you; eh, Dick?"

"It sounds like it," replied Turpin; "but I advise you not to become too intimate with Jack Ketch. He may prove your best friend after all."

"Why, faith, that's true," replied King, laughing; "and if I must ride backwards up Holborn Hill, I'll do the thing in style, and honest Jack Ketch shall never want his dues. A man should always die game. We none of us know how soon our turn may come; but come when it will, I shall never flinch from it.

> As the highwayman's life is the fullest of zest,
> So the highwayman's death is the briefest and best;
> He dies not as other men die, by degrees,
> But *at once!* without flinching—and quite at his ease!

as the song you are so fond of says. When I die, it will not be of consumption. And if the surgeon's knife must come near me, it will be after death. There's some comfort in that reflection, at all events."

"True," replied Turpin; "and, with a little alteration, my song would suit you capitally:

> There is not a king, should you search the world round,
> So blithe as the king's king, Tom King, to be found;
> Dear woman's his empire, each girl is his own,
> And he'd have a long reign if he'd let 'em alone!

Ha, ha!"

"Ha, ha!" laughed Tom. "And now, Dick, to change the subject. You are off, I understand, to Yorkshire tonight. 'Pon my soul, you are a wonderful fellow—an *alibi* personified! here and everywhere at the same time. No wonder you are called the flying highwayman. To-day in town, to-morrow at York, the day after at Chester. The devil only knows where you will pitch your quarters a week hence. There are rumours of you in all counties at the same moment. This man swears you robbed him at Hounslow; that, on Salisbury Plain; while another avers you monopolise Cheshire and Yorkshire, and that it isn't safe even to *hunt* without pops in your pocket. I heard some devilish good stories of you at D'Osyndar's t'other day; the fellow who told them to me little thought I was a brother blade."

"You flatter me," said Dick, smiling complacently; "but it's no merit of mine. Black Bess alone enables me to do it, and hers be the credit. Talking of being everywhere at the same time, you shall hear what she once did for me in Cheshire. Meantime, a glass to the best mare in England. You won't refuse that toast, Tom. Ah! if your mistress is only as true to you as my nag to me, you might set at nought the tightest hempen cravat that was ever twisted, and defy your best friend to hurt you. Black Bess! and God bless her! And now for the song." Saying which, with much emotion, Turpin chanted the following rhymes:

BLACK BESS.*

Let the lover his mistress's beauty rehearse,
And laud her attractions in languishing verse;
Be it mine in rude strains, but with *truth* to express,
The love that I bear to my bonny Black Bess.

From the West was her dam, from the East was her sire,
From the one came her swiftness, the other her fire;
No peer of the realm better blood can possess
Than flows in the viens of my bonny Black Bess.

Look! look! how that eyeball glows bright as a brand!
That neck proudly arches, those nostrils expand!
Mark that wide-flowing mane! of which each silky tress
Might adorn prouder beauties—though none like Black Bess!

Mark that skin sleek as velvet, and dusky as night,
With its jet undisfigured by one lock of white;
That throat branched with veins, prompt to charge or caress:
Now is she not beautiful?—bonny Black Bess!

Over highway and by-way, in rough and smooth weather,
Some thousands of miles have we journeyed together;
Our couch the same straw, and our meal the same mess:
No couple more constant than I and Black Bess!

---

* Set to music by Mr. F. Romer.

By moonlight, in darkness, by night, or by day,
Her headlong career there is nothing can stay;
She cares not for distance, she knows not distress.
Can you show me a courser to match with Black Bess?

"Egad! I should think not," exclaimed King; "you are as
sentimental on the subject of your mare as I am when I think
of my darling Susan. But pardon my interruption. Pray,
proceed."

"Let me first clear my throat," returned Dick; "and now,
to resume :"

Once it happened in Cheshire, near Dunham, I popped
On a horseman alone, whom I suddenly stopped;
That I lightened his pockets you'll readily guess—
Quick work makes Dick Turpin when mounted on Bess.

Now it seems the man knew me; "Dick Turpin," said he,
"You shall swing for this job, as you live, d'ye see;"
I laughed at his threats and his vows of redress;
I was sure of an *alibi* then with Black Bess.

The road was a hollow, a sunken ravine,*
Overshadowed completely by wood like a screen;
I clambered the bank, and I needs must confess
That one touch of the spur grazed the side of Black Bess.

Brake, brook, meadow, and plough'd field, Bess fleetly bestrode,
As the crow wings her flight we selected our road;
We arrived at Hough Green in five minutes, or less—
My neck it was saved by the speed of Black Bess.

Stepping carelessly forward, I lounge on the green,
Taking excellent care that by all I am seen;
Some remarks on time's flight to the squires I address,
But I say not a word of the flight of Black Bess.

I mention the hour—it was just about four—
Play a rubber at bowls—think the danger is o'er;
When athwart my next game, like a checkmate at chess,
Comes the horseman in search of the rider of Bess.

What matter details? Off with triumph I came;
He swears to the hour, and the squires swear the same;
I had robbed him at *four!*—while at four *they* profess
I was quietly bowling—all thanks to Black Bess!

Then one halloo, boys, one loud cheering halloo!
To the swiftest of coursers, the gallant, the true!
For the sportsman unborn shall the memory bless
Of the horse of the highwayman—bonny Black Bess!

---

* The exact spot where Turpin committed the robbery, which has often
been pointed out to us, lies in what is now a wooden hollow, though once the
old road from Altringham to Knutsford, skirting the rich and sylvan domains of
Dunham, and descending the hill that brings you to the bridge crossing the
little river Bollin. With some difficulty we penetrated this ravine. It is
just the place for an adventure of the kind. A small brook wells through it; and
the steep banks are overhung with timber, and were, when we last visited the
place, in April, 1831, a perfect nest of primroses and wild flowers. Hough
(pronounced Hoo) Green lies about three miles across the country—the way
Turpin rode. The old Bowling-green is one of the pleasantest inns in
Cheshire.

Loud acclamations rewarded Dick's performance. Awakened from his doze, Zoroaster beat time to the melody, the only thing, Jerry said, he was capable of *beating* in his present shattered condition. After some little persuasion, the Magus was prevailed upon to enliven the company with a strain, which he trolled forth after a maudlin manner:

THE DOUBLE CROSS.

Though all of us have heard of *crost* fights,
And certain *gains*, by certain *lost* fights;
I rather fancies that it's news,
How in a mill, *both* men should *lose*;
For vere the *odds* are thus made even,
It plays the dickens with the *steven*;*
Besides, against all rule they're sinning,
Vere *neither* has no chance of vinning.   *Ri, tol, lol, &c.*

Two *milling cores*, each vide avake,
Vere backed to fight for heavy stake;
But in the mean time, so it vos,
Both *kids* agreed to *play a cross*;
Bold came each *buffer*† to the *scratch*,
To make it look a *tightish match*;
They *peeled*‡ in style, and bets vere making,
'Twos six to four, but few were *taking*.   *Ri, tol, lol, &c.*

Quite cautiously the mill began,
For neither knew the other's plan;
Each *cull*§ completely in the *dark*,
Of vot might be his neighbour's *mark*;
Resolved his *jibbing*‖ not to mind,
Nor yet to *pay him back in kind*;
So on each other *kept the tout*,¶
And *sparred* a bit and *dodged* about.   *Ri, tol, lol, &c.*

Vith *mawleys*** raised, Tom bent his back,
As if to plant a heavy thwack:
Vile Jem, with neat left-handed *stopper*,
Straight threatened Tommy with a *topper*;
'Tis all my eye! no claret flows,
No *facers* sound—no smashing blows,
Five minutes past, yet not a *hit*,
How can it end, pals?—vait a bit.   *Ri, tol, lol, &c.*

Each cove vos *teazed* with double duty,
To please his backers, yet *play booty*;††
Ven, luckily for Jem, a *teller*
Vos planted right upon his *smeller*;
Down dropped he, stunned; ven time was called,
Seconds in vain the *seconds* bawled;
The *mill* is o'er, the crosser *crost*,
The loser's *von*, the vinner's *lost!*   *Ri, tol, lol, &c.*

The party assumed once more a lively air, and the glass was circulated so freely, that at last a final charge drained the ample bowl of its contents.

---

* Money.   † Man.   ‡ Stripped.   § Fellow.
A particular kind of pugilistic punishment.
¶ Kept each an eye upon the other.   ** Hands.   †† Deceive them.

"The best of friends must part," said Dick; "and I would willingly order another whiff of punch, but I think we have all had *enough to satisfy us*, as you milling coves have it, Zory! Your one eye has got a drop in it already, old fellow; and, to speak the truth, I must be getting into the saddle without more delay, for I have a long ride before me. And now, friend Jerry, before I start, suppose you tip us one of your merry staves; we haven't heard you pipe to-day, and never a cross cove of us all can throw off so prime a chant as yourself. A song! a song!"

"Ay, a song," reiterated King and the Magus.

"You do me too much honour, gemmen," said Jerry, modestly taking a pinch of snuff; "I am sure I shall be most happy. My chants are all of a sort. You must make all due allowances—hem!" And clearing his throat, he forthwith warbled

THE MODERN GREEK.

(*Not* translated from the Romaic.)

Come, gemmen, name, and make your game,
　See, round the ball is spinning.
Black, red, or blue, the colours view,
　Un, deux, cinque, 'tis beginning.
　　　　Then make your game,
　　　　The colour name,
　　While round the ball is spinning.

This sleight of hand my *flat* shall *land*,
　While *covered* by my *bonnet*,*
I *plant* my ball, and boldly call,
　Come make your game upon it!
　　　　Thus rat-a-tat!
　　　　I land my flat!
　　'Tis black—not red—is winning.

At gay *roulette* was never met
　A lance like mine for *bleeding!*
I'm ne'er *at fault*, at nothing halt,
　All other *legs* preceding.
　　　　To all awake,
　　　　I never shake
　　A *mag*† unless I nip it.

Blind-hookey sees how well I squeeze
　The *well-packed* cards in shuffling,
Ecarté, whist, I never missed,
　And nick the *broads*‡ while ruffling.
　　　　Mogul or loo,
　　　　The same I do,
　　I am down to trumps as trippet!

French hazard ta'en I *nick the main*,
　Was ne'er so prime a *caster,*

---

* Accomplice　　　　† A farthing.　　　　‡ Cards.

u 2

No *crabs* for me, I'm fly, d'ye see ;
  The bank shall change its master.
            Seven *quatre, trois,*
              The stakes are high !
          Ten *aaaes !* ten *aaaas* are mine, pals.

At *Rouge et Noir,* you *hell ite** choir
  I'll make no bones of stripping ;
One glorious *corp* for me shall *do,*
  While they may deal each *pip* in.
            Trente-un-après
              Ne'er clogs my way ;
          The game—the game's divine, pals.

At billiards set I make my bet,
  I'll *score* and win the *rub*, pals ;
I miss my cue, my *hazard*, too,
  But yet my foe I'll drub, pals.
            That *cannon-twist,*
              I ne'er had missed,
          Unless to suit my views, pals.

To make all right, the match look *tight,*
  This trick you know is done, pals ;
But now be gay, I'll *show* my play—
  Hurrah ! the game is won, pals.
            No hand so fine,
              No wrist like mine,
          No odds I e'er refuse, pals.

Then choose your game ; whate'er you name.
  To me alike all offers ;
Chick-hazard, whist, whate'er you list,
  Replenish quick your coffers.
            Thus, rat-a-tat !
              I *land* my *flat !*
          To every purse I *speak*, pals.

Cramped boxes 'ware, all's right and fair,
  Barred balls I bar when goaded ;
The deuce an ace is out of place !
  The deuce a die is *loaded !*
            Then make your game,
              Your colour name ;
          Success attend the *Greek*, pals.

"Bravo, Jerry ; bravissimo !" chorused the party.

"And now, pals, farewell !—a long farewell !" said Dick, in a tone of theatrical valediction. "As I said before, the best friends must separate. We may soon meet again, or we now may part for ever. We cannot command our luck ; but we can make the best of the span allotted to us. You have your game to play. I have mine. May each of us meet with the success he deserves."

"Egad, I hope not," said King. "I'm afraid in that case the chances would be against us."

"Well, then, the success we anticipate, if you prefer it,"

* Qy. *élite.*—PRINTERS' DEVIL.

rejoined Dick. "I have only to observe one thing more, namely, that I must insist upon standing Sam upon the present occasion. Not a word. I won't hear a syllable. Landlord, I say—what ho! continued Dick, stepping out of the arbour. "Here, my old Admiral of the White, what's the reckoning?—what's to pay, I say?"

"Let ye know directly, sir," replied mine host of the Falstaff.

"Order my horse—the black mare," added Dick.

"And mine," said King, "the sorrel colt. I'll ride with you a mile or two on the road, Dick; perhaps we may stumble upon something."

"Very likely."

"We meet at twelve, at D'Osyndar's, Jerry," said King, "if nothing happens."

"Agreed," responded Juniper."

"What say you to a rubber at bowls, in the mean time?" said the Magus, taking his everlasting pipe from his lips.

Jerry nodded acquiescence. And while they went in search of the implements of the game, Turpin and King sauntered gently on the green.

It was a delicious evening. The sun was slowly declining, and glowed like a ball of fire amid the thick foliage of a neighbouring elm. Whether, like the robber Moor, Tom King was touched by this glorious sunset, we pretend not to determine. Certain it was that a shade of inexpressible melancholy passed across his handsome countenance as he gazed in the direction of Harrow-on-the-Hill, which, lying to the west of the green upon which they walked, stood out with its pointed spire and lofty college against the ruddy sky. He spoke not. But Dick noticed the passing emotion.

"What ails you, Tom?" said he, with much kindness of manner—"are you not well, lad?"

"Yes, I am well enough," said King; "I know not what came over me, but looking at Harrow, I thought of my school-days, and what I was *then*, and that bright prospect reminded me of my boyish hopes."

"Tut, tut," said Dick, "this is idle; you are a man now."

"I know I am," replied Tom, "but I *have* been a boy. Had I any faith in presentiments, I should say this is the last sunset I shall ever see."

"Here comes our host," said Dick, smiling. "I've no presentiment that this is the last bill I shall ever pay."

The bill was brought and settled. As Turpin paid it, the man's conduct was singular, and awakened his suspicions.

"Are our horses ready?" asked Dick, quickly.

"They are, sir," said the landlord.

"Let us be gone," whispered Dick to King; "I don't like this fellow's manner. I thought I heard a carriage draw up at the inn door just now—there may be danger. Be fly!" added he to Jerry and the Magus. "Now, sir," said he to the landlord, "lead the way. Keep on the alert, Tom."

Dick's hint was not lost upon the two bowlers. They watched their comrades; and listened intently for any manifestation of alarm.

III.

A SURPRISE.

Was this well done, Jenny?   Captain Macheath.

WHILE Turpin and King are walking across the bowling-green, we will see what has taken place outside the inn. Tom's presentiments of danger were not, it appeared, without foundation. Scarcely had the ostler brought forth our two highwaymen's steeds, when a post-chaise, escorted by two or three horsemen, drove furiously up to the door. The sole occupant of the carriage was a lady, whose slight and pretty figure was all that could be distinguished, her face being closely veiled. The landlord, who was busied in casting up Turpin's account, rushed forth at the summons. A word or two passed between him and the horsemen, upon which the former's countenance fell. He posted in the direction of the garden; and the horsemen instantly dismounted.

"We have him now, sure enough," said one of them, a very small man, who looked, in his boots, like Buckle equipped for the Oaks.

"By the powers! I begin to think so," replied the other horseman. "But don't spoil all, Mr. Coates, by being too precipitate."

"Never fear that, Mr. Tyrconnel," said Coates, for it was the gallant attorney: "he's sure to come for his mare. That's a *trap* certain to catch him, eh, Mr. Paterson? With the chief constable of Westminster to back us, the devil's in it if we are not a match for him."

"And for Tom King, too," replied the chief constable; "since his blowen's peached, the game's up with him, too

We've long had an eye upon him, and now we'll have a finger. He's one of your dashing trouts to whom we always give a long line, but we'll *land* him this time, anyhow. If you'll look after Dick Turpin, gemmen, I'll make sure of Tom."

"I'd rather you would help *us*, Mr. Paterson," said Coates; "never mind Tom King; another time will do for him."

"No such thing," said Paterson; "one *weighs* just as much for that matter as t'other. I'll take Tom to myself, and surely you two, with the landlord and ostler, can manage Turpin amongst you."

"I don't know that," said Coates, doubtfully; "he's a devil of a fellow to deal with."

"Take him quietly," said Paterson. "Draw the chaise out of the way, lad. Take our tits to one side, and place their nags near the door, ostler. Shall you be able to see him, ma'am, where you are?" asked the chief constable, walking to the carriage, and touching his hat to the lady within. Having received a satisfactory nod from the bonnet and veil, he returned to his companions. "And now, gemmen," added he, "let's step aside a little. Don't use your fire-arms too soon."

As if conscious of what was passing around her, and of the danger that awaited her master, Black Bess exhibited so much impatience, and plunged so violently, that it was with difficulty the ostler could hold her. "The devil's in the mare," said he; "what's the matter with her? She was quiet enough a few minutes since. Soho! lass, stand."

Turpin and King, meanwhile, walked quickly through the house, preceded by the host, who conducted them, not without some inward trepidation, towards the door. Arrived there, each man rushed swiftly to his horse. Dick was in the saddle in an instant, and stamping her foot upon the ostler's leg, Black Bess compelled the man, yelling with pain, to quit his hold of the bridle. Tom King was not equally fortunate. Before he could mount his horse, a loud shout was raised, which startled the animal, and caused him to swerve, so that Tom lost his footing in the stirrup, and fell to the ground. He was instantly seized by Paterson, and a struggle commenced, King endeavouring, but in vain, to draw a pistol.

"Flip him,* Dick; fire, or I'm taken," cried King. "Fire!

* Shoot him.

damn you, why don't you fire?" shouted he, in desperation, still struggling vehemently with Paterson, who was a strong man, and more than a match for a light weight like King.

"I can't," cried Dick; "I shall hit you if I fire."

"Take your chance," shouted King. "Is *this* your friendship?"

Thus urged, Turpin fired. The ball ripped up the sleeve of Paterson's coat, but did not wound him.

"Again!" cried King. "Shoot him, I say. Don't you hear me? Fire again!"

Pressed as he was by foes on every side, himself their mark, for both Coates and Tyrconnel had fired upon him, and were now mounting their steeds to give chase, it was impossible that Turpin could take sure aim; added to which, in the struggle, Paterson and King were each moment changing their relative positions. He, however, would no longer hesitate, but again, at his friend's request, fired. The ball lodged itself in King's breast. He fell at once. At this instant a shriek was heard from the chaise: the window was thrown open, and her thick veil being drawn aside, the features of a very pretty female, now impressed with terror and contrition, were suddenly exhibited.

King fixed his glazing eyes upon her.

"Susan!" sighed he, "is it you that I behold?"

"Yes, yes, 'tis she, sure enough," said Paterson. "You see, ma'am, what you and suchlike have brought him to. However, you'll lose your reward; he's going fast enough."

"Reward!" gasped King; "reward! Did she betray me?"

"Ay, ay, sir," said Paterson, "she blowed the gaff, if it's any consolation to you to know it."

"Consolation!" repeated the dying man; "perfidious!—oh!—the prophecy—my best friend—Turpin—I die by his hand."

And vainly striving to raise himself, he fell backwards and expired. Alas, poor Tom!

"Mr. Paterson! Mr. Paterson!" cried Coates; "leave the landlord to look after the body of that dying ruffian, and mount with us in pursuit of the living rascal. Come, sir; quick! mount! despatch! You see he is yonder; he seems to hesitate; we shall have him now."

"Well, gemmen, I'm ready," said Paterson; "but how the devil came you to let him escape?"

"Saint Patrick only knows!" said Titus; "he's as slippery

as an eel; and, like a cat, turn him which way you will, he is always sure to alight upon his legs. I wouldn't wonder but we lose him now, after all, though he has such a small start. That mare flies like the wind."

"He shall have a tight run for it, at all events," said Paterson, putting his spurs into his horse. "I've got a good nag under me, and you are neither of you badly mounted. He's only three hundred yards before us, and the devil's in it if we can't run him down. It's a three hundred pound job, Mr. Coates, and well worth a race."

"You shall have another hundred from me, sir, if you take him," said Coates, urging his steed forward.

"Thank you, sir, thank you. Follow my directions, and we'll make sure of him," said the constable. "Gently, gently, not so fast up the hill; you see he's breathing his horse. All in good time, Mr. Coates; all in good time, sir."

And maintaining an equal distance, both parties cantered leisurely up the ascent now called Windmill Hill. We shall now return to Turpin.

Aghast at the deed he had accidentally committed, Dick remained for a few moments irresolute; he perceived that King was mortally wounded, and that all attempts at rescue would be fruitless; he perceived, likewise, that Jerry and the Magus had effected their escape from the bowling-green, as he could detect their figures stealing along the hedge-side. He hesitated no longer. Turning his horse, he galloped slowly off, little heeding the pursuit with which he was threatened.

"Every bullet has its billet," said Dick; "but little did I think that I really should turn poor Tom's executioner. To the devil with this rascally snapper," cried he, throwing the pistol over the hedge. "I could never have used it again. 'Tis strange, too, that he should have foretold his own fate—devilish strange! And then that he should have been betrayed by the very blowen he trusted! that's a lesson, if I wanted any. But trust a woman! not I, the length of my little finger."

IV.

THE HUE AND CRY.

Six gentlemen upon the road
  Thus seeing Gilpin fly,
With postboy scampering in the rear,
  They raised the hue and cry :

Stop thief! stop thief! a highwayman!
  Not one of them was mute ;
And all and each that pass'd that way
  Did join in the pursuit.
               John Gilpin.

ARRIVED at the brow of the hill, whence such a beauiful view of the country surrounding the metropolis is obtained,* Turpin turned for an instant to reconnoitre his pursuers. Coates and Titus he utterly disregarded ; but Paterson was a more formidable foe, and he well knew that he had to deal with a man of experience and resolution. It was then, for the first time, that the thoughts of executing his extraordinary ride to York first flashed across him ; his bosom throbbed high with rapture, and he involuntarily exclaimed aloud, as he raised himself in the saddle, " By God! I will do it!"

He took one last look at the great Babel that lay buried in a world of trees beneath him ; and as his quick eye ranged over the magnificent prospect, lit up by that gorgeous sunset, he could not help thinking of Tom King's last words. " Poor fellow!" thought Dick, " he said truly. He will never see another sunset." Aroused by the approaching clatter of his pursuers, Dick struck into a lane which lies on the right of the road, now called Shoot-up-hill Lane, and set off at a good pace in the direction of Hampstead.

" Now," cried Paterson, " put your tits to it, my boys. We must not lose sight of him for a second in these lanes."

Accordingly, as Turpin was by no means desirous of inconveniencing his mare at this early stage of the business, and as the ground was still upon an ascent, the parties preserved their relative distances.

At length, after various twistings and turnings in that deep and devious lane ; after scaring one or two farmers, and riding over a brood or two of ducks ; dipping into the verdant valley of West End, and ascending another hill, Turpin burst upon the gorsy, sandy, and beautiful heath of

---

* Since the earlier editions of this Romance were published, we regret to state (for to us, at least, it is matter of regret, though probably not to the travellers along the Edgware-road) that this gentle ascent has been cut through, and the fair prospect from its brow utterly destroyed.

Hampstead. Shaping his course to the left, Dick then made for the lower part of the heath, and skirted a part that leads towards North End, passing the furze-crowned summit which is now crested by a clump of lofty pines.

It was here that the chase first assumed a character of interest. Being open ground, the pursued and pursuers were in full view of each other; and as Dick rode swiftly across the heath, with the shouting trio hard at his heels, the scene had a very animated appearance. He crossed the hill—the Hendon-road — passed Crackskull Common—and dashed along the cross road to Highgate.

Hitherto no advantage had been gained by the pursuers; they had not lost ground, but still they had not gained an inch, and much spurring was required to maintain their position. As they approached Highgate, Dick slackened his pace; and the other party redoubled their efforts. To avoid the town, Dick struck into a narrow path at the right, and rode easily down the hill.

His pursuers were now within a hundred yards, and shouted to him to stand. Pointing to a gate which seemed to bar their further progress, Dick unhesitatingly charged it, clearing it in beautiful style. Not so with Coates's party; and the time they lost in unfastening the gate, which none of them chose to leap, enabled Dick to put additional space betwixt them. It did not, however, appear to be his intention altogether to outstrip his pursuers; the chase seemed to give him excitement, which he was willing to prolong, as much as was consistent with his safety. Scudding rapidly past Highgate, like a swift-sailing schooner, with three lumbering Indiamen in her wake, Dick now took the lead along a narrow lane that threads the fields in the direction of Hornsey. The shouts of his followers had brought others to join them, and as he neared Crouch End, traversing the lane which takes its name from Du-Val, and in which a house, frequented by that gayest of robbers, stands, or stood, "A highwayman! a highwayman!" rang in his ears, in a discordant chorus of many voices.

The whole neighbourhood was alarmed by the cries, and by the tramp of horses; the men of Hornsey rushed into the road to seize the fugitive; and women held up their babes to catch a glimpse of the flying cavalcade, which seemed to gain number and animation as it advanced. Suddenly three horsemen appear in the road; they hear the uproar and the din. "A highwayman! a highwayman!" cry the voices: "stop

him, stop him!" But it is no such easy matter. With a pistol
in each hand, and his bridle in his teeth, Turpin passed
boldly on. His fierce looks—his furious steed—the impetus
with which he pressed forward, bore down all before him.
The horsemen gave way, and only served to swell the list of
his pursuers.

"We have him now! we have him now!" cried Paterson,
exultingly. "Shout for your lives. The turnpike-man will
hear us. Shout again—again! The fellow has heard it. The
gate is shut. We have him. Ha! ha!"

The old Hornsey toll-bar was a high gate, with *chevaux-de-
frize* in the upper rail. It may be so still. The gate was
swung into its lock, and like a tiger in his lair, the prompt
custodian of the turnpike trusts, ensconced within his doorway, held himself in readiness to spring upon the runaway.
But Dick kept steadily on. He coolly calculated the height
of the gate; he looked to the right and to the left; nothing
better offered; he spoke a few words of encouragement to
Bess; gently patted her neck; then struck spurs into her
sides, and cleared the spikes by an inch. Out rushed the
amazed turnpike-man, thus unmercifully bilked, and was
nearly trampled to death under the feet of Paterson's horse.

"Open the gate, fellow, and be expeditious," shouted the
chief constable.

"Not I," said the man, sturdily, "unless I get my dues.
I've been done once already. But strike me stupid if I'm
done a second time."

"Don't you perceive that's a highwayman? Don't you
know that I'm chief constable of Westminster?" said Paterson, showing his staff. "How dare you oppose me in the
discharge of my duty?"

"That may be, or it may not be," said the man, doggedly.
"But you don't pass, unless I gets the blunt, and that's the
long and short on it."

Amidst a storm of oaths Coates flung down a crown piece,
and the gate was thrown open.

Turpin took advantage of this delay to breathe his mare;
and, striking into a by-lane at Duckett's Green, cantered
easily along in the direction of Tottenham. Little repose
was allowed him. Yelling like a pack of hounds in full cry,
his pursuers were again at his heels. He had now to run the
gauntlet of the long straggling town of Tottenham, and
various were the devices of the populace to entrap him. The
whole place was up in arms, shouting, screaming, running,

dancing, and hurling every possible description of missile at
the horse and her rider. Dick merrily responded to their
clamour as he flew past, and laughed at the brickbats that
were showered thick as hail, and quite as harmlessly, around
him.

A few more miles' hard riding tired the volunteers, and
before the chase reached Edmonton most of them were "*nowhere.*" Here fresh relays were gathered, and a strong field
was again mustered. John Gilpin himself could not have
excited more astonishment amongst the good folks of Edmonton, than did our highwayman as he galloped through
their town. Unlike the men of Tottenham, the mob received
him with acclamations, thinking, no doubt, that, like "the
citizen of famous London Town," he rode for a wager. Presently, however, borne on the wings of the blast, came the
cries of "Turpin! Dick Turpin!" and the hurrahs were
changed to hootings; but such was the rate at which our
highwayman rode, that no serious opposition could be offered
to him.

A man in a donkey-cart, unable to get out of the way,
drew himself up in the middle of the road. Turpin treated
him as he had done the *dub* at the *knapping jigger*, and
cleared the driver and his little wain with ease. This was a
capital stroke, and well adapted to please the multitude, who
are ever taken with a brilliant action. "Hark away, Dick!"
resounded on all hands; while hisses were as liberally bestowed upon his pursuers.

V.

THE SHORT PIPE.

The Peons are capital horsemen, and several times we saw them, at a
gallop, throw the rein on the horse's neck, take from one pocket a bag of
loose tobacco, and, with a piece of paper, or a leaf of Indian corn, make a
cigar, and then take out a flint and steel and light it.

HEAD's *Rough Notes.*

AWAY they fly past scattered cottages, swiftly and skim-
mingly, like eagles on the wing, along the Enfield highway.
All were well mounted, and the horses, now thoroughly
warmed, had got into their paces, and did their work beautifully. None of Coates's party lost ground; but they maintained it at the expense of their steeds, which were stream-

ing like water-carts, while Black Bess had scarcely turned a hair.

Turpin, the reader already knows, was a crack rider; he was *the* crack rider of England of his time, and, perhaps, of any time. The craft and mystery of jockeyship was not then so well understood in the eighteenth as it is in the nineteenth century; men treated their horses differently; and few rode then as well as many ride now, when every youngster takes to the field as naturally as if he had been bred a Guacho. Dick Turpin was a glorious exception to the rule, and anticipated a later age. He rode wonderfully lightly, yet sat his saddle to perfection; distributing the weight so exquisitely, that his horse scarcely felt his pressure; he yielded to every movement made by the animal, and became, as it were, part and parcel of itself; he took care Bess should be neither strained nor wrung. Freely, and as lightly as a feather, was she borne along; beautiful was it to see her action; to watch her style and temper of covering the ground; and many a first-rate Meltonian might have got a wrinkle from Turpin's seat and conduct.

We have before stated that it was not Dick's object to *ride away* from his pursuers; he could have done that at any moment. He liked the fun of the chase, and would have been sorry to put a period to his own excitement. Confident in his mare, he just kept her at such speed as should put his pursuers completely *to it*, without in the slightest degree inconveniencing himself. Some judgment of the speed at which they went may be formed, when we state that little better than an hour had elapsed, and nearly twenty miles had been ridden over. "Not bad travelling that," methinks we hear the reader exclaim.

"By the mother that bore me," said Titus, as they went along in this slapping style—Titus, by the bye, rode a big, Roman-nosed, powerful horse, well adapted to his weight, but which required a plentiful exercise both of leg and arm to call forth all his action, and keep his rider alongside his companions—"by the mother that bore me," said he, almost thumping the wind out of his flea-bitten Bucephalus with his calves, after the Irish fashion, "if the fellow isn't lighting his pipe! I saw the sparks fly on each side of him, and there he goes like a smoky chimney on a frosty morning! See, he turns his impudent phiz, with the pipe in his mouth! Are we to stand that, Mr. Coates?"

"Wait awhile, sir; wait awhile," said Coates: "we'll smoke *him* by-and-by."

"Pæans have been sung in honour of the Peons of the Pampas by the *Headlong* Sir Francis; but what the gallant major extols so loudly in the South American horsemen, viz., the lighting of a cigar when in mid career, was accomplished with equal ease by our English highwayman a hundred years ago, nor was it esteemed by him any extravagant feat either. Flint, steel, and tinder were bestowed within Dick's ample pouch; the short pipe was at hand; and within a few seconds there was a stream of vapour exhaling from his lips, like the smoke from a steam-boat shooting down the river, and tracking his still rapid course through the air.

"I'll let 'em see what I think of 'em!" said Dick, coolly, as he turned his head.

It was now grey twilight. The mists of coming night were weaving a thin curtain over the rich surrounding landscape. All the sounds and hum of that delicious hour were heard, broken only by the regular clatter of the horses' hoofs. Tired of shouting, the chasers now kept on their way in deep silence. Each man held his breath, and plunged his spurs rowel-deep into his horse; but the animals were already at the top of their speed, and incapable of greater exertion. Paterson, who was a hard rider, and perhaps a thought better mounted, kept the lead. The rest followed as they might.

Had it been undisturbed by the rush of the cavalcade, the scene would have been still and soothing. Overhead, a cloud of rooks were winging their garrulous flight to the ancestral avenue of an ancient mansion to the right; the bat was on the wing; the distant lowing of a herd of kine saluted the ear at intervals; the blithe whistle of the rustic herdsman, and the merry chime of waggon bells rang pleasantly from afar. But these cheerful sounds, which make the still twilight hour delightful, were lost in the tramp of the horsemen, now three abreast. The hind fled to the hedge for shelter; and the waggoner pricked up his ears, and fancied he heard the distant rumbling of an earthquake.

On rush the pack, whipping, spurring, tugging for very life. Again they gave voice, in hopes the waggoner might succeed in stopping the fugitive. But Dick was already by his side. "Harkee, my tulip," cried he, taking the pipe from his mouth as he passed, "tell my friends behind they will hear of me at York."

"What did he say?" asked Paterson, coming up the next moment.

"That you'll find him at York," replied the waggoner.

"At York!" echoed Coates, in amaze.

Turpin was now out of sight; and although our trio flogged with might and main, they could never catch a glimpse of him until, within a short distance of Ware, they beheld him at the door of a little public-house, standing with his bridle in his hand, coolly quaffing a tankard of ale. No sooner were they in sight than Dick vaulted into the saddle, and rode off.

"Devil seize you, sir! why didn't you stop him?" exclaimed Paterson, as he rode up. "My horse is dead lame. I cannot go any further. Do you know what a prize you have missed? Do you know who that was?"

"No, sir, I don't," said the publican. "But I know he gave his mare more ale than he took himself, and he has given me a guinea instead of a shilling. He's a regular good 'un."

"A good 'un!" said Paterson; "it was Turpin, the notorious highwayman. We are in pursuit of him. Have you any horses? Our cattle are all blown."

"You'll find the post-house in the town, gentlemen. I'm sorry I can't accommodate you. But I keeps no stabling. I wish you a very good evening, sir." Saying which the publican retreated to his domicile.

"That's a flash crib, I'll be bound," said Paterson. I'll chalk you down, my friend, you may rely upon it. Thus far we're done, Mr. Coates. But curse me if I give in. I'll follow him to the world's end first."

"Right, sir; right," said the attorney. "A very proper spirit, Mr. Constable. You would be guilty of neglecting your duty were you to act otherwise. You must recollect my father, Mr. Paterson; Christopher, or Kit Coates; a name as well known at the Old Bailey as Jonathan Wild's. You recollect him—eh?"

"Perfectly well, sir," replied the chief constable.

"The greatest thief-taker, though I say it," continued Coates, "on record. I inherit all his zeal—all his ardour. Come along, sir. We shall have a fine moon in an hour—bright as day. To the post-house! to the post-house!"

Accordingly, to the post-house they went; and, with as little delay as circumstances admitted, fresh hacks being procured, accompanied by a postilion, the party again pursued their onward course, encouraged to believe they were still in the right scent.

Night had now spread her mantle over the earth; still it was not wholly dark. A few stars were twinkling in the deep, cloudless heavens, and a pearly radiance in the eastern horizon heralded the rising of the orb of night. A gentle breeze was stirring; the dews of evening had already fallen; and the air felt bland and dry. It was just the night one would have chosen for a ride, if one ever rode by choice at such an hour; and to Turpin, whose chief excursions were conducted by night, it appeared little less than heavenly.

Full of ardour and excitement, determined to execute what he had mentally undertaken, Turpin held on his solitary course. Everything was favourable to his project; the roads were in admirable condition, his mare was in like order; she was inured to hard work, had rested sufficiently in town to recover from the fatigue of her recent journey, and had never been in more perfect training. " She has now got her wind in her," said Dick; "I'll see what she can do—hark away, lass—hark away! I wish they could see her now," added he, as he felt her almost fly away with him.

Encouraged by her master's voice and hand, Black Bess started forward at a pace which few horses could have equalled, and scarcely any have sustained so long. Even Dick, accustomed as he was to her magnificent action, felt electrified at the speed with which he was borne along. " Bravo! bravo!" shouted he; " hark away, Bess!"

The deep and solemn woods through which they were rushing, rang with his shouts, and the sharp rattle of Bess's hoofs; and thus he held his way, while, in the words of the ballad :

> Fled past, on right and left, how fast.
> Each forest, grove, and bower;
> On right and left, fled past, how fast,
> Each city, town, and tower.

VI.

BLACK BESS.

Dauphin. I will not change my horse with any that treads but on four pasterns. *Ca, ha!* He bounds from the earth as if his entrails were hairs; *le cheval volant*, the Pegasus *qui a les narines de feu!* When I bestride him I soar. I am a hawk; the earth sings when he touches it; the basest horn of his hoof is more musical than the pipe of Hermes.
SHAKSPEARE.— *Henry V., Act III.*

BLACK BESS being undoubtedly the heroine of the Fourth Book of this Romance, we may, perhaps, be pardoned for here expatiating a little in this place upon her birth, parentage,

X

breeding, appearance, and attractions.   And first as to her
pedigree; for in the horse, unlike the human species, nature
has strongly impressed the noble or ignoble caste.   He is the
real aristocrat, and the pure blood that flows in the veins of
the gallant steed will infallibly be transmitted, if his mate be
suitable, throughout all his line. Bess was no *cock-tail*. She
was thorough-bred; she boasted blood in every bright and
branching vein :

> If blood can give nobility
>   A noble steed was she ;
> Her sire was blood, and blood her dam,
>   And all her pedigree.

As to her pedigree.   Her sire was a desert Arab, renowned
in his day, and brought to this country by a wealthy traveller; her dam was an English racer, coal-black as her child.
Bess united all the fire and gentleness, the strength and
hardihood, the abstinence and endurance of fatigue of the
one, with the spirit and extraordinary fleetness of the other.
How Turpin became possessed of her is of little consequence. We never heard that he paid a heavy price for her;
though we doubt if any sum would have induced him to part
with her.   In colour, she was perfectly black, with a skin
smooth on the surface as polished jet ; not a single white hair
could be detected in her satin coat.   In make, she was magnificent.   Every point was perfect, beautiful, compact; mo-
delled, in little, for strength and speed.   Arched was her
neck, as that of the swan ; clean and fine were her lower
limbs, as those of the gazelle ; round and sound as a drum
was her carcase, and as broad as a cloth-yard shaft her width
of chest.   Hers were the " *pulchræ clunes, breve caput, ardua-
que cervix,*" of the Roman bard.   There was no redundancy
of flesh, 'tis true ; her flanks might, to please some tastes,
have been rounder, and her shoulder fuller; but look at the
nerve and sinew, palpable through the veined limbs ! She
was built more for strength than beauty, and yet she *was*
beautiful.   Look at that elegant little head ; those thin
tapering ears, closely placed together ; that broad snorting
nostril, which seems to snuff the gale with disdain ; that eye,
glowing and large as the diamond of Giamschid ! Is she not
beautiful ? Behold her paces ! how gracefully she moves !
She is off !—no eagle on the wing could skim the air more
swiftly. Is she not superb ? As to her temper, the lamb is
not more gentle. A child might guide her.

But hark back to Turpin.   We left him rattling along

in superb style, and in the highest possible glee. He could not, in fact, be otherwise than exhilarated; nothing being so wildly intoxicating as a mad gallop. We seem to start out of ourselves—to be endued, for the time, with new energies. Our thoughts take wings rapid as our steed. We feel as if his fleetness and boundless impulses were for the moment our own. We laugh; we exult; we shout for very joy. We cry out with Mephistopheles, but in anything but a sardonic mood. " What I enjoy with spirit, is it the less my own on that account? If I can pay for six horses, are not their powers mine? I drive along, and am a proper man, as if I had four-and-twenty legs!" These were Turpin's sentiments precisely. Give him four legs and a wide plain, and he needed no Mephistopheles to bid him ride to perdition as fast as his nag could carry him. Away, away!—the road is level, the path is clear. Press on, thou gallant steed, no obstacle is in thy way!—and, lo! the moon breaks forth! Her silvery light is thrown over the woody landscape. Dark shadows are cast athwart the road, and the flying figures of thy rider and thyself are traced, like giant phantoms in the dust!

Away, away! our breath is gone, in keeping up with this tremendous run. Yet Dick Turpin has not lost his wind, for we hear his cheering cry—hark! he sings. The reader will bear in mind that Oliver means the moon; to " whiddle" is to blab.

OLIVER WHIDDLES!

Oliver Whiddles—the tattler old !
Telling what best had been left untold.
Oliver ne'er was a friend of mine ;
All glims I hate that so brightly shine.
Give me a night black as hell, and then
See what I'll show to you, my merry men.

Oliver Whiddles !—who cares—who cares,
If down upon us he peers and stares?
Mind him who will, with his great white face,
Boldly *I'll* ride by his glim to the chase ;
Give him a Rowland, and loudly as ever
Shout, as I show myself, " Stand and deliver !"

" Egad," soliloquized Dick, as he concluded his song, look-ing up at the moon, " Old Noll's no bad fellow either. I would't be without his white face to-night for a trifle. He's as good as a lamp to guide one, and let Bess only hold on as she goes now, and I'll do it with ease. Softly, wench, softly ; dost not see it's a hill we're rising. The devil's in the mare, she cares for nothing." And as they ascended the hill, Dick's voice once more awoke the echoes of the night.

WILL DAVIES AND DICK TURPIN.

Hodiè mihi, cràs tibi. — SAINT AUGUSTIN.

One night when mounted on my mare,
To Bagshot Heath I did repair,
And saw Will Davis hanging there,
Upon the gibbet bleak and bare,
   With a rustified, justified, mustified air.

Within his chains bold Will looked blue,
Gone were his sword and snappers too,
Which served their master well and true ;
Says I, " Will Davies, how are you?
   With your rustified, justified, mustified air !"

Says he, " Dick Turpin, here I be,
Upon the gibbet, as you see ;
I take the matter easily ;
You'll have your turn as well as me,
   With your whistle-me, pistol-me, cut-my-throat-air !"

Says I, " That's very true, my lad ;
Meantime, with pistol and with prad,
I'm quite contented as I am,
And heed the gibbet not a d—n !
   With its rustified, justified, mustified air !"

"**Poor Will Davies !**" sighed Dick ; "Bagshot ought never
to forget him."*

For never more shall Bagshot see
A highwayman of such degree,
Appearance, and gentility,
As Will, who hangs upon the tree.
   With his rustified, justified, mustified air !"

"Well," mused Turpin, "I suppose one day it will be with
me like the rest of 'em, and that I shall dance a long lavolta
to the music of the four whistling winds, as my betters have
done before me ; but I trust, whenever the chanter-culls and
last-speech scribblers get hold of me, they'll at least put no
cursed nonsense into my mouth, but make me speak, as I
have ever felt, like a man who never either feared death, or
turned his back upon his friend. In the mean time I'll give

* This, we regret to say, is not the case. The memory of bold Will Davis,
the "*Golden Farmer*" (so named from the circumstance of his always paying his rent in gold), is fast declining upon his peculiar domain, Bagshot.
The inn, which once bore his name, still remains to point out to the traveller
the dangers his forefathers had to encounter in crossing this extensive heath.
Just beyond this house the common spreads out for miles on all sides in a
most gallop-inviting style ; and the passenger, as he gazes from the box of
some flying coach, as we have done, upon the gorse-covered waste, may, without much stretch of fancy, imagine he beholds Will Davies careering like the
wind over its wild and undulating expanse. We are sorry to add that the
"*Golden Farmer*" has altered its designation to the "*Jolly Farmer*." This
should be amended ; and when next we pass that way, we hope to see the
original sign restored. We cannot afford to lose our *golden* farmers.

them something to talk about. This ride of mine shall
ring in their ears long after I'm done for—put to bed with a
mattock, and tucked up with a spade.

> And when I am gone boys, each huntsman shall say,
> None rode like Dick Turpin so far in a day.

And thou, too, brave Bess! thy name shall be linked with
mine, and we'll go down to posterity together; and what,"
added he despondingly, "if it should be too much for thee?
what if—— but no matter. Better die now, while I am with
thee, than fall into the knacker's hands. Better die with all
thy honours upon thy head, than drag out thy old age at the
sand-cart. Hark forward, lass—hark forward!"

By what peculiar instinct is it that this noble animal, the
horse, will at once perceive the slightest change in his rider's
physical temperament, and allow himself so to be influenced
by it, that, according as his master's spirits fluctuate, will his
own energies rise and fall, wavering

> From walk to trot, from canter to full speed?

How is it, we ask of those more intimately acquainted with
the metaphysics of the Huoyhnymn than we pretend to be?
Do the saddle or the rein convey, like metallic tractors,
vibrations of the spirit betwixt the two? We know not; but
this much is certain, that no servant partakes so much of the
character of his master as the horse. The steed we are wont
to ride becomes a portion of ourselves. He thinks and feels
with us. As we are lively, he is sprightly; as we are de-
pressed, his courage droops. In proof of this, let the reader
see what horses some men make—*make* we say, because in
such hands their character is wholly altered. Partaking,
in a measure, of the courage and the firmness of the hand
that guides them, and of the resolution of the frame that
sways them—what their rider wills they do, or strive to do.
When that governing power is relaxed, their energies are relaxed likewise; and their fine sensibilities supply them with
an instant knowledge of the disposition and capacity of the
rider. A gift of the gods is the gallant steed, which, like any
other faculty we possess, to use or to abuse—to command or
to neglect—rests with ourselves; he is the best general test
of our own self-government.

Black Bess's action amply verified what we have just
asserted; for during Turpin's momentary despondency, her
pace was perceptibly diminished, and her force retarded; but

as he revived, she rallied instantly, and, seized apparently
with a kindred enthusiasm, snorted joyously, as she recovered
her speed. Now was it that the child of the desert showed
herself the undoubted offspring of the hardy loins from
whence she sprung. Full fifty miles had she sped, yet she
showed no symptom of distress. If possible, she appeared
fresher than when she started. She had breathed; her limbs
were suppler; her action was freer, easier, lighter. Her sire,
who, upon his trackless wilds, could have outstripped the
pestilent simoom; and with throat unslacked, and hunger un-
appeased, could thrice have seen the scorching sun go down,
had not greater powers of endurance. His vigour was her
heritage. Her dam, who upon the velvet sod was of almost
unapproachable swiftness, and who had often brought her
owner golden assurances of her worth, could scarce have kept
pace with her, and would have sunk under a third of her
fatigue. But Bess was a paragon. We ne'er shall look upon
her like again, unless we can prevail upon some Bedouin
chief to present us with a brood mare, and then the racing
world shall see what a breed we will introduce into this
country. Eclipse, Childers, or Hambletonian, shall be nothing to our colts, and even the railroad slow travelling compared with the speed of our new nags!

But to return to Bess, or rather to go along with her, for
there is no halting now; we are going at the rate of twenty
knots an hour—sailing before the wind; and the reader must
either keep pace with us, or drop astern. Bess is now in her
speed, and Dick happy. Happy! he is enraptured—maddened—furious—intoxicated as with wine. Pshaw! wine
could never throw him into such a burning delirium. Its
choicest juices have no inspiration like this. Its fumes are
slow and heady. This is ethereal, transporting. His blood
spins through his veins; winds round his heart; mounts to
his brain. Away! away! He is wild with joy. Hall, cot,
tree, tower, glade, mead, waste, or woodland, are seen, passed,
left behind, and vanish as in a dream. Motion is scarcely
perceptible—it is impetus! volition! The horse and her
rider are driven forward, as it were, by self-accelerated
speed. A hamlet is visible in the moonlight. It is scarcely
discovered ere the flints sparkle beneath the mare's hoofs.
A moment's clatter upon the stones, and it is left behind.
Again, it is the silent, smiling country. Now they are buried
in the darkness of woods; now sweeping along on the
wide plain; now clearing the unopened toll-bar, now tramp-

ling over the hollow-sound'ng bridge, their shadows momently reflected in the placid mirror of the stream ; now
scaling the hill-side a thought more slowly ; now plunging,
as the horses of Phœbus into the ocean, down its precipitous
sides.

The limits of two shires are already past. They are within
the confines of a third. They have entered the merry county
of Huntingdon ; they have surmounted the gentle hill that
slips into Godmanchester. They are by the banks of the
rapid Ouse. The bridge is past ; and as Turpin rode through
the deserted streets of Huntingdon, he heard the eleventh
hour given from the iron tongue of St. Mary's spire. In four
hours (it was about seven when he started), Dick had accomplished full sixty miles !

A few reeling topers in the streets saw the horseman flit
past, and one or two windows were thrown open ; but Peeping Tom of Coventry would have had small chance of beholding the unveiled beauties of Queen Godiva had she ridden at
the rate of Dick Turpin. He was gone, like a meteor, almost
as soon as he appeared.

Huntingdon is left behind, and he is once more surrounded
by dew-gemmed hedges and silent slumbering trees. Broad
meadows, or pasture land, with drowsy cattle, or low bleating
sheep, lie on either side. But what to Turpin, at that moment, is nature, animate or inanimate? He thinks only of
his mare—his future fame. None are by to see him ride ; no
stimulating plaudits ring in his ears ; no thousand hands are
clapping ; no thousand voices huzzaing ; no handkerchiefs
are waved ; no necks strained ; no bright eyes rain influence
upon him ; no eagle orbs watch his motions ; no bells are
rung ; no cup awaits his achievement ; no sweepstakes—no
plate. But his will be renown—everlasting renown ; his will
be fame which will not die with him—which will keep his
reputation, albeit a tarnished one, still in the mouths of men.
He wants all these adventitious excitements, but he has that
within which is a greater excitement than all these. He is
conscious that he is doing a deed to live by. If not riding
for *life*, he is riding for *immortality ;* and as the hero may
perchance feel (for even a highwayman may feel like a hero)
when he willingly throws away his existence in the hope
of earning a glorious name, Turpin cared not what might
befall himself, so he could proudly signalise himself as the
first of his land,

And witch the world with noble horsemanship !

What need had he of spectators? *The eye of posterity* was upon him; he felt the influence of that Argus glance which has made many a poor wight spur on his Pegasus with not half so good a chance of reaching the goal as Dick Turpin. Multitudes, yet unborn, he knew would hear and laud his deeds. He trembled with excitement, and Bess trembled under him. But the emotion was transient—on, on they fly! The torrent leaping from the crag—the bolt from the bow—the air-cleaving eagle—thoughts themselves are scarce more winged in their flight!

VII.

THE YORK STAGE.

YORK, FOUR DAYS!—*Stage Coach begins on Friday, the 18th of April, 1706.* All that are desirous to pass from London to York, or from York to London, or any other place on that road, let them repair to the Black Swan, in Holborn, in London, or the Black Swan, in Coney-street, in York. At both which places they may be received in a *Stage Coach*, every Monday, Wednesday, and Friday, which performs the whole journey in four days (if God permits!) and sets forth at five in the morning. And returns from York to Stamford in two days, and from Stamford, by Huntingdon in two days more. And the like stages in their return. Allowing each passenger fourteen pounds' weight, and all above, three-pence per pound. Performed by Benjamin Kingman, Henry Harrison, and Walter Baynes.—*Placard, preserved in the coffee-room of the Black Swan Inn at York.*

THE night had hitherto been balmy and beautiful, with a bright array of stars, and a golden harvest moon, which seemed to diffuse even warmth with its radiance; but now Turpin was approaching the region of fog and fen, and he began to feel the influence of that dank atmosphere. The intersecting dykes, yawners, gullies, or whatever they are called, began to send forth their steaming vapours, and chilled the soft and wholesome air, obscuring the void, and in some instances, as it were, choking up the road itself with vapour. But fog or fen was the same to Bess; her hoofs rattled merrily along the road, and she burst from a cloud, like Eöus at the break of dawn.

It chanced, as he issued from a fog of this kind, that Turpin burst upon the York stage coach. It was no uncommon thing for the coach to be stopped; and so furious was the career of our highwayman, that the man involuntarily drew up his horses. Turpin had also to draw in the rein, a task of no little difficulty, as charging a huge lumbering coach, with its full complement of passengers, was more than even Bess could accomplish. The moon shone brightly on Turpin and his mare. He was unmasked, and his features were distinctly visible. An exclamation was uttered by a gentleman on the box, who it appeared instantly recognised him.

"Pull up—draw your horses across the road!" cried the gentleman; "that's Dick Turpin, the highwayman. His capture would be worth three hundred pounds to you," added he, addressing the coachman, "and is of equal importance to me. Stand!" shouted he, presenting a cocked pistol.

This resolution of the gentleman was not apparently agreeable, either to the coachman or the majority of the passengers; the name of Turpin acting like magic upon them. One man jumped off behind, and was with difficulty afterwards recovered, having tumbled into a deep ditch at the road side. An old gentleman with a cotton nightcap, who had popped out his head to swear at the coachman, drew it suddenly back. A faint scream in a female key issued from within, and there was a considerable hubbub on the roof. Amongst other ominous sounds, the guard was heard to click his long horse-pistols. "Stop the York four-day stage!" said he, forcing his smoky voice through a world of throat-embracing shawl; "the fastest coach in the kingdom: vos ever sich atrocity heard of? I say, Joe, keep them ere leaders steady; we shall all be in the ditch. Don't you see where the hind wheels are? Who—whoop, I say."

The gentleman on the box now discharged his pistol, and the confusion within was redoubled. The white nightcap was popped out like a rabbit's head, and as quickly popped back on hearing the highwayman's voice. Owing to the plunging of the horses, the gentleman had missed his aim.

Prepared for such emergencies as the present, and seldom at any time taken aback, Dick received the fire without flinching. He then lashed the horses out of his course, and rode up, pistol in hand, to the gentleman who had fired

"Major Mowbray," said he, in a stern tone, "I know you. I meant not either to assault you or these gentlemen. Yet you have attempted my life, sir, a second time. But you are now in my power, and by hell! if you do not answer the questions I put to you, nothing earthly shall save you."

"If you ask aught I may not answer, fire!" said the major; "I will never ask life from such as you."

"Have you seen aught of Sir Luke Rookwood?" asked
Dick.

"The villain you mean is not yet secured," replied the
major, "but we have traces of him. 'Tis with the view of
procuring more efficient assistance that I ride to town."

"They have not met then since?" said Dick, carelessly.

"Met! whom do you mean?"

"Your sister and Sir Luke," said Dick.

"My sister meet him?" cried the major, angrily; "think
you he dare show himself at Rookwood?"

"Ho! ho!" laughed Dick; "she *is* at Rookwood, then?
A thousand thanks, major. Good night to you, gentlemen."

"Take that with you, and remember the guard," cried the
fellow, who, unable to take aim from where he sat, had crept
along the coach roof, and discharged thence one of his large
horse-pistols at what he took to be the highwayman's head,
but which, luckily for Dick, was his hat, which he had raised
to salute the passengers.

"Remember you," said Dick, coolly replacing his perforated
beaver on his brow; "you may rely upon it, my fine fellow,
I'll not forget you the next time we meet."

And off he went like the breath of the whirlwind.

VIII.

A ROADSIDE INN.

Moor. Take my horse, and dash a bottle of wine over him. 'Twas hot work.
                                                 SCHILLER.—*The Robbers.*

WE will now make inquiries after Mr. Coates and his party,
of whom both we and Dick Turpin have for some time lost
sight. With unabated ardour the vindictive man of law and
his myrmidons pressed forward. A tacit compact seemed to
have been entered into between the highwayman and his pursuers, that he was to fly while they were to follow. Like
bloodhounds, they kept eadily upon his trail; nor were
they so far behind as Dick imagined. At each post-house
they passed they obtained fresh horses, and, while these
were saddling, a postboy was despatched *en courier* to order
relays at the next station. In this manner they proceeded
after the first stoppage without interruption. Horses were
in waiting for them, as they, "bloody with spurring, fiery

hot with haste," and their jaded hacks arrived. Turpin had been heard or seen in all quarters. Turnpike-men, waggoners, carters, trampers, all had seen him. Besides, strange as it may sound, they placed some faith in his word. York they believed would be his destination.

At length the coach which Dick had encountered hove in sight. There was another stoppage and another hubbub. The old gentleman's nightcap was again manifested, and suffered a sudden occultation, as upon the former occasion. The postboy, who was in advance, had halted, and given up his horse to Major Mowbray, who exchanged his seat on the box for one on the saddle, deeming it more expedient after his interview with Turpin, to return to Rookwood, rather than to proceed to town. The postboy was placed behind Coates, as being the lightest weight; and, thus reinforced, the party pushed forward as rapidly as heretofore.

Eighty and odd miles had now been traversed—the boundary of another county, Northampton, passed; yet no rest nor respite had Dick Turpin or his unflinching mare enjoyed. But here he deemed it fitting to make a brief halt.

Bordering the beautiful domains of Burleigh House stood a little retired hostelrie of some antiquity, which bore the great Lord Treasurer's arms. With this house Dick was not altogether unacquainted. The lad who acted as ostler was known to him. It was now midnight, but a bright and beaming night. To the door of the stable then did he ride, and knocked in a peculiar manner. Reconnoitring Dick through a broken pane of glass in the lintel, and apparently satisfied with his scrutiny, the lad thrust forth a head of hair as full of straw as Mad Tom's is represented to be upon the stage. A chuckle of welcome followed his sleepy salutation. "Glad to see you, Captain Turpin," said he; "can I do anything for you?"

"Get me a couple of bottles of brandy and a beefsteak," said Dick.

"As to the brandy, you can have that in a jiffy; but the steak, Lord love ye, the old 'ooman won't stand it at this time; but there's a cold round, mayhap a slice of that might do; or a knuckle of ham?"

"D—n your knuckles, Ralph," cried Dick; "have you any raw meat in the house?"

"Raw meat?" echoed Ralph, in surprise. "Oh, yes, there's a rare rump of beef. You can have a cut off that, if you like."

"That's the thing I want," said Dick, ungirthing his mare. "Give me the scraper. There, I can get a wisp of straw from your head. Now run and get the brandy. Better bring three bottles. Uncork 'em, and let me have half a pail of water to mix with the spirit."

"A pail full of brandy and water to wash down a raw steak! My eyes!" exclaimed Ralph, opening wide his sleepy peepers; adding, as he went about the execution of his task, "I always thought them Rum-padders, as they call themselves, rum fellows, but now I'm sartin sure on it."

The most sedulous groom could not have bestowed more attention upon the horse of his heart than Dick Turpin now paid to his mare. He scraped, chafed, and dried her, sounded each muscle, traced each sinew, pulled her ears, examined the state of her feet, and, ascertaining that her "withers were unwrung," finally washed her from head to foot in the diluted spirit, not, however, before he had conveyed a thimbleful of the liquid to his own parched throat, and replenished what Falstaff calls a "pocket-pistol," which he had about him. While Ralph was engaged in rubbing her down after her bath, Dick occupied himself, not in dressing the raw steak in the manner the stable-boy had anticipated, but in rolling it round the bit of his bridle.

"She will go as long as there's breath in her body," said he, putting the flesh-covered iron within her mouth.

The saddle being once more replaced, after champing a moment or two at the bit, Bess began to snort and paw the earth, as if impatient of delay; and, acquainted as he was with her indomitable spirit and power, her condition was a surprise even to Dick himself. Her vigour seemed inexhaustible, her vivacity was not a whit diminished, but, as she was led into the open space, her step became as light and free as when she started on her ride, and her sense of sound as quick as ever. Suddenly she pricked her ears, and uttered a low neigh. A dull tramp was audible.

"Ha!" exclaimed Dick, springing into his saddle; "they come."

"Who come, captain?" asked Ralph.

"The road takes a turn here, don't it?" asked Dick— "sweeps round to the right by the plantations in the hollow?"

"Ay, ay, captain," answered Ralph; "it's plain you knows the ground."

"What lies beyond yon shed?"

"A stiff fence, captain—a reg'lar rasper. Beyond that a hill-side steep as a house; no oss as was ever shoed can go down it."

"Indeed!" laughed Dick.

A loud halloo from Major Mowbray, who seemed advancing upon the wings of the wind, told Dick that he was discovered. The major was a superb horseman, and took the lead of his party. Striking his spurs deeply into his horse, and giving him bridle enough, the major seemed to shoot forward like a shell through the air. The Burleigh Arms retired some hundred yards from the road, the space in front being occupied by a neat garden, with low clipped hedges. No tall timber intervened between Dick and his pursuers, so that the motions of both parties were visible to each other. Dick saw in an instant that if he now started he should come into collision with the major exactly at the angle of the road, and he was by no means desirous of hazarding such a rencontre. He looked wistfully back at the double fence.

"Come into the stable. Quick, captain, quick!" exclaimed Ralph.

"The stable?" echoed Dick, hesitating.

"Ay, the stable; it's your only chance. Don't you see he's turning the corner, and they are all coming. Quick, sir, quick!"

Dick, lowering his head, rode into the tenement, the door of which was most unceremoniously slapped in the major's face, and bolted on the other side.

"Villain!" cried Major Mowbray, thundering at the door, "come forth. You are now fairly trapped at last—caught like the woodcock, in your own springe. We have you. Open the door, I say, and save us the trouble of forcing it. You cannot escape us. We will burn the building down but we will have you."

"What do you want, measter?" cried Ralph, from th lintel, whence he reconnoitred the major, and kept the door fast. "You're clean mistaken. There be no one here."

"We'll soon see that," said Paterson, who had now arrived; and leaping from his horse, the chief constable took a short run, to give himself impetus, and with his foot burst open the door. This being accomplished, in dashed the major and Paterson, but the stable was vacant. A door was open at the back; they rushed to it. The sharply sloping sides of a hill slipped abruptly downwards, within a yard of the door. It was a perilous descent to the horseman, yet the print of a horse's heels was visible in the dislodged turf and scattered soil.

"Confusion!" cried the major, "he has escaped us."

"He is yonder," said Paterson, pointing out Turpin moving swifty through the steaming meadow. "See, he makes again for the road—he clears the fence. A regular throw he has given us, by the Lord!"

"Nobly done, by Heaven!" cried the major. "With all his faults, I honour the fellow's courage, and admire his prowess. He's already ridden to-night as I believe never man rode before. I would not have ventured to slide down that wall, for it's nothing else, with the enemy at my heels. What say you, gentlemen, have you had enough? Shall we let him go, or——"

"As far as chase goes, I don't care if we bring the matter to a conclusion," said Titus. "I don't think, as it is, that I shall have a *sate* to sit on this week to come. I've lost leather most confoundedly."

"What says Mr. Coates?" asked Paterson. "I look to him."

"Then mount, and off," cried Coates. "Public duty requires that we should take him.'

"And *private pique*," returned the major. "No matter! The end is the same. Justice shall be satisfied. To your steeds, my merry men all. Hark, and away."

Once more upon the move, Titus forgot his distress, and addressed himself to the attorney, by whose side he rode.

"What place is that we're coming to?" asked he, pointing to a cluster of moonlit spires belonging to a town they were rapidly approaching.

"Stamford," replied Coates.

"Stamford!" exclaimed Titus; "by the powers! then we've ridden a matter of ninety miles. Why, the great deeds of Redmond O'Hanlon were nothing to this! I'll remember it to my dying day, and with reason," added he, uneasily shifting his position on the saddle.

IX.

EXCITEMENT.

> How fled what moonshine faintly showed!
> How fled what darkness hid !
> How fled the earth beneath their feet.
> The heaven above their head.   *William and Ellen.*

DICK TURPIN, meanwhile, held bravely on his course. Bess was neither strained by her gliding passage down the slippery hill-side, nor shaken by *larking* the fence in the meadow. As Dick said, "It took a devilish deal to take it out of her." On regaining the high road she resumed her old pace, and once more they were distancing Time's swift chariot in its whirling passage o'er the earth. Stamford, and the tongue of Lincoln's fenny shire, upon which it is situated, are passed almost in a breath. Rutland is won and passed, and Lincolnshire once more entered. The road now verged within a bowshot of that sporting Athens (Corinth, perhaps, we should say), Melton Mowbray. Melton was then unknown to fame, but, as if inspired by that *furor venaticus* which now inspires all who come within twenty miles of this Charybdis of the chase, Bess here *let out* in a style with which it would have puzzled the best Leicestershire squire's best prad to have kept pace. The spirit she imbibed through the pores of her skin, and the juices of the meat she had champed, seemed to have communicated preternatural excitement to her. Her pace was absolutely terrific. Her eye-balls were dilated, and glowed like flaming carbuncles; while her widely-distended nostril seemed, in the cold moonshine, to snort forth smoke, as from a hidden fire. Fain would Turpin have controlled her; but, without bringing into play all his tremendous nerve, no check could be given her headlong course, and for once, and the only time in her submissive career, Bess resolved to have her own way—and she had it. Like a sensible fellow, Dick conceded the point. There was something even of conjugal philosophy in his self-communion upon the occasion. "E'en let her take her own way, and be hanged to her, for an obstinate, self-willed jade as she is," said he: "now her back is up there'll be no stopping her, I'm sure: she rattles away like a woman's tongue, and when that once begins, we all know what chance the curb has. Best to let her have it out, or rather to lend her a lift. 'Twill be over the sooner. Tantivy, lass! tantivy! I know which of us will tire first."

We have before said that the vehement excitement of continued swift riding produces a paroxysm in the sensorium amounting to delirium. Dick's blood was again on fire. He was first giddy, as after a deep draught of kindling spirit; this passed off, but the spirit was still in his veins—the *estro* was working in his brain. All his ardour, his eagerness, his fury, returned. He rode like one insane, and his courser partook of his frenzy. She bounded; she leaped; she tore up the ground beneath her; while Dick gave vent to his exultation in one wild prolonged halloo. More than half his race is run. He has triumphed over every difficulty. He will have no further occasion to halt. Bess carries her forage along with her. The course is straightforward—success seems certain—the goal already reached—the path of glory won. Another wild halloo, to which the echoing woods reply, and away!

Away! away! thou matchless steed! yet brace fast thy sinews—hold, hold thy breath, for, alas, the goal is not yet attained!

> But forward! forward, on they go,
>   High snorts the straining steed,
> Thick pants the rider's labouring breath,
>   As headlong on they speed!

X.

THE GIBBET.

> See there, see there, what yonder swings
>   And creaks 'mid whistling rain,
> Gibbet and steel—the accursed wheel—
>   A murderer in his chain.   *William and Ellen.*

As the eddying currents sweep over its plains in howling bleak December, the horse and her rider passed over what remained of Lincolnshire. Grantham is gone, and they are now more slowly looking up the ascent of Gonerby Hill, a path well known to Turpin; where often, in bygone nights, many a purse had changed its owner. With that feeling of independence and exhilaration which every one feels, we believe, on having climbed the hill-side, Turpin turned to gaze around. There was triumph in his eye. But the triumph was checked as his glance fell upon a gibbet near him to the right, on the round point of hill which is a landmark to the wide vale of Belvoir. Pressed as he was for time, Dick immediately struck out of the road, and approached the spot where it stood. Two scarecrow objects, covered with rags and rusty links of chains, depended from the tree. A night crow screaming around the carcasses added to the hideous effect of the scene. Nothing but the living highwayman and his skeleton brethren were visible upon the solitary spot. Around him was the lonesome waste of hill, o'erlooking the moonlit valley: beneath his feet, a patch of bare and lightning-blasted sod: above, the wan declining moon and skies, flaked with ghostly clouds: before him, the bleached bodies of the murderers, for such they were.

"Will this be my lot, I marvel?" said Dick, looking upwards, with an involuntary shudder.

"Ay, marry will it," rejoined a crouching figure, suddenly springing from beside a tuft of briers that skirted the blasted ground.

Dick started in his saddle, while Bess reared and plunged at the sight of this unexpected apparition.

"What ho! thou devil's dam, Barbara, is it thou?" exclaimed Dick, re-assured upon discovering it was the gipsy queen, and no spectre whom he beheld. "Stand still, Bess —stand, lass. What dost thou here, mother of darkness? Art gathering mandrakes for thy poisonous messes, or pilfering flesh from the dead? Meddle not with their bones, or I will drive thee hence. What dost thou here, I say, old dam of the gibbet?"

"I came to die here," replied Barbara, in a feeble tone; and, throwing back her hood, she displayed features well-nigh as ghastly as those of the skeletons above her.

"Indeed," replied Dick. "You've made choice of a pleasant spot, it must be owned. But you'll not die yet."

"Do you know whose bodies these are?" asked Barbara, pointing upwards.

"Two of your race," replied Dick; "right brethren of the blade."

"Two of my sons," returned Barbara; "my twin children. I am come to lay my bones beneath their bones: my sepulchre shall be their sepulchre; my body shall feed the fowls of the

Y

air as theirs have fed them. And if ghosts can walk, we'll scour this heath together. I tell you what, Dick Turpin," said the hag, drawing as near to the highwayman as Bess would permit her; "dead men walk and ride—ay, *ride!*— there's a comfort for you. I've seen these do it. I have seen them fling off their chains, and dance—ay, dance with me—with their mother. No revels like dead men's revels, Dick. I shall soon join 'em."

"You will not lay violent hands upon yourself, mother?" said Dick, with difficulty mastering his terror.

"No," replied Barbara, in an altered tone. "But I will let nature do her task. Would she could do it more quickly. Such a life as mine won't go out without a long struggle. What have I to live for now? All are gone—*she and her child!* But what is this to you? You have no child; and if you had, you could not feel like a father. No matter. I rave. Listen to me. I have crawled hither to die. 'Tis five days since I beheld you, and during that time food has not passed these lips, nor aught of moisture, save Heaven's dew, cooled this parched throat, nor shall they to the last. That time cannot be far off; and now can you not guess *how* I mean to die? Begone, and leave me, your presence troubles me. I would breathe my last breath alone, with none to witness the parting pang."

"I will not trouble you longer, mother," said Dick, turning his mare; "nor will I ask your blessing."

"My blessing!" scornfully ejaculated Barbara. "You shall have it if you will, but you will find it a curse. Stay! a thought strikes me. Whither are you going?"

"To seek Sir Luke Rookwood," replied Dick; "know you aught of him?"

"Sir Luke Rookwood! You seek him, and would find him?" screamed Barbara.

"I would," said Dick.

"And you *will* find him," said Barbara; "and that ere long. I shall ne'er again behold him. Would I could. I have a message for him—one of life and death. Will you convey it to him?"

"I will," said the highwayman.

"Swear by those bones to do so," cried Barbara, pointing with her skinny fingers to the gibbet; "that you will do my bidding."

"I swear," cried Dick.

"Fail not, or *we* will haunt thee to thy life's end," cried

Barbara; adding, as she handed a sealed package to the high-wayman, "Give this to Sir Luke—to him alone. I would have sent it to him by other hands ere this, but my people have deserted me—have pillaged my stores—have rifled me of all, save this. Give this, I say, to Sir Luke, with your own hands. You have sworn it, and will obey. Give it to him, and bid him think of Sibyl as he opens it. But this must not be till Eleanor is in his power; and she must be present when the seal is broken. It relates to both. Dare not to tamper with it, or my curse shall pursue you. That packet is guarded with a triple spell, which to you were fatal. Obey me, and my dying breath shall bless thee."

"Never fear," said Dick, taking the packet; "I'll not disappoint you, mother, depend upon it."

"Hence!" cried the crone; and as she watched Dick's figure lessening upon the waste, and at length beheld him finally disappear down the hill-side, she sank to the ground, her frail strength being entirely exhausted. "Body and soul may now part in peace," gasped she. "All I live for is accomplished." And ere one hour had elapsed, the night crow was perched upon her still breathing frame.

Long pondering upon this singular interview, Dick pursued his way. At length he thought fit to examine the packet with which the old gipsy had intrusted him.

"It feels like a casket," thought he. "It can't be gold. But then it may be jewels, though they don't rattle, and it ain't quite heavy enough. What can it be? I should like to know. There is some mystery, that's certain, about it; but I will not break the seal, not I. As to her spell, that I don't value a rush; but I've sworn to give it to Sir Luke, and deliver her message, and I'll keep my word if I can. He shall have it." Saying which he replaced it in his pocket.

XI.

THE PHANTOM STEED.

> I'll speak to thee, though hell itself should gape,
> And bid me hold my peace.   *Hamlet.*

TIME presses. We may not linger in our course. We must fly on before our flying highwayman. Full forty miles shall we pass over in a breath. Two more hours have elapsed, and he still urges his headlong career, with heart resolute as ever, and purpose yet unchanged. Fair Newark and the dashing Trent, "most loved of England's streams," are gathered to his laurels. Broad Notts, and its heavy paths and sweeping glades; its waste (forest no more) of Sherwood past; bold Robin Hood and his merry men, his Marian and his moonlight rides, recalled, forgotten, left behind. Hurrah! hurrah! That wild halloo, that waving arm, that enlivening shout—what means it? He is once more upon Yorkshire ground; his horse's hoof beats once more the soil of that noble shire. So transported was Dick, that he could almost have flung himself from the saddle to kiss the dust beneath his feet. Thrice fifty miles has he run, nor has the morn yet dawned upon his labours. Hurrah! the end draws nigh; the goal is in view. Halloo! halloo! on!

Bawtrey is past. He takes the lower road by Thorne and Selby. He is skirting the waters of the deep-channelled Don.

Bess now began to manifest some slight symptoms of distress. There was a strain in the carriage of her throat, a dulness in her eye, a laxity in her ear, and a slight stagger in her gait, which Turpin noticed with apprehension. Still she went on, though not at the same gallant pace as heretofore. But, as the tired bird still battles with the blast upon the ocean, as the swimmer still stems the stream, though spent, on went she; nor did Turpin dare to check her, fearing that, if she stopped, she might lose her force, or, if she fell, she would rise no more.

It was now that grey and grimly hour ere one flicker of orange or rose has gemmed the east, and when unwearying nature herself seems to snatch brief repose. In the roar of restless cities, this is the only time when the strife is hushed. Midnight is awake—alive; the streets ring with laughter and with rattling wheels. At the third hour, a dead, deep silence prevails; the loud-voiced streets grow dumb. They are deserted of all, save the few guardians of the night and the skulking robber. But even far removed from the haunts of men and hum of towns it is the same. "Nature's best nurse" seems to weigh nature down, and stillness reigns throughout. Our feelings are, in a great measure, influenced by the hour. Exposed to the raw crude atmosphere, which has neither the nipping, wholesome shrewdness of morn, nor the profound chillness of night, the frame vainly struggles against the dull, miserable sensations engendered by the damps, and at once communicates them to the spirits. Hope forsakes us. We are weary, exhausted. Our energy is dispirited. Sleep does "not weigh our eyelids down." We stare upon the vacancy. We conjure up a thousand restless, disheartening images. We abandon projects we have formed, and which, viewed through this medium, appear fantastical, chimerical, absurd. We want rest, refreshment, energy.

We will not say that Turpin had all these misgivings. But he had to struggle hard with himself to set sleep and exhaustion at defiance.

The moon had set. The stars,

> Pinnacled deep in the intense main,

had all—save one, the herald of the dawn—withdrawn their lustre. A dull mist lay on the stream, and the air became piercing cold. Turpin's chilled fingers could scarcely grasp the slackening rein, while his eyes irritated by the keen atmosphere, hardly enabled him to distinguish surrounding objects, or even to guide his steed. It was owing, probably, to this latter circumstance, that Bess suddenly floundered and fell, throwing her master over her head.

Turpin instantly recovered himself. His first thought was for his horse. But Bess was instantly upon her legs—covered with dust and foam, sides and cheeks—and with her large eyes glaring wildly, almost piteously, upon her master.

"Art hurt, lass?" asked Dick, as she shook herself, and slightly shivered. And he proceeded to the horseman's scrutiny. "Nothing but a shake; though that dull eye—those quivering flanks——" added he, looking earnestly at her. "She won't go much further, and I must give it up—what! give up the race just when it's won? No, that can't be. Ha! well thought on. I've a bottle of liquid given me by an old fellow, who was a knowing cove and famous jockey in his day, which he swore would make a horse go as long as he'd a leg to carry him, and bade me keep it for some great occasion. I've never used it: but I'll try it now. It should be in this pocket. Ah! Bess, wench, I fear I'm using thee, after all, as Sir Luke did his mistress, that I thought so like thee. No matter! It will be a glorious end."

Raising her head upon his shoulder, Dick poured the contents of the bottle down the throat of his mare. Nor had he to wait long before its invigorating effects were instantaneous. The fire was kindled in the glassy orb; her crest was once more erected; her flank ceased to quiver; and she neighed loud and joyously.

"Egad, the old fellow was right," cried Dick. "The drink has worked wonders. What the devil could it have been? It smells like spirit," added he, examining the bottle. "I wish I'd left a taste for myself. But here's that will do as well." And he drained his flask of the last drop of brandy.

Dick's limbs were now become so excessively stiff, that it was with difficulty he could remount his horse. But this necessary preliminary being achieved by the help of a stile, he found no difficulty in resuming his accustomed position upon the saddle. We know not whether there was any likeness between our Turpin and that modern Hercules of the sporting world, Mr. Osbaldeston. Far be it from us to institute any comparison, though we cannot help thinking that, in one particular, he resembled that famous "copper-bottomed" squire. This we will leave to our reader's discrimination. Dick bore his fatigues wonderfully. He suffered somewhat of that martyrdom which, according to Tom Moore, occurs "to weavers and M.P.'s from sitting too long;" but again on his courser's back, he cared not for anything.

Once more, at a gallant pace he traversed the banks of the Don, skirting the fields of flax that bound its sides, and hurried far more swiftly than its current to its confluence with the Aire.

Snaith was past. He was on the road to Selby when dawn first began to break. Here and there a twitter was heard in the hedge; a hare ran across his path, grey looking as the morning self; and the mists began to rise from the earth. A bar of gold was drawn against the east, like the roof of a gorgeous palace. But the mists were heavy in this world of rivers and their tributary streams. The Ouse was before him, the Trent and Aire behind; the Don and Derwent on either hand, all in their way to commingle their currents ere they formed the giant Humber. Amid a region so prodigal of water, no wonder the dews fell thick as rain. Here and there the ground was clear; but then again came a volley of vapour, dim and palpable as smoke.

While involved in one of these fogs, Turpin became aware of another horseman by his side. It was impossible to discern the features of the rider, but his figure in the mist seemed gigantic; neither was the colour of his steed distinguishable. Nothing was visible except the meagre-looking phantom-like outline of a horse and his rider, and, as the unknown rode upon the turf that edged the way, even the sound of his horse's hoofs was scarce audible. Turpin gazed, not without superstitious awe. Once or twice he essayed to address the strange horseman, but his tongue clove to the roof of his mouth. He fancied he discovered in the mist-exaggerated lineaments of the stranger a wild and fantastic resemblance to his friend Tom King. "It must be Tom," thought Turpin; "he is come to warn me of my approaching end. I will speak to him."

But terror o'ermastered his speech. He could not force out a word, and thus side by side they rode in silence. Quaking with fears he would scarcely acknowledge to himself, Dick watched every motion of his companion. He was still, stern, spectre-like, erect; and he looked for all the world like a demon on his phantom steed. His courser seemed, in the indistinct outline, to be huge and bony, and, as he snorted furiously in the fog, Dick's heated imagination supplied his breath with a due proportion of flame. Not a word was spoken—not a sound heard, save the sullen dead beat of his hoof upon the grass. It was intolerable to ride thus cheek by jowl with a goblin. Dick could stand it no longer. He put spurs to his horse, and endeavoured to escape. But it might not be. The stranger, apparently without effort, was still by his side, and Bess's feet, in her master's apprehensions, were nailed to the ground. By-and-by, however, the atmosphere became clearer. Bright quivering beams burst through the vaporous shroud, and then it was that Dick discovered that the apparition of Tom King was no other than Luke Rookwood. He was mounted on his old horse, Rook, and looked grim and haggard as a ghost vanishing at the crowing of the cock.

"Sir Luke Rookwood, by this light!" exclaimed Dick, in astonishment. "Why, I took you for——"

"The devil, no doubt?" returned Luke, smiling sternly, "and were sorry to find yourself so hard pressed. Don't disquiet yourself; I am still flesh and blood."

"Had I taken you for one of mortal mould," said Dick, "you should have soon seen where I'd have put you in the race. That confounded fog deceived me, and Bess acted the fool as well as myself. However, now I know you, Sir Luke, you must spur alongside, for the hawks are on the wing; and though I've much to say, I've not a second to lose." And Dick briefly detailed the particulars of his ride, concluding

with his rencontre with Barbara. "Here's the packet," said
he, "just as I got it. You must keep it till the proper
moment. And here," added he, fumbling in his pocket for
another paper, "is the marriage document. You are now
your father's lawful son, let who will say you nay. Take it
and welcome. If you are ever master of Miss Mowbray's
hand, you will not forget Dick Turpin."

"I will not," said Luke, eagerly grasping the certificate
"but she never may be mine."

"You have her oath?"

"I have."

"What more is needed?"

"Her hand."

"That will follow."

"It *shall* follow," replied Sir Luke, wildly. "You are
right. She is my affianced bride—affianced before hell, if not
before heaven. I have sealed the contract with blood—with
Sibyl's blood—and it shall be fulfilled. I have her oath—
her oath—ha, ha! Though I perish in the attempt, I will
wrest her from Ranulph's grasp. She shall never be his. I
would stab her first. Twice have I failed in my endeavours
to bear her off. I am from Rookwood even now. To-morrow night I shall renew the attack. Will you assist me?"

"To-morrow night!" interrupted Dick.

"Nay, I should say to-night. A new day has already
dawned," replied Luke.

"I will: she is at Rookwood?"

"She languishes there at present, attended by her mother
and her lover. The hall is watched and guarded. Ranulph
is ever on the alert. But we will storm their garrison. I have
a spy within its walls—a gipsy girl, faithful to my interests.
From her I have learnt that there is a plot to wed Eleanor to
Ranulph, and that the marriage is to take place privately to-
morrow. This must be prevented."

"It must. But why not boldly appear in person at the
hall and claim her?"

"Why not? I am a proscribed felon. A price is set upon
my head. I am hunted through the country—driven to concealment, and dare not show myself for fear of capture.
What could I do now? They would load me with fetters,
bury me in a dungeon, and wed Eleanor to Ranulph. What
would my rights avail? What would her oath signify to
them? No; she must be mine by force. *His* she shall never
be. Again, I ask you, will you aid me?"

"I have said—I will. Where is Alan Rookwood?"

"Concealed within the hut on Thorne Waste. You know it—it was one of your haunts."

"I know it well," said Dick, "and Conkey Jem, its keeper, into the bargain: he is a knowing file. I'll join you at the hut at midnight, if all goes well. We'll bring off the wench, in spite of them all—just the thing I like. But in case of a break-down on my part, suppose you take charge of my purse in the mean time."

Luke would have declined this offer.

"Pshaw!" said Dick. "Who knows what may happen? and it's not ill lined either. You'll find an odd hundred or so in that silken bag—it's not often your highwayman gives away a purse. Take it, man—we'll settle all to-night; and if I don't come, keep it—it will help you to your bride. And now off with you to the hut, for you are only hindering me. Adieu! My love to old Alan. We'll do the trick to-night. Away with you to the hut. Keep yourself snug there till midnight, and we'll ride over to Rookwood."

"At midnight," replied Sir Luke, wheeling off, "I shall expect you."

"'Ware hawks!" hallooed Dick.

But Luke had vanished. In another instant Dick was scouring the plain as rapidly as ever. In the mean time, as Dick has casually alluded to the hawks, it may not be amiss to inquire how they had flown throughout the night, and whether they were still in chase of their quarry.

With the exception of Titus, who was completely done up at Grantham, "having got," as he said, "a complete bellyful of it," they were still on the wing, and resolved sooner or later to pounce upon their prey, pursuing the same system as heretofore in regard to the post-horses. Major Mowbray and Paterson took the lead, but the irascible and invincible attorney was not far in their rear, his wrath having been by no means allayed by the fatigue he had undergone. At Bawtrey they held a council of war for a few minutes, being doubtful which course he had taken. Their incertitude was relieved by a foot traveller, who had heard Dick's loud halloo on passing the boundary of Nottinghamshire, and had seen him take the lower road. They struck, therefore, into the path to Thorne, at a hazard, and were soon satisfied they were right. Furiously did they now spur on. They reached Selby, changed horses at the inn in front of the venerable cathedral church, and learned from the postboy that a toil-

worn horseman, on a jaded steed, had ridden through the
town about five minutes before them, and could not be more
than a quarter of a mile in advance. "His horse was so dead
beat," said the lad, "that I'm sure he cannot have got far;
and, if you look sharp, I'll be bound you'll overtake him before
he reaches Cawood Ferry."

Mr. Coates was transported. "We'll lodge him snug in
York Castle before an hour, Paterson," cried he, rubbing his
hands.

"I hope so, sir," said the chief constable, "but I begin to
have some qualms."

"Now, gentlemen," shouted the postboy, "come along.
I'll soon bring you to him."

XII.

CAWOOD FERRY.

> The sight renewed my courser's feet,
> A moment, staggering feebly fleet,
> A moment, with a faint low neigh,
> He answered, and then fell.
> With gasps and glazing eyes he lay,
> And reeking limbs immovable.—
> His first, and last career was done.   *Mazeppa.*

THE sun had just o'ertopped the "high eastern hill," as
Turpin reached the Ferry of Cawood, and his beams were
reflected upon the deep and sluggish waters of the Ouse.
Wearily had he dragged his course thither—wearily and
slow. The powers of his gallant steed were spent, and he
could scarcely keep her from sinking. It was now midway
'twixt the hours of five and six. Nine miles only lay before
him, and that thought again revived him. He reached the
water's edge, and hailed the ferry-boat, which was then on
the other side of the river. At that instant a loud shout
smote his ear; it was the halloo of his pursuers. Despair
was in his look. He shouted to the boatman, and bade him
pull fast. The man obeyed; but he had to breast a strong
stream, and had a lazy bark and heavy sculls to contend with.
He had scarcely left the shore, when another shout was raised

from the pursuers. The tramp of their steeds grew louder and louder.

The boat had scarcely reached the middle of the stream. His captors were at hand. Quietly did he walk down the bank, and as cautiously enter the water. There was a plunge, and steed and rider were swimming down the stream.

Major Mowbray was at the brink of the stream. He hesitated an instant, and stemmed the tide. Seized, as it were by a mania for equestrian distinction, Mr. Coates braved the torrent. Not so Paterson. He very coolly took out his bull-dogs, and, watching Turpin, cast up in his own mind the *pros* and *cons* of shooting him as he was crossing. " I could certainly hit him," thought, or said, the constable ; " but what of that ? A dead highwayman is worth nothing—alive, he *weighs* 300*l.* I won't shoot him, but I'll make a pretence." And he fired accordingly.

The shot skimmed over the water, but did not, as it was intended, do much mischief. It, however, occasioned a mishap, which had nearly proved fatal to our aquatic attorney. Alarmed at the report of the pistol, in the nervous agitation of the moment Coates drew in his rein so tightly that his steed instantly sank. A moment or two afterwards he rose, shaking his ears, and floundering heavily towards the shore ; and such was the chilling effect of this sudden immersion, that Mr. Coates now thought much more of saving himself than of capturing Turpin. Dick, meanwhile, had reached the opposite bank, and, refreshed by her bath, Bess scrambled up the sides of the stream, and speedily regained the road. I shall do it, yet," shouted Dick; " that stream has saved her. Hark away, lass ! Hark away !"

Bess heard the cheering cry, and she answered to the call. She roused all her energies ; strained every sinew ; and put forth all her remaining strength. Once more, on wings of swiftness, she bore him away from his pursuers, and Major Mowbray, who had now gained the shore, and made certain of securing him, beheld him spring, like a wounded hare, from beneath his very hand.

" It cannot hold out," said the major ; " it is but an expiring flash ; that gallant steed must soon drop."

" She be regularly booked, that's certain," said the postboy. " We shall find her on the road."

Contrary to all expectation, however, Bess held on, and set pursuit at defiance. Her pace was swift as when she started. But it was unconscious and mechanical action. It wanted

the ease, the lightness, the life of her former riding. She
seemed screwed up to a task which she must execute. There
was no flogging, no gory heel; but her heart was throbbing,
tugging at the sides within. Her spirit spurred her onwards.
Her eye was glazing; her chest heaving; her flank quivering;
her crest again fallen. Yet she held on. "She is dying, by
God!" said Dick. "I feel it——" No, she held on.

Fulford is past. The towers and pinnacles of York burst
upon him in all the freshness, the beauty, and the glory of a
bright, clear, autumnal morn. The ancient city seemed to
smile a welcome—a greeting. The noble Minster and its
serene and massive pinnacles, crocketed, lantern-like, and
beautiful; Saint Mary's lofty spire, All-Hallows Tower, the
massive mouldering walls of the adjacent postern, the grim
castle, and Clifford's neighbouring keep—all beamed upon
him, "like a bright-eyed face, that laughs out openly."

"It is done—it is won," cried Dick. "Hurrah, hurrah!"
And the sunny air was cleft with his shouts.

Bess was not insensible to her master's exultation. She
neighed feebly in answer to his call, and reeled forwards. It
was a piteous sight to see her,—to mark her staring, pro-
truding eyeball,—her shaking flanks; but, while life and limb
held together, she held on.

Another mile is past. York is near.

"Hurrah!" shouted Dick; but his voice was hushed. Bess
tottered—fell. There was a dreadful gasp—a parting moan
—a snort; her eye gazed, for an instant, upon her master,
with a dying glare; then grew glassy, rayless, fixed. A
shiver ran through her frame. Her heart had burst.

Dick's eyes were blinded, as if with rain. His triumph,
though achieved, was forgotten—his own safety was disregarded. He stood weeping, and swearing, like one beside
himself.

"And art thou gone, Bess!" cried he in a voice of agony,
lifting up his courser's head, and kissing her lips, covered
with blood-flecked foam. "Gone, gone! and I have killed
the best steed that was ever crossed! And for what?" added
Dick, beating his brow with his clenched hand—"for what?
for what?"

At that moment the deep bell of the Minster clock tolled
out the hour of six.

"I am answered," gasped Dick; "*it was to hear those
strokes!*"

Turpin was roused from the state of stupefaction into which

he had fallen by a smart slap on the shoulder. Recalled to himself by the blow, he started at once to his feet, while his hands sought his pistols; but he was spared the necessity of using them, by discovering in the intruder the bearded visage of the gipsy Balthazar. The patrico was habited in mendicant weeds, and sustained a large wallet upon his shoulders.

"So it's all over with the best mare in England, I see," said Balthazar; "I can guess how it has happened—you are pursued?"

"I am," said Dick, roughly.

"Your pursuers are at hand?"

"Within a few hundred yards."

"Then why stay here? Fly while you can."

"Never—never," cried Turpin; "I'll fight it out here by Bess's side. Poor lass! I've killed her—but she has done it —ha! ha! we have won—what!" And his utterance was again choked.

"Hark! I hear the tramp of horses, and shouts," cried the patrico, "Take this wallet. You will find a change of dress within it. Dart into that thick copse—save yourself."

"But Bess—I cannot leave her," exclaimed Dick, with an agonizing look at his horse.

"And what did Bess die for, but to save you?" rejoined the patrico.

"True, true," said Dick; "but take care of her. Don't let those dogs of hell meddle with her carcass."

"Away," cried the patrico; "leave Bess to me."

Possessing himself of the wallet, Dick disappeared in the adjoining copse.

He had not been gone many seconds when Major Mowbray rode up.

"Who is this?" exclaimed the major, flinging himself from his horse, and seizing the patrico: "this is not Turpin."

"Certainly not," replied Balthazar, coolly. "I am not exactly the figure for a highwayman."

"Where is he? what has become of him?" asked Coates, in despair, as he and Paterson joined the major.

"Escaped, I fear," replied the major. "Have you seen any one, fellow?" added he, addressing the patrico.

"I have seen no one," replied Balthazar. "I am only this instant arrived. This dead horse lying in the road attracted my attention."

"Ha!" exclaimed Paterson, leaping from his steed; "this may be Turpin after all. He has as many disguises as the devil himself, and may have carried that goat's hair in his pocket." Saying which, he seized the patrico by the beard, and shook it with as little reverence as the Gaul handled the hirsute chin of the Roman senator.

"The devil! hands off!" roared Balthazar. "By Salamon I won't stand such usage. Do you think a beard like mine is the growth of a few minutes? Hands off, I say."

"Regularly done!" said Paterson, removing his hold of the patrico's chin, and looking as blank as a cartridge.

"Ay," exclaimed Coates; "all owing to this worthless piece of carrion. If it were not that I hope to see him dangling from those walls" (pointing towards the castle), "I should wish her master were by her side now. To the dogs with her." And he was about to spurn the breathless carcass of poor Bess, when a sudden blow, dealt by the patrico's staff, felled him to the ground.

"I'll teach you to molest me," said Balthazar, about to attack Paterson.

"Come, come," said the discomfited chief constable, "no more of this. It's plain we're in the wrong box. Every bone in my body aches sufficiently without the aid of your cudgel, old fellow. Come, Mr. Coates, take my arm, and let's be moving. We've had an infernal long ride for nothing."

"Not so," replied Coates; "I've paid pretty dearly for it. However, let us see if we can get any breakfast at the Bowling-green, yonder; though I've already had my morning draught," added the facetious man of law, looking at his dripping apparel.

"Poor Black Bess!" said Major Mowbray, wistfully regarding the body of the mare, as it lay stretched at his feet. "Thou deservedst a better fate and a better master. In thee Dick Turpin has lost his best friend. His exploits will, henceforth, want the colouring of romance, which thy unfailing energies threw over them. Light lie the ground over thee, thou matchless mare!"

To the Bowling-green the party proceeded, leaving the patrico in undisturbed possession of the lifeless body of Black Bess. Major Mowbray ordered a substantial repast to be prepared with all possible expedition.

A countryman in a smock-frock was busily engaged at his morning's meal.

"To see that fellow bolt down his breakfast, one would

think he had fasted for a month," said Coates; "see the wholesome effects of an honest, industrious life, Paterson. I envy him his appetite—I should fall to with more zest were Dick Turpin in his place."

The countryman looked up. He was an odd-looking fellow, with a terrible squint, and a strange, contorted countenance.

"An ugly dog!" exclaimed Paterson; "what a devil of a twist he has got!"

"What's that you says about Dick Taarpin, measter?" asked the countryman, with his mouth half-full of bread.

"Have you seen aught of him?" asked Coates.

"Not I," mumbled the rustic; "but I hears aw the folk hereabouts talk on him. They say as how he sets all the lawyers and constables at defiance, and laughs in his sleeve at their efforts to cotch him—ha, ha! He gets over more ground in a day than they do in a week—ho, ho!"

"That's all over now," said Coates, peevishly. "He has cut his own throat—ridden his famous mare to death."

The countryman almost choked himself, in the attempt to bolt a huge mouthful. "Ay—indeed, measter! How happened that?" asked he, so soon as he recovered speech.

"The fool rode her from London to York last night," returned Coates; "such a feat was never performed before. What horse could be expected to live through such work as that?"

"Ah, he were a foo' to attempt that," observed the countryman; "but you followed belike?"

"We did."

"And took him arter all, I reckon?" asked the rustic, squinting more horribly than ever.

"No," returned Coates, "I can't say we did; but we'll have him yet. I'm pretty sure he can't be far off. We may be nearer him than we imagine."

"May be so, measter," returned the countryman; "but might I be so bold as to ax how many horses you used i' the chase—some half-dozen, may be?"

"Half a dozen!" growled Paterson; "we had twenty at the least."

"And I one!" mentally ejaculated Turpin, for he was the countryman.

Book the Fifth.

THE OATH.

> It was an ill oath better broke than kept—
> The laws of nature, and of nations, do
> Dispense with matters of divinity
> In such a case.   TATEHAM.

I.

THE HUT ON THORNE WASTE.

> *Hind.* Are all our horses and our arms in safety?
> *Furbo.* They feed, like Pluto's palfreys, under ground.
> Our pistols, swords, and other furniture,
> Are safely locked up at our rendezvous.
>   *Prince of Prigs' Revels.*

The hut on Thorne Waste, to which we have before incidentally alluded, and whither we are now about to repair, was a low, lone hovel, situate on the banks of the deep and oozy Don, at the eastern extremity of that extensive moor. Ostensibly its owner fulfilled the duties of ferryman to that part of the river; but as the road, which skirted his tenement, was little frequented, his craft was, for the most part, allowed to sleep undisturbed in her moorings.

In reality, however, he was the inland agent of a horde of smugglers who infested the neighbouring coast; his cabin was their rendezvous; and not unfrequently, it was said, the depository of their contraband goods. Conkey Jem (so was he called by his associates, on account of the Slawkenbergian promontory which decorated his countenance) had been an old hand at the same trade; but having returned from a seven years' leave of absence from his own country, procured by his lawless life, now managed matters with more circumspection and prudence, and had never since been detected in his former illicit traffic; nor, though so marvellously gifted in that particular himself, was he ever known to *nose* upon any of his accomplices; or, in other words, to betray them. On the contrary, his hut was a sort of asylum for all fugitives from justice; and although the sanctity of his walls would, in all probability, have been little regarded, had any one been detected within them, yet, strange to say, even if a robber had been tracked (as it often chanced) to Jem's immediate neighbourhood, all traces of him were sure to be lost at the ferryman's hut; and further search was useless.

Within, the hut presented such an appearance as might be expected, from its owner's pursuits and its own unpromising exterior. Consisting of little more than a couple of rooms, the rude, whitewashed mud walls exhibited, in lieu of prints of more pretension, a gallery of choicely-illustrated ballads, celebrating the exploits of various highwaymen, renowned in song, amongst which, our friend Dick Turpin figured conspicuously upon his sable steed, Bess being represented by a huge rampant black patch, and Dick, with a pistol considerably longer than the arm that sustained it. Next to this curious collection was a drum-net, a fishing-rod, a landing-net, an eel-spear, and other piscatorial apparatus, with a couple of sculls and a boat-hook, indicative of Jem's ferryman's office, suspended by various hooks; the whole blackened and begrimed by peat smoke, there being no legitimate means of *exit* permitted to the vapour generated by the turf-covered hearthstone. The only window, indeed, in the hut, was to the front; the back apartment, which served Jem for dormitory, had no aperture whatever for the admission of light, except such as was afforded through the door of communication between the rooms. A few broken rush-bottomed chairs, with a couple of dirty tables, formed the sum total of the ferryman's furniture.

Notwithstanding the grotesque effect of his exaggerated nasal organ, Jem's aspect was at once savage and repulsive; his lank black hair hung about his inflamed visage in wild elf locks, the animal predominating throughout; his eyes were small, red, and wolfish, and glared suspiciously from beneath his scarred and tufted eyebrows; while certain of his teeth projected, like the tusks of a boar, from out his coarse-lipped sensual mouth. Dwarfish in stature, and deformed in person, Jem was built for strength; and what with his width of shoulder and shortness of neck, his figure looked as square and solid as a cube. His throat and hirsute chest, constantly exposed to the weather, had acquired a glowing tan, while his arms, uncovered to the shoulders, and clothed with fur like a bear's hide, down, almost, to the tips of his fingers, presented a knot of folded muscles, the concentrated force of which few would have desired to encounter in action.

z

It was now on the stroke of midnight; and Jem, who had been lying extended upon the floor of his hovel, suddenly aroused by that warning impulse which never fails to awaken one of his calling at the exact moment when they require to be upon the alert, now set about fanning into flame the expiring fuel upon his hearth. Having succeeded in igniting further portions of turf, Jem proceeded to examine the security of his door and window, and satisfied that lock and bolt were shot, and that the shutter was carefully closed, he kindled a light at his fire, and walked towards his bedroom. But it was not to retire for the night that the ferryman entered his dormitory. Beside his crazy couch stood a litter of empty bottles and a beer cask, crowding the chamber. The latter he rolled aside, and pressing his foot upon the plank beneath it, the board gave way, and a trap-door opening, discovered a ladder, conducting, apparently, into the bowels of the earth. Jem leaned over the abyss, and called in hoarse accents to some one below.

An answer was immediately returned, and a light became soon afterwards visible at the foot of the ladder. Two figures next ascended; the first who set foot within the ferryman's chamber was Alan Rookwood; the other, as the reader may perhaps conjecture, was his grandson.

"Is it the hour?" asked Luke, as he sprang from out the trap-door.

"Ay," replied Jem, with a coarse laugh; "or I had not disturbed myself to call you. But, may be," added he, softening his manner a little; "you'll like some refreshment before you start? A stoup of Nantz will put you in cue for the job, ha, ha!"

"Not I," replied Luke, who could ill tolerate his companion's familiarity.

"Give me to drink," said Alan, walking feebly towards the fire, and extending his skinny fingers before it. "I am chilled by the damps of that swampy cave—the natural heat within me is nigh extinguished."

"Here is that shall put fresh marrow into your old bones," returned Jem, handing him a tumbler of brandy; "never stint it. I'll be sworn you'll be the better on't, for you look desperate queer, man, about the mazzard."

Alan was, in sooth, a ghastly spectacle. The events of the last few days had wrought a fearful change. His countenance was almost exanimate; and when, with shaking hand

and trembling lips, he had drained the fiery potion to the dregs, a terrible grimace was excited upon his features, such as is produced upon the corpse by the action of the galvanic machine. Even Jem regarded him with a sort of apprehension. After he had taken breath for a moment, Alan broke out into a fit of wild and immoderate laughter.

"Why, ay," said he, "this is indeed to grow young again, and to feel fresh fire within one's veins. Who would have thought so much of life and energy could reside in this little vessel? I am myself once more, and not the same soulless, pulseless lump of clay I was a moment or two back. The damps of that den had destroyed me—and the solitude—the *waking dreams* I've had—the visions! horrible! I will not think of them. I am better now—ready to execute my plans —*your* plans I should say, grandson Luke. Are our horses in readiness? Why do we tarry? The hour is arrived, and I would not that my new-blown courage should evaporate, ere the great work, for which I live, be accomplished. That done, I ask no further stimulant. Let us away."

"We tarry but for Turpin," said Luke, "I am as impatient as yourself. I fear some mischance must have befallen him, or he would have been true to his appointment. Do you not think so?" he added, addressing the ferryman.

"Why," replied Jem, reluctantly; "since you put it home to me, and I can't conceal it no longer, I'll tell you what I didn't tell afore, for fear you should be down in the mouth about it. Dick Turpin can do nothing for you—he's grabb'd."

"Turpin apprehended!" ejaculated Luke.

"Ay," returned Jem. "I learnt from a farmer, who crossed the ferry at night-fall, that he were grabb'd this morning at York, after having ridden his famous cherry-coloured prad to death—that's what hurts me more nor all the rest; though I fear Dick will scarce cheat the nubbing cheat this go. His time's up, I calculate."

"Will you supply his place and accompany us?" asked Luke, of the ferryman.

"No, no," replied Jem, shaking his head; "there's too much risk, and too little profit, in the business for me—it won't pay."

"And what might tempt you to undertake the enterprise?" asked Alan.

"More than you have to offer, Master Peter," replied Jem,

z 2

who had not been enlightened upon the subject of Alan's real
name or condition.

"How know you that?" demanded Alan. "Name your
demand."

"Well, then, I'll not say but a hundred pounds, if you had
it, might bribe me——"

"To part with your soul to the devil, I doubt not," said
Luke, fiercely stamping the ground. "Let us be gone. We
need not his mercenary aid. We will do without him."

"Stay," said Alan, "you shall have the hundred, provided
you will assure us of your services."

"Cut no more blarneyfied whids, Master Sexton," replied
Jem, in a gruff tone. "If I'm to go, I must have the chink
down, and that's more nor either of you can do, I'm
thinking."

"Give me your purse," whispered Alan to his grandson.
"Pshaw," continued he, "do you hesitate? This man can
do much for us. Think upon Eleanor, and be prudent. You
cannot accomplish your task unaided." Taking the amount
from the purse, he gave it to the ferryman, adding, "if we
succeed, the sum shall be doubled, and now let us set out."

During Alan's speech, Jem's sharp eyes had been fastened
upon the purse, while he mechanically clutched the bank
notes which were given to him. He could not remove his
gaze, but continued staring at the treasure before him, as if
he would willingly, by force, have made it all his own.

Alan saw the error he had committed, in exposing the contents of the purse to the avaricious ferryman, and was about
to restore it to Luke, when the bag was suddenly snatched
from his grasp, and himself levelled by a blow upon the floor.
Conkey Jem found the temptation irresistible. Knowing
himself to be a match for both his companions, and imagining
he was secure from interruption, he conceived the idea of
making away with them, and possessing himself of their
wealth. No sooner had he disposed of Alan, than he assailed
Luke, who met his charge half way. With the vigour and
alacrity of the latter the reader is already acquainted, but he
was no match for the Herculean strength of the double-
jointed ferryman, who, with the ferocity of the boar he so
much resembled, thus furiously attacked him. Nevertheless,
as may be imagined, he was not disposed to yield up his life
tamely. He saw at once the villain's murderous intentions,
and, well aware of his prodigious power, would not have

risked a close struggle could he have avoided it. Snatching
the eel-spear from the wall, he had hurled it at the head of
his adversary, but without effect. In the next instant he was
locked in a clasp terrible as that of a polar bear. In spite of
all his struggles, Luke was speedily hurled to the ground;
and Jem, who had thrown himself upon him, was apparently
searching about for some weapon, to put a bloody termination
to the conflict, when the trampling of a horse was heard at
the door, three taps were repeated slowly, one after the other,
and a call resounded from a whistle.

"Damnation!" ejaculated Jem, gruffly, "interrupted!"
And he seemed irresolute, slightly altering his position on
Luke's body.

The moment was fortunate for Luke, and, in all probability, saved his life. He extricated himself from the ferryman's grasp, regained his feet, and, what was of more
importance, the weapon he had thrown away.

"Villain!" cried he, about to plunge the spear with all his
force into his enemy's side. "You shall——"

The whistle was again heard without.

"Don't you hear that?" cried Jem; "'tis Turpin's call."

"Turpin!" echoed Luke, dropping the point of his weapon.
"Unbar the door, you treacherous rascal, and admit him."

"Well, say no more about it, Sir Luke," said Jem, fawn-
ingly; "I knows I owes you my life, and I thank you for it.
Take back the lowre. He should not have shown it me—it
was that as did all the mischief."

"Unbar the door, and parley not," said Luke, contemptuously.

Jem complied with pretended alacrity, but real reluctance,
casting suspicious glances at Luke as he withdrew the bolts.
The door at length being opened, haggard, exhausted, and
covered with dust, Dick Turpin staggered into the hut.

"Well, I am here," said he with a hollow laugh. "I've
kept my word—ha, ha! I've been damnably put to it; but
here I am, ha, ha!" and he sank upon one of the stools.

"We heard you were apprehended," said Luke. "I am
glad to find the information was false," added he, glancing
angrily at the ferryman.

"Whoever told you that, told you a lie, Sir Luke," replied
Dick; "but what are you scowling at, old Charon?—and
you, Sir Luke? Why do you glower at each other? Make
fast the door—bolt it, Cerberus—right! Now give me a

glass of brandy, and then I'll talk—a bumper—so—another.
What's that I see—a dead man? Old Peter—Alan I mean—
has anything happened to him, that he has taken his measure
there so quietly?"

"Nothing, I trust," said Luke, stooping to raise up his
grandsire. "The blow has stunned him."

"The blow?" repeated Turpin. "What! there *has* been
a quarrel then? I thought as much from your amiable looks
at each other. Come, come, we must have no differences.
Give the old earthworm a taste of this—I'll engage it will
bring him to fast enough. Ay, rub his temples with it if
you'd rather; but it's a better remedy down the gullet—the
natural course; and hark ye, Jem, search your crib quickly,
and see if you have any *grub* within it, and any more *bub* in
the cellar: I'm as hungry as a hunter, and as thirsty as a
camel."

II.

MAJOR MOWBRAY.

Mephistopheles. Out with your toasting-iron! Thrust away!
           FAUST.—*Hayward's Translation.*

CONKEY JEM went in search of such provisions as his hovel
afforded. Turpin, meantime, lent his assistance towards the
revival of Alan Rookwood; and it was not long before his
efforts, united with those of Luke, were successful, and Alan
restored to consciousness. He was greatly surprised to find
the highwayman had joined them, and expressed an earnest
desire to quit the hut as speedily as possible.

"That shall be done forthwith, my dear fellow," said Dick.
"But if you had fasted as long as I have done, and gone
through a few of my fatigues into the bargain, you would
perceive, without difficulty, the propriety of supping before
you started. Here comes Old Nosey, with a flitch of bacon
and a loaf. Egad, I can scarce wait for the toasting. In my
present mood, I could almost devour a grunter in the sty."
Whereupon he applied himself to the loaf, and to a bottle of
stout March ale, which Jem placed upon the table, quaffing

copious draughts of the latter, while the ferryman employed himself in toasting certain rashers of the flitch upon the hissing embers.

Luke, meanwhile, stalked impatiently about the room. He had laid aside his tridental spear, having first, however, placed a pistol within his breast to be ready for instant service, should occasion demand it, as he could now put little reliance upon the ferryman's fidelity. He glanced with impatience at Turpin, who pursued his meal with steady voracity, worthy of a half-famished soldier; but the highwayman returned no answer to his looks, except such as was conveyed by the incessant clatter of his masticating jaws, during the progress of his, apparently, interminable repast.

"Ready for you in a second, Sir Luke," said Dick; "all right now—capital ale, Charon—strong as Styx—ha, ha!—one other rasher, and I've done. Sorry to keep you—can't conceive how cleverly I put the winkers upon 'em at York, in the dress of a countryman; all owing to old Balty, the patrico, an old pal—ha, ha! My old pals never *nose* upon me—eh, Nosey—always help one out of the water—always stanch. Here's health to you, old crony."

Jem returned a sulky response, as he placed the last rasher on the table, which was speedily discussed.

"Poor Bess!" muttered Dick, as he quaffed off the final glass of ale. "Poor lass! we buried her by the roadside, beneath the trees—deep—deep. Her remains shall never be disturbed. Alas! alas! my bonnie Black Bess! but no matter, her name is yet alive—her deeds will survive her—the trial is over. And now," continued he, rising from his seat, " I'm with you. Where are the tits?"

"In the stable, underground," growled Jem.

Alan Rookwood, in the mean time, had joined his grandson, and they conversed an instant or two apart.

"My strength will not bear me through the night," said he. "That fellow has thoroughly disabled me. You must go without me to the hall. Here is the key of the secret passage. You know the entrance. I will await you in the tomb."

"The tomb!" echoed Luke.

"Ay, our family vault," returned Alan, with a ghastly grin; "it is the only place of security for me now. Let me see *her* there. Let me know that my vengeance is complete, that I triumph in my death over him, the accursed *brother*, through you, my grandson. *You* have a rival brother—a successful one; you know what hatred is."

"I do," returned Luke, fiercely.

"But not such a hate as mine, which, though a life, a long life, hath endured, intense as when 'twas first engendered in my bosom; which *from one* hath spread o'er all my race—o'er all save *you*—and which even now, when death stares me in the face—when the spirit pants to fly from its prison-house, burns fiercely as ever. You cannot know what hate like that may be. *You* must have wrongs—such wrongs as *mine* first."

"My hate to Ranulph is bitter as your own to Sir Reginald."

"Name him not," shrieked Alan. "But, oh! to think upon the bride he robbed me of—the young—the beautiful!—whom I loved to madness; whose memory is a barbed shaft, yet rankling keen as ever in my heart. God of Justice! how is it that I have thus long survived? But some men die by inches. My dying lips shall name him once again, and then 'twill be but to blend his name with curses."

"I speak of him no more," said Luke. "I will meet you in the vault."

"Remember, to-morrow is her wedding-day with Ranulph."

"Think you I forget it?"

"Bear it constantly in mind. To-morrow's dawn must see her *yours* or *his*. You have her oath. To you or to death she is affianced. If she should hesitate in her election, do not you hesitate. Women's will is fickle; her scruples of conscience will be readily overcome; she will not heed her vows; but let her not escape you. Cast off all your weakness. You are young, and not as I am, age-enfeebled. Be firm, and," added he, with a look of terrible meaning, "if all else should fail—if you are surrounded—if you cannot bear her off—use this," and he placed a dagger in Luke's hands. "It has avenged me, ere now, on a perjured wife, it will avenge you of a foresworn mistress, and remove all obstacle to Rookwood."

Luke took the weapon.

"Would you have me kill her?" demanded he.

"Sooner than she should be Ranulph's."

"Ay, aught sooner than that. But I would not murder both."

"Both !" echoed Alan. "I understand you not."

"Sibyl and Eleanor," replied Luke : " for, surely as I live, Sibyl's death will lie at my door."

"How so ?" asked Alan ; "the poison was self-ministered."

"True," replied Luke, with terrible emphasis, " but I *spoke daggers.* Hearken to me," said he, hollowly whispering in his grandsire's ears. "Methinks I am not long for this world. I have seen her since her death."

"Tut, tut," replied Alan. " 'Tis not for you (a man) to talk thus. A truce to these womanish fancies."

"Womanish or not," returned Luke ; "either my fancy has deceived me, or I beheld her, distinctly as I now behold you, within yon cave, while you were sleeping by my side."

"It is disordered fancy," said Alan Rookwood. "You will live—live to inherit Rookwood—live to see them fall, crushed beneath your feet. For myself, if I but see you master of Eleanor's hand, or know that she no longer lives to bless your rival, or to mar your prospects, I care not how soon I brave my threatened doom."

"Of one or other you shall be resolved to-night," said Luke, placing the dagger within his vest.

At this moment a trampling of a horse was heard before the hovel, and in another instant a loud knocking resounded from the door. The ferryman instantly extinguished the light, motioning his companions to remain silent.

"What ho !" shouted a voice. "Ferry wanted."

"Gad zooks !" exclaimed Dick. "As I live, 'tis Major Mowbray."

"Major Mowbray !" echoed Alan, in amazement. "What doth he here ?"

"He must be on his way from York to Rookwood, I conclude," said Dick. "If he's here, I'll engage the others are not far off."

Scarcely were the words out of Dick's mouth, when further clatter was heard at the door, and the tones of Coates were heard in *altissimo* key, demanding admittance.

"Let us retire into the next room," whispered Turpin, "and then admit them, by all means, Conkey. And hark ye, manage to detain them a few seconds."

"I'll do it," said Jem. "There's a bit of a hole you can peep through."

Another loud rat-tat was heard at the door, threatening to burst it from its hinges.

"Well, I be coming," said Jem, seeing the coast was clear, in a drowsy, yawning tone, as if just awakened from sleep. "You'll cross the river none the faster for making so much noise." With these words he unbarred the door, and Coates and Paterson, who, it appeared, were proceeding to Rookwood, entered the hovel. Major Mowbray remained on horseback at the door.

"Can you find us a glass of brandy, to keep out the fog ?" said Coates, who knew something of our ferryman's vocations. "I know you to be a lad of amazing *spirit*."

"May be I can, master, if I choose. But won't the other gemman walk in doors likewise ?"

"No, no," said Coates; "Major Mowbray don't choose to dismount."

"Well, as you please," said Jem. "It 'll take me a minute or two to get the punt in order for all them prads."

"The brandy in the first place," said Coates. "What's here ?" added the loquacious attorney, noticing the remnants of Turpin's repast. "But that we're hurried, I should like a little frizzled bacon myself."

Jem opened the door of his dormitory with the greatest caution, though apparent indifference, and almost instantly returned with the brandy. Coates filled a glass for Paterson, and then another for himself. The ferryman left the house apparently to prepare his boat, half closing the door after him.

"By my faith! this is the right thing. Paterson," said the attorney. "We may be sure the strength of this was never tested by a gauger's proof. Take another thimbleful. We've twelve miles and a heavy pull to go through ere we reach Rookwood. After all, we made but a poor night's work of it, master constable. Cursed stupid in us to let him escape. I only wish we had such another chance. Ah, if we had him within reach now, how we would spring upon him—secure him in an instant. I should glory in the encounter. I tell you what, Paterson, if ever he is taken, I shall make a point of attending his execution, and see whether he dies game. Ha! ha! You think he is sure to swing, Paterson, eh ?"

"Why, yes," replied the chief constable. "I wish I was as certain of my reward as that Turpin will eventually figure at the scragging-post."

"Your reward!" replied Coates. "Make yourself easy on

that score, my boy; you shall have your dues, depend upon it. Nay, for the matter of that, I'll give you the money now, if you think proper."

"Nothing like time present," said Paterson. "We'll make all square at once."

"Well, then," said Coates, taking out a pocket-book, "you shall have the hundred I promised. You won't get Turpin's reward, the three hundred pounds; but that can't be helped. You shall have mine—always a man of my word, Paterson," continued the attorney, counting out the money. "My father, the thief-taker, was a man of his word before me."

"No doubt," said the chief constable; "I shall always be happy to serve you."

"And then there's that other affair," said the attorney, mysteriously, still occupied in doling out his bank notes, "that Luke Bradley's case; the fellow, I mean, who calls himself Sir Luke Rookwood—ha, ha! A rank imposter! Two fives, that makes fifty: you want another fifty, Paterson. As I was saying, we may make a good job of that—we must ferret him out. I know who will come down properly for that; and if we could only tuck him up with his brother blade, why it would be worth double. He's all along been a thorn in my Lady Rookwood's side; he's an artful scoundrel."

"Leave him to me," said Paterson; "I'll have him in less than a week. What's your charge against him?"

"Felony, burglary, murder, every description of crime under the heavens," said Coates. "He's a very devil incarnate. Dick Turpin is as mild as milk compared with him. By the bye, now I think of it, this Jem, Conkey Jem, as folks call him, may know something about him; he's a keen file, I'll sound him. Thirty, forty, fifty—there's the exact amount. So much for Dick Turpin."

"Dick Turpin thanks you for it in person," said Dick, suddenly snatching the whole sum from Paterson's hands, and felling the chief constable with a blow of one of his pistols. "I wish I was as sure of escaping the gallows as I am certain that Paterson has got his reward. You stare, sir. You are once more in the hands of the Philistines. See who is at your elbow."

Coates, who was terrified almost out of his senses at the sight of Turpin, scarcely ventured to turn his head; but when he did so, he was perfectly horror-stricken at the threatening aspect of Luke, who held a cutlass in his hand, which he had picked up in the ferryman's bedroom.

"So you would condemn me for crimes I have never committed," said Luke. "I am tempted, I own, to add the destruction of your worthless existence to their number."

"Mercy, for God's sake, mercy!" cried Coates, throwing himself at Luke's feet. "I meant not what I said."

"Hence, reptile," said Luke, pushing him aside; "I leave you to be dealt upon by others."

At this juncture, the door of the hut was flung open, and in rushed Major Mowbray, sword in hand, followed by Conkey Jem.

"There he stands, sir," cried the latter; "upon him."

"What! Conkey Jem turned snitch upon his pals?" cried Dick; "I scarce believe my own ears."

"Make yourself scarce, Dick," growled Jem; "the jigger's open, and the boat loose. Leave Luke to his fate. He's sold."

"Never, vile traitor," shouted Dick; "'tis thou art *sold*, not he;" and, almost ere the words were spoken, a ball was lodged in the brain of the treacherous ferryman.

Major Mowbray, meanwhile, had rushed furiously upon Luke, who met his assault with determined calmness. The strife was sharp, and threatened a speedy and fatal issue. On the major's side it was a desperate attack of cut and thrust, which Luke had some difficulty in parrying; but as yet no wounds were inflicted. Soldier as was the major, Luke was not a whit inferior to him in his knowledge of the science of defence, and in the exercise of the broadsword he was perhaps the more skilful of the two: upon the present occasion his coolness stood him in admirable stead. Seeing him hard pressed, Turpin would have come to his assistance; but Luke shouted to him to stand aside, and all that Dick could do, amid the terrific clash of steel, was to kick the tables out of the way of the combatants. Luke's arm was now slightly grazed by a cut made by the major, which he had parried. The smart of the wound roused his ire. He attacked his adversary in his turn, with so much vigour and good-will, that, driven backwards by the irresistible assault, Major Mowbray stumbled over the ferryman's body, which happened to lie in his way; and his sword being struck from his grasp, his life became at once at his assailant's disposal.

Luke sheathed his sword. "Major Mowbray," said he, sternly, "your life is in my power. I spare it for the blood that is between us—for your sister's sake. I would not raise my hand against her brother."

"I disclaim your kindred with me, villain!" wrathfully exclaimed the major. "I hold you no otherwise than as a wretched impostor, who has set up claims he cannot justify; and as to my sister, if you dare to couple her name——" and the major made an ineffectual attempt to raise himself, and to regain his sword, which Turpin, however, removed.

"Dare!" echoed Luke, scornfully; "hereafter, you may learn to fear my threats, and acknowledge the extent of my daring; and in that confidence I give you life. Listen to me, sir. I am bound for Rookwood. I have private access to the house—to your sister's chamber—*her chamber*—marked you that? I shall go armed—attended. This night she shall be mine. From you—from Ranulph—from Lady Rookwood, from all will I bear her off. She shall be mine, and you, before the dawn, my brother, or ——" and Luke paused.

"What further villany remains untold?" inquired the major, fiercely.

"You shall bewail your sister's memory," replied Luke, gloomily.

"I embrace the latter alternative with rapture," replied the major—"God grant her firmness to resist you. But I tremble for her;" and the stern soldier groaned aloud in his agony.

"Here is a cord to bind him," said Turpin; "he must remain a prisoner here."

"Right," said Alan Rookwood, "unless—but enough blood has been shed already."

"Ay, marry has there," said Dick, "and I had rather not have given Conkey Jem a taste of blue plumb, had there been any other mode of silencing the snitching scoundrel, which there was not. As to the major, he's a gallant enemy, and shall have fair play as long as Dick Turpin stands by. Come, sir," added he, to the major, as he bound him hand and foot with the rope, "I'll do it as gently as I can. You had better submit with a good grace. There's no help for it. And now for my friend Paterson, who was so anxious to furnish me with a hempen cravat, before my neck was in order, he shall have an extra twist of the rope himself, to teach him the inconvenience of a tight neckcloth, when he recovers." Saying which, he bound Paterson in such manner, that any attempt at liberation on the chief constable's part would infallibly strangle him. "As to you, Mr. Coates," said he, addressing the trembling man of law, "you shall proceed to Rookwood with us. You may yet be useful, and I'll accommodate you

with a seat behind my own saddle—a distinction I never yet
conferred upon any of your tribe. Recollect the countryman
at the Bowling-green at York—ha, ha! Come along, sir."
And having kicked out the turf fire, Dick prepared to
depart.

It would be vain to describe the feelings of rage and
despair which agitated the major's bosom, as he saw the
party quit the hovel, accompanied by Coates. Aware as he
was of their destination, after one or two desperate but ineffectual attempts to liberate himself, by which he only
increased the painful constriction of his bonds without in the
slightest degree ameliorating his condition, he resigned himself, with bitterest forebodings, to his fate. There was no
one even to sympathise with his sufferings. Beside him lay
the gory corpse of the ferryman, and, at a little distance, the
scarcely more animate frame of the chief constable. And here
we must leave him, to follow, for a short space, the course of
Luke and his companions.

Concerning themselves little about their own steeds, the
party took those which first offered, and embarking man and
horse in the boat, soon pushed across the waters of the
lutulent Don. Arrived at the opposite banks of the river,
they mounted, and, guided by Luke, after half an hour's sharp
riding, arrived at the skirts of Rookwood Park. Entering
this beautiful sylvan domain, they rode for some time silently
among the trees, till they reached the knoll, whence Luke
had beheld the hall, on the eventful night of his discovery of
his mother's wedding-ring. A few days only had elapsed,
but during that brief space what storms had swept over his
bosom—what ravages had they not made! He was then all
ardour—all impetuosity—all independence. The future presented a bright unclouded prospect. Wealth, honours, and
happiness apparently awaited him. It was still the same
exquisite scene, hushed, holy, tranquil—even solemn, as upon
that glorious night. The moon was out, silvering wood and
water, and shining on the white walls of the tranquil mansion. Nature was calm, serene, peaceful as ever. Beneath
the trees, he saw the bounding deer—upon the water, the
misty wreaths of vapour — all, all was dreamy, delightful,
soothing, all save his heart—*there* was the conflict—*there* the
change. Was it a troubled dream, with the dark oppression
of which he was struggling, or was it stern, waking, actual
life? That moment's review of his wild career was terrible.

He saw to what extremes his ungovernable passions had hurried him; he saw their inevitable consequences; he saw also his own fate; but he rushed madly on.

He swept round the park, keeping under the covert of the wood, till he arrived at the avenue leading to the mansion. The stems of the aged limes gleamed silvery white in the moonshine. Luke drew in the rein beneath one of the largest of the trees.

"A branch has fallen," said he, as his grandsire joined him.

"Ha!" exclaimed Alan, "a branch from that tree?"

"It bodes ill to Ranulph," whispered Luke, "does it not?"

"Perchance," muttered Alan. "'Tis a vast bough!"

"We meet within an hour," said Luke, abruptly.

"Within the tomb of our ancestry," replied Alan; "I will await you there."

And as he rode away, Alan murmured to himself the following verse from one of his own ballads:

> But whether gale or calm prevail, or threatening cloud hath fled,
> By hand of Fate, predestinate, a limb that tree will shed—
> A verdant bough, untouched, I trow, by axe or tempest's breath—
> To Rookwood's head an omen dread of fast-approaching death.

III.

HANDASSAH.

> I have heard it rumoured for these many years,
> None of our family dies but there is seen
> The shape of an old woman, which is given
> By tradition to us to have been murthered
> By her nephews for her riches. Such a figure
> One night, as the prince sat up late at 's book,
> Appeared to him; when, crying out for help,
> The gentleman of his chamber found his Grace
> All in a cold sweat, altered much in face
> And language; since which apparition
> He hath grown worse and worse, and much I fear
> He cannot live. *Duchess of Malfy.*

IN one of those large antique rooms belonging to the suite of apartments constituting the eastern wing of Rookwood

Place—upon the same night as that in which the events just detailed took place, and it might be about the same time, sat Eleanor, and her now attendant, the gipsy Handassah. The eyes of the former were fixed, with a mixture of tenderness and pity, upon the lineaments of another lovely female countenance, bearing a striking resemblance to her own, though evidently, from its attire, and bygone costume, not intended for her, depicted upon a tablet, and placed upon a raised frame. It was nigh the witching hour of night. The room was sombre and dusky, partially dismantled of its once flowing arras, and the lights set upon the table feebly illumined its dreary extent. Tradition marked it out as the chamber in which many of the hapless dames of Rookwood had expired; and hence Superstition claimed it as her peculiar domain. The room was reputed to be haunted, and had for a long space shared the fate of haunted rooms—complete desertion. It was now tenanted by one too young, too pure, to fear aught unearthly. Eleanor seemed, nevertheless, affected by the profound melancholy of the picture upon which she gazed. At length, Handassah observed her start, and avert her eye shudderingly from the picture.

"Take it hence," exclaimed Eleanor; "I have looked at that image of my ancestress, till it has seemed endowed with life—till its eyes have appeared to return my gaze, and weep. Remove it, Handassah."

Handassah silently withdrew the tablet, placing it against the wall of the chamber.

"Not there—not there," cried Eleanor; "turn it with its face to the wall. I cannot bear those eyes. And now come hither, girl—draw nearer—for I know not what of sudden dread has crossed me. This was *her* room, Handassah—the chamber of my ancestress—of all the Ladies Rookwood—where they say—ha!—did you not hear a noise?—a rustle in the tapestry—a footstep near the wall? Why, you look as startled as I look, wench; stay by me—I will not have you stir from my side—'twas mere fancy."

"No doubt, lady," said Handassah, with her eyes fixed upon the arras.

"Hist!" exclaimed Eleanor. "There 'tis again."

"'Tis nothing," replied Handassah. But her looks belied her words.

"Well, I will command myself," said Eleanor, endeavouring to regain her calmness; "but the thoughts of the Lady

Eleanor—for *she* was an Eleanor like to me, Handassah—and ah! even more ill-fated and unhappy—have brought a whole train of melancholy fancies into my mind. I cannot banish them; nay, though painful to me, I recur to these images of dread, with a species of fascination, as if in their fate I contemplated mine own. Not one, who hath wedded a Rookwood, but hath rued it."

"Yet you will wed one," said Handassah.

"He is not like the rest," said Eleanor.

"How know you that, lady?" asked Handassah. "His time may not yet be come. See what to-morrow will bring forth."

"You are averse to my marriage with Ranulph, Handassah."

"I was Sybil's handmaid, ere I was yours, lady. I bear in mind a solemn compact with the dead, which this marriage will violate. You are plighted by oath to another, if he should demand your hand."

"But he has not demanded it."

"Would you accept him were he to do so?" asked Handassah, suddenly.

"I meant not that," replied Eleanor. "My oath is annulled."

"Say not so, lady," cried Handassah—"'twas not for this that Sybil spared your life. I love you, but I loved Sybil, and I would see her dying behests complied with."

"It may not be, Handassah," replied Eleanor. "Why, from a phantom sense of honour, am I to sacrifice my whole existence to one, who neither can love me, nor whom I myself could love? Am I to wed this man because, in her blind idolatry of him, Sybil enforced an oath upon me which I had no power to resist, and which was mentally cancelled while taken? Recall not the horrors of that dreadful cell—urge not the subject more. 'Tis in the hope that I may be freed for ever from this persecution, that I have consented thus early to wed with Ranulph. This will set Luke's fancied claims at rest for ever."

Handassah answered not, but bent her head, as if in acquiescence.

Steps were now heard near the door, and a servant ushered in Doctor Small and Mrs. Mowbray.

"I am come to take leave of you for the night, my dear young lady," said the doctor; "but before I start for the

Vicarage, I have a word or two to say, in addition to the advice you were so obliging as to receive from me this morning. Suppose you allow your attendant to retire for a few minutes. What I have got to say concerns yourself solely. Your mother will bear us company. There," continued the doctor, as Handassah was dismissed—"I am glad that dark-faced gipsy has taken her departure. I can't say I like her sharp suspicious manner, and the first exercise I should make of my powers, were I to be your husband, should be to discharge the hand-maiden. To the point of my visit. We are alone, I think. This is a queer old house, Miss Mowbray; and this is the queerest part of it. Walls have ears, they say; and there are so many holes and corners in this mansion, that one ought never to talk secrets above one's breath."

"I am yet to learn, sir," said Eleanor, "that there is any secret to be communicated."

"Why, not much, I own," replied the doctor; "at least, what has occurred is not a secret in the house by this time. What do you think *has* happened?"

"It is impossible for me to conjecture. Nothing to Ranulph, I hope."

"Nothing of consequence, I trust,—though he is in part concerned with it."

"What is it?" asked Eleanor.

"Pray, satisfy her curiosity, doctor," interposed Mrs. Mowbray.

"Well, then," said Small, rather more gravely, "the fact of the matter stands thus:—Lady Rookwood, who, as you know, was not the meekest wife in the world, now turns out by no means the gentlest mother, and has within this hour found out that she has some objection to your union with her son."

"You alarm me, doctor."

"Don't alarm yourself at all. It will be got over without difficulty, and only requires a little management. Ranulph is with her now, and I doubt not will arrange all to her satisfaction."

"What was her objection?" asked Eleanor; "was it any one founded upon my obligation to Luke—my oath?"

"Tut, tut! dismiss that subject from your mind entirely," said the doctor. "That oath is no more binding on your conscience than would have been the ties of marriage had you been wedded by yon recusant Romish priest, Father

Checkley, upon whose guilty head the Lord be merciful!
Bestow not a thought upon it. My anxiety, together with
that of your mother, is to see you now, as speedily as may be,
wedded to Ranulph, and then that idle question is set at rest
for ever; and, therefore, even if such a thing were to occur
as that Lady Rookwood should not yield her consent to your
marriage, as that consent is totally unnecessary, we must go
through the ceremonial without it."

"The grounds of Lady Rookwood's objections——" said
Mrs. Mowbray.

" Ay, the grounds of her ladyship's objections," interposed
Small, who, when he had once got the lead, liked nobody to
talk but himself, " are simply these, and exactly the sort of
objections one would expect her to raise. She cannot bear
the idea of abandoning the control of the house and estates
to other hands. She cannot, and will not relinquish her
station, as head of the establishment, which Ranulph has
insisted upon as your right. I thought, when I conversed
with her on this subject, that she was changed, but

Naturam expellas furcâ, tamen usque recurret.

I beg your pardon. She is, and always will be the same."

" Why did not Ranulph concede the point to her? I wish
not to dwell here. I care not for these domains—for this
mansion. They have no charms for me. I could be happy
with Ranulph anywhere—happier anywhere than here."

The kind-hearted doctor squeezed her hand in reply, brush-
ing a tear from his eyes.

" Why did he not concede it?" said Mrs. Mowbray,
proudly. " Because the choice remained not with him. It
was not his to concede. This house—these lands—all—all
are yours; and it were poor requital indeed, if, after they
have so long been wrongfully withheld from us, you should
be a dependent on Lady Rookwood."

" Without going quite so far as that, madam," said the doctor, " it is but justice to your daughter that she should be put
in full possession of her rights; nor should I for one instant
advise, or even allow her to inhabit the same house with Lady
Rookwood. Her ladyship's peculiarities of temper are such
as to preclude all possibility of happiness. At the same time,
I trust by management—always by management, madam—
that her ladyship's quiet departure may be insured. I understand that all such legal arrangements in the way of

settlements as could be entered into between your daughter and her future husband are completed. I have only to regret the absence of my friend, Mr. Coates, at this momentous conjuncture. It will be a loss to him. But he inherits from his father a taste for thief-taking, which he is at present indulging, to the manifest injury of his legitimate practice. Hark! I hear Ranulph's step in the gallery. He will tell us the result of his final interview. I came to give you advice, my dear," added the doctor in a low tone to Eleanor; "but I find you need it not. 'Whoso humbleth himself, shall be exalted.' I am glad you do not split upon the rock which has stranded half your generation."

At this moment Ranulph Rookwood entered the room, followed by Handassah, who took her station at the back of the room, unperceived by the rest of the party, whose attention was attracted by Ranulph's agitated manner.

"What has happened?" asked Doctor Small and Mrs. Mowbray, in the same breath.

Ranulph hesitated for a moment in his answer, during which space he regarded Eleanor with the deepest anxiety, and seemed revolving within himself, how he could frame his reply in such way as should be least painful to her feelings; while, with instinctive apprehension of coming misfortune, Miss Mowbray eagerly seconded the inquiries of her friends.

"It is with great pain," said he at length, in a tone of despondency, not unmingled with displeasure, "that I am obliged to descant upon the infirmities of a parent, and to censure her conduct as severely as I may do now. I feel the impropriety of such a step, and I would willingly avoid it, could I do so in justice to my own feelings—and especially at a moment like the present—when every hope of my life is fixed upon uniting myself to you, dear Eleanor, by ties as near as my own to that parent. But the interview which I have just had with Lady Rookwood—bitter and heart-breaking as it has been—compels me to reprobate her conduct in the strongest terms, as harsh, unjust, and dishonourable; and if I could wholly throw off the son, as she avows she has thrown off the mother, I should unhesitatingly pronounce it as little short of——"

"Dear Ranulph," said Eleanor, palpitating with apprehension, "I never saw you so much moved."

"Nor with so much reason," rejoined Ranulph. "For myself, I could endure anything—but for *you*——"

"And does your dispute relate to *me?*" asked Eleanor.
"Is it for *my* sake you have braved your mother's displeasure? Is it because Lady Rookwood is unwilling to resign
the control of this house and these lands to *me*, that you have
parted in anger with her? Was this the cause of your
quarrel?"

"It was the origin of it," replied Ranulph.

"Mother," said Eleanor, firmly, to Mrs. Mowbray, "go
with me to Lady Rookwood's chamber."

"Wherefore?" demanded Mrs. Mowbray.

"Question me not, dear mother, or let me go alone."

"Daughter, I guess your meaning," said Mrs. Mowbray,
sternly. "You would relinquish your claims in favour of
Lady Rookwood. Is it not so?"

"Since you oblige me to answer you, mother," said Eleanor,
crimsoning, "I must admit that you have guessed my meaning. To Lady Rookwood, as to yourself, I would be a
daughter, as far as is consistent with my duty," added she,
blushing still more deeply, "but my first consideration
shall be my husband. And if Lady Rookwood can be content—but pray question me not further—accompany me to
her chamber."

"Eleanor," interposed Ranulph, "dearest Eleanor, the
sacrifice you would make is unnecessary—uncalled for. You
do not know my mother. She would not, I grieve to say it,
appreciate the generosity of your motives. She would not
give you credit for your feelings. She would only resent
your visit, as an intrusion."

"My daughter comprehends you, sir," said Mrs. Mowbray,
haughtily. "I will take care that, in her own house, Miss
Mowbray shall remain free from insult."

"Mother, dear mother," said Eleanor, "do not wilfully
misunderstand him."

"You can be little aware, madam," said Ranulph, calmly,
yet sadly, "how much I have recently endured—how much
of parental anger—how much of parental malediction I have
incurred, to save you and your daughter from the indignity
you apprehend. As I before said, you do not know my
mother; nor could it enter into any well-regulated imagination to conceive the extremities to which the violence of her
passion will, when her schemes are thwarted, hurry her. The
terms upon which you met together will not escape your
recollection: nor shall I need to recall to your mind her
haughtiness, her coldness. That coldness has since ripened

into distrust; and the match which she was at first all
anxiety to promote, she would now utterly set aside, were it
in her power to do so. Whence this alteration in her views
has arisen, I have no means of ascertaining; it is not my
mother's custom to give a reason for her actions or her
wishes: it is all-sufficient to express them. I have perceived,
as the time has drawn nigh for the fulfilment of my dearest
hopes, that her unwillingness has increased; until to-day
what had hitherto been confined to hints has been openly
expressed, and absolute objections raised. Such, however, is
the peculiarity of her temper, that I trusted, even at the
eleventh hour, I should be able to work a change. Alas!
our last meeting was decisive. She commanded me to break
off the match. At once, and peremptorily, I refused. Pardon
me, madam, pardon me, dearest Eleanor, if I thus enter into
particulars; it is absolutely necessary I should be explicit.
Enraged at my opposition to her wishes, her fury became
ungovernable. With appalling imprecations upon the memory
of my poor father, and upon *your* father, madam, whose chief
offence in her eyes was, it seems, the disposition of his property to Eleanor, she bade me begone, and take her curses as
my wedding portion. Beneath this roof—beneath *her* roof,
she added—no marriage of mine should e'er take place. I
might go hence, or might stay, as I thought fitting; but you
and your daughter, whom she characterized as intruders,
should not remain another hour within her house. To this
wild raving, I answered, with as much composure as I could
command, that she entirely mistook her own position; and
that so far from the odium of intrusion resting with you, if
applicable to any one, the term must necessarily affix itself
on those who, through ignorance, had for years unjustly
deprived the rightful owners of this place of their inheritance. Upon this, her wrath was boundless. She disowned
me as her son; disclaimed all maternal regard; and heaped
upon my head a frightful malediction, at the recollection of
which I still tremble. I will spare you further details of this
dreadful scene. To me it is most distressing; for, however
firmly resolved I may be to pursue a line of conduct which
every sound principle within me dictates as the correct one,
yet I cannot be insensible to the awful responsibility I shall
incur in bringing down a mother's curse upon my head, nor
to the jeopardy in which her own excessive violence may
place her."

Mrs. Mowbray listened to Ranulph's explanation in haughty

displeasure; Eleanor with throbbing, tearful interest; Doctor Small with mixed feelings of anger and astonishment.

"Lady Rookwood's conduct," said the doctor, "is, you must forgive me, my dear Sir Ranulph, for using strong expressions, outrageous beyond all precedent, and only excusable on the ground of insanity, to which I wish it were possible we could attribute it. There is, however, too much method in her madness to allow us to indulge any such notion; she is shrewd, dangerous, and designing; and, since she has resolved to oppose this match, she will leave no means untried to do so. I scarcely know how to advise you under the circumstances—that is, if my advice were asked."

"Which I scarcely think it is likely to be, sir," said Mrs. Mowbray, coldly. "After what has occurred, *I* shall think it my duty to break off this alliance, which I have never considered to be so desirable that its rupture will occasion me an instant's uneasiness."

"A plague on all these Rookwoods!" muttered Small. "One would think all the pride of the Prince of Darkness were centred in their bosoms. But, madam," continued the benevolent doctor, "have you no consideration for the feelings of your daughter, or for those of one who is no distant relation to you—your nephew? Your son, Major Mowbray, is, if I mistake not, most eager for this union to take place between his sister and his friend."

"My children have been accustomed to yield implicit obedience to my wishes," said Mrs. Mowbray; "and Major Mowbray, I am sure, will see the propriety of the step I am about to take. I am content, at least, to abide by *his* opinion."

"Snubbed again!" mentally ejaculated the doctor, with a shrug of despair. "It is useless attempting to work upon such impracticable material."

Ranulph remained mute, in an attitude of profound melancholy. An eloquent interchange of glances had passed between him and Eleanor, communicating to each the anxious state of the other's feelings.

At this crisis the door was suddenly opened, and old Agnes, Lady Rookwood's aged attendant, rushed into the room, and sank upon her knees on the floor, her limbs shaking, her teeth chattering, and every feature expressive of intense terror. Ranulph went instantly towards her, to demand the cause of her alarm.

"No, let me pray," cried Agnes, as he took her hand in

the attempt to raise her; "let me pray while there is yet
time; let the worthy doctor pray beside me. . Pray for an
overladen soul, sir; pray heartily, as you would hope for
mercy yourself; ah! little know the righteous of the terrors
of those that are beyond the pale of mercy. The Lord pardon
me my iniquities, and absolve *her*.'

"Whom do you mean?" asked Ranulph, in agitation.
"You do not allude to my mother?"

"You have no longer a mother, young man," said Agnes,
solemnly.

"What!" exclaimed Ranulph, terror-stricken; "is she
dead?"

"She is gone."

"Gone! How? Whither?" exclaimed all, their amazement increasing each instant at the terror of the old woman,
and the apparently terrible occasion of it.

"Speak!" exclaimed Ranulph; "but why do I loiter?
my mother, perchance, is dying—let me go."

The old woman maintained her clutching grasp, which was
strong and convulsive as that of one struggling betwixt life
and death. "It's of no use, I tell you; it's all over," said
she; "the dead are come—the dead are come—and she is
gone."

"Whither?—whither?"

"To the grave—to the tomb," said Agnes, in a deep and
hollow tone, and with a look that froze Ranulph's soul.
"Listen to me, Ranulph Rookwood, my child, my nursling;
listen while I *can* speak. We were alone, your mother and
I, after that scene between you—after the dark denunciations
she had heaped upon the dead—when I heard a low and
gasping kind of sob, and there I saw your mother, staring
wildly upon the vacancy, as if she saw that of which I dare
not think."

"What think you she beheld?" asked Ranulph, quaking
with apprehension.

"That which had been your father," returned Agnes, in a
hollow tone. "Don't doubt me, sir—you'll find the truth of
what I say anon. I am sure he was there. There was a
thrilling, speechless horror in the very sight of her countenance that froze my old blood to ice—to the ice in which 'tis
now—ough! ough! Well, at length she arose, with her eyes
still fixed, and passed through the paneled door without a
word. She is gone!"

"What madness is this?" cried Ranulph.

"Let me go, woman—'tis that ruffian in disguise—she may be murdered."

"No, no," shrieked Agnes; "it was no disguise. She is gone, I tell you—the room was empty, all the rooms were empty—the passage was void—through the door they went together—silently, silently—ghostlike, slow. Ha! that tomb —they are there together now—he has her in his arms—see, they are here—they glide through the door—do you not see them now? Did I not speak the truth? She is dead—ha, ha!" And with a frantic and bewildering laugh the old woman fell upon her face.

Ranulph raised her from the floor; but the shock of what she had beheld had been too much for her. She was dead!

IV.

THE DOWER OF SYBIL.

Card. Now thou art come? Thou look'st ghastly;
There sits in thy face some great determination,
Mixed with some fear.
Bos. Thus it lightens into action:
I am come to kill thee.   *Duchess of Malfy.*

RANULPH ROOKWOOD was for some moments so much stunned by the ghastly fate of Agnes, connected, as it appeared to be, with a supernatural summons similar to that which he imagined he had himself received, that he was incapable of stirring from the spot, or removing his gaze from the rigid features of the corpse, which, even in death, wore the strong impress of horror and despair. Through life he knew that Agnes, his own nurse, had been his mother's constant and faithful attendant; the unhesitating agent of her schemes, and it was to be feared from the remorse she had exhibited, the participator of her crimes; and Ranulph felt, he knew not why, that in having witnessed her terrible end, he beheld the ultimate condition of his own parent. Conquering, not without great effort, the horror which had

rivetted him to the spot, he turned to look towards Eleanor.
She had sunk upon a chair, a silent witness of the scene. Mrs.
Mowbray and Doctor Small having, upon the first alarm
given by Agnes respecting Lady Rookwood's departure from
the house, quitted the room to ascertain the truth of her
statement. Ranulph immediately flew to Eleanor.

"Ranulph," said she, though almost overcome by her
alarm, "stay not an instant here with me. I am sure from
that poor woman's dreadful death, that something terrible
has occurred, perhaps to Lady Rookwood. Go to her chamber. Tarry not, I entreat of you."

"But will you, can you, remain here alone with that body?"
asked Ranulph.

"I shall not be alone. Handassah is within call—nay, she
is here. Oh, what an eve of our espousals has this been, dear
Ranulph! Our whole life is a troubled volume, of which each
successive leaf grows darker. Fate is opposed to us. It is
useless to contend with our destiny. I fear we shall never be
united."

"Dismiss me not with words like those, dear Eleanor,"
returned Ranulph. "Fate cannot have greater woes in store
for us than those by which we are now oppressed. Let us
hope that we are now at that point whence all must brighten.
Once possessed of you, assured of thus much happiness, I
would set even fate at defiance. And you will be mine to-
morrow."

"Ranulph, dear Ranulph, your suit at this moment is
desperate. I dare not, cannot pledge myself. You yourself
heard, even now, my mother's sentiments, and I cannot marry
without her consent."

"Your mother, like my own, regards not the feelings of
her children. Forgive my boldness, Eleanor; forgive me if
I linger now, when duty calls me hence; but I cannot tear
myself away. Your mother may return — my hopes be
crushed; for even your love for me seems annihilated in her
presence."

"Ranulph, your vehemence terrifies me," rejoined Eleanor.
"I implore you, by the tender affection which you know I
bear you, not to urge me further at this moment. Recall
your firmer feelings, and obtain some mastery over yourself.
I repeat, I am yours only, if I am bride of any one. But when
our union can take place rests not with myself. And now, I
entreat you, leave me."

"You are mine," said Ranulph, with fervour; "mine only."

"Yours only," replied Eleanor.

"Be this the earnest of my happiness!" exclaimed Ranulph, imprinting a long and impassioned kiss upon her lips.

The lovers were startled from their embrace by a profound sigh; it proceeded from Handassah, who, unbidden, had replaced the picture of the Lady Eleanor upon its frame. The augury seemed sinister. Every one who has gazed steadfastly upon a portrait must have noticed the peculiar and lifelike character which, under certain aspects, the eyes will assume. Seen by the imperfect light upon the table, the whole character of the countenance of the Lady Eleanor seemed changed; the features appeared to be stamped with melancholy, and the eyes to be fixed with pitying tenderness upon her descendants. Both gazed at each other and at the picture, struck with the same sentiment of undefined awe. Beside them stood the dark figure of the gipsy girl, watching, with ill-concealed satisfaction, the effect of her handiwork. Ranulph was aroused from his abstraction by hearing a loud outcry in Mrs. Mowbray's voice. Hastily committing Eleanor to the care of her attendant, he left the room. Handassah followed him to the door, closed it after him, and then locked it within side. This done, she walked back hastily towards Eleanor, exclaiming, in a tone of exultation, "You have parted with him for ever."

"What mean you, girl?" cried Eleanor, alarmed at her manner. "Why have you fastened the door? Open it, I command you."

"Command *me!*" laughed Handassah, scornfully. "What if I refuse your mandate? What if, in my turn, I bid *you* obey me? I never owned but one mistress. If I have bowed my neck to you for a time, 'twas to fulfil her dying wishes. If I have submitted to your control, it was to accomplish what I have now accomplished. Your oath! Remember your oath. The hour is come for its fulfilment."

With these words Handassah clapped her hands. A panel in the wall opened, and Luke stood suddenly before them. Silently and with stern deliberation he strode towards Eleanor, and seizing one of her hands, drew her forcibly toward him. Eleanor resisted not; she had not the power; neither did she scream, for so paralysing was her terror, that for the moment it took away all power of utterance. Luke

neither stirred nor spoke, but, still maintaining his hold,
gazed searchingly upon her features, while Eleanor, as if
spell-bound, could not withdraw her eyes from him. Nothing
more terribly impressive could be conceived than Luke's
whole appearance. Harassed and exhausted by the life he
had recently led; deprived almost of natural rest; goaded
by remorse, his frame was almost worn to the bone, while his
countenance, once dark and swarthy, was now blanched and
colourless as marble. This pallid and deathlike hue was, in
all probability, owing to the loss of blood he had sustained
from the wound inflicted by Major Mowbray, with the stains
of which his apparel was dyed; for, though stanched, the
effusion had been sufficient to cause great faintness. His
dark eyes blazed with their wonted fire—nay, they looked
darker and larger from his exceeding paleness, and such
intense mental and bodily suffering was imprinted upon his
countenance, that, despite its fierceness and desperation, few
could have regarded him without sympathy. Real desperation has so much of agony in its character, that no one can
witness it unmoved. His garb was not that in which the
reader first beheld him, but a rich, dark, simple suit of velvet,
corresponding more with his real rank in life than his former
peasant's attire; but it was disordered by his recent conflict,
and stained with bloody testimonials of the fray; while his
long sable curls, once his pride and ornament, now hung in
intertangled elf-locks, like a coil of wreathed water-snakes.
Even in her terror, as she dwelt upon his noble features,
Eleanor could not help admitting that she beheld the undoubted descendant and the living likeness of the handsomest
and most distinguished of her house—the profligate and
criminal Sir Reginald. As her eye, mechanically following
this train of thought, wandered for an instant to the haughty
portraiture of Sir Reginald, which formed part of the family
pictures, and thence to those of his unfortunate lady, she was
struck with the fancy that, by some terrible fatality, the
tragic horrors of bygone days were to be again enacted in
their persons, and that they were in some way strangely
identified with their unfortunate progenitors. So forcibly
was this idea impressed upon her features, that Luke, who
had followed the direction of her glances, became instantly
aware of it. Drawing her nearer to the portrait of the Lady
Eleanor, he traced the resemblance in mute wonder; thence,
turning towards that of Sir Reginald, he proudly exclaimed:

"You doubted once my lineage, maiden—can you gaze on those features, which would almost seem to be a reflection of mine own, and longer hesitate whose descendant I am? I glory in my likeness. There is a wild delight in setting human emotions at nought, which he was said to feel—which I feel now. Within these halls I seem to breathe an atmosphere congenial to me. I visit what I oft have visited in my dreams; or as in a state of pre-existence. Methinks, as I gaze on you, I could almost deem myself Sir Reginald, and you his bride, the Lady Eleanor. Our fates were parallel: *she* was united to her lord by ties of hatred—by a *vow*—a *bridal vow*. So are you to me. And she could ne'er escape him—could ne'er throw off her bondage—nor shall you. I claim the fulfilment of *your* oath; you are *mine*."

"Never, never!" shrieked Eleanor, struggling to disengage herself. But Luke laughed at her feeble efforts. Handassah stood by, a passive spectatress of the scene, with her arms folded upon her bosom.

"You refuse compliance!" said Luke, scornfully. "Have you no hopes of heaven, no fears of perdition, that you dare to violate your vow? Bethink you of the awful nature of that obligation; of the life which was laid down to purchase it; of the blood which will cry out for vengeance 'gainst the *murderess*, should you hesitate. By that blood-cemented sacrament, I claim you as my own. You are mine." And he dragged her towards the opening.

Eleanor uttered a prolonged and terrific scream.

"Be silent, on your life," added he, searching for the dagger given to him by Alan Rookwood, when, as his hand sought the weapon, Eleanor escaped from his grasp, and fled towards the door. But Handassah had anticipated her intention. The key was withdrawn from the lock, and the wretched maiden vainly tried to open it.

At this instant Turpin appeared at the sliding panel.

"Quick, quick!" cried he, impatiently—"despatch, in the devil's name; the house is alarmed. I hear young Ranulph's voice in the gallery."

"Ranulph!" shrieked Eleanor—"then I am saved." And she redoubled her outcries for assistance.

Luke again seized his victim. Her hands clutched so convulsively fast in her despairing energy against the handle of the door that he could not tear her thence. By this time Ranulph Rookwood, who had caught her reiterated screams for help, was at the entrance. He heard her struggles; he heard Luke's threats—his mockery—his derisive laughter—but vainly, vainly did he attempt to force it open. It was of the strongest oak, and the bolts resisted all his efforts. A board alone divided him from his mistress. He could hear her sobs and gasps. He saw, from the action of the handle, with what tenacity she clung to it; and, stung to frenzy by the sight, he hurled himself against the sturdy plank, but all in vain. At length the handle was still. There was a heavy fall upon the floor—a stifled scream—and a sound as of a body being dragged along. The thought was madness.

"To the panel! to the panel!" cried a voice (it was that of Turpin) from within.

"The panel!—ha!" echoed Ranulph, with a sudden gleam of hope. "I may yet save her." And he darted along the corridor with the swiftness of thought.

Luke, meanwhile, had for some minutes fruitlessly exhausted all his force to drag Eleanor from the door. Despair gave her strength; she clutched at the door; but she felt her strength failing her—her grasp was relaxing. And then the maddening thought that she would be shortly his—that he would slay her—while the idea that Ranulph was so near, and yet unable to protect her, added gall even to her bitterness. With savage delight Luke exulted in the lover's tortures. He heard Ranulph's ineffectual attempts; he heard his groans; he heard their mutual cries. Inflamed by jealousy, he triumphed in his power of vengeance, and even prolonged the torture which accident had given him the means of inflicting. He stood like the inquisitor who marks his victim's anguish on the rack, and calculates his powers of further endurance. But he could no longer dally, even with this horrible gratification. His companion grew impatient. Eleanor's fair long tresses had escaped from their confinement in the struggle, and fell down her neck in disorder. Twining his fingers amidst its folds, Luke dragged her backwards from her hold, and, incapable of further resistance, her strength completely exhausted, the wretched girl fell to the ground.

Luke now raised her almost inanimate form in his arms, and had nigh reached the aperture, when a crash was heard in the panel opposite to that by which he was about to escape, and communicating with a further apartment. It was thrown open, and Ranulph Rookwood presented himself at the narrow partition. An exclamation of joy, that he was yet in time, escaped his lips; and he was about to clear the partition at a bound, and to precipitate himself upon Luke, when, as suddenly as his own action, was the person of the unfortunate Mr. Coates wedged into the aperture.

"Traitor!" cried Ranulph, regarding Coates with concentrated fury, "dare you to oppose me?—hence! or, by Heaven, I will cut you down!"

"'Tis impossible," ejaculated the attorney. "For your own sake, Sir Ranulph—for my sake—I entreat—implore of you—not to attempt to pass this way. Try the other door."

Ranulph said no more. He passed his sword through the body of the miserable attorney, who, with a deep groan, fell. The only obstacle to his passage being thus removed, he at once leaped into the room.

The brothers were now confronted together, but little of brotherly love mingled with the glances which they threw upon each other. Ranulph's gentle, but withal enthusiastic temperament, had kindled, under his present excitement, like flax at the sudden approach of flame. He was wild with frenzy. Luke was calmer, but his fury was deadly and inextinguishable. The meeting was terrible on both sides.

With one arm Luke enfolded Eleanor, with the other he uplifted the dagger. Its point was towards her bosom. Scowling grim defiance at Ranulph, he exclaimed, in a determined tone, "Advance a footstep, and my dagger descends into her heart."

Ranulph hesitated, uncertain how to act; foaming with rage, yet trembling with apprehension.

"Ranulph," gasped Eleanor, "life without you were valueless. Advance—avenge me!"

Ranulph still hesitated. He could not, by any act of his own, compromise Eleanor's safety.

Luke saw his advantage, and was not slow to profit by it. "You seal her destruction if you stir," said he.

"Villain," returned Ranulph, between his ground teeth, and with difficulty commanding sufficient coolness to speak with deliberation, "you perceive your power. Injure her, and nothing earthly shall protect you. Free her, and take your life and liberty; nay, reward if you will. You cannot otherwise escape me."

"Escape you!" laughed Luke, disdainfully. "Stand aside, and let me pass. Beware," added he, sternly, "how you oppose me. I would not have a brother's blood upon **my** soul."

"Nor I," cried Ranulph; "but you pass not." And he placed himself full in Luke's path.

Luke, however, steadily moved forward, holding Eleanor between himself and Ranulph, so as to shield his own person; but, fancying he saw an opportunity of dealing a blow without injury to his mistress, the latter was about to hazard the thrust, when his arms were seized behind, and he was rendered powerless.

"Lost, lost," groaned he; "she is lost to me for ever!"

"I fear that's but too true," replied Turpin, for it was the highwayman whose grasp confined Ranulph.

"Must I see her borne away before my eyes?" cried Ranulph. "Release me—set me free."

"Quite impossible at present," returned Dick. "Mount and away, Sir Luke," continued he; "never mind me. Leave me to shift for myself."

"Eleanor!" cried Ranulph, as she passed close by his side.

"Ranulph!" shrieked Eleanor, with a loud scream, recalled to consciousness by his voice, "farewell for ever."

"Ay, for ever," responded Luke, triumphantly. "You meet no more on earth."

He was about to pass through the panel, when Eleanor exerted all her remaining strength in a last futile attempt at liberation. In the struggle, a packet fell from Luke's bosom.

Handassah stooped to pick it up.

"From Sybil!" exclaimed she, glancing at the superscription.

"Remember my promise to old Barbara," roared Dick, who had some curiosity, as the reader knows, to learn what the package contained. "The time is arrived. Eleanor is in your power—in your presence."

"Give me the packet," said Luke, resigning Eleanor for the instant to Handassah's custody; "take the steel, and grasp her firmly."

Handassah, who, though slight of figure, was of singular personal strength, twined her arms about Miss Mowbray in such a manner as to preclude all possibility of motion.

Luke tore open the package. It was a box carefully enclosed in several folds of linen, and lastly within a sheet of paper, on which were inscribed these words:

THE DOWER OF SYBIL.

Hastily, and with much curiosity, Luke raised the lid of the box. It contained one long silken tress of blackest hair, curiously braided. It was Sybil's. His first impulse was to cast it from him; his next, reproachfully to raise it to his lips. He started as if a snake had stung him.

At this moment a loud clamour was heard in the gallery. In the next, the door was assailed by violent strokes, evidently proceeding from some weighty instrument, impelled by the united strength of several assailants.

The voice of Turpin rose above the deafening din. "A bullet for the first who enters," shouted he. "Quick, Sir Luke, and the prize is safe—away, and——"

But as he seconded his exhortation with a glance at Luke, he broke off the half-uttered sentence, and started with horror and amazement. Ere the cause of his alarm could be expressed, the door was burst open, and a crowd of domestics, headed by Major Mowbray and Titus Tyrconnel, rushed into the room.

"Nay, then, the game's up!" exclaimed Dick; "I have done with Rookwood." And, springing through the panel, he was seen no more.

When the new-comers first looked around, they could perceive only two figures besides themselves—those of the two lovers—Eleanor having sunk pale, exhausted, and almost senseless, into the arms of Ranulph. Presently, however, a ghastly object attracted their attention. All rushed towards it—all recoiled, as soon as they discovered that it was the lifeless body of Luke Rookwood. His limbs were stiff, like those of a corpse which has for hours been such; his eyes protruded from their sockets; his face was livid and blotched. All bespoke, with terrible certainty, the efficacy of the poison, and the full accomplishment of Barbara's revenge.

Handassah was gone. Probably she had escaped ere Turpin fled. At all events, she was heard of no more at Rookwood.

It required little to recall the senses of Eleanor. Shortly she revived, and as she gazed around, and became conscious of her escape, she uttered exclamations of thanksgiving, and sank into the embraces of her brother.

Meanwhile Mrs. Mowbray and Doctor Small had joined the assemblage.

The worthy doctor had been full of alarm; but his meditated condolences were now changed to congratulations, as

he heard the particulars of the terrible scene that had occurred, and of Eleanor's singular and almost providential
deliverance.

"After what has befallen, madam," said the doctor to Mrs.
Mowbray, slightly coughing, "you can no longer raise any
objections to a certain union, eh?"

"I will answer for my mother in that particular," said
Major Mowbray, stepping forward.

"She will answer for herself, my son," said Mrs. Mowbray. "The match has her full and entire consent. But
to what am I to attribute the unexpected happiness of your
return?"

"To a chain of singular circumstances," replied the major,
"which I will hereafter detail to you. Suffice it to say, that
but for this gentleman's fortunate arrival," added he, looking
at Titus Tyrconnel, "at the hut on Thorne Waste, I might
have been detained a prisoner, without *parole*, and, what is
worse, without provision perhaps for days; and to add to my
distress, fully acquainted with the meditated abduction of my
sister. It was excessively lucky for me, Mr. Tyrconnel, that you
happened to pass that way, and for poor Paterson, likewise."

"Arrah, by my *soul*, major, and you may say that with
safety; and it was particularly fortunate that we stumbled
upon the tits in the cellar, or we'd never have been here just
in the nick of it. I begin to think we've lost all chance of
taking Dick Turpin this time. He's got clean away."

"I am not sorry for his escape," said the major. "He's a
brave fellow; and I respect courage wherever I find it, even
in a highwayman. I should be sorry to appear as a witness
against him; and I trust it will never be my fate to do so."

We shall not pause to describe the affectionate meeting
which now ensued between the brother and sister—the congratulations upon Eleanor's escape from peril, intermingled
with the tenderest embraces, and the warmest thanks offered
to Ranulph for his gallant service. "She is yours, my dear
boy," said the major; "and though you are a Rookwood, and
she bears the ill-fated name of Eleanor, I predict that, contrary to the usual custom of our families in such cases, all your
misfortunes will have occurred *before* marriage."

"There is only one thing," said Small, with a very peculiar
expression, which might almost be construed into serio-
comic, could we suspect the benevolent doctor of any such
waggery, "that can possibly throw a shade over our present
felicity. Lady Rookwood is not to be found."

"My poor mother," said Ranulph, starting.

"Make yourself easy," said the doctor; "I doubt not we shall hear of her to-morrow. My only apprehension," added he, half aside, "is, that she may be heard of before."

"One other circumstance afflicts me," said Ranulph. "Poor Mr. Coates!"

"What's that you say of Mr. Coates, Sir Ranulph?" exclaimed Titus.

"I fear he is killed in the recent affray," said Ranulph. "Let some one search for the body."

"Kilt!" echoed Titus. "Is it kilt that Mr. Coates is? Ah! *ullagone*, and is it over with him entirely? Is he gone to rejoin his father, the thief-taker? Bring me to his remains."

"He will bring them to you himself," said the attorney, stepping forward. "Luckily, Sir Ranulph," said the incurable punster, "it was merely the *outer coats* that your sword passed through; the *inner* remains uninjured, so that you did not act as my *conveyancer* to eternity. Body o' me! I've as many lives as a cat—ha, ha!"

Ranulph welcomed the facetious man of law with no little satisfaction.

We think it unnecessary to enter into further detail. Another chamber was prepared for Eleanor's reception, to which she was almost immediately transported. The remains of the once fierce and haughty Luke, now stiff and stark, but still wearing, even in death, their proud character, were placed upon the self-same bier, and covered with the self-same pall which, but a week ago, had furnished forth his father's funeral. And as the domestics crowded round the corpse, there was not one of them but commented upon his startling resemblance to the grandsire, Sir Reginald; nor, amongst the superstitious, was the falling of the fatal bough forgotten.

Tranquillity was at length restored at the hall. Throughout the night, and during the next day, Ranulph made every search for his mother, but no tidings could be learned of her. Seriously alarmed, he then caused more strict and general inquiry to be instituted, but with like unsuccessful effect. It was not, indeed, till some years afterwards that her fate was ascertained.

V.

THE SARCOPHAGUS.

So now 'tis ended, like an old wife's story.—WEBSTER.

NOTWITHSTANDING the obscurity which hung over the fate of Lady Rookwood, the celebration of the nuptials of Sir Ranulph and Eleanor was not long delayed; the ceremony took place at the parish church, and the worthy vicar offiated upon the occasion. It was a joyous sight to all who witnessed it, and not few were they who did so, for the whole neighbourhood was bidden to the festival. The old avenue was thronged with bright and beaming faces, rustic maidens decked out in ribands of many-coloured splendour, and stout youths in their best holiday trim; nor was the lusty yeoman and his buxom spouse—nor yet the patriarch of the village, nor prattling child, wanting. Even the ancestral rooks seemed to participate in the universal merriment, and returned from their eyries a hoarse greeting, like a lusty chorus of laughter, to the frolic train. The churchyard path was strewn with flowers—the church itself a complete garland. Never was there seen a blither wedding: the sun smiled upon the bride—accounted a fortunate omen, as dark lowering skies and stormy weather had, within the memory of the oldest of the tenantry, inauspiciously ushered in all former espousals. The bride had recovered her bloom and beauty, while the melancholy which had seemingly settled for ever upon the open brow of the bridegroom, had now given place to a pensive shade, that only added interest to his expressive features; and, as in simple state, after the completion of the sacred rites, the youthful pair walked, arm in arm, amongst their thronging and admiring tenants towards the hall, many a fervent prayer was breathed that the curse of the house of Rookwood might be averted from their heads; and, not to leave a doubt upon the subject, we can add that these aspirations were not in vain, but that the day, which dawned so brightly, was one of serene and unclouded happiness to its close.

After the ceremonial, the day was devoted to festivity. Crowded with company, from the ample hall to the kitchen ingle, the old mansion could scarce contain its numerous

guests, while the walls resounded with hearty peals of
laughter, to which they had been long unaccustomed. The
tables groaned beneath the lordly baron of beef, the weighty
chine, the castled pasty flanked on the one hand with neat's
tongue, and on the other defended by a mountainous ham,
an excellent *pièce de résistance*, and every other substantial
appliance of ancient hospitality. Barrels of mighty ale were
broached, and their nut-brown contents widely distributed,
and the health of the bride and bridegroom was enthusiasti-
cally drunk in a brimming wassail cup of spicy wine with
floating toast. Titus Tyrconnel acted as master of the cere-
monies, and was, Mr. Coates declared, " *quite in his element.*"
So much was he elated, that he ventured to cut some of his
old jokes upon the vicar, and, strange to say, without incurring the resentment of Small.

To retrace the darker course of our narrative, we must
state that some weeks before this happy event the remains of
the unfortunate Sir Luke Rookwood had been gathered to
those of his fathers. The document that attested his legitimacy being found upon his person, the claims denied to him
in life were conceded in death ; and he was interred with all
the pomp and peculiar solemnity proper to one of the house,
within the tomb of his ancestry.

It was then that a discovery was made respecting Alan
Rookwood, in order to explain which we must again revert
to the night of the meditated *enlèvement* of Eleanor.

After quitting his grandson in the avenue, Alan shaped
his course among the fields in the direction to the church.
He sought his own humble, but now deserted dwelling. The
door had been forced ; some of its meagre furniture was removed ; and the dog, his sole companion, had fled. " Poor
Mole !" said he ; "thou hast found, I trust, a better master."
And having possessed himself of what he came in search—
namely, a bunch of keys and his lantern, deposited in an
out-of-the-way cupboard, that had escaped notice, he quickly
departed.

He was once more within the churchyard ; once more upon
that awful stage whereon he had chosen to enact, for a long
season, his late fantastical character ; and he gazed upon the
church tower, glistening in the moonshine, the green and undulating hillocks, the " chequered cross-sticks," the clustered
head-stones, and the black and portentous yew-trees, as upon
" old familiar faces." He mused, for a few moments, upon

the scene, apparently with deep interest. He then walked
beneath the shadow of one of the yews, chanting an odd
stanza or so of one of his wild staves, wrapped the while, it
would seem, in affectionate contemplation of the subject-
matter of his song:

THE CHURCHYARD YEW.

—— Metuendaque succo
Taxus.

A noxious tree is the churchyard yew,
As if from the dead its sap it drew;
Dark are its branches, and dismal to see,
Like plumes at Death's latest solemnity.
Spectral and jagged, and black as the wings
Which some spirit of ill o'er a sepulchre flings:
Oh! a terrible tree is the churchyard yew;
Like it is nothing so grimly to view.

Yet this baleful tree hath a core so sound,
Can nought so tough in the grove be found:
From it were fashioned brave English bows,
The boast of our isle, and the dread of its foes.
For our sturdy sires cut their stoutest staves
From the branch that hung o'er their fathers' graves;
And though it be dreary and dismal to view,
Stanch at the heart is the churchyard yew.

His ditty concluded, Alan entered the churchyard, taking
care to leave the door slightly ajar, in order to facilitate his
grandson's entrance. For an instant he lingered in the
chancel. The yellow moonlight fell upon the monuments of
his race; and, directed by the instinct of hate, Alan's eye
rested upon the gilded entablature of his perfidious brother,
Reginald, and muttering curses, "not loud but deep," he
passed on. Having lighted his lantern in no tranquil mood,
he descended into the vault, observing a similar caution with
respect to the portal of the cemetery, which he left partially
unclosed, with the key in the lock. Here he resolved to abide
Luke's coming. The reader knows what probability there
was of his expectations being realized.

For a while he paced the tomb, wrapped in gloomy meditation, and pondering, it might be, upon the result of Luke's
expedition, and the fulfilment of his own dark schemes,
scowling from time to time beneath his bent eyebrows, counting the grim array of coffins, and noticing, with something
like satisfaction, that the shell which contained the remains
of his daughter had been restored to its former position. He
then bethought him of Father Checkley's midnight intrusion

upon his conference with Luke, and their apprehension of a
supernatural visitation, and his curiosity was stimulated to
ascertain by what means the priest had gained admission
to the spot unperceived and unheard. He resolved to sound
the floor, and see whether any secret entrance existed; and
hollowly and dully did the hard flagging return the stroke of
his heel as he pursued his scrutiny. At length the metallic
ringing of an iron plate, immediately behind the marble
effigy of Sir Ranulph, resolved the point. There it was that
the priest had found access to the vault; but Alan's disappointment was excessive, when he discovered that this
plate was fastened on the underside, and all communication
thence with the churchyard, or to wherever else it might
conduct him, cut off; but the present was not the season for
further investigation, and tolerably pleased with the discovery
he had already made, he returned to his silent march around
the sepulchre.

At length a sound, like the sudden shutting of the church
door, broke upon the profound stillness of the holy edifice.
In the hush that succeeded, a footstep was distinctly heard
threading the aisle.

"He comes—he comes!" exclaimed Alan, joyfully; adding, an instant after, in an altered voice, "but he comes
alone."

The footstep drew near to the mouth of the vault—it was
upon the stairs. Alan stepped forward to greet, as he supposed, his grandson, but started back in astonishment and
dismay as he encountered in his stead Lady Rookwood. Alan
retreated, while the lady advanced, swinging the iron door
after her, which closed with a tremendous clang. Approaching the statue of the first Sir Ranulph, she paused, and Alan
then remarked the singular and terrible expression of her
eyes, which appeared to be fixed upon the statue, or upon
some invisible object near it. There was something in her
whole attitude and manner calculated to impress the deepest
terror on the beholder. And Alan gazed upon her with an
awe which momently increased. Lady Rookwood's bearing
was as proud and erect as we have formerly described it to
have been—her brow was as haughtily bent—her chiselled lip
as disdainfully curled; but the staring, changeless eye, and
the deep-heaved sob which occasionally escaped her, betrayed
how much she was under the influence of mortal terror.
Alan watched her in amazement. He knew not how the

scene was likely to terminate, nor what could have induced her to visit this ghostly spot at such an hour, and alone; but he resolved to abide the issue in silence—profound as her own. After a time, however, his impatience got the better of his fears and scruples, and he spoke.

"What doth Lady Rookwood in the abode of the dead?" asked he, at length.

She started at the sound of his voice, but still kept her eye fixed upon the vacancy.

"Hast thou not beckoned me hither, and am I not come?" returned she, in a hollow tone. "And now thou askest wherefore I am here. I am here because, as in thy life I feared thee not, neither in death do I fear thee. I am here because——"

"What seest thou?" interrupted Alan, with ill-suppressed terror.

"What see I—ha—ha!" shouted Lady Rookwood, amidst discordant laughter; "that which might appal a heart less stout than mine—a figure anguish-writhen, with veins that glow as with a subtle and consuming flame. A substance, yet a shadow, in thy living likeness. Ha—frown if thou wilt; I can return thy glances."

"Where dost thou see this vision?" demanded Alan.

"Where!" echoed Lady Rookwood, becoming for the first time sensible of the presence of a stranger. "Ha—who are you that question me?—what are you?—speak!"

"No matter who or what I am," returned Alan; "I ask you what you behold."

"Can you see nothing?"

"Nothing," replied Alan.

"You knew Sir Piers Rookwood?"

"Is it he?" asked Alan, drawing near her.

"It is," replied Lady Rookwood; "I have followed him hither, and I will follow him whithersoever he leads me, were it to——"

"What doth he now?" asked Alan; "do you see him still?"

"The figure points to that sarcophagus," returned Lady Rookwood—"can you raise up the lid?"

"No," replied Alan; "my strength will not avail to lift it."

"Yet let the trial be made," said Lady Rookwood; "the figure points there still—my own arm shall aid you."

Alan watched her in dumb wonder. She advanced towards the marble monument, and beckoned him to follow. He reluctantly complied. Without any expectation of being able to move the ponderous lid of the sarcophagus, at Lady Rookwood's renewed request he applied himself to the task. What was his surprise, when, beneath their united efforts, he found the ponderous slab slowly revolve upon its vast hinges, and, with little further difficulty, it was completely elevated; though it still required the exertion of all Alan's strength to prop it open, and prevent its falling back.

"What does it contain?" asked Lady Rookwood.

"A warrior's ashes," returned Alan.

"There is a rusty dagger upon a fold of faded linen," cried Lady Rookwood, holding down the light.

"It is the weapon with which the first dame of the house of Rookwood was stabbed," said Alan, with a grim smile:

> " Which whoso findeth in the tomb
> Shall clutch until the hour of doom ;
> And when 'tis grasped by hand of clay,
> The curse of blood shall pass away.

So saith the rhyme. Have you seen enough?"

" No," said Lady Rookwood, precipitating herself into the marble coffin. " That weapon shall be mine."

" Come forth—come forth," cried Alan. " My arm trembles —I cannot support the lid."

"I will have it, though I grasp it to eternity," shrieked Lady Rookwood, vainly endeavouring to wrest away the dagger, which was fastened, together with the linen upon which it lay, by some adhesive substance to the bottom of the shell.

At this moment Alan Rookwood happened to cast his eye upward, and he then beheld what filled him with new terror. The axe of the sable statue was poised above its head, as in the act to strike him. Some secret machinery, it was evident, existed between the sarcophagus lid and this mysterious image. But in the first impulse of his alarm Alan abandoned his hold of the slab, and it sunk slowly downwards. He uttered a loud cry as it moved. Lady Rookwood heard this cry. She raised herself at the same moment—the dagger was in her hand—she pressed it against the lid, but its downward force was too great to be withstood. The light was within the sarcophagus, and Alan could discern her features.

The expression was terrible. She uttered one shriek, and the lid closed for ever.

Alan was in total darkness. The light had been inclosed with Lady Rookwood. There was something so horrible in her probable fate, that even *he* shuddered as he thought upon it. Exerting all his remaining strength, he essayed to raise the lid, but now it was more firmly closed than ever. It defied all his power. Once, for an instant, he fancied that it yielded to his straining sinews, but it was only his hand that slided upon the surface of the marble. It was fixed—immovable. The sides and lid rang with the strokes which the unfortunate lady bestowed upon them with the dagger's point; but these sounds were not long heard. Presently all was still; the marble ceased to vibrate with her blows. Alan struck the lid with his knuckles, but no response was returned. All was silent.

He now turned his attention to his own situation, which had become sufficiently alarming. An hour must have elapsed, yet Luke had not arrived. The door of the vault was closed —the key was in the lock, and on the outside. He was himself a prisoner within the tomb. What if Luke should *not* return? What if he were slain, as it might chance, in the enterprise? That thought flashed across his brain like an electric shock. None knew of his retreat but his grandson. He might perish of famine within this desolate vault.

He checked this notion as soon as it was formed—it was too dreadful to be indulged in. A thousand circumstances might conspire to detain Luke. He was sure to come. Yet the solitude—the darkness was awful, almost intolerable. The dying and the dead were around him. He dared not stir.

Another hour—an age it seemed to him—had passed. Still Luke came not. Horrible forebodings crossed him; but he would not surrender himself to them. He rose, and crawled in the direction, as he supposed, of the door—fearful even of the stealthy sound of his own footsteps. He reached it, and his heart once more throbbed with hope. He bent his ear to the key; he drew in his breath; he listened for some sound, but nothing was to be heard. A groan would have been almost music in his ears.

Another hour was gone! He was now a prey to the most frightful apprehensions, agitated in turns by the wildest emotions of rage and terror. He at one moment imagined that

Luke had abandoned him, and heaped curses upon his head ; at the next, convinced that he had fallen, he bewailed with equal bitterness his grandson's fate and his own. He paced the tomb like one distracted ; he stamped upon the iron plate ; he smote with his hands upon the door ; he shouted, and the vault hollowly echoed his lamentations. But Time's sand ran on, and Luke arrived not.

Alan now abandoned himself wholly to despair. He could no longer anticipate his grandson's coming—no longer hope for deliverance. His fate was sealed. Death awaited him. He must anticipate his slow but inevitable stroke, enduring all the grinding horrors of starvation. The contemplation of such an end was madness, but he was forced to contemplate it now; and so appalling did it appear to his imagination, that he half resolved to dash out his brains against the walls of the sepulchre, and put an end at once to his tortures; and nothing, except a doubt whether he might not, by imperfectly accomplishing his purpose, increase his own suffering, prevented him from putting this dreadful idea into execution. His dagger was gone, and he had no other weapon. Terrors of a new kind now assailed him. The dead, he fancied, were bursting from their coffins, and he peopled the darkness with grisly phantoms. They were around about him on each side, whirling and rustling, gibbering, groaning, shricking, laughing, and lamenting. He was stunned, stifled. The air seemed to grow suffocating, pestilential; the wild laughter was redoubled ; the horrible troop assailed him ; they dragged him along the tomb, and amid their howls he fell, and became insensible.

When he returned to himself, it was some time before he could collect his scattered faculties ; and when the agonising consciousness of his terrible situation forced itself upon his mind, he had nigh relapsed into oblivion. He arose. He rushed towards the door ; he knocked against it with his knuckles till the blood streamed from them ; he scratched against it with his nails till they were torn off by the roots. With insane fury he hurled himself against the iron frame ; it was in vain. Again he had recourse to the trap-door. He searched for it ; he found it. He laid himself upon the ground. There was no interval of space in which he could insert a finger's point. He beat it with his clenched hand ; he tore it with his teeth ; he jumped upon it ; he smote it with his heel. The iron returned a sullen sound.

He again essayed the lid of the sarcophagus. **Despair**
nerved his strength. He raised the slab a few inches. He
shouted, screamed, but no answer was returned; and again
the lid fell.

"She is dead!" cried Alan. "Why have I not shared her
fate? But mine is to come. And such a death!—oh, oh!"
And, frenzied at the thought, he again hurried to the door,
and renewed his fruitless attempts to escape, till nature gave
way, and he sank upon the floor, groaning and exhausted.

Physical suffering now began to take the place of his mental
tortures. Parched and consumed with a fierce internal fever,
he was tormented by unappeasable thirst—of all human ills
the most unendurable. His tongue was dry and dusty, his
throat inflamed; his lips had lost all moisture. He licked
the humid floor; he sought to imbibe the nitrous drops from
the walls; but, instead of allaying his thirst, they increased
it. He would have given the world, had he possessed it, for
a draught of cold spring-water. Oh, to have died with his
lips upon some bubbling fountain's marge! But to perish
thus—— !

Nor were the pangs of hunger wanting. He had to endure
all the horrors of famine, as well as the agonies of quenchless
thirst.

In this dreadful state three days and nights passed over
Alan's fated head. Nor night nor day had he. Time, with
him, was only measured by its duration, and that seemed
interminable. Each hour added to his suffering, and brought
with it no relief. During this period of prolonged misery
reason often tottered on her throne. Sometimes he was
under the influence of the wildest passions. He dragged
coffins from their recesses, hurled them upon the ground,
striving to break them open and drag forth their loathsome
contents. Upon other occasions he would weep bitterly and
wildly; and once—once only—did he attempt to pray; but
he started from his knees with an echo of infernal laughter,
as he deemed, ringing in his ears. Then, again, would he
call down imprecations upon himself and his whole line,
trampling upon the pile of coffins he had reared; and, lastly,
more subdued, would creep to the boards that contained the
body of his child, kissing them with a frantic outbreak of
affection.

At length he became sensible of his approaching dissolu-
tion. To him the thought of death might well be terrible;

but he quailed not before it, or rather seemed, in his latest moments, to resume all his wonted firmness of character. Gathering together his remaining strength, he dragged himself towards the niche wherein his brother, Sir Reginald Rookwood, was deposited, and placing his hand upon the coffin, solemnly exclaimed, "My curse—my dying curse—be upon thee evermore!"

Falling with his face upon the coffin, Alan instantly expired. In this attitude his remains were discovered.

L'Cnbop.

Our tale is told. Yet, perhaps, we may be allowed to add
a few words respecting two of the subordinate characters of
our drama (melo-drama we ought to say), namely, Jerry
Juniper and the knight of Malta. What became of the
Caper Merchant's son after his flight from Kilburn Wells we
have never been able distinctly to ascertain. Juniper, however, would seem to be a sort of Wandering Jew ; for certain
it is that *somebody very like him* is extant still, and to be met
with at Jerry's old haunts ; indeed, we have no doubt of
encountering him at the ensuing meetings of Ascot and
Hampton.

As regards the knight of Malta — (Knight of *Roads*
"Rhodes" as he should have been)—we are sorry to state
that the career of the Ruffler terminated in a madhouse, and
the poor knight became in reality a *Hospitaller!* According to
the custom observed in those establishments, the knight was
deprived of his luxuriant locks, and the loss of his beard
rendered his case incurable ; but, in the mean time, the
barber of the place made his fortune by retailing the materials of all the black wigs he could collect to the impostor's
dupes.

Such is the latest piece of intelligence that has reached us
of the *Arch-hoaxer* of Canterbury !

Turpin (why disguise it ?) was hanged at York in 1739.
His firmness deserted him not at the last. When he mounted
the fatal tree his left leg trembled ; he stamped it impatiently
down, and, after a brief chat with the hangman, threw him-

self suddenly and resolutely from the ladder. His sufferings would appear to have been slight : as he himself sang :

He died, not as other men, by *degrees*,
But *at once*, without wincing, and quite at his ease !

We may, in some other place, lay before the reader the particulars (and they are not incurious) of the "night before Larry was stretched."

The remains of the vagrant highwayman found a final resting-place in the desecrated churchyard of Saint George, without the Fishergate postern, a green and grassy cemetery, but withal a melancholy one. A few recent tombs mark out the spot where some of the victims of the pestilence of 1832-33 have been interred ; but we have made vain search for Turpin's grave—unless (as is more than probable) the plain stone with the simple initials R. T. belongs to him.

The gyves by which he was fettered are still shown at York Castle, and are of prodigious weight and strength ; and though the herculean robber is said to have moved in them with ease, the present turnkey was scarcely able to lift the ponderous irons. An old woman of the same city has a lock of hair, said to have been Turpin's, which she avouches her grandfather cut off from the body after the execution, and which the believers look upon with great reverence. O rare Dick Turpin !

We shall, perhaps, be accused of dilating too much upon the character of the highwayman, and we plead guilty to the charge. But we found it impossible to avoid running a little into extremes. Our earliest associations are connected with sunny scenes in Cheshire, said to have been haunted by Turpin ; and with one very dear to us (from whose lips, now, alas! silent, we have listened to many stories of his exploits) he was a sort of hero. We have had a singular delight recounting his feats and hair-breadth escapes ; and if the reader derives only half as much pleasure from the perusal of his adventures as we have had in narrating them, our satisfaction will be complete. Perhaps, we may have placed him in too favourable a point of view ; and yet we know not.

As upon those of more important personages, many doubts rest upon his history. Such as we conceive him to have been, we have drawn him—hoping that the benevolent reader, upon finishing our Tale, will arrive at the same conclusion; and, in the words of the quaint old Prologue to the Prince of Prigs' Revels,

———————— Thank that man,
Can make each thief a complete Roscian !

THE END.

LONDON:
WHITING AND CO., 30 & 32, SARDINIA STREET, LINCOLN'S-INN-FIELDS.

www.ingramcontent.com/pod-product-compliance
Lightning Source LLC
Chambersburg PA
CBHW030819110726
47900CB00006B/1670